Detective Agency

Woodlawn
843-5939

DETECTIVE AGENCY

Women Rewriting the Hard-Boiled Tradition

Priscilla L. Walton
and
Manina Jones

UNIVERSITY OF CALIFORNIA PRESS

Berkeley   Los Angeles   London

University of California Press
Berkeley and Los Angeles, California

University of California Press, Ltd.
London, England

Library of Congress Cataloging-in-Publication Data

Walton, Priscilla L.
    Detective agency : women rewriting the hard-boiled
tradition / Priscilla L. Walton and Manina Jones.
        p.   cm.
    Includes bibliographic references and index
    ISBN 0-520-21507-9 (alk. paper). —
    ISBN 0-520-21508-7 (alk. paper)
    1. Detective and mystery stories, American—History
and criticism.   2. Women and literature—United
States—History—20th century.   3. American fiction—
Women authors—History and criticism.   I. Jones, Manina.
II. Title.
PS374.D4W35   1999
813'.0872099287—dc21   98-22739
                                                 CIP

Printed in the United States of America
9 8 7 6 5 4 3 2 1

The paper used in this publication is both acid-free and
totally chlorine-free. It meets the minimum requirements of
American Standard for Information Sciences—Permanence
of Paper for Printed Library Materials, ANSI Z39.48-1984.

To our (not-so-silent) partners in crime,
Neal and Michael

Contents

Figures

Acknowledgments

We are deeply indebted to Linda Hutcheon for being our ever-vigilant guardian angel, and to Linda Norton, Will Murphy, and Suzanne Rancourt for their encouragement and editorial assistance. Friends and colleagues like Nancy Adamson, Jamie Barlowe, Peter Rabinowitz, Cheryl Torsney, Ann Wilson, Lee Person, Matthew Okuloski, Kim Lister, Lynne Magnusson, and Illona Haus provided mysteries, clues, and lots of support. Much credit goes to our students and especially to our research assistants at Carleton University, the University of Western Ontario, and the University of Waterloo: Andrew Fieldsend, Catherine Hatt, Shelley Hulan, Marsha Jackson, Jason Kuzminski, and Tracy Whalen. Kathleen Gregory Klein and Rebecca Pope offered valuable commentary; we are most grateful for their contributions. We are indebted to Rose Anne White, project editor at University of California Press, for her efficiency and good judgment, and to copyeditor Alice Falk for her sharp eye and astute sense of style. We would like to thank our families for their support of our academic work. Priscilla especially thanks her grandmother, Adele Hallett, who, in more ways than one, was the foremother of this study. We offer our warmest appreciation to the authors, editors, agents, and readers and DorothyLers who made this study possible. Together they constitute a detective agency of the highest order.

We would also like to express our thanks to the Social Sciences and Humanities Research Council of Canada for their generous funding of this project, as well as to both Carleton University and the University of Western Ontario for their support.

Grateful acknowledgment is made to the following for permission to reprint previously published material: Plangent Visions Music Limited: excerpt from "Watching the Detectives" by Elvis Costello. Copyright © 1977 by Sideways Songs administered by Plangent Visions Music Limited. Reprinted with permission.

Introduction

> My name is Kinsey Millhone. I'm a private investigator,
> licensed by the state of California. I'm thirty-two
> years old, twice-divorced, no kids. The day before
> yesterday I killed someone and the fact weighs heavily
> on my mind.
>
> Sue Grafton, *"A" Is for Alibi*

So begins the first of Sue Grafton's best-selling "alphabetized" detective series, featuring private investigator Kinsey Millhone. Successful in its own right, Grafton's series both participates in and is representative of a larger publishing phenomenon: the emergence of the female hard-boiled series detective. Since the late 1970s, this subgenre of the crime novel, written by women and centering on the professional woman investigator, has virtually exploded onto the popular fiction market. Grafton is perhaps the most remarkable case study, in part because of her marketable series titles (*"A" Is for Alibi, "B" Is for Burglar, "C" Is for Corpse* . . .), her exceptional sales figures, and her self-conscious status as a "professional" writer. Grafton, who had already established a career as a Hollywood and television screenwriter before she began writing mysteries, clearly saw *"A" Is for Alibi* not simply as an isolated creative act but as part of a professional project that had its context within the economic

1

conditions of the publishing world. Grafton says, "I was accustomed to being paid lots for what I wrote. When I decided to write mysteries, I said to myself, 'Well, I'm going to write 65 pages of this book, and if it never sells, I won't have to finish it.' I was worried I'd devote a year of my life to 'A' and the publishers would tell me they'd done a book just like it, or, 'sorry, we're not doing private eye novels this year'" ("G Is for (Sue) Grafton" 7–8). Her long-term plan "to do a mystery series based on the alphabet" defines Grafton as an author of series fiction, aware that "marketing is as important as the writing when it comes right down to it. . . . I am, in effect, in business with Henry Holt and Bantam [her publishers]. We're partners" ("G Is for (Sue) Grafton" 10, 11). The alphabet series, then, is a carefully premeditated—and profitable—set of "serial murders" in which both Grafton and her publishers (not to mention her readers) are implicated.

The opening paragraph of *"A" Is for Alibi* inaugurates the first-person female voice of Grafton's protagonist. As a significant primary gesture, the detective names herself. She goes on to establish her identity in relation to her profession: Kinsey tells us what she *does* as an integral part of who she is, leaving conventional "personal details" ("I'm a nice person and I have lots of friends") for later in her self-portrait. Kinsey's introduction constitutes the opening frame for the story of her investigation of a crime. It is, moreover, *her own* story of her investigation, as distinguished from other accounts of the facts of the case: "I've already given a statement to the police, which I initialed page by page and then signed. I filled out a similar report for the office files. The language in both documents is neutral, the terminology oblique, and neither says quite enough" (1). The initial(ed) statement Kinsey endorses for the authorities and the report she simply fills out (rather than composes) for her office files are somehow inadequate to her experience of the crime and its solution: "neither says quite enough." Her own telling, as conveyed in the novel's narrative, both supplements and counters these "official" records. In it, a woman emerges into her own language, using the *non*neutral first-person gendered voice and a more "direct" terminology that evokes her complex responses to the case, responses the official documents literally do not take into (their) account. This voice is, ironically, made possible by the traditionally masculine tradition of male "tough guy" hard-boiled fiction.

In *"A" Is for Alibi*, Kinsey's *un*official report is designated neither for officers nor office but for her female client, Nikki Fife. Indeed, each of Grafton's novels identifies itself as the report Kinsey presents to her clients at the termination of her investigations in order to conclude her contract with them, and each novel ends with her "signature" closing, "Respectfully submitted, Kinsey Millhone." The frame explains that the narrative as report is directed to a paying audience who has, both literally and figuratively, an investment in the case: the client. A succession of novels written for a popular market, the alphabet series is also self-consciously directed toward consumers, who contract for Grafton's literary services every time they purchase and read her books. What is the role of these consumers, and what is the nature of *their* personal, social, and economic investment in Kinsey's cases? What kind of "work" do the novels perform? What, in other words, are the aesthetic and ideological dimensions of the "contract" established between the novelist and her reading public, a contract that is in large measure defined by a dynamic relation between (female) gender and (private eye) genre? These are some of the questions that have generated *Detective Agency*.

Our names are Manina Jones and Priscilla Walton. We are literary scholars "licensed" in our investigations, not by the state of California but by the University of California Press and the academic institution for which it stands. The title of this study is meant to hint at the institutional agencies of publishing, marketing, and consumerism in which the hard-boiled detective tradition—and, more specifically, the re-visioning of that tradition as exemplified by writers like Grafton—originates. Our title also speaks of a concern with women's ability to exercise individual and collective agency (the ability to act, to intervene) within the prescribed structures of such institutions. Writing for a popular market and within the confines of both formula and series fiction, authors such as Sara Paretsky, Marcia Muller, Linda Barnes, Liza Cody, and Sue Grafton have strategically redirected the masculinist trajectory of the American hard-boiled detective novel of the 1930s and 1940s to what we would argue are feminist ends. Their writing, in other words, uses an established popular formula in order to investigate not just a particular crime but the more general offenses in which the patriarchal power structure of contemporary society itself is potentially incriminated. They use the popular novel as a lens through which to filter cultural issues and theoretical problems, providing a forum in which such issues and problems might be negotiated (if not solved) as part of the narrative of investigation. The feminist impetus of these novels, we contend, is established in the ambivalent relationship between contemporary works and the literary tradition, in the intimate connection between the individual reader and the novel in the act of reading, and in the more systemic interdependence of novelist, publisher, and audience. We would like to explore the dynamics of these relationships.

The title *Detective Agency* also suggests what we see as an important aspect of the feminist impulse of these novels in terms both of their content and their form. We do not want simply to discuss how any given novel details the process of setting up business as a female private eye, or establishing a woman's detective agency. Rather, we intend to examine the strategic means by which this group of novels confronts in an entertaining and accessible medium questions of women's agency in general. As Delys Bird and Brenda Walker put it in their introduction to *Killing Women*, "Women's crime fiction tells women readers a story about their own lives. It presents the fictional possibility of controlling events and issues that affect our lives and of bringing a measure of understanding to them" (38). These works also establish the distinctive voice of an empowered female subject, and this, clearly, is not just a formal but is also a political gesture. When Sue Grafton comments in an interview that "Voice is a big issue. Until I found the right voice for Kinsey Millhone, I wasn't in business" ("G Is for (Sue) Grafton" 10), she too connects voice and the economy of publishing. The feminine voice of these novels, somehow, is literally what puts them in business, making them salable to what appears to have been a previously untapped readership.

Popular formula fiction is by its nature a kind of writing in which the writer's individual creative process must be seen in relation to the collectivity of authors who work, in effect, collaboratively to generate and modify the parameters and possibilities of the genre. For us, as co-authors of this project, the title *Detective Agency* points to the ways in which collaboration involves breaking down the illusion of the "heroic" academic who acts alone in producing a unique scholarly work: "agency" implies a social context rather than an individual effort. It is thus a term that can work at several levels to foreground our own self-consciousness about working within the institutional and communal structure of the academy. For example, this project has generated for us a community of people—both within our universities and outside them—who have chosen to take their private passion for reading detective fiction public, coming out of the academic closet as readers of popular fiction to contribute in "unauthorized" ways to this work. Writing not just as scholars but as members of a community of enthusiastic readers of detective fiction, we are thereby implicated as both subjects and objects of this study. A few moments ago we referred to being "licensed" by both the press and the university system. By this we meant that the developing fields of both feminist and cultural studies have opened a space (albeit a limited one, and one fraught with disciplinary and ideological tensions) within the academy at large and departments of English in particular to engage in the study of popular texts. This movement is reflected in the unprecedented growth of scholarly publications focusing on evaluative analyses of popular media of various kinds. As authors, therefore, we are implicated in a preexistent academic culture that licenses us to speak.

The practices of contemporary cultural studies make possible both an alternative field of vision and provocative new ways of envisioning "field" itself, since cultural studies works the borders between conventional academic disciplines, using a "bricolage" of methodologies, including semiotics, textual analysis, survey research, and interviews in order to offer a self-consciously "positioned" analysis of cultural practices of all kinds (Nelson, Treichler, and Grossberg 2). As Tony Bennett puts it, such analyses tend to demonstrate the degree to which cultural phenomena are "intricated" with, and within, relations of power ("Policy" 23). Our field of vision here owes a great deal to work being done in cultural studies. Its specifically literary point of view takes in the realm of popular formula fiction, a class of writing best explained, as John Cawelti observes, by seeing the success of individual works in terms of analogy and comparison with others (*Adventure* 21). Cawelti argues that formula fiction is sustained by a reciprocal relationship with culture at large, both affirming existing values and beliefs and, potentially, helping readers assimilate changes to traditional ways of seeing (*Adventure* 35–36). While we certainly want to appreciate and explore the unique, aesthetically appealing qualities of the individual works under study, we are primarily interested in the elements they share. These elements are implicitly "underwritten" by the reading public, which systematically reinforces them as aspects of the formula through their buying habits. Our work is especially concerned with how these shared qualities relate to the kinds of beliefs and values they both reproduce and transform, particularly when it comes to issues of gender. Our methodology is deeply indebted to the formidable "detective agency" comprising the authors, editors, agents, and publicists who so generously contributed their time and astute perceptions in the interviews they allowed us to conduct with them, as well as to the mystery fiction readers who responded with such enthusiasm and openness to our reader survey. We have attempted to integrate the diverse voices of these communities into the texture of this study. Their insights are as important to our understanding of the genre as any provided by more conventionally scholarly commentary.

The list of works cited at the end of this book includes the writers who form the core of our study. Each is the female author of a detective series published by a mainstream press that centers on a professional woman investigator and that, in terms of the generic conventions it exploits as well as those it subverts, must be seen in ambivalent relation to what has come to be known as the American hard-boiled literary tradition, a tradition best exemplified by "tough guy" writers such as Dashiell Hammett, Raymond Chandler, and Mickey Spillane. The historical and economic trajectory of this re-vision of the masculine genre is explored in chapter 1, "The Private Eye and the Public: Professional Women Detectives and the Business of Publishing." This chapter explores the advent in the late 1970s of what Maureen Reddy would call a "feminist counter-tradition" of women writing along hard-boiled formal and stylistic lines who are at the same time challenging the gender boundaries demarcated in earlier male writers and, indeed, potentially undermining the very system of values on which the male hard-boiled tradition is founded.

Chapter 2, "Gumshoe Metaphysics: Reading Popular Culture and Formula Fiction," expands on the significance of formula fiction as a cultural product driven by popular demand and situates our analysis in relation to theories of gender, genre, and popular culture. Chapter 3, "Does She or Doesn't She?: The Problematics of Feminist Detection," uses the framework of feminist politics and counterdiscursive practice to delve into the subversive potential of women's crime novels. Critics are certainly not unanimous in their appraisal of the women's hard-boiled novel as an aspect of cultural critique; this chapter sets out the terms of the debate over the politics of the subgenre and positions our argument within it. In chapter 4, "The Text as Evidence: Linguistic Subversions," we look at the specific ways that women writers both use and strategically alter the formal conventions of hard-boiled writing, considering questions relating to voice and style, while in chapter 5, "Private I: Viewing (through) the (Female) Body," we examine the revisionary role of autobiographical form in women's private eye fiction, considering the implications of the repositioned subjectivity made possible by locating narrative voice in the female body. We make a connection between the scene/seen of the crime and "woman's place"—and by this phrase we mean women's place with reference to the narrative of detection, as well as to the publishing world. It is important to remember that behind the professional woman detective of fiction stands the professional woman writer, and this chapter confronts the role of both as working women: as novelist Julie Smith puts it in the cover blurb to Janet Dawson's *Till the Old Men Die*, "With both author and sleuth, you know you're in the hands of true professionals." Chapter 6, "Plotting against the Law: Outlaw Agency," looks at the private eye novel's social and historical contexts. It also explores the female private eye's ambivalent position in relation to the historicized "laws" of gender and genre, considering ways in which that "outlaw" status offers the potential for altering both the narrative and ideological paradigms offered by the traditional masculine hard-boiled novel. Chapter 7 directs its attention specifically to the eye of the viewer of film and television representations of the female detective since the 1970s.

This last chapter draws its title ("'She's Watching the Detectives': The Woman PI in Film and Television") from Elvis Costello's memorable musical evocation of the traditional hard-boiled narrative in "Watching the Detectives." The title of Costello's song elides the subject of the verb "watching" so as to allow it to take as its subject both the woman in the song, a classic femme fatale in the hard-boiled mold (the chorus begins with the line "She's watching the detectives . . .") *and*, arguably, that of the male "speaker"/singer who, in effect, subsumes her gaze when he places the woman under surveillance in his narration of the song's story. In the song, as in the hard-boiled novel, the femme fatale provokes the male gaze with her "looks" ("She pulls their eyes out with a face like a magnet") and is ultimately punished for her potentially subversive subjectivity: when she's watching the detective in the first chorus, "He's so cute," but she is finally warned "Don't get cute" . . . on pain of death— "cute," after all, in the song is rhymed with "Shoot! Shoot! Shoot!"

What happens to this model, though, in a version of the detective narrative where both the fictional private investigator and her author are women? How does the first realize subversive power through the agency of the private eye, and the second achieve it when she uses the agency of publishing to take the female private eye to the public? In this study, we're watching the detectives to find out.

Chapter 1

THE PRIVATE EYE AND THE PUBLIC

Professional Women Detectives and the Business of Publishing

Women who write crime fiction may yet be the ultimate subversives. The shock troops of feminists come and go, the backlash swells, but, ignoring the tumult, nice women sit down to typewriters and word processors and create deceptions.

Claire McNab

BREAKING IN

In its April 1990 review of the mystery fiction market, *Publishers Weekly* magazine declared that "the woman as tough professional investigator has been the single most striking development in the detective novel in the past decade" (Anthony, "Mystery Books" 28). The following month, an article in *Newsweek* announced, "Call her Samantha Spade or Philippa Marlowe and she would deck you. A tough new breed of detective is re-forming the American mystery novel: smart, self-sufficient, principled, stubborn, funny—and female." The same article named Sara Paretsky and Sue Grafton, along with Tony Hillerman, as "the best American mystery novelists working today" (Ames and Sawhill 66). Sue Grafton's female private eye series first appeared on the *New York Times* hardcover best-seller list with her seventh novel, *"G" Is for Gumshoe*, in 1990, and it stayed for seven weeks; Grafton's previous novel, *"F" Is for Fugitive*, was on the paperback list for a total of eight weeks that year. Every Grafton novel since then has landed on both best-seller lists. When mass-market rights to *"G" Is for Gumshoe* were offered in a November 1990 publishers' auction, the winning press, Fawcett, offered Grafton a two-book deal for one million dollars (Anthony, "Mystery Books" 24–25). Julie Smith's *New Orleans Mourning*, featuring female detective Skip Langdon, won the respected Edgar Allan Poe Award for Best Mystery Novel of 1990—the first time, in the almost fifty years of the prize, that an American woman had garnered the award, and only the fourth time it had been won by a woman writing alone.[1] Janet Dawson's first novel, *Kindred Crimes* (1990), featuring female private investigator Jeri Howard, won the St. Martin's Press Private Eye Writer's Contest and a Private Eye Writers of America Shamus Award, and it was nominated for both the Anthony Award (given at the World Mystery Convention) and the MacCavity Award (presented by the Mystery Readers of America). In the same year, it was announced that a major motion picture starring Kathleen Turner would be based on Sara Paretsky's V. I. Warshawski detective series. Two years earlier, Paretsky had been named one of *Ms.* magazine's Women of the Year, "For bringing a woman detective and feminist themes to murder mysteries, and for championing women writers in this mostly male genre" (Shapiro, "Sara Paretsky" 66). Paretsky's series would make the crossover from simple category fiction to the best-seller lists in 1992.

Clearly, something significant was afoot in the mystery world: by 1990 the female "tough gal" outgrowth of the male hard-boiled novel was making waves in the mainstream of American popular culture. The subgenre of the professional woman investigator had become well-established and was being publicly celebrated through unprecedented

sales and economic rewards, as well as literary prestige and popular re-
nown. Moreover, its popularization of feminist issues was being recognized. But this explosion of interest in the female private eye did not happen overnight. The fiction had been consistently building an author and
reader base and a reputation in the publishing industry—gradually since
the late 1970s, and dramatically since the mid-1980s. The subgenre's
immediate literary and social genealogy may be traced back to the 1960s
and early 1970s; while it has become a critical commonplace to observe
that the phenomenon of feminist activism and changes in society and
gender roles occurring during that period made possible shifts in the
conception of the fictional detective hero, it is also a commonplace
whose truth must be acknowledged at the outset of our discussion.
These shifts in perception were both produced by and reflected in such
events as the establishment of a Presidential Commission on the Status
of Women in 1961; the publication in 1963 of Betty Friedan's immensely
influential *Feminine Mystique*, with its indictment of systemic sexism in
American society; the passage of the American Equal Pay Act of 1963
and the Civil Rights Act of 1964, which prohibited sex discrimination
in employment and mandated a government agency to enforce its policies; and the incorporation of the National Organization for Women
(NOW) in 1966, "to take action to bring women into full participation
in the mainstream of American society *now*, exercising all the privileges
and responsibilities thereof in truly equal partnership with men" (founding statement, qtd. in Mandle 161). In addition, more general social
movements—including the development of consciousness-raising and
self-help groups for women, and the rise of the activist and social protest
movements of the 1960s—"advanced new definitions, personalities, and
roles for women in American society" (Mandle 170).

Trends in popular fiction, especially realist fiction, are driven by
changes in society and in what readers are willing to "buy" in both the
literal and metaphoric sense of that word. In one sense, realist fiction
defines and conventionalizes the limits of its audience's shifting conceptions of reality at the same time that it allows its readers to explore, me-

diate, and manage their fantasies and fears about those limits. Popular fictions are thus, as François Truffaut described popular films, not just aesthetic objects but "sociological events" (qtd. in Schatz 4) that build up a credibility and significance of their own, because they negotiate and renegotiate both the aesthetic expectations and ideological invest-ments of their readers in a pleasurable—and, for authors and publish-ers, *profitable*—way. Popular genres are thus very much economic events too. Discussing the debates over feminism carried out during the early 1970s, Barbara Ryan remarks cynically that "women's lib had become big business" (68). Popular formula novels featuring professional women investigators—who were, after all, working women in traditionally male fields—are very much the product of a combination of economic and social factors and have continuing investments in those fields. These novels are reflections of and on the changes in women's roles and per-ceptions of them(selves) and their abilities inaugurated in the 1960s and 1970s. Canadian novelist Elisabeth Bowers characterizes the trend as "if not consciously feminist, then very obviously influenced by the feminist movement of the 1970s. But this trend was also a reflection of what was happening in society—women were entering the workforce and train-ing for jobs they'd never held before: as cops, firefighters, machinists, soldiers, etc. It was inevitable that popular fiction should reflect this change."[2]

A CHANGE IN PROCEDURES

Crime fiction was most likely to reflect societal change in the first oc-cupational category Bowers lists: cops. The professional woman investi-gator makes her first featured appearances in the police procedural genre, a version of the crime novel in which the mystery is unraveled by the police and in which much of the reader's pleasure is derived from the novel's focus on police teamwork, techniques of investigation, and rou-tines of crime solving. In these books the central character is tradition-ally viewed as part of a collectivity, integrated into the state structures of law and order that function as the corporate hero of the novels, thereby inspiring reader confidence in the ability of such structures to administer justice and control social disorder. As Robert P. Winston and Nancy C. Mellerski point out, by shifting the reader's focus from the criminal to the institutional apparatus that opposes him or her, "the procedural reshapes the potentially destructive impulses of individualism into successful participation in a corporate structure, the police squad." At the same time, the genre offers the possibility of debunking the image of social harmony that is generally seen as key in managing the social problems embodied in the individual criminal (Winston and Mellerski 2). When the central police officer is female, this genre can represent both the possibility of women's integration into "the mainstream of American society" in "equal partnership with men" (the goal of NOW) and the disruption of perceived social harmony within law enforcement agencies themselves. The genre is thus able to portray the resistance of such agencies (and, by implication, of the society they represent and preserve) to women's participation and women's concerns. The female police procedural begins to negotiate in fictional form anxieties about two issues central to the women's liberation movement of the 1960s and 1970s: women's equal access to the institutional workplace and problems of social justice—justice both as it is administered *by* the law and as it is conducted *within* the law itself.

The female police officer makes early appearances in the work of British author Jennie Melville (the pseudonym of Gwendoline Butler) and of Americans Dorothy Uhnak and Lillian O'Donnell. The investigation of women's place in the institutions of law enforcement is perhaps most obvious in the case of Uhnak, whose best-selling first novel *The Bait*, featuring New York City Detective Christine Opara, appeared in 1968, when it won the Edgar Allan Poe Award for Best First Novel. Uhnak, a former police officer, had documented the discrimination she had herself faced as a member of the force in a nonfiction book, *Policewoman: A Young Woman's Initiation into the Realities of Justice* (1964). *The Bait* redeveloped some of these themes, and the series format allowed ongoing elaboration. There were two other installments in the Christine Opara police series, *The Witness* (1969) and *The Ledger* (1970). Lillian O'Donnell's series featuring police officer Norah Mulcahaney made its debut four years after Uhnak's in *The Phone Calls* (1972), and the series continues into the 1990s. O'Donnell observed that in creating her character,

> I wasn't interested then in making Norah a spokeswoman for women's lib, nor am I now. However, I did want her to be part of the real world, and the facts of the case are that at the time Norah joined the force, "police officers, female" were just breaking out of the traditional mould of matron and juvenile work. The evolution of women's responsibilities within the New York Police Department is perforce a part of Norah's story. ("Norah Mulcahaney" 119)

O'Donnell insists, in effect, on the sociological rather than self-consciously "political" origins of her police officer character, but her statement also acknowledges the degree to which her fictional narratives cultivated a quasi-documentary quality ("I did want her to be part of the real world"), which enabled her to dramatize an institutional politics of gender relations and roles. As Christine Gledhill argues of the television police show *Cagney and Lacey*, "when female protagonists have to operate in a fictional world organized by male authority and criminality, gender conflict is inevitable," and the credibility of that conflict relies in part on discourses about sexism made current by the American women's movement (70). "The case," as O'Donnell herself implies, involves not just the crime under investigation but also the position of women in the police force—and, by extension, in middle-class American urban society at large. Marcia Muller, whose first novel featuring PI Sharon McCone appeared in 1977, and who is often heralded as "the founding 'mother' of the contemporary female hard-boiled private eye" (as Sue Grafton put it in a book jacket blurb), affirms that Uhnak and O'Donnell were important models for her own work: in effect, they exceeded the technically oriented aspects of the police procedural formula in favor of developing female characters who tread the boundaries between the real and fictional—as well as the conventionally masculine and feminine— realms. She explains, "They were both writing about New York police women, and while there was a lot of procedure involved there, the characters were rounded characters. They were tough but they also were vulnerable. They proved that women could actually do this job, and do it well."

AN UNSUITABLE JOB FOR A WOMAN?

In 1972 British mystery novelist P. D. James published the first novel by a woman author featuring a "countertraditional" professional female private investigator, *An Unsuitable Job for a Woman*. As Lyn Pykett observes, James's novel makes the connection between gender and genre a central element of its narrative and characterization (64)—the paid work of investigation is "unsuitable" for a woman both in the gender stereotypes of the "real" world and in the stereotypical world of genre fiction, in which the PI (and by implication his author and readership) must be a tough *guy*. In *An Unsuitable Job for a Woman*, Cordelia Gray, James's hero, inherits a detective agency when her former employer, Bernie Pryde, commits suicide. Cordelia is something of an unwilling convert to the profession, and her character owes much to the tradition of the disingenuous amateur sleuth who, however clever she may be, tends to solve her cases by intuition and luck, rarely using the active physical intervention so frequently resorted to by the male heroes of hard-boiled stories. The novel is also in some sense an adjunct to James's popular Inspector Adam Dalgleish police procedural series, since Dalgleish plays a pivotal and authoritative role at the conclusion of the plot and since, for many years, *An Unsuitable Job for a Woman* appeared to be a once-on, stand-alone novel, rather than an installment in a series.

Nevertheless, the novel, like Cordelia herself, inherited and made effective, innovative, and popular use of a masculine generic inheritance, claiming "equal access" to the popular discourse of the private eye novel. In addition, *An Unsuitable Job for a Woman*'s emphasis on professional equality (Cordelia's ability to do "an unsuitable job") and the detective's solidarity with other women, particularly the female murderer, makes Cordelia, according to Nicola Nixon, "a touchstone of early seventies feminism" (30–31). Nixon links the sustained popularity of the novel to the way it fictionally dramatizes social circumstances and concerns of the period in Britain and elsewhere: "It seems hardly surprising, then, that the single, working Cordelia Gray, as a harbinger or prototype of the seventies new woman, should sustain and indeed increase in popularity throughout the decade which saw the agitation of the women's liberation movement force such crucial parliamentary legislation as Britain's Equal Pay Act of 1970 and Sex Discrimination Act of 1975" (32). After a decade of encouragement and anticipation from her readers (Nixon 32), James finally produced a second Cordelia Gray novel, *The Skull beneath the Skin*, but the later novel is much more indebted to the British cozy or "country house" murder mystery tradition than it is to the American private eye novel. Consider its setting, for example: it takes place on an isolated rural island temporarily populated by a closed community of theatrical eccentrics. Furthermore, Cordelia's "professional" status as an investigator has been diminished; she is now a "detective" who specializes in locating lost pets or, in the central role she adopts in the novel, what amounts to a gentlewoman's companion, a task for which she does not finally accept a fee. This generic shift also represents a conservative shift in the politics of the novel, reflected in the characterization of Cordelia—rewritten, Nixon argues, less as a detective than as a heroine of domestic fiction or gothic romance (41). Cordelia's role, she asserts, has been altered to reflect Tory doctrine of 1980s Britain:

> Appearing first in the seventies and then in the eighties, Cordelia does actually offer a representative touchstone for the political shift

in Britain: first she eschews conventional feminine roles and works as a private detective, and then she embraces domesticity and dedicates herself to re-establishing domestic harmony. This trajectory, this transformation of the model of femininity from equal opportunity worker to upholder of domestic family values, is the very transformation that [Margaret] Thatcher advocated every time she spoke to the female electorate or every time she gave interviews for women's magazines. (43)

While the conservative transformation of Cordelia in James's second novel, interestingly, does not mirror the developments in the genre in North America, *An Unsuitable Job for a Woman* certainly does set a significant—and popular—early precedent for them. Indeed, in her female private eye series, J. M. Redmann pays oblique tribute to Cordelia and her author in a character (who becomes the detective's lover) named "Cordelia James."

Maxine O'Callaghan's first Delilah West short story appeared in *Alfred Hitchcock Magazine* in November 1974. Delilah is thus the first American incarnation in fiction of the hard-boiled female private eye. As Marcia Muller observes, this appearance "was an event little noted by the world, simply because the world wasn't yet ready for the fictional female private investigator. Possibly many readers ignored the fact that its protagonist *was* a licensed investigator. After all, she didn't fit into the tradition of the private eye—a male loner striding down the mean streets in a hurry to get to the bottle in the desk drawer of his shabby urban office" ("Appreciation" 9). Muller's comments on readers' difficulty in recognizing O'Callaghan's adaptation of the private eye genre are certainly apt, although we might also point to the short story form of Delilah's first appearance as contributing to the lack of initial acclaim. However, O'Callaghan's first Delilah West novel, *Death Is Forever*, appeared in 1980, and the sketchy early publishing history of the series reflects the difficulty both readers and publishers had in recognizing and categorizing O'Callaghan's new twist on an eminently recognizable male fictional form.[3] In the early 1980s, as O'Callaghan herself recalls, "Editors were not lining up to buy female PI novels" ("Delilah, Then and Now" 4).

Nor were such books widely promoted or hailed by reviewers when they did appear. Former president of Sisters in Crime Linda Grant observes that as late as 1988, when she was finishing her first Catherine Sayler novel, she was unaware that other American women had experimented in an extended way with the series PI genre: "I think that goes back to the fact that books by women were not being promoted at that time." Browsing in a used book store, Grant stumbled across Marcia Muller's first Sharon McCone PI novel, *Edwin of the Iron Shoes,* which was then over ten years old: "And I was absolutely amazed, and immediately started asking if there were other books by Marcia Muller. . . . In retrospect the smart thing would have been to talk to booksellers and talk to librarians, but I just sort of browsed around and those books were not widely distributed so I didn't see them." Most of the major early innovators in the female private eye genre seem to have produced their first novels largely in isolation from one another, suggesting that the advent of the female PI in the 1970s and early 1980s was not a matter of authors directly influencing one another or self-consciously participating in a widely hailed trend. To a much greater degree, they *independently* perceived a gap in what popular fiction had to offer and decided that the hard-boiled detective genre could uniquely accommodate their interests at a particular moment in history. As Wendy Hornsby remarks in her tribute to O'Callaghan, "the issue is not who came first, but why it took so long for anyone to notice that the traditions of mystery fiction were about to be shaken off their foundations" ("Afterword" 49). It wasn't until 1987 that the newly founded organization Sisters in Crime investigated one answer to Hornsby's question: inequities in the reviewing process, they demonstrated, gave disproportionate space to male writers in the mystery genre.

Janice Law's first novel featuring investigator Anna Peters, *The Big Payoff,* appeared in 1976. This series is rarely acknowledged in accounts

of the genre; though Anna Peters ultimately heads up an investiga-
tion/security firm, in the first novel she is still employed as an oil company researcher. All the novels in the series use a first-person narrative
in a hard-boiled tone, and all develop professional investigation plots.
They may (especially early on in the series) have been designed to appeal as novels of suspense or thrillers, often taking place in international
settings—their cover art and titles such as *Gemini Trip* sometimes give
them the appearance of spy novels—and the marriage of the main character during the course of the series further complicates its generic designation, since the private eye is typically a loner. Law's series, however,
definitely offers an early prototype for the female professional investigator, and continues to develop it: the series currently includes nine
novels, the most recent being *Cross-check* (1997).

In 1977 Marcia Muller's immensely influential series made its first appearance with *Edwin of the Iron Shoes*, which featured Sharon McCone,
the staff investigator for a legal cooperative in San Francisco. In her 1978
essay "Creating a Female Sleuth," Muller observed that prior to em-
barking on her career as a novelist she and her friends were already avid
fans of mysteries. They perceived, however, a significant deficiency in
the genre: "There were scores of male sleuths, both hard- and soft-
boiled. There were old ladies with knitting needles and noses for secrets.
There were even a few dedicated and hard-working policewomen. But
nowhere, at that time, could we find a female private eye." Muller, in effect, used her own desires as a consumer of popular fiction (and those of
her friends) as a guide for her project as a writer, working actively as a
literary producer to address the deficiency: "Obviously, I decided, if I
wanted to read about such a character, I would first have to write about
her" (20). In 1994 the writers of *Library Journal* pointed to an amus-
ing but significant figurative correspondence between Sharon McCone's
bold incursion into the macho terrain of the private eye and Muller's
similarly bold infiltration of the masculine market for private eye fiction:
"In 1977 Marcia Muller's first mystery featuring Sharon McCone was
filled with policemen and lawyers all asking, 'What's a nice girl like you

doing in a business like this?' Shopping the manuscript, Muller may well have provoked the same response from more than a few mystery editors. But as Mysterious Press releases the 15th title in the series this July . . . neither Muller nor her editor, Sara Ann Freed, need be bothered by such quaint attitudes" (Annichiarico et al. 120). Muller herself described the collective efforts of women beginning to write in the private eye genre in the early 1980s: "We wanted to write about people like us, like the women around us. The time was ripe" (qtd. in Brainard 362).

No sooner had the private eye genre been adapted to the figure of the heterosexual woman investigator than it was given another important shift in perspective. In 1978 the first lesbian private eye novel appeared: *A Reason to Kill,* by Canadian Eve Zaremba, was published by the Canadian press Paperjacks, though Zaremba comments that this mainstream press debut was "an aberration"; her four subsequent novels have been published by feminist presses. Like Muller, Zaremba saw her series as redressing an absence in traditional crime narratives, which had tended to ignore or offer only negative, criminalized stereotypes of homosexual characters: "For most of my life lesbian detectives did not exist and lesbians generally were invisible in genre fiction, except for their rare appearance in character parts of 'perverts.' So I wanted to write mysteries about a dyke Private Eye. Period. No overt political messages—lesbian, feminist or otherwise. Just a middle-aged lesbian matter-of-factly going about her job as a PI. Of course, that simple ambition has turned out problematic" ("A Canadian Speaks" 45). As Zaremba's comments imply, the "simple" act of representation has complex effects. Her simple ambition matter-of-factly to feature a lesbian character is perhaps "problematic" in part because in shifting perspective—making the traditional "other" of crime fiction the focus of the private eye narrative—she necessarily involves a politics of identity, for lesbian writers as for women writers in general.

Other lesbian professionals eventually followed Zaremba's Helen Keremos. Katherine V. Forrest's lesbian homicide detective Kate Delafield first appeared in *Amateur City* (1984). Canadian Lauren Wright

Douglas's detective Caitlin Reece, American Mary Wings's private eye Emma Victor, and Briton Val McDermid's journalist-investigator Lindsay Gordon—all lesbian characters—did not make their initial appearances until 1987 (in *The Always Anonymous Beast*, *She Came Too Late*, and *Report for Murder*, respectively). J. M. Redmann's private eye Micky Knight and Pat Welch's Helen Black came onto the scene in 1990 (in *Death by the Riverside* and *Murder by the Book*, respectively), and the market has since expanded considerably. However, the next appearance of the lesbian private eye published by a mainstream press didn't occur until more than ten years after Zaremba's first novel, when Sandra Scoppettone's popular Lauren Laurano series, published by Little, Brown, made its debut in 1991 with *Everything You Have Is Mine*.

EXPANDED INVESTMENTS

During the early 1980s, novels featuring a female professional investigator began to multiply and achieve some recognition in the network of authors, publishers, and readers that constitutes the world of popular fiction. For example, Liza Cody's important British series featuring detective Anna Lee, a security firm employee, began with *Dupe* in 1980; a decade later the popularity of the novels had been translated into a television series, produced for ITV and aired in North America on the Arts & Entertainment Channel (see chapter 7). In 1981 Elizabeth Atwood Taylor told the story of her character Maggie Elliott's initiation into private investigation in *The Cable Car Murder* (1981), and Julie Smith inaugurated her feminist lawyer-investigator Rebecca Schwartz in that year too, with *Death Turns a Trick*, though Smith's agent told her that "female private investigators don't sell" and suggested that she create a male protagonist instead (qtd. in Isaac, "Investigator of Mean Rooms" 5).[4] At about the same time, Linda Barnes, who had been writing a popular series featuring amateur detective Michael Spraggue, informed her agent of her aspirations to create a female investigator—and was told that no one would buy a book about a woman detective. Sara Paretsky also reputedly had difficulty selling her first V. I. Warshawski novel (completed in 1980), in part because publishers were uncomfortable with her fiercely independent female character and wanted to equip V.I. with a male partner (Shapiro, "The Lady Is a Gumshoe" 64). Despite its proliferation, then, in the early 1980s the genre was still not widely recognized, even within the publishing world.

"Little did he know," Julie Smith muses wryly of her agent, "in 1982 Sue Grafton, Sara Paretsky, and I all published our first books, and Muller's second, *Ask the Cards a Question*, also came out. All of a sudden, instead of being alone, each of us had company, and soon after, followers" (qtd. in Isaac, "Investigator of Mean Rooms" 5). In other words, the corporate "generic effect" of multiple novelists employing and revising the same conventions to accommodate similar concerns (though using uniquely interesting characters, settings, and situations), began to be recognized and reinforced among authors, readers, and publishers. As Fred Isaac puts it, "Interest in the serious woman as a PI was born, and the movement was on" ("Investigator of Mean Rooms" 5). Even then, though, the development of the genre was cumulative rather than precipitous and instantly heralded. The first novels of Muller, Grafton, and Paretsky were each reviewed by Newgate Callendar in the *New York Times'* prestigious crime column, but the pseudonymous reviewer's comments reveal a failure to perceive the substitution of a female protagonist as a significant innovation on the conventions of the private eye novel. Callendar commented in 1977 of *Edwin of the Iron Shoes*, "No new ground here"; of Paretsky's novel the column remarked that "there really are few original things in *Indemnity Only*"; in answer to the question "Will the series take hold?" it responded that Grafton's *"A" Is for Alibi* "is competent enough, but not particularly original."

Nevertheless, the practitioners of the genre continued to multiply and develop their own variations. To cite but a few examples: Susan Dunlap began her homicide detective Julie Smith series with *Karma* in 1981 (her private eye series began in 1989); Carolyn Wheat's series featuring attorney-investigator Cass Jameson was initiated with *Dead Man's*

Thoughts in 1983; expatriate South African Gillian Slovo's Kate Baeier private eye series, set in London, began in 1984 with *Morbid Symptoms;* in Katherine V. Forrest's 1984 *Amateur City* lesbian police officer Kate Delafield emerged; and Barbara Paul's Marian Larch police series debuted in the same year, with *The Renewable Virgin.* In 1985 the fourth of the best-known American female private eye novelists (the others are Grafton, Paretsky, and Muller) asserted her presence: Linda Barnes published her first Carlotta Carlyle short story, "Lucky Penny," followed in 1987 by her first private eye novel featuring Carlotta, *A Trouble of Fools,* which won the American Mystery Award. By the later 1980s Karen Kijewski's first Kat Colorado PI novel *Katwalk* (1988) appeared, winning the St. Martin's Press Award, a Shamus, and an Anthony. The first installment in Linda Grant's Catherine Sayler series, *Random Access Murder,* was also issued in 1988. Elisabeth Bowers and Marele Day produced private eye novels in Canada and Australia, respectively: Bowers's *Ladies' Night* featured Meg Lacey, and Day's *The Life and Crimes of Harry Lavender* starred Claudia Valentine. In 1988 the first African American fictional female private eye appeared, in Dolores Komo's *Clio Browne: Private Investigator.* In that novel, Clio, named for the muse of history, carries on the tradition established by her father, running the detective agency he founded in 1947 as "the first black private investigator in the city of St. Louis—maybe in the whole country" (2). Komo, similarly, extends and varies a literary tradition (the hard-boiled detective novel) that flourished during the same period, linking it with an African American heritage and perspective.

RECASTING THE GOLDEN AGE

These releases coincide with a more general boom in the market for mystery fiction in the 1980s. The trend, hailed by *Publishers Weekly* as a "New Golden Age of Mysteries," was characterized by breakthrough sales by crime fiction writers including P. D. James, Dick Francis, and Elmore Leonard, all of whom appeared on the hardcover best-seller lists

(Anthony, "Mystery Books" 24; Herbert 17). Magazines and newspapers heralded the change; publishers began to buy more heavily in the mystery genre; membership in the Mystery Guild (a book club devoted to the genre) rose sharply; the Book-of-the-Month Club featured crime fiction as its main selection and set up its own mystery club (Anthony, "Mystery Books" 24). Traditionally, the mystery novel (if not its hard-boiled variant) has proved extraordinarily profitable for women novelists—writers such as Agatha Christie and Dorothy L. Sayers, Josephine Tey, and later Ngaio Marsh and Margery Allingham had driven the first "Golden Age" of mystery fiction between the two world wars with successful series heroes—Miss Marple and Hercule Poirot (Christie), Lord Peter Wimsey and Harriet Vane (Sayers), Alan Grant (Tey), Inspector Alleyn (Marsh), and Albert Campion (Allingham). It was also the product of changes in readership, publishing, and marketing that made the field particularly attractive and accessible to new women writers and readers. David Glover observes, for example, that at the same time as the Golden Age "feminized detective fiction" by focusing on domestic crime, it participated in a more general shift in the production and consumption of popular literature that was geared specifically to appeal to women readers (71). Indeed, many of the developments in the publishing industry of the 1920s and 1930s that created the first golden age are the very staples of the contemporary crime fiction industry: the maximization of sales to libraries, reader participation in book clubs, the inception of distinctive mystery "lines" within publishing houses, the proliferation of specialty genre magazines, the marketing of cheap mass-market paperback editions of novels, and the cultivation by publishers of popular authors and series characters.

Mystery fiction was particularly welcoming to new writers and new series in the 1980s in part because of the resurgence in crime fiction sales during the period, which heightened its appeal to women who wanted to break into publishing. Ruth Cavin, senior editor at St. Martin's Press, reported in 1989 that over the preceding two years, she had seen a 25 percent increase in manuscript submissions featuring a female sleuth, while

Scribners' senior editor Susanne Kirk attested to a 30 percent increase (E. Gibson 37). In recessionary times genre fiction, and crime fiction in particular, is not just economically stable but expands significantly, perhaps because the pleasure of formula fiction is a "sure bet" economically—the reader's financial investment is based on predictable rewards in entertainment value. The appeal of the cheap mass-market paperbacks that are the stock-in-trade of the genre is also a significant factor. Certainly, the formulaic approach of genre fiction both offers readers consistency and a sense of reassurance and provides publishers with "reproducibility" (see chapter 2). These novels are thus able to perpetuate their own market, since readers will buy books of the same genre over and over in what has often been described as addicted behavior. Series fiction is another version of this self-sustaining function, since the backlist of a reputable author's previously published work in a continuing series promised consistent, cumulative sales. Author J. A. Jance testifies, for instance, that while her first novel featuring J. P. Beaumont (a male investigator) had an initial print run of 35,000 in 1985, the runs for new novels in the series (which in 1995 included thirteen novels) have gradually increased to about 195,000. In addition, she notes that the backlist sales of the series have consistently grown, so that the cumulative print run for each novel is about 200,000. Jance's more recent female investigator series featuring Sheriff Joanna Brady capitalized both on the earlier series and on the demand for strong female protagonists—Jance's agent had actually suggested a female series hero to her; it began with a run of 400,000, an exceptional figure for a mystery.

As publishing analyst Carolyn Anthony puts it, "The series character (or characters) has been the lynchpin of successful mystery writing since the invention of Sherlock Holmes, the Hardy Boys and Miss Marple. The ability to do such continuity publishing—to keep selling the old books once the new one is published—is one of today's most important marketing considerations for mass market firms" ("Mystery Books" 25). This phenomenon gives formula fiction an extended shelf life. Series sales are notably augmented by book club selections—the Mystery Guild monthly selections, for example, are clearly dominated by series characters (Isaac, "What Do They Want?"). Library purchases too are an important market, since libraries usually respond to client demand by acquiring all the books in a popular series, often in hardcover; the *Library Journal* confirms that "Libraries are a haven for mid-list fiction, into which much category fiction falls, and they nurture and build writers in these fields" (Annichiarico et al. 120, 121). While publishers are not known for investing heavily in first novels, series do allow first-time authors a sort of proving ground: publishers can produce them relatively inexpensively, with minimal promotion budgets, but if a series builds an audience and reputation over several novels, then the series may be given more extensive support. To cite an extreme example, while the first installment of Sue Grafton's alphabet series (published in 1982) was signed by the publisher for less than $7,000 (Molly Friedrich), in 1989 the sixth installment, *"F" Is for Fugitive,* had a $100,000 promotion budget (Chambers 81); and by 1990 Marion Woods, Grafton's editor, commented that "with *'G' Is for Gumshoe* . . . we are aiming for the national best-seller lists and promoting and advertising to get there" (qtd. in Anthony, "Mystery Books" 26).

Women mystery authors in general clearly rode the crest of escalating mystery fiction sales and crossovers onto the best-seller lists in the latter-day golden age of mystery fiction. Manuscript submissions by women increased, mystery lines actively sought submissions from women authors, sales expanded, and the numbers of mysteries by women authors escalated (E. Gibson 37). "Women mystery writers and their books with female protagonists have become the hottest segment of the market," Kate Miciak, senior editor at Bantam Books commented in 1989: "Where women authors once sold 20,000–25,000 copies in mass market paperback, sales have climbed to 40,000–45,000, and, in some instances, 60,000–65,000 or more" (qtd. in E. Gibson 37). All this activity created a second-wave "feminisation of crime writing" that Delys Bird and Brenda Walker see as an effect of feminist politics of the 1960s and 1970s (11), which stimulated feminist theorizing and provoked energetic debates that crossed the boundary between the academic realm and the popular media. Feminist politics also prompted the founding of women's presses—many of which, including the Crossing Press, Seal, Women's Press, Naiad, New Victoria, and Spinster's Ink, published feminist crime fiction—that cultivated women writers, encouraged the use of fictional forms to advance political themes, and stressed women's different approaches to writing itself. Nicole Décuré characterizes the recent proliferation of feminist crime fiction as a fusion of the golden age of women's detective fiction between the two world wars and the 1970s golden age of the American feminist novel (comprising novelists like Marge Piercy, Marilyn French, and Lisa Alther) (227).

But the rise of the professional female investigator is a unique new element, and the growth of the subgenre exceeded even the startling increase in the production of women's mystery in general.[5] Between 1966 and 1970, 145 books were published by women writers of mystery series; only 6 of those featured professional women investigators. Between 1971 and 1975 the number of novels in mystery series written by women and female professional investigator novels remained relatively stable at 142 and 5, respectively. During the period between 1976 and 1980, 13 of the 166 mystery novels published by women writers featured professional female investigators. The number of women's mystery novels in general increases sharply, from 166 to 299, with the boom between 1981 and 1985. The figure more than doubles between 1986 and 1990, to 623, then doubles again between 1991 and 1995. But the increase in professional investigators is even more remarkable: it more than triples from 13 (between 1976 and 1980) to 43 titles between 1981 and 1985, and continues at the same rate—almost tripling again from 1986 to 1990, to 124, and again in the (incompletely documented) period between 1991 and 1995, to 366 (see figures 1, 2, and 3). The genre had become so well-established and well-populated that by 1993 one editor complained she was seeing too many manuscripts whose authors had obviously targeted

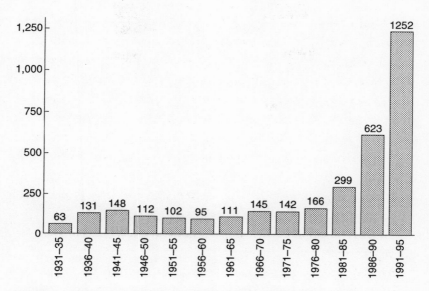

Figure 1. Series novels by women writers of mystery fiction, 1931–95. Source: Heising and authors.

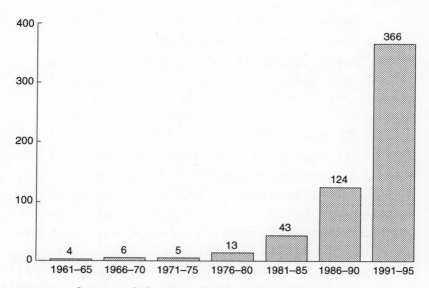

Figure 2. Series novels featuring a female professional investigator, 1961–95. Source: Heising and authors.

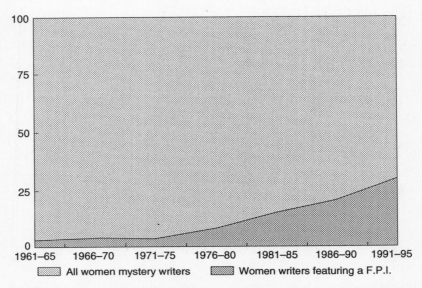

Figure 3. Series novels featuring a female professional investigator, 1961–95
(percentage). Source: Heising and authors.

the genre as "marketable": "It's like some authors are working from a
checklist. Female protagonist. Check. Feisty. Check. Has trouble with
men. Check. Has drinking problem or jogs. Check" (M. Hall 5).

MEANING BUSINESS

The professional investigator novel apparently tapped into a previously
unexploited market for series detective fiction. Like works by writers of
the first golden age, these books appealed particularly to women—but
not because they domesticated crime fiction. Rather, they professionalized it, as the hard-boiled novels of the 1930s and 1940s had done. They
put an independent working woman detective at the center of the narrative of investigation, and the first-person or focalized narration of the
traditional hard-boiled form, along with its distinctive stylistic qualities,
provided a unique avenue for exploring the difference of women's expe-

riences, from their own point of view and in a positioned, personalized voice (see chapters 4 and 5). In addition, the investigative narrative of the novel by definition *is* the paid work of the woman detective. Furthermore, the private detective, as an independent operator, is a professional woman who lives with but does not rely on male support—institutional, emotional, or physical. The narratives of such novels thus enable a broad analogy to be drawn between the professional detective('s) agency and the agency of the independent working woman: these narratives are thus able to dramatize fears and fantasies of and about that figure in a way possible for no other genre.

In describing the features of the popular female private eye novel, literary agent Susan Ann Protter draws attention to the similarities between the professional detective and working women at large. Her language also hints at the distinction between the "cozy" tradition of the more passive amateur detective and the contemporary integration of working women into the hard-boiled tradition. The suspense developed by the latter narratives, she remarks, is "not like that soft, sweet, you know, 'have a cup of tea and what do you think happens' [kind of suspense]. I mean, [the hero has] got to be someone who moves fast, is smart. You know, like a woman executive today, only those qualities turned into a sleuth or detective." Sara Paretsky's description of her early struggles with the genre confirms the connection. While she was still working in an insurance company, Paretsky experimented unsuccessfully with simple gender role reversals in the hard-boiled story, finally arriving at a moment of insight that would pave the way for her V. I. Warshawski series: "Suddenly I realized, what I really need is a woman who's doing what I'm doing—trying to work in a world that is predominantly male, and raising hackles" (qtd. in Shapiro, "Sara Paretsky" 67).

The professional female detective character is also a fictional site where the link between gender, capital, and power central to Western economies may be both foregrounded and arbitrated. Economic validation is itself almost always a central thematic element of private eye fiction, since the genre relies on the figure of the economically motivated detective, the nonamateur investigator. That motivation is emphasized in the narratives, which customarily include details of completing the contractual process with clients, salary negotiations, comments on hours spent, expenses incurred, and payment of fees. For instance, in Sara Paretsky's *Indemnity Only* (as in Dana Stabenow's more recent *Play with Fire*), such details become a professional point of principle. When the detective takes a case on behalf of a child, she demands nevertheless a token payment: "If you want to hire me," V.I. tells the young Jill Thayer, "give me a dollar and I'll give you a receipt, and that will mean you've hired me" (110). The transaction implicitly distinguishes between the detective as a by nature maternal protector and the detective as a professional advocate. The distinction between professional and amateur is highlighted again in *Indemnity Only* after the climax of the novel, when V.I.'s lover Ralph Devereux admits that he put himself in jeopardy because he didn't have enough confidence in her professional capabilities: "I couldn't believe you knew what you were talking about. I guess deep down I didn't take your detecting seriously. I thought it was a hobby" (208).

While the private eye's private status signifies a profoundly ambivalent relation to the law (which we will explore in chapter 6), her professional status tends to indicate, above all else, competence and independence, dramatizing the fantasy of both having access to the material/ political economy and possessing the ability to act independently and ethically within it. Elisabeth Bowers, author of the Meg Lacey books, explains, "I did follow the American tradition in having my detective be a professional private eye, rather than an amateur sleuth—but I did this for feminist reasons, because I wanted my female detective to be a pro, i.e. someone to be taken seriously." Private detectives tend to keep their investigations relatively independent from governing institutional structures. Sandra Tomc observes, "With any one crime only symptomatic of a systemic abuse of women and minorities, with the government, the law courts, the police, big business, even husbands and boyfriends all implicated in a 'patriarchal' orthodoxy, the detective finds her political purpose in the rejection of institutional and organized authority. As Grafton's Kinsey Millhone puts it, 'I like being by myself' (*'E' Is for Evidence* 70)" (47). Valerie Wilson Wesley also confirms that in creating her detective, "I wanted to make a professional woman. She has her own business, which is very important to her. And she's independent in this sense. She left the cops because they were sexist and they were racist. . . . She is a woman who has her own, makes her own way." Marcia Muller, who has written both professional and amateur detective series, stresses a central difference between them: the professional is the subject of knowledge. Because she understands the system of legal and social rules that govern her, she may become adept at bending them: "Sharon [McCone] is a professional, and she won't let you forget it. She knows what is legal and what is not, what can and cannot be done in a given instance. When she takes a chance she recognizes the problems that can result if she botches it. Elena [Oliverez], on the other hand, is an amateur, so she doesn't have the knowledge of investigations. She tries to get by on instinct and savvy" (qtd. in Isaac, "Situation, Motivation, Resolution" 30).

A BLAST FROM THE PAST

While the appearance of the female professional investigator in fiction coincides with the spread of the feminist movement in North America and Britain, the genre became popular only during and after the movement's initial energy and effectiveness had dissipated. The period following the mid-1970s saw the rise of antifeminist backlash from a number of quarters, and slightly later on a distinct shift to the right occurred in the politics of the United States, Canada, and Britain; conservative governments were elected, and some of the significant ground gained for women in the 1960s and 1970s was lost. Chapter 6 explores the conflicts these ideological shifts introduced into the discourse of equality and democratic access that liberal feminist activism had circulated in the

1970s, focusing on how women's private eye fiction mediates those conflicts in terms of the detective's ambivalent relationship to the law. The female private eye genre as it evolved in the 1980s was also fueled by a nostalgia for the idealistic social action of the 1960s and early 1970s, when the women's movement (and activism more generally) seemed to hold so much promise for changing both society as a whole and individual lives. In an article in the *Voice Literary Supplement*, Ruby B. Rich discusses the impetus behind the emergence of fictional "lady dicks" (though her discussion is largely limited to the small press publications):

> The new genre plays with a nostalgia for the 1960s and '70s even as it flagrantly owes its very revisionist existence to the 1980s. . . . It plays with the layers of our subjectivities, literalizing them into actual landscapes in which the trials and tribulations of the present turn out to have roots in the past's unfinished business. This time-travel must account for some of the genre's success: balm poured on our contemporary schizophrenia, it allows a recuperation of the past without giving in to either Movement nostalgia or regressive fault-finding. (24)

A number of successful writers in the subgenre explicitly develop this theme of working through the inheritance of the 1960s in the very different social climate of the 1980s and 1990s. In Paretsky's *Killing Orders*, for example, in telling a police officer about her relationship with her friend Agnes, V.I. revisits their college days together:

> "I'm not going to try to describe to you what it felt like in those days—you don't have much sympathy for the causes that consumed us. I think sometimes that I'll never feel so—so alive."
>
> A wave of bittersweet memory swept over me and I closed my eyes tightly to keep tears at bay. "Then the dream started falling apart. We had Watergate and drugs and the deteriorating economy, and racism and sexual discrimination continued despite our enthusiasm. So we all settled down to deal with reality and earn a living. You know my story. I guess my ideals died the hardest." (106)

The nostalgic allure of the activist 1960s may even contribute to the frequent use of San Francisco settings. Established as a conventional locale of the traditional private eye story by writers such as Dashiell Hammett, more recent novels often combine that association with the city's latter-day reputation as a mecca of 1960s arts-activist culture. Marcia Muller's Sharon McCone, for example, begins the series as an in-house investigator for the All Souls legal cooperative, a San Francisco legal services plan run by liberal lawyers who also function as a kind of support group and collective conscience. In the first novel Sharon wryly describes their typical client as one who "entertained liberal sentiments, toyed with the idea for an 'alternative' lifestyle, and would never get busted for anything more serious than growing marijuana plants on the fire escape" (*Edwin of the Iron Shoes* 11). Later books deal in part with Sharon's response to changes in the cooperative structure of All Souls. Lia Matera's *Where Lawyers Fear to Tread* (1986), set in 1980s San Francisco, introduces lawyer-investigator Willa Jansen. The book begins with an impromptu debate, during a law school review editorial meeting, over the aftermath of American involvement in Vietnam; one of the participants, Jane Day, is a representative of the backlash in the feminist movement of the 1980s, whom Willa calls "one of those damned Republican feminists. You know, get women out of the home and into the Mercedes for luncheon with the Ladies Against Drug Abuse ('Madame Chairman, I'd like to propose a toast to the eradication of drug abuse')" (6). In the second installment of the series, significantly titled *A Radical Departure*, Willa's genetic/social inheritance is described: she is the daughter of Haight-Ashbury radical activist parents who, Willa tells us, "met at a Ban the Bomb meeting and conceived me shortly thereafter; this was probably the last thing they ever did that was unpreceded by moral debate" (9). Lia Matera's second series, featuring lawyer Laura Di Palma, begins in 1988 with *The Smart Money*, centering on a case that requires Laura to revisit the early years of her marriage—"Dropping mescaline in a room with red light bulbs; discussing J. D. Salinger and listening to Leon Russell; going to sleazy dockside bars to prove we'd severed our middle-class roots; opening a 'Peace Center' and running off 'Peace Letters' on an ancient Gestetner; George Carlin records, Firesign Theater . . ." (23). Both of Matera's series discuss the difficult transition between the idealism of the 1960s and the materialism of the 1980s.

The radical roots of Linda Barnes's private eye, Carlotta Carlyle, go even deeper: in the first installment of that series she tells us that she owns a parakeet named "Red Emma," after Emma Goldman, her labor-activist mother's hero. Carlotta attests to "gr[owing] up on my mom's glorious tales about her mom and the New York garment workers' strike" (*A Trouble of Fools* 12). Early in Carolyn Wheat's first Cass Jameson novel, *Dead Man's Thoughts*, the protagonist talks about why she entered the legal profession. Her friend suggests: "Because you wanted to save the whales, end the war, and stop pollution, all in your first year of practice?" and Cass replies, "Something like that. . . . After the shootings at Kent, which the legal system did nothing but cover up, I decided to learn the language, get my union card, and do what I could" (12).

WORKING THEORY

Sara Paretsky's first novel, *Indemnity Only*, also takes her back to the scene of her college activist days, and the period is often revisited and reconsidered in her other novels. Here, V.I. visits a "University Women United" meeting to gather information about a missing woman who had been a member. At the meeting, the women discuss their support of a NOW booth to promote the Equal Rights Amendment at a state fair, but the simple decision gets tangled up in a familiar debate between differing feminist perspectives and nothing is settled. "This was an old argument," V.I. observes to herself, "it went back to the start of radical feminism in the late sixties: Do you concentrate on equal pay and equal legal rights, or do you go off and try to convert the whole society to a new set of sexual values?" (161–62). Not only does the meeting fail to resolve the practical issue with which it began, but when V.I. identifies herself as an investigator, the women refuse to help her protect their missing friend—in part because they suspect her of being a "cop," no matter who is paying her salary. V.I. is expelled from the meeting; frustrated with their inability to execute their theories, she remarks ironically, "Thanks for the time, sisters," as she takes her exit (164). This scene draws attention to the female private eye's role as a practical feminist whose investigations advance, in effect, a *working* feminism that seems to reconcile feminist theory and everyday practice. It offers the hope that the political activism of the 1960s might somehow be integrated with the renewed rhetoric of entrepreneurial capitalism that dominated the conservative 1980s. The figure of the female professional investigator dramatizes, in other words, the hope that somewhere between the apparently outmoded idealist philosophy of the former and the materialist individualism of the latter there might be a space for feminist agency.

Catherine Dain's fifth detective novel, *Bet against the House*, actually comments directly on the professional demeanor that characterizes her investigator's personality and the revisionist possibilities it offers for integrating a feminist sensibility with capitalist enterprise. In that novel Dain's private investigator, Freddie O'Neal, describes a blind date with a business school professor who impresses her by using his expertise in the field of business leadership to develop an accurate thumbnail sketch of her personality, including her emphasis on work and her need for achievement and control, for taking responsibility and preserving her independence (71–72). When Freddie jokingly asks him if he tells fortunes at the carnival on his days off, he replies:

> "Social sciences aren't always exact, but they're a little more certain than tarot cards. I just described the profile of successful women entrepreneurs. There haven't been many studies done, and they're all first generation, but the results have been consistently replicated. We're seeing a second generation of women managers now, and they're significantly different from their predecessors. The same will probably be true with women entrepreneurs." (72)

The private investigator has long been considered a mythologized representation of the self-sufficient, entrepreneurial hero, but that hero has typically been exclusively male. Because of this association, private eye writing by and about women produces female subjects who are "licensed" in the economy; it posits a viable, or "working," subjective space for the working woman. This is by no means a radical gesture, based as it is on the liberal feminist goal of equal access to work and capital, but it is nevertheless significant: it offers readers the tantalizing possibility that a version of the heroic (capitalist) individualism taken for granted in male private eye novels might be not only accessible to women but also open to their manipulation and reshaping. It is important to note, then, that Freddie O'Neal's dinner companion is not simply describing a reproduction or gender role reversal of the male entrepreneurial myth. When Freddie asks him what she would learn if she took a course in leadership from him, he takes her question seriously and replies in a manner that deflates his professorial position of authority. "I don't know," he admits frankly, explaining that while he can teach his male students to alter their detrimental socially conditioned behavior, his female students already seem to have a distinctive set of leadership resources on which to draw. Their unconventional definitions and practices of authority mean that he can only tell them "to go for it and not let the boys stand in their way" (73–74).

DIVERSIFIED CORPORATE BODIES

The professor's advice is also played out in the role of the professional woman writer, whose successful appropriation and reshaping of the role of authorship and the masculine private eye genre gives her access to the discursive, monetary, and broadly political economy offered by publishing success. The popular genre of hard-boiled fiction itself, in other words, offers a potential source of agency, suggesting that it is possible to appropriate liberal discursive structures in order to reshape and perhaps even destabilize them. Our study tends to focus on women writers published by mainstream presses, in part as a method of refining the definition of "popular writing." We take seriously Anne Cranny-Francis's suggestion that the consequences of more avant-garde feminist subversions of genre "may be a loss of readership so severe as to call into question the whole concept of the feminist appropriation of popular fiction. If the appropriation is such that the fiction is no longer popular, where then?" (20). If women's appropriation of the hard-boiled tradition is indeed a viable feminist gesture, even when it is not explicitly intended as such, it has the potential both to work *for* (i.e., to satisfy) and to work *on* (i.e., to renegotiate the attitudes and perceptions of) its audience. Lyn Pykett points out that the more radical novels that appear on the genre fiction lists of small feminist publishers tend to have "a smaller and more self-selected readership" than those of mainstream houses (65–66). A focus on the wider audience of mainstream publications offers several strategic possibilities. In fact, novels that appeal to this audience act out the revisionist feminist goal of working through or subverting existing systems by, in effect, infiltrating rather than overthrowing them. One of these systems, as Kathleen Gregory Klein perceives, is the publishing industry and popular fiction market (*Woman Detective* 200). Another is that of genre itself, with its long-standing gender coding. Each allows access to the other.

As the figures indicate, the female private investigator continues to be popular, though editors and agents agree that the proliferation of authors will probably result in a winnowing process. Natalee Rosenstein of Berkley's Prime Crime mystery line observes that "it's an established subgenre now and it's not going to go away," and Ruth Cavin of St. Martin's affirms that "the professional woman detective is solidly entrenched in the genre. . . . There's no reason for them [the good ones] not to stay, because they reflect their society." As recently as May 1996, *Publishers Weekly*'s review of mysteries affirmed that "the powerful subgenre of American female PI's—Muller's Sharon McCone, Grafton's Kinsey Millhone, Paretsky's V. I. Warshawski, etc.—continues to show muscle" (Dahlin 45). Indeed, beginning in the 1990s, the journal began to note innovations in the mystery genre that further strengthened the female private eye novel: in 1994 an article titled "Many Ways to Mayhem" announced, "Business, booksellers report, is resoundingly good in the mystery category. Many credit the current good health of the crime novel to a parade of energetic and imaginative new crime writers, Americans for the most part, who are infusing the genre with multi-cultural, multi-ethnic, multi-lifestyle settings and characters" (Anthony 43).

Such writers found the private eye an accommodating genre, for many of the same reasons that had attracted their predecessors. It is, for example, a genre that actually prescribes that a marginal figure lay claim to the narrative's central perspective. Discussing recent ethnic, racial, and gay alternatives to the prototypical investigator, novelist Elizabeth Pincus, author of the Nell Fury private eye series (which features a lesbian detective), notes that "as well as being accessible, detective fiction almost always deals with marginal characters. Those of us outside the mainstream can feel a keen affinity with the rebel PI bumping up against the status quo" (qtd. in Anthony, "Many Ways to Mayhem" 43). J. M. Redmann designates her lesbian detective "the lavender sheep of the family" (*Intersection of Law and Desire* 23). The status quo Pincus points to is simultaneously generic and social—it takes in the private eye, the public sphere in general, and its readers in particular. Harry Helm, mystery buyer for Waldenbooks, is quoted in *Publishers Weekly* as saying that "the increase of women writers in the field helped move the category beyond its traditional parameters," allowing a variety of sociological and cultural backgrounds to enter mainstream fiction (Anthony, "Many Ways to Mayhem" 43). This is due in part to the crossover potential of genre fiction, which appeals both to readers who identify with the often marginalized identity of the detective and to those who identify with the conventions of the genre itself. As Bob Mecoy, vice president and senior editor at Simon and Schuster, puts it, "Mysteries are wonderfully inclusive. Readers rally around tough guys, tough women, gay cops, you name it. The mystery has always been an autodidact's paradise. They're for people looking for fun and for a window into something new" (qtd. in Langstaff 43).

In particular, gay and lesbian detective fiction has been touted as "a subgenre flexing considerable muscle" in category fiction (Langstaff 43), and African American mystery novels dealing with racial issues and featuring black characters "have taken a major position in the mystery category" (Anthony, "Many Ways to Mayhem" 50). The novels featuring lesbian private investigators and, on a much smaller scale, those featuring characters who are racial or ethnic minorities seem to be creating a second wave within the trend established by female private investigators in general, as the numbers of titles published continues to grow. For example, books featuring lesbian professional detectives have increased from a negligible number in the 1970s and early 1980s, to 14 from 1986 to 1990, tripling to 43 between 1991 and 1995 (see figures 4 and 5). And, as Avon editor Marjorie Braman remarked in 1993, these characters are becoming more mainstream (M. Hall 5). Indeed, by the 1990s such writers as Katherine V. Forrest, Mary Wings, and J. M. Redmann were moving from feminist presses to mainstream presses; others, including Phyllis Knight and Sandra Scoppettone, were being published by mainstream presses at the outset of their series, changes that imply a widening of the audience for such novels. Kate Mattes of Kate's Mystery Bookstore in Cambridge, Massachusetts, perceives the shift in her own bookstore clientele: "Gay and lesbian books have come out of the closet and are being read by not just the gay constituency but a considerable number of straight readers who read them to learn about a world they don't know much about" (qtd. in Anthony, "Many Ways to Mayhem" 52). The increase in titles featuring racial and ethnic minority investigators shows similar potential (see figures 4 and 5). In particular, Valerie Wilson Wesley's series, centering on African American ex-cop private eye Tamara Hayle, and Eleanor Taylor Bland's Marti MacAlister police series have been widely acclaimed, as have Jean Hager's Molly Bearpaw series and Dana Stabenow's Kate Shugak series, both of which feature

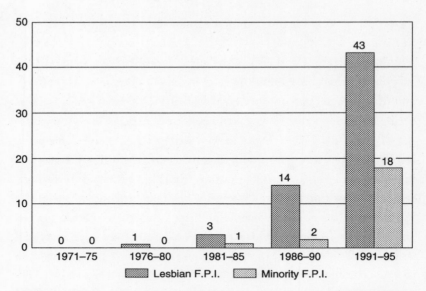

Figure 4.   Series novels featuring a lesbian or racial minority female professional investigator, 1971–95. Source: Heising and authors.

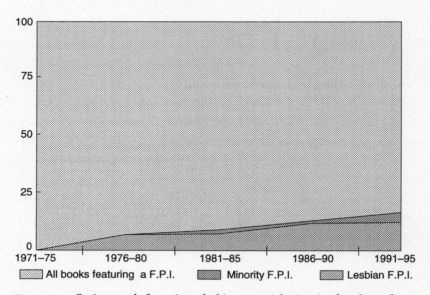

Figure 5.   Series novels featuring a lesbian or racial minority female professional investigator, 1971–95 (percentage). Source: Heising and authors.

Native American female investigators. Leslie Glass's April Woo series featuring a Chinese American homicide detective and S. J. Rozan's series starring Lydia Chin, a Chinese American private eye, also offer readers alternative cultural viewpoints, as does Irene Lin-Chandler's Holly-Jean Ho series, whose hero is half-English and half-Chinese.

It is difficult to know much about the constituency represented by the readership of these works, except that it is largely composed of women—significantly more than half, by all accounts from booksellers, authors, editors, and agents.[6] Literary agent Susan Ann Protter, who believes that the majority of mystery readers are women, speculates that "one of the reasons that there are so many female protagonists in the mystery genre right now is because there are so many women readers. And the women got tired of reading these tough guys." The progenitors of the female private eye novel and their readers demonstrated that there was a market for this variant on the genre. As we discuss in chapter 2, genre fiction, like genre film, is constituted by the active but indirect participation of audiences (Schatz 12), since successful formulas tend to reproduce themselves through multiple installments in a series or through other books of a similar kind. Readers, in other words, are not simply a market that passively consumes a simply defined, static product. Rather, they are women and men who are actively engaged in a social and economic process—not to mention the process of negotiating meaning—and are thus part of the industry that produces genre fiction: they are, quite simply, what makes it *work*. Readers exercise agency in popular genres every time they buy a book, or recommend one to a friend, or ask that it be ordered by their local library. How and why their choices work in the economic, aesthetic, and social realms are among the questions addressed in chapter 2.

Chapter 2

GUMSHOE METAPHYSICS

Reading Popular Culture and Formula Fiction

> Popular fiction, popular art in general, is the very air a
> civilization breathes. . . . It reaffirms our values as they
> change, and dramatizes the conflicts of those values. It
> absorbs and domesticates the spoken language, placing it
> in meaningful context with traditional language, form-
> ing new linguistic synapses in the brain and body of the
> culture. It describes new modes of behavior, new ver-
> sions of human character, new shades and varieties of
> good and evil, and implicitly criticizes them. It holds
> us still and contemplative for a moment, caught like
> potential shoplifters who see their own furtive images
> in a scanning mirror, and wonder if the store detective
> is looking.
>
> Ross MacDonald, "The Writer as Detective Hero"

In Orania Papazoglou's *Wicked, Loving Murder*, romance writer and amateur sleuth Patience C. McKenna muses on the feelings of guilt induced
in writers of women's genre fiction by proponents of "higher," more
"progressive" forms of literary culture:

They *know* people are trying to make them look stupid. They *know* critics are lurking in broom closets, waiting for a chance to blame the decline of Western civilization and the erosion of world capitalism on the latest Silhouette Desire. They *know* there are traitors in their midst, spies, Quality Lit thugs who swoop into the world of love and lust to make a few thousand dollars under a pseudonym and then swoop out again, to surface in the pages of the *Village Voice* with articles accusing category romance of destroying the future of the women's movement. (32)

While Patience McKenna is speaking specifically about the romance genre here, her comments also speak to the climate in which formula writers of other genres—including detective fiction, thrillers, and westerns—create.[1] Patience's perception that her literary activities are under surveillance and thus cast as "criminal" by a disciplinary cultural body is to a large degree legitimated by the widespread perception that formula fiction—and especially women's genres—is not just escapist and apolitical but politically retrograde.

MASS PRODUCTIONS

To "do" popular literature, whether as consumer or creator, is often to be subject to derision, as engaging in an activity that is at best trivial and self-indulgent, at worst destructively regressive. And, as Scott R. Christianson points out, "popular fiction is definitively *generic*," generic being a term traditionally used as a blanket indictment ("Talkin' Trash" 128). Posited as lacking the seriousness of "high" art, genre fiction is often construed as an addictive "habit," a vice that needs to be concealed and controlled, if not curtailed. In one of the earliest essays on modern detective fiction, for example, "The Guilty Vicarage" (1938), W. H. Auden begins his discussion with "A Confession" in which he calls attention to the similarity in the guilty pleasures he derives from his addiction to detective novels and his addictions to tobacco and alcohol (15). Sparkle Hayter weaves a similar notion into her novel *What's a Girl Gotta Do?*

when her protagonist, Robin Hudson, ironically enumerates the myriad flaws of her ex-husband, implicitly equating the reading of popular literature with a private life lacking in the propriety of his public persona: "I know lots of his secrets: that his given name is Heinrich Albert Stedlbauer IV, changed to Burke Avery for television; that at home he belches without excusing himself and secretly reads Judith Krantz. I know his guilty pleasures" (31).

The guilt that accompanies such pleasures exists in part because generic texts are not "individualized" after the fashion of "high" literature: they are formulaic; they are mass-produced; they appeal to a "mass" audience; readers consume them quickly and in quantity, rather than for their enduring value as discrete aesthetic texts; and their production is economically motivated—their success is judged not by literary standards but by the sheer volume of their sales. Given these characteristics, formula works are often viewed, almost by definition, as extremely conservative modes of expression, since they are invested in (commercially) reproducing, rather than changing, the hegemonic literary and social values of the past. Genre writings, therefore, are texts in which readers may safely dip (while on vacation, say, at the beach) but in which "serious" readers immerse themselves at their peril.

The nonindividualized conception of genre fiction, however, may itself be the key to renegotiating its social value. In order to accomplish this renegotiation, we will examine three aspects of formula works: the ways readers participate in the "writing" of the genre and the recognition of its variants, the series production of generic texts, and the reflexivity of generic works. All these elements enable the texts to be conceived as a space of negotiation in which communities of readers and writers, far from being passive reproducers or consumers of preexistent forms and values, can exercise a kind of collective agency. Hard-boiled detective fiction written by women can thus merit the label "feminist" because it admits the possibility of altering the "generic"—and *gendered*—conventions of both literary and social behavior.

It is important to recognize from the start that the supposedly "simple" conventions of genre formulas are in fact complicated and contradictory. If readers of popular fiction are passive, even addicted consumers, then they are at the mercy of the cultural industries and the messages those industries formulaically market. But this assumption ignores a contradiction inherent in the texts, one that Stuart M. Kaminsky and Jeffrey H. Mahan foreground in their study of television:

> When we encounter any work of popular art, whether it is a nursery rhyme from early antiquity or television coverage of a baseball game, we are dealing with an apparent contradiction. The work of popular art is two things at the same time: it is like many other things that have preceded it; yet is also unique, not a precise duplication of anything that has been presented before. This leads to the basic debate about whether examination of works of popular art, or any art, should emphasize their familiarity or their uniqueness. (3)

The duality that they perceive arises because authors of popular genres both must follow recognizable generic conventions and must build upon and alter what has gone before.

What gets lost in Kaminsky and Mahan's argument about familiarity and uniqueness, however, is the role of the reader. Umberto Eco picks up this thread when he suggests that a "modern conception of aesthetic value" is endowed with two characteristics:

> 1. It must achieve a dialectic between order and novelty—in other words between scheme and innovation;
>
> 2. This dialectic must be perceived by the consumer, who must not only grasp the contents of the message, but also the way in which the message transmits these contents. (173–74)

Eco draws attention to the role of the reader, who must recognize the generic conventions at play in a work and who thus takes on an active role in the construction of the popular text. And, as Christianson perceives,

> Contrary to "popular" belief—in this case, the belief of critics preferring "high" or "serious" culture—readers of popular fiction are

critically comparative readers. For whatever reasons and with whatever outcomes, readers of popular fiction are highly cognizant of the
forms and conventions of the genres they read. Far from the limited
view that such readers will tolerate only those works which "cor-
rectly" conform to the rules of formation of their favored genres,
the proliferation and development of popular fictional genres suggests that playing off and even violating norms of genres are essential aspects of reader enjoyment. ("Talkin' Trash" 128)

Indeed, while formula texts must be recognizable to their audience as a
"type" or genre of fiction, they must also add to or strategically alter that
genre. The development of the hard-boiled form itself demonstrates the
possibility of strategic change within the generic paradigm, for in subverting the "rules" of the British cozy, it gave rise to a "new" American
subgenre. Shifting the locale and the ideological impetus of the British
genre, the hard-boiled novelists moved its focus from an upper-class to
a lower-class milieu, and from the rural "country house" or English village environment to an urban one, at the same time altering the genre's
narrative strategies and language.

The hard-boiled form thus renegotiated its own "generic rules" ex-
pressive of a differing social context and sensibility. These rules are sum-
marized by Arthur Asa Berger:

The tough guy detective has to solve the crime to avoid being sus-
pected or convicted by the dumb cops. In the same way, the individual must prove himself or herself by being a success in the world;
otherwise there is doubt that cannot be allayed. [Such heroes are]
paradigmatic . . . and reflect basic American personality traits and
philosophical beliefs. . . . [The hard-boiled hero] shows the virtue
of a principled individualism for . . . the rules motivating his behav-
iour . . . [demonstrate] what political scientists call *a theory of obligation.* He may be cynical and sceptical and stoical, but he also has a
sense of duty and loyalty. (116–17)

The hard-boiled innovations in mystery fiction to which Berger draws attention spoke to a particular time—the late 1920s and the early 1930s—

in which increasing corporatization, economic instability, and flux in gender roles made the affirmation of the power of the "common man" particularly important. In their time, therefore, hard-boiled novels worked to reinforce the social role of many of the readers to whom they appealed, but they also helped to ease transitions into a trans- formed social situation and to confront the problems resulting from that transformation.

In his analysis of formula fiction, John G. Cawelti maps out four im- portant functions that genre works fulfill:

1.   Formula stories affirm existing interests and attitudes by pre- senting an imaginary world that is aligned with these interests and attitudes. . . .

2.   Formulas resolve tensions and ambiguities resulting from the conflicting interests of different groups within the culture or from ambiguous attitudes toward particular values.

3.   Formulas enable the audience to explore in fantasy the bound- ary between the permitted and the forbidden and to experience in a carefully controlled way the possibility of stepping across this boundary.

4.   Finally, literary formulas assist in the process of assimilating changes in values to traditional imaginative constructs. . . . [L]iterary formulas ease the transition between old and new ways of expressing things and thus contribute to cultural continuity. (*Adventure* 35–36)

As Cawelti contends, formula fiction serves different and conflicting functions: it affirms norms and values at the same time that it enables readers to assimilate changes (though perhaps not as simply as Cawelti implies). It therefore is (or can be) both conservative and innovative— at the same time. While the overall movement of the particular genre may work to affirm the ideological norms of its consumers, subtle changes within it also reflect changes in the social climate and provide a means of working through those changes in a "controlled fashion." Cawelti thus demonstrates the ways in which formulaic conventions speak to and from a cultural demand: "allowing for a certain degree of inertia in the process, the production of formulas is largely dependent on audience response" (*Adventure* 34).

That the audience might participate in the construction of a genre itself contradicts the notion that the readers of popular works are simply passive consumers. Thomas Schatz cites the critic Henry Nash Smith to demonstrate the ways in which writers of the western participated in a creative celebration and perpetuation of certain values and myths central to the culture, particularly those concerning westward expansion: "He contends that the public writer is not pandering to his market by lowering himself to the level of the mass audience, but rather that he or she is cooperating with it in formulating and reinforcing collective values and ideals" (11). Extending Smith's thesis, Schatz goes on to discuss how consumers often participate in the construction of these texts, and even set (rather than simply follow) market trends:

> In underscoring the relationship of pulp Western novels to a mass audience and hence to American folklore, however, Smith's study adds an important dimension to our discussion. He suggests that these novels were written not only for the mass audience, but *by* them as well. Produced by depersonalized representatives of the collective, anonymous public and functioning to celebrate basic beliefs and values, their formulas might be regarded not only as popular or even elite art but also as *cultural ritual*—as a form of collective expression seemingly obsolete in an age of mass technology and a genuinely "silent majority." . . . The basis for this viewpoint is the level of *active but indirect audience participation* in the formulation of any popular commercial form. (11–12)

With a commercial genre, reader input (through demand and consumption) is important because the bottom line of mass-market publishing is sales. Consequently, the ideological service that the original hard-boiled novels performed had to shift with the times, for the subgenre's initial movement to affirm the male hard-boiled hero and his code of ethics ceased to speak to a wide readership. Other aspects of the genre, however, continued to speak powerfully indeed.

MONEY TALKS

By the early 1980s, the date we have pinpointed as marking the emergence of the hard-boiled female investigator as a significant phenomenon, women had established their presence not simply as consumers of household items but as buyers with significant disposable incomes whose needs were independent of the domestic context; this status as consumer helped generate the shift to a "tough gal" hero. Indeed, in "Murder Most Foul and Fair," Katrine Ames and Ray Sawhill note that the active female detective arose in part because female readers were clamoring for representations of strong women characters. They suggest that this demand was made possible by the expansion of feminism itself: "As the women's movement grew, so did the demand for female protagonists. Carol Brener, former proprietor of the Manhattan bookstore Murder Ink, remembers customers so desperate 'they didn't even care if the killer was a woman, as long it was a strong character'" (67).

In an article in the *Voice Literary Supplement*, B. Ruby Rich also comments on the appeal and the sales potential of the subgenre: "Women's and gay bookstores, from Old Wives' Tales in San Francisco to the new Judith's Room in Greenwich Village, report that woman-detective novels are walking out the door as fast as they arrive on the shelves" (24). Rich's observation is confirmed by a 1990 *Publishers Weekly* article. In "Mystery Books," Carolyn Anthony surveys and quotes publishing and marketing experts: St. Martin's Press editor Ruth Cavin declares, "Books with a woman as central sleuth are very popular with us right now"; Janet Hutching of Walker Publishing testifies, "our biggest sellers last year were those with strong female characters"; and Susan Sandler of the book club Mystery Guild comments, "Women writers in general are selling better than ever before. . . . Having a woman detective puts special demands on the writer to be more imaginative" (28). Such observations suggest that consumers are more than the targets of publishers' marketing campaigns: they also play an active role in directing the industry simply because of their purchasing power. As subjects, these readers effected and reinforced a shift in the form of generic conventions, which in turn affirmed their empowered subject position as readers: "Just the fact that these books exist feels like an achievement," writes Rich. "The woman-detective genre can take on anything currently being peddled at airport bookshops or supermarket checkout counters, accommodating any style or level of quality" (26). Indeed, the *professional* status of the female investigator in the tough gal genre epitomized the economic power such change reflected.

Without a doubt, consumerism is a problematic space from which to construct subjectivity, but the shifts in subject matter urged by buying power can work to ease women's problems in entering what had previously been a "man's world." As Rich comments:

> The woman who's been happily seduced by years of soap operas, *telenovelas*, and romance novels now gets a different thrill—the old formulas turned inside out, with gutsy heroines instead of trembling maidens, yet with the same page-turning appeal intact. Each volume offers itself to the willing reader like a safe-deposit box of feminist possibilities, a place where real problems can be play-acted and strategies tested. (24)

In offering this insight into the feminist possibilities implicit in each volume, Rich's language designates the reading of the novels as a kind of performance that engages the reader in a reciprocal relationship with the revisionary version of the genre, a relationship that involves the active rereading of both genre and self. Novelist Shelley Singer (author of the Barrett Lake and Jake Sampson–Rosie Vincente series) echoes Rich's "performative" language when she observes that the hard-boiled genre isn't a static form ("you know, the guy in his office with the bottle in the drawer") and is thus open to the kind of gender reversals Rich perceives: "performance," Singer notes, "is elastic."

SERIAL INTERVENTIONS

The series format of the novels is an important element of the genre's elasticity. The subgenre of the feminist hard-boiled detective novel, and arguably other forms of formula fiction including science fiction, westerns, and so on, departs from the individualistic emphasis of the self-contained novel. That "high" cultural form is seen in modernist terms as a discrete aesthetic. Umberto Eco notes that the products of the mass media were traditionally "equated with the products of industry insofar as they were produced *in series*, the 'serial' production was considered as alien to the artistic invention" (162). Yet, precisely because it *was* alien to conventional ideas about "artistic invention," serial formula fiction enabled readers to adapt a different kind of reading strategy and to influence the shape of the genre itself.[2] As John Fiske observes, "The reader of the aesthetic text attempts to read it on *its* terms, to subjugate him- or herself to its aesthetic discipline. The reader reveres the text. The popular reader, on the other hand, holds no such reverence for the text but views it as a resource to be used at will" (106). The series format of genre fiction in fact engenders innovations because it encourages such readerly involvement. Not surprisingly, then, Fiske goes on to contend that "genres are the result of a three-way contract between audience, producer, and text" (108).

Reader involvement in serial fiction may directly affect the development of both series and genre. People in the publishing industry acknowledge that series fiction is driven by reader expectations and demands in a way quite unlike any other form.[3] Natalee Rosenstein of Berkley Prime Crime, for example, observes that mystery fiction "is very much a word-of-mouth kind of genre," and that word of mouth is integral to its series form:

> A first mystery is not going to be something that any publishing house is going to support with a lot of advertising or promotion. And you really need to have two, three, four books out there. . . .

[W]e rely a lot on the mystery specialty stores as well as other inde-
pendents, even though a lot of our distribution goes to the chains
and bigger stores. But we rely on, to build someone's career initially,
that . . . a customer comes in and says "Oh, what's good?" and they
[the booksellers] say, "Oh, I just [got] in this great new writer." And
a lot of people talking to each other are recommending the books to
their friends and beginning to get some familiarity. So what we find
a lot is that maybe it won't be until the third book that somebody
will pick it up, at which point, if they like it, hopefully, they then
want to go back and read the first and the second.

One of our reader survey respondents described an ongoing commitment to individual series authors: "I have a fairly limited interest in that
I rarely start reading a new author, but, once started, read everything I
can by that person" (respondent 26).

Katherine V. Forrest, author of the Kate Delafield mysteries, sees the
relationship between author and reader as part of a kind of generic "contract" that makes it possible for her to bring issues important to the lesbian community to public light. In effect, the generic conventions on
which readers of series fiction insist create an ongoing performative
space in which Forrest can act out lesbian feminist political narratives.
She notes that in one sense dealing with the series format and the conventions of the genre is limiting, since readers have fixed expectations:
"There just are certain aspects that you know you need to meet. It's not
enough to want to make a statement in a book, you still have to fulfill
that contract with the reader. But yet at the same time . . . it's given me
an almost unparalleled opportunity to really convey some issues that
matter, that matter to me and matter to my community, in a way that I
think has a great deal of impact."

The series structure of female hard-boiled PI novels plays an important role in shifting reader expectations. Because of the form, authors
can explore the varieties and nuances of the genre and its themes in an
extended way and from a single point of view to which readers develop

both a personal attachment and a political engagement. The serial form generates a relationship of trust and identification between the reader and both the series protagonist *and* her author. Ruth Cavin of St. Martin's Press describes the process: "You establish a rapport with the reader and then the reader is on the lookout not only for books by you which they like, because they like the first book, but also because they're anxious to deal with a character again." Or, as Phyllis Grann of Putnam says of readers' relationship to series characters, "People get attached. It's like a family, you know."

Identification, an important aspect of the dynamic, is particularly pronounced in this genre because the narrative is typically either first-person or third-person, consistently focalized through a single sensibility (see chapter 5). One survey respondent observed that "feminism means to focus on women's experiences and feelings which is what these authors do" (respondent 11). The practical, everyday ways in which this identification can empower readers is suggested by a respondent who gained a sense of vindication that countered the vulnerability often felt by urban women: "I enjoy mystery/detective novels with women as the main character (detective) because I enjoy seeing women do well, especially in a 'man's world.' Having been the victim of crime and living in a large city with a high crime/murder rate I enjoy seeing women 'getting the best' of criminals" (respondent 39). On a slightly different note, Eileen Massucco, a contributor to the e-mail discussion group DorothyL, wrote the group that during a difficult set of long-distance negotiations to sell her house, her "personal stress buster" was reading a Janet Dawson book, *Till the Old Men Die*.

> That book travelled all over Seattle with me to every appointment, event, etc. (It was my personal security blanket ;-) It was wonderful reading. And just when you think it is all resolved, it has a wonderful twist that shows the perseverance and clear thinking of Dawson's female private eye, Jeri Howard. (I used Jeri Howard as my role model to help me with the million decisions I had to make during the house

negotiations!!) Thanks again, Janet/Jeri, for getting me through another big step in my life!![4]

Indeed, Massucco wrote that the *series* of Jeri Howard novels took her through the traumatic experience, since their ongoing serial narratives formed a parallel with the stages and ongoing difficulties of her move. Sara Paretsky confirms the phenomenon: "A lot of women write and tell me that V.I. helped them get through some difficulty in their own lives by making them feel they could resolve their own problems. I think that women are getting the message of empowerment" (Paretsky, "What Do Women Really Want?" 13).

The series structure of detective fiction allows authors room to develop and extend reader identification, providing room to explore the character and through her confront a variety of issues and concerns. Sue Grafton signals the connection between series writing and the emotional investments of readers in a *Writer's Digest* interview in which she comments on how the simple hard work of series writing pays off in reader identification: "If it's a character readers like, they look forward to the next book. They become interested in that character's life and, since the groundwork has been already laid out, I can focus each book on larger issues" (Carcaterra 45). Indeed, that investment and payoff should be seen in both emotional and economic terms, since series fiction is driven by the response of authors and publishers to reader demand: as Bantam associate editor Kate Miciak notes, "There are not many bestselling mystery authors who don't do series. Once readers have made a commitment to an author and his or her other characters, they become fanatically loyal. Writers simply have to write series to keep them satisfied" (qtd. in Summer 44).

Laurie King, author of the Kate Martinelli series, emphasizes the advantages of the form: "Because I write about people and how they move and change, 300 pages isn't enough to complete a good, strong character. A series is a sort of mega-fiction: 3,000 pages, divided into 10 episodes!" Dana Stabenow, who writes the Kate Shugak series, also comments on the character possibilities she enjoys, drawing attention to how readers identify with the central character: "I love writing series fiction. I love being able to peel back another layer of a character with every book, to allow them to tell me things about themselves I never knew, to watch them grow. The challenge is to keep the characters fresh. The reward is when a fan says, 'I miss Kate. When do I get to visit with her again?'" Valerie Wilson Wesley, author of the Tamara Hayle novels, the first female African American private eye series in the mainstream,[5] explains her preference for series novels in similar terms: "I think that it allows you to develop a character in ways that you may not be able to in a different kind of book. . . . [I]n each book I reveal more about Tamara's character and her past . . . because I think we're all so much a part of our past in our present . . . and I think a series allows you the freedom to do that with not only your main character but also with other characters." In other words, the serial narrative—and especially detective narratives, which focus on the reconstruction of past events—enables the historical-biographical, and even sociological, "grounding" of characters.

Like Grafton, Sara Paretsky has isolated the ongoing character as an aspect of the series form particularly accommodating to her interest in developing broader themes:

> In my own work, I didn't set out to create a series character. I was trying to prove to myself that I could write a novel. I wanted to write a crime novel with a woman protagonist. And because I live in the ultimate hard-boiled city, Chicago, it was impossible to think of my protagonist except as a hard-boiled detective.
>
> As time has passed, though, the kinds of crimes that interest me, and the perspective that interests me, make the voice of my PI hero the most effective one to use. I find that she gives me the opportunity to look in depth, and over time, at issues of law, society and justice. I wouldn't be able to explore these as effectively in a stand-alone thriller. ("Writing a Series Character" 60)

Because readers form an attachment to them, series characters become mediators, helping those who might not be interested in works with a more identifiable orientation toward "social problems" to negotiate political issues *through* personal space. And the private eye's social mobility enables her to take the middle-class reader places she might otherwise never go—both literally and figuratively. Elisabeth Bowers's detective Meg Lacey's initiation into the private eye business in *Ladies' Night*, for example, marks the opening of her perspective from the limitations of her middle-class domestic world to other cultures, classes, and locales; and the reader follows her character.

Nancy Baker Jacobs, author of the Devon MacDonald series, compares her approach to genre fiction with the strategies she used as a teacher of a course on women and the media offered by a university journalism department. Because she was careful not to alienate her more conservative (often male) students, she felt her teaching was able to reach a wider audience while maintaining its integrity: "I've tried to put that [approach] in the Devon books, where she might well be making the same point that some other character might be making in somebody else's books, but perhaps make it in a way that people are more able to hear." It is important to remember that mainstream genre fiction must affirm the values of its wide readership; at the same time, such fiction can explore and expand the limits of those values. It must, as Jacobs implies, provoke readers to listen to something new, but speak to them in ways they can hear.

USING THE "F" WORD

This equivocal position allows novels to dramatize feminist politics for readers who may not consider themselves "feminists." Indeed, while many of the readers who responded to our survey clearly derived pleasure from the portrayal of female autonomy and a woman-centered perspective in detective novels written by women, they were, by and large, reluctant to acknowledge a connection between pleasure and ideology.

One wrote, "I read them [detective novels featuring strong female protagonists] for pleasure and I don't spend a lot of time thinking about political ramifications" (respondent 7), though she also made it clear that she would not enjoy a novel about a woman who didn't think for herself. Another stated simply, "I read for pleasure, not social politics" (respondent 64). Readers were generally reluctant to conceive of their own "entertainment" reading as in itself politically positioned. Only two respondents clearly aligned themselves with or against feminism as a cause. Interestingly, both responded positively to detective novels with strong female protagonists, and both saw their responses as "natural" rather than political: respondent 8 commented that "I'm no real feminist and I just enjoy strong female heroes, women who don't always cry for help and can cope with problems," and respondent 72 wrote that "I am a feminist, and so naturally find especially appealing the many excellent books now focussed on various aspects of the current revolutions in women's lives and roles, and the impact of that on society and ideas." Obviously, the books can function as a common ground for readers who read from a variety of positions.

One of the pleasures of reading novels with strong female detectives, it seems, lies in the ability of these works to negotiate what we would call the territory of gender politics in a manner that readers saw as "normal" rather than "political," one identified with "realism" rather than "ideology." Almost unanimously, mystery readers stated that they greatly enjoyed detective novels with strong female heroes (all but two agreed), but they divided on the issue of whether or not these works should be designated "feminist."[6] Those readers who thought it was appropriate to think of novels portraying female detectives as feminist did so largely because of their emphasis on a strong, active, independent protagonist who pursues the goal of equality with men. They identified these broad goals with feminism. As one reader put it, "Women taking an active role as detectives in books is to me a pragmatic, de facto form of feminism" (respondent 36). Another wrote, "I have just about decided that whether or not a woman self-identifies as feminist, if she has somehow furthered the cause of equal opportunity for women, even if only by being a groundbreaker, then she is a feminist in my book" (respondent 55). Yet another suggests,

> A story with a woman as the central character will usually have to examine or comment on how the woman operates in a traditionally male environment, whether it be her reaction to authority structures or male colleagues in her profession—we also see the reaction of clients and other characters in the yarn in their perception of a female detective. These explorations (although maybe not their outcomes) are feminist intentions, even if unconscious, on the part of the author. (respondent 73)

Thus for some readers in the matter-of-fact realism of these books feminist issues are an integral component, even if they are not overtly theorized. They are, in other words, books in which a kind of working feminism is a normalized part of the "reality" constructed by the story.

Those readers who did not find the feminist label appropriate often distanced themselves from the term and cause itself. In order to explain their pleasure, they seemed to need to separate the novels and themselves from *any* overt political cause: "I simply don't think about feminist issues when reading mysteries" (respondent 14). Often they associated feminist writing with "soap box" politicking or "propaganda"; because they did not detect any overt attempt to convert them to a political cause, these readers eschewed the ideologically charged word "feminist."[7] If the gender issues in the novels were normalized (i.e., portrayed in a "realistic" manner), or if readers could identify with the central female characters, then they did not see them as overtly (or troublingly) political. One of our respondents, for example, commented that the strong female detectives "just seem like normal people to me, women who do what they have to do, not because they're feminist" (respondent 35). Other respondents wrote:

> Some novels are written by authors reflecting strong feminist views however most novels I read tend to portray females in situations that

I can relate to or believe in without having to be hit over the head by strong feminist propaganda. Women have as much power as they believe they have. I don't think that many female authors push a strong feminist theme. That is not to say they do not have strong female protagonists but they just do not overburden the point. (respondent 9)

It depends mostly on the author, but I don't think most women authors are trying to ram that particular point down the reader's throat. The books may help the feminist cause by portraying women not as victims but as problem-solvers, but since I'm a woman and already know that, I don't need convincing. I read them for a good read about characters with which I can identify. (respondent 32)

I see women writing detective fiction about female characters to be part of the social conditions of our times. I see this as a reflection of the fact that women are tired of the old stereotypes and want to read about capable female characters. I would not see this as feminism but a sign of the times. (respondent 63)

It's not necessarily feminist to portray women as strong—many women ARE strong. (respondent 38)

I don't think that portraying women as strong, competent professionals is feminist. It's reality. (respondent 89)

Respondents in the camp that resisted the feminist label often used violent imagery to describe their conception of feminist political discourse: phrases like "hit over the head" and "ram that particular point down the reader's throat" abound. Others felt there had to be an "anti-male theme" or "male bashing" to merit the "feminist" label (e.g., respondents 22 and 69). These readers saw a clear disjunction between their own perceived norms and realities—which determined the characters they could "relate" to—and a version of "feminism" they identified as harsh, strident, or proselytizing. It is our contention that women's detective fiction, working through the "reader recognition" effects of identification, techniques of realism, and the conventions of genre, at the same time may subtly open up the nature of subjectivity and social "reality" to analysis and reinterpretation. Fiction (a somewhat less politically charged "f" word than feminism, for most readers) becomes a locus where feminist politics can be practiced in a nonthreatening manner.

The conventions of genre fiction are, of course, not "realistic" at all— they are social and aesthetic constructs—but readers apparently associate the generic qualities of these novels with a kind of comforting, normalizing process: if the recognizable narrative and discursive strategies of the generic novel are conventional, then the central female character's behavior and the ideological position she occupies are by extension conventionalized too. The strategies of the feminist novel of investigation thus involve a dialogue between discourses of realism and reflexivity, a balance between simply reproducing and renegotiating recognizable generic conventions, and an erasure of the distinction between theory and practice, politics and fiction. This, we suggest, is why readers can use diametrically opposed political language to describe such fiction, while in many ways coming to similar conclusions about its pleasurable effects on them. The result is a working definition of feminism, a kind of theory-in-practice that is both accessible and enjoyable—even to readers reluctant to confront the politics of popular entertainment.

COLLABORATIVE COMPOSITIONS

The series structure of the feminist hard-boiled detective novel makes it possible to explore social issues in an entertaining fashion: because a single book need not evoke every possibility afforded by the subgenre, a variety of cultural problems can be woven into the series. Clearly, engagement with social issues is important for the authors. As Kathy Hogan Trocheck notes of her Callahan Garrity novels: "Issues of race, class and gender always seem to be important in my books. Race especially, since my books are set in Atlanta, the capital of the New South. . . . I can't seem to not write about the issues affecting the society I live in."

For Trocheck, social issues automatically figure into her description of the world her characters inhabit, especially since her novels share a sociogeographic locale. Authors also perceive the benefit of writing in a popular format, which enables them to reach an audience that might not otherwise integrate politics and pleasure. Elizabeth Pincus, author of the Nell Fury series, observes, "I like the idea of writing in a popular genre, something that would be very accessible to readers while being political/contemporary at the same time. Dare I say subversive . . ." (her ellipsis). Sandra Scoppettone deliberately draws attention to the way she uses the familiar space of the genre novel to develop her lesbian detective Lauren Laurano's life story. The series, she says, "seems to have crossed over in the mystery field. . . . I want to entertain and I also want to show that lesbians are just people. . . . That there's nothing so frightening here, and basically just to show the characters as regular people, leading a life. That's I guess the major thing."

Hard-boiled detective fiction thus generates a "common space" in which concerns and social issues can be addressed and negotiated by readers who would not necessarily read about them elsewhere. That common space is the arena of genre. Valerie Wilson Wesley finds (much like Scoppettone) that her novels function as crossover texts. She uses the detective genre both to draw attention to the ways racial and gender differences are constructed and to interrogate such barriers:

> I think my readers are primarily, at this point, African American women. It also crosses over, because many white women enjoy my books too and some white men. . . . White readers read black mysteries, black mystery readers read white writers. So it's not the same kind of barriers that I think often separate us when we choose our literature. . . . So it's not the same kind of lines, of fences that we build. And I think that's a good thing. To be able to cross into other people's worlds and walk in their shoes for a while.

The effect of genre also relies on its production by authors working as a de facto community. Linda Grant observes that a number of authors who have created a strong female protagonist write about similar issues:

> We come up with common kinds of concerns and common ways of dealing with things; we each put our individual stamp on them but we're concerned, many of us are concerned with similar issues. I think one of the, for want of a better word, trends among women writers is that . . . the kinds of issues that we address are slightly different from the ones that men have traditionally addressed. We're more apt to be concerned about issues like domestic violence, children at risk, that sort of thing.

And Grant explicitly acknowledges her debt to other writers (of whose texts she acts as a reader). In a gesture frequently used by authors of the private eye genre, Grant dedicates *A Woman's Place* to Susan Dunlap, the author of the Jill Smith and Kiernan O'Shaughnessy series. Grant's acknowledgment performs a dual purpose: it expresses her personal indebtedness to another author, and it also points to the growing community of female writers "collaboratively" engaged in genre writing. Marcia Muller calls attention to the fact that many members of this community know one another and are thus "constantly swapping ideas." Although personal knowledge and interaction need not be part of the more general intertextual processes of reading and rewriting that drive the development and proliferation of a genre, the act of collaboration is an apt metaphor for the way genres are written not by individuals but by virtual communities of writers and readers. Muller herself literally collaborated on two early unpublished novels with Sue Dunlap, and their subsequent "recycling" of those works is an apt figure for the sharing of generic features: "we since have dismantled them, taking different characters or different parts, and recycled them into individual works. . . . There was a time when one or the other [of us] would call up and say 'Hey, have you used so and so? Well do you mind if I take her for this story line?'"

Interestingly, novels themselves alert readers not just to the notion of a community of authors who are also readers of one another's work but also to a broader community of readers who can actively recognize and decode generic markers. As Sarah Dunant's investigator comments after she unsuccessfully tries to perform for an oblivious waitress the "hold the mayonnaise scene" from the film *Five Easy Pieces*, "homage only works when you both know what you're worshipping" (*Fatlands* 7). In Elizabeth Pincus's *Two-Bit Tango*, protagonist Nell Fury comments that "I'd stayed up late reading the night before, wanting to find out if Kinsey Millhone would go to bed with this fellow Dietz. Then I woke early out of anxiousness—whether for Kinsey or myself, I wasn't sure" (87). This kind of reflexive technique is a kind of in-joke: it acknowledges the author's sense of her place in the subgenre, and its effect hinges on the reader's awareness of other works in that subgenre. In this case, Pincus's reference also draws attention to the reader's responsive relationship with the "reality" of the fiction, even as it disturbs that reality by referring to another fictional text. In Michelle Spring's *Every Breath You Take*, the reader's recognition of a metatextual reference actually functions as a clue in the investigation: PI Laura Principal uncovers the killer of a former roommate, Monica Harcourt, by deducing that Monica's penchant for reading Katherine V. Forrest's novels (the murderer tampers with a copy of *Murder at the Nightwood Bar* found on the victim's bedside table) has been misinterpreted as a sign of her lesbianism by a homophobic and homicidal admirer. In solving the mystery, readers acknowledge that not only lesbian readers enjoy lesbian novels.

Metatextual references are scattered throughout Sandra Scoppettone's novels. By evoking other female PIs, Scoppettone helps establish the role of Lauren Laurano in relation to a tradition of other female investigators who authorize her in her investigations. This is a particularly self-conscious evocation of the way in which characterizations in genre fiction are always established relationally—readers understand characters both as individuals and as generic types. Scoppettone sets up specifically female generic standards to which her character must be compared. In *Everything You Have Is Mine*, Laurano's inquiry is guided by the thought, "Would Kiernan O'Shaughnessy leave without talking to this woman, even if there was nothing to gain?" (244). She also keeps herself in line with the reminder that "Meg Lacey would never get sidetracked this way" (277); and when she self-deprecatingly examines a disguise, she muses, "I wonder if Kat Colorado would ever dress like this" (284). Sara Paretsky's V. I. Warshawski, similarly, comments that "I've always been a little jealous of Kinsey Milhone's [sic] immaculate record-keeping; I didn't even have receipts for meals or gas" (*Blood Shot* 159).

Lesley Grant-Adamson, one of the few female hard-boiled novelists in England, gives her character Laura Flynn a friend named "Anna Lee," thereby providing an intertextual nod both to Liza Cody's detective character of the same name and to Cody's position as Grant-Adamson's collaborator in the British tradition. Cody's own recent novels *Bucket Nut*, *Monkey Wrench*, and *Musclebound*, which follow the life and investigations of Eva Wylie, a professional wrestler, also refer back to her earlier private eye series, since Anna Lee appears as a secondary character who contracts with Eva for security services. J. M. Redmann, as noted earlier, uses a similar intertextual device in *The Intersection of Law and Desire* when she names her detective's lover Cordelia James, paying tribute both to P. D. James and her heroine, Cordelia Gray—and, perhaps, suggesting a dynamic of lesbian desire possible in a reading of James's Cordelia Gray novels: lesbian readers read "straight" novels, too. In *Double*, a novel written collaboratively by Marcia Muller and her husband Bill Pronzini, Muller's character Sharon McCone, attending a private investigator's convention, chats briefly with "a woman named Kinsey Millhone, who had her own agency in Santa Teresa" (56), calling attention to the importance of such generic encounters within the "conventions" of the private eye novel itself.

CRIMINAL COLLECTIVES

In addition to such literary and intertextual "meetings," there are also important *literal* conventions, readings, and meetings, which often function as a support network and lobbying group. The general failure of publishers to market and publicize writers early in their careers has tended to stimulate an ethos of self-help among less-established writers, and authors actively work at being professionals in the fields of publishing and marketing. For example, they often engage in self and mutual promotion—setting up tours and readings, creating promotional devices like newsletters and bookmarks, attending conventions, and establishing professional networks and organizations with other authors and readers. The remarks of novelist T. J. MacGregor (who writes her detective Aline Scott series under the pseudonym Alison Drake) counter the image of the mystery writer as dilettante: "It's not enough anymore that you sit down and write a book. Now you have to figure out how you're going to market it. . . . I know quite a few writers who, for them it's like a second job."

Perhaps the most significant of the organizations for women writers in the genre is Sisters in Crime, which offers a handbook on self-promotion—wittily titled "Shameless Promotion for Brazen Hussies," as if to make obsolete stereotypical ideas about the modesty and amateur status of women writers. The group was founded at the Bouchercon World Mystery Conference in 1986 specifically "to combat discrimination against women in the mystery field, educate publishers and the general public as to inequalities in the treatment of female authors, and raise the level of awareness of their contribution to the field" (D'Amato, "Welcome"). Thus, its motivating principle was an interest in the "representation" of women in the mystery field at several levels: as characters in novels written by male authors, as readers, and as authors of stature—especially as represented by reviews of their books:

> By 1986, probably a third of American mysteries were by women, but women were getting less than a fifth of the reviews. Sara Paretsky, concerned about issues including the number of books that reveled in "the graphic abuse of women," founded Sisters in Crime. The watchdog and networking organization has more than 600 members. . . . Women are more frequently reviewed now. And Kate

Mattes [of Kate's Mystery Books in Cambridge, Mass.] says, "Publishers are saying, 'Gee, we ought to promote these women.' They hadn't before. If I had a book signing, generally the author got herself here and paid for it." (Ames and Sawhill 67)

The organization is one example of the ongoing efforts of female mystery writers and their readers to fashion a *collective* space in which readers and writers can effect change, largely through its role as a practical support group. Jean Taylor, author of a lesbian private eye series that began in 1995 with *We Know Where You Live*, declared that "What has taken the place of publisher's support for me in many ways is the mystery writers' organization. Sisters in Crime and Mystery Writers of America, on both the national level and locally, have been life-savers for friendly advice as well as help with promotion." More generally, Sisters in Crime succeeded in pressuring publishers to promote books more intensively and publications to review them more widely. These reviews are particularly important since, as Linda Grant indicates, often public libraries require at least two reviews of any work being considered for acquisition. Without reviews, the librarians could not order the books, thereby preventing many mystery readers who depended on libraries from gaining access to them. Library purchases also make up a significant proportion of the sales of hardcover novels.

On another front, writers in the mystery genre have been aided in their demand for greater visibility by bibliographers. In 1994 Kathleen Gregory Klein edited a comprehensive biocritical dictionary of women crime writers, which she titled *Great Women Mystery Writers*. In turn, librarians Jean Swanson and Dean James produced a popular guide to female authors of mystery fiction, *By a Woman's Hand*. Their book consists of author entries and brief summaries of their series, along with notes at the bottom of each entry offering the readers advice (i.e., "If this writer interests you, you might also want to look at the following writers") that affirms a continuity or connectedness among writers in the various mystery subgenres. Also in print is Willetta L. Heising's exhaustive work, first published as *Detecting Women: A Readers' Guide and Checklist for Mystery Fiction Written by Women* and now in its second edition as *Detecting Women 2*. The compilation lists female authors by subgenre, profession, and so on, and features (at an additional cost) an accompanying pocket-size volume that readers can take to their bookstore or library to follow up on the suggestions provided in the larger book.[8] These volumes also highlight readers' roles as active and discriminating investigators of the genre, able to identify and pursue in the work of other writers the elements of a particular series that they find appealing, such as the specific kind of character, the setting, themes, or styles.

Such activities underscore the importance of genre in general and each text in particular as communal enterprises in which readers, writers, and characters meet. And the political impetus that propels the novels inspires groups such as Sisters in Crime in which writers and readers work together to bring their concerns to the attention of the publishing industry and the public. Indeed, the emergence of the subgenre that involves an active female investigator has repercussions beyond the intervention of any one woman author or character into mainstream narratives: these books offer empowering possibilities to the readers who consume them, and whose purchasing power supports (both economically and as a more general endorsement) the professional women writers who produce them. This ongoing process is exemplified both in the interactive nature of the texts and in the interactive community to which they give rise, a community that en/genders an extended circle of partners—and sisters—in crime.

ACADEMIC INTERVENTIONS

Popular culture has fit uneasily into the *academic* realm, where its nature and value have often been hotly disputed. It is important to understand this locus too as a collective space in which the engaged reading of popular culture—and women's popular culture in particular—may take place in a variety of ways; such readings of popular texts have a controversial history. To better establish the context of the present study, we here briefly examine some of its historical and theoretical grounding; in the process, we demonstrate the ways in which theory, practice, and history are intimately engaged with one another. Academic critics of the popular certainly do not escape the notion of "guilty pleasure" with which this chapter began. Indeed, they are sometimes represented as operating within a perceived contradiction between the "academic" and "popular," "work" and "play," or "serious" and "trivial" pursuits. Susan J. Douglas begins her study, *Where the Girls Are: Growing Up Female with the Mass Media*, with a mock-confession that comments on representations in the mass media of the mass media theorist:

> I am one of those people *The Wall Street Journal*, CBS News, and *Spy* magazine love to make fun of: I am a professor of media studies. You know what that means. I probably teach entire courses on the films of Connie Francis, go to academic conferences where the main intellectual exchange is trading comic books, never make my students read books, and insist that Gary Lewis and the Playboys were more important than Hegel, John Dos Passos, or Frances Perkins. All I do now, of course, is study Madonna. . . . This anyway is the caricature of people like me. (10–11)

Douglas's opening is deliberately provocative, but it astutely points out both a general perception of theorists of the popular and, implicitly, their ambivalent position within academic circles. More important, it strategically resists rigid distinctions between (academic) labor and (popular) pleasure, or between "intellectual" readers and readings and those of the "real" consumers of popular culture outside the academy. Douglas, significantly, places herself "where the girls are"—as a female scholar who *is* a female consumer of popular culture, who takes active pleasure in popular texts, and who takes that pleasure seriously indeed.

The construction of theorists and theories of popular culture, of course, varies from discipline to discipline; and its place in the academy is, by and large, an interstitial one whose currency is defined by its defiance of disciplinary boundaries. Debates over its status and value have taken different forms in different venues (in departments of literature, film, fine arts, history, anthropology, women's studies, etc.). Disciplines like Douglas's (media and American studies), for example, have stimulated questions about not just *if* but *how* works of popular culture should be situated and interpreted, what aspects of those works should be the focus of attention (e.g., their audience, text, or mode of production), and how their study should "fit" within the academic structure and academic discourses. Until quite recently universities, like Western cultural ideology at large, have tended to dismiss popular forms as "low-class" entertainment, undeserving of rigorous critique (e.g., journal and newspaper reviews of "highbrow" and "lowbrow" films often differ markedly in tone). Feminist critics have been particularly sensitive to this tendency because of its larger context: a modernist tradition of literature and scholarship that has often positioned woman as the paradigmatic consumer of "inferior" cultural products, while man has been constructed as the authoritative producer and scholarly explicator of "genuine," "authentic" art (see Huyssen).

As we have already suggested, our interest in the political potential of formula texts arises in large part from their very *lack* of "originality" or individuation in the traditional sense: the generic or formulaic status for which they are often dismissed is, we submit, precisely what makes them socially engaged and potentially empowering. While academic critics traditionally have been either explicitly or implicitly trained to dismiss popular culture as irrelevant—or even antithetical—to academic study, over the past thirty-odd years it has become the focus of an increasing number of academic studies and successful course offerings at many colleges and universities. Both disdained and glorified, popular culture illustrates a striking dichotomy at the heart of academic studies today.

"Even bubblegum has a metaphysics" (T. W. Adorno)

There are historical reasons for the conventional schism between "high" and "low" culture. In many ways, popular culture has functioned as high culture's "other," the derided low(er-class) counterpart that establishes the intellectual and moral superiority of privileged aesthetic standards and products: high culture can exist, in effect, only in relation to what it is not—low culture. Thus popular culture is defined by its "mass" status: its very popularity restricts it from the realm of elite art. The myth persists that reading popular fiction is not "real" reading—or not reading "real" literature—at all; but this myth strategically writes off a huge portion of the reading public, along with the pleasure, power, and diversity of their acts of interpretation. "Mass" appeal makes cultural products both popular and financially viable, a category of "success" rarely acknowledged as relevant when literary merit is determined. In *The Field of Cultural Production*, French sociologist Pierre Bourdieu suggests that there is actually an inverse correlation between the artistic and the economic criteria of judgment: "The artist can triumph on the symbolic terrain only to the extent that he loses on the economic one, and vice versa"; hence, the artistic world is "the economic world reversed" (169). Historically, formula texts have been regarded as banal because they are consumer-oriented and mass-produced. At one level, this judgment simply reveals a strategic elision in the way so-called high culture has traditionally been considered in isolation from its contexts of socioeconomic production and reception. As Orania Papazoglou's amateur detective Patience McKenna observes wryly at one point in the novel *Wicked, Loving Murder*, "it's all a business . . . even ['high'] literary publishing" (10).

While the battle for the legitimacy of different generic forms has been fought for hundreds of years,[9] we begin with the late nineteenth and early twentieth centuries, when the split between the artistic and the popular widens significantly. The post-Darwinian nineteenth century was a period in which, for perhaps the first time in history, religion had ceased to provide social stability and cohesion. At the same time, economic value increasingly was defining standards of achievement for industrialized culture at large; mass production and consumption were central to economic exchange. And, as Andreas Huyssen points out, the threat of being consumed by consumer culture was often portrayed during this period as feminine, especially since consumer culture was associated with the uncontrollable "masses," commodification, and a sense of (mechanical and thus inauthentic) reproduction that was out of control. Magazines and periodicals of this time, Huyssen observes, often represent the figure of woman "as a receptacle for all kinds of projections, displaced fears, and anxieties (both personal and political), which were brought about by modernization and the new social conflicts" (195). One response to such generalized fears about the repercussions of mass-market production and the concomitant loss of "civilizing" social forces (like religion) was put forward by such cultural critics as Matthew Arnold, who proposed that literature might fill the void religion had left.[10] Authentic literature, Arnold argued in his preface to *Culture and Anarchy*, could serve as a means of instilling and preserving a set of common cultural values.

In effect, the advent of the modern university and the study of English in the early twentieth century institutionalized such ideas, especially in validating the study of "modern" works (as opposed to the classical works of Greece and Rome) and accepting the argument in favor of literature's ability to establish social and moral precepts, to "civilize" readers (see Eagleton). T. S. Eliot and other critics praised the literary tradition for consolidating and conserving a certain set of authoritative values and beliefs. Ironically, though, the artistic products of modernism became more and more erudite and self-consciously complex, and hence accessible to smaller and smaller audiences. Modernist writers came consciously to promote—indeed insist on—a certain kind of education and values in their readers. As Donald Davie has noted, Ezra Pound believed that if his poetry sent one reader to the library, he would feel his writings had achieved their purpose (317). Eliot's emphasis on the continuity, stability, and cultural centrality (not to mention the implicit masculinity) of the established Western literary tradition might well be seen as part of modernism's more general compensatory response to the "increasingly marginal position of literature and the arts in a society in which masculinity is identified with action, enterprise, and progress—with the realms of business, industry, science, and law" (Huyssen 189).

Industrial Productions

While it might be argued that the poetry since the nineteenth century has been received with a simultaneous decrease in audience size and increase in high culture stature, the novel has followed a different course. Materializing in the eighteenth century as a form that crossed the class lines of its audience, it appeared transgressive because of its popular appeal (see Watts) and its attempt to represent in a "realistic" manner the material details of the "everyday" lives of characters of different social strata. But by the end of the nineteenth century, the days of the popular novel that appealed to audiences across class lines (as had the writings of Dickens) were ending. Modernist writings and modernist critics, despite their theoretical emphasis on instilling value in the society at large, in practice reinforced cultural divisions among readers: even the "civilizing" project of high literature designated one class the producer of legitimate culture (and the values it authorized), while another class was that culture's consumer and beneficiary.[11]

"Low" culture in the form of popular prose narrative, which had earlier been available in such forms as eighteenth-century Gothic novels and Victorian novels of sensation, became increasingly prominent in the late nineteenth and early twentieth centuries in immensely successful cheap mass-market publications, including dime novels and "pulp" magazines.[12] Particularly important for our purposes are the detective-adventure magazines, such as *Black Mask* and *Dime Detective*, that produced the hard-boiled school of fiction. The evolution of modern-day formula fiction began with such publications, which were directed at a mass audience, written with a recognizable vernacular and "corporate" style and structure, and marketed in an inexpensive periodical format. Formula literature is, in one sense, a standardized industrial product made possible at a particular moment in the history of the publishing industry, one marked by technological innovations that made cheap merchandise possible, by an expanding population, by an increasing level of education and literacy, and by growing urbanization, which made the distribution and sale of magazines and books easier and more economical (Hamilton 55). Thus the "massification" of detective fiction takes place with the paperback revolution after World War I, touched off by Penguin and by Simon and Schuster—firms that adapted mass-marketing techniques to publishing (Mandel 66). Cynthia Hamilton affirms that marketing "was another way of providing the potential book-buyer with a reliable 'brand name': formula fiction came as close to providing uniformity of product as it was possible to get in the publishing business" (60).

The industrial model of literary production was, not surprisingly, viewed with suspicion by the Marxist-oriented theorists associated with the Frankfurt Institute for Social Research, founded at the University of Frankfurt in 1923. The Frankfurt School regarded mass-produced works as an outgrowth of "high capitalism"; therefore by definition they reproduced the hegemonic values of monopoly capitalism and served as opiates of the masses who passively consumed them. The end result of this system of production and consumption, these theorists claimed, was the perpetuation of the existing social order. As Theodor W. Adorno argues in *The Culture Industry:*

> Today the commercial production of cultural goods has become
> streamlined, and the impact of popular culture upon the individual
> has concomitantly increased. This process has not been confined to
> quantity, but has resulted in new qualities. While recent popular cul-
> ture has absorbed all the elements and particularly all the "don'ts"
> of its predecessor, it differs decisively inasmuch as it has developed
> into a system. Thus, popular culture is no longer confined to certain

forms such as novels or dance music, but has seized all media of artistic expression. . . . Above all, this rigid institutionalization transforms modern mass culture into a medium of undreamed of psychological control. The repetitiveness, the selfsameness, and the ubiquity of modern mass culture tend to make for automatized reactions and to weaken the forces of individual resistance. (137–38)

Adorno's is certainly not a simple analysis, nor is it an elitist dismissal of popular culture's potential. It offers, among other things, a resolutely ideological reading of popular culture, as well as a careful distinction between social *significance* and aesthetic/social *value*. Furthermore, Adorno was deeply concerned with the political potential of "the populace," which he saw as subordinated by the capital-driven "cultural industries." But he continued to perceive the "individualized" construction of elite culture as the means by which a popular audience could be educated, elevated, and empowered by literature. Proponents of the Frankfurt School, in effect, could not see beyond the standardized nature of mass culture and its capitalist basis to its potential as a resistant artistic form. Many critics have taken issue with Adorno's position (see, for example, the essays in Modleski's *Studies in Entertainment*), but here we will note just one of the problems with his argument: the idea that mass culture is simply imposed from "above," a form that audiences can only passively consume. What gets left out of this account are the ways in which genre can be a subversive performance (rather than a simple reproduction) of literary conventions and hegemonic values. Popular fiction's ability to draw attention to—and take advantage of—the role of genre as a powerful but necessarily mutable social construction does not figure in this paradigm. It also diminishes the ways in which authors and audiences can and do interact with cultural industries generally, with the formulas of fiction, and with individual texts, thereby "performing" resistant readings of dominant culture.

But to imply that all consumers of popular culture are actively and effectively resistant obviously would be naive. The tendency in some cultural studies scholarship to idealize and uncritically celebrate the audience's potential for resistant readings has recently produced work that reflects both a simplistic notion of the political efficacy of literature and an idealized, conflict-free—and potentially elitist—construction of the "real folks" who read it. Indeed, as Jim McGuigan has charged, a contextless and "resistant" model of cultural studies "merely produces a simple inversion of the [Frankfurt School–style] mass culture critique at its worst," applauding popular readings without considering "the possibility that a popular reading could be anything other than 'progressive'" (72). For Alan Stanbridge, the conflation of diverse approaches and terminologies—including ethnography, semiotics, Barthesian pleasure, postmodern subjectivity, and Bakhtinian carnivalesque—in the absence of critical readings and economic and political analyses of material conditions of production has resulted in "a consumptionist utopia, in which people 'make their own meanings,' thereby 'subverting' and 'resisting' dominant ideologies" (44–45).[13]

Have Theory, Will Travel

Important readings of popular culture alternative to (though often influenced by) the Frankfurt School have developed over the last several decades, and we will sketch here both the historical grounding of cultural studies and its role as an interdisciplinary locus that continues to generate and test competing ideas about popular culture's relation to power and pleasure. In the early 1970s work began at the Birmingham Centre for Contemporary Cultural Studies in England. Stuart Hall, Richard Hoggart, Richard Johnson, and other scholars, countering the high culture focus of conventional university syllabi, reengaged with the Frankfurt School's perception of popular culture as a product of the capitalist system. Drawing on the work of writers such as historian E. P. Thompson (*The Making of the English Working Class* [1963]) and literary scholar Raymond Williams (e.g., *Culture and Society* [1958] and *The Long Revo-*

lution [1961])—particularly on Williams's suggestion that popular culture might be valued as an expression of the working class (see Easthope)—the critics of the Birmingham School formulated a conception of popular culture as a locus of both containment and resistance. Stuart Hall, for example, attempted to account for the complexities of mass media reception in multidimensional ways. In "Encoding and Decoding," he describes three kinds of reading a single text might produce: the "encoded" reading, which adopts meanings embedded in the text; the "negotiated" reading, which accepts some of the precepts of the encoded meaning but contests others; and the "oppositional" reading, which challenges the assumptions of the work. Associated with efforts to break down the class biases of British higher education, the Birmingham School challenged the traditional subject matter studied at Oxford and Cambridge, and even the Oxbridge institutional structure itself, by promoting an access-oriented system, exemplified by the Open University. Among other things, the Birmingham School focused its research and teaching on analyses of television news (e.g., the Glasgow News Group) and audience responses to it (e.g., David Morley's *"Nationwide" Audience* [1980]). Incorporating ethnographic studies as a means of understanding the ways in which popular media were actually interpreted by consumers, critics in the Birmingham School theorized audience interpretive practice in a manner that itself resisted the conservative political ethos then beginning its ascendancy in Britain. Tony Bennett (in work such as his *Formalism and Marxism* [1979]) and others suggested that texts do not "issue" meanings on a simple production-consumption model but rather perform as sites in which meanings may be produced by audiences in various ways. In Australia (where Bennett moved), this theoretical focus was further complicated by a postcolonial context—complications evidenced, for example, in the early work of John Fiske.

North America came somewhat later to the field of cultural studies; and when the kind of theoretical work initiated in Australia and the United Kingdom traveled to North America, it was largely isolated from its origins in working-class culture, educational reform, and social activism. Its theoretical precepts thus lost some of their material political grounding. North American literary theory in the 1970s and 1980s was much more engaged with a range of continental poststructuralist philosophies and linguistic theories that had begun attracting attention during the 1960s. While the influence of early poststructuralist theories resulted in intricate readings of texts and the processes by which they produced meaning, these texts in general were canonical literary artifacts, largely considered apart from their social and historical circumstances and their relation to other works.

The influential work of structuralist theorist Tzvetan Todorov, however, translated from French into English in 1977, is an important exception to such isolated analyses. Todorov significantly anticipates some of the concerns of more recent popular culture and genre critics. His interest in certain forms of popular culture—especially fantasy and detective fiction—led him not just to reactivate theories of genre but to develop such a theory specific to popular art. Todorov recognized that "for nearly two centuries, there has been a powerful reaction in literary studies against the very notion of genre. We write either about literature in general or about a single work, and it is a tacit convention that to classify several works in a genre is to devalue them" (42). The appreciation of popular art, he realized, was restricted by the criteria used to evaluate high culture, since popular art is a field in which strict conformity to the conventions of genre is a mark of success. Todorov also recognized the necessity of developing suitable analytical tools precisely to describe generic features.

Despite their de-historicizing tendencies, poststructuralist theories did make possible an emphasis on and analysis of the formation of subjectivity and its relation to linguistic practice. The relationship between subjectivity and language was important to the political and cultural interrogations that arose out of "identity politics": the analysis of the power dynamics of subject formation and its grounding in such categories as race, class, and gender. George Lipsitz's *Time Passages*, for example, which analyzes ethnicity and the cold war in relation to early

American prime-time television, specifically situates its discussion in the American material conditions in which that relationship is produced. Houston A. Baker, Jr.'s scholarship on the blues, rap, and African American culture; studies like James Snead's investigation of race in popular film; and queer theorists' rereadings of popular culture's relation to sexual orientation also represent important theoretical directions. Of most interest to us at this point, however, are the ways in which cultural studies converges with feminism.

Mediating Women

Feminism intersected with cultural studies through feminist literary scholarship's efforts to recuperate works by women authors and so-called women's genres. Such works had been relegated to the margins of the canon of high culture, apparently doubly condemned by their status as popular and their association with women authors or audiences. Film studies was a particularly fertile ground of inquiry. Popular American genre film had been accommodated to academic study in the 1960s, in part through auteurist studies that tended to focus on the distinctive styles of individual (and almost exclusively male) film directors working within the formulaic constraints and industrial modes of the Hollywood system. The film theorists and critics Teresa de Lauretis, Mary Ann Doane, and Kaja Silverman, among others, significantly altered that emphasis as they attended to the psychological, aesthetic, and political dimensions of "women's films," cinematic modes that spoke largely to women. Laura Mulvey and others took an interest in the gendered representational dynamics of Hollywood films. Drawing on poststructuralist and psychoanalytic theories, Mulvey developed an influential theory that visual pleasure in mainstream Hollywood films originates in a gendered structure of spectatorship that constructs the spectator's gaze as male and the object of the gaze as female.

Theorists such as Tania Modleski undertook studies of the popular

romance in order to explore the genre's value to its predominantly female readership. One of the few works produced in the 1980s that combined textual analysis with ethnographic material was Janice Radway's
Reading the Romance, which built on Modleski's earlier work, *Loving with
a Vengeance*. Radway's study was distinctive in that it examined in empirical detail the responses of a target group of women romance readers
in Smithton, New York. In her conclusion, Radway argues for the importance of understanding the production of meaning as constituted by
a reciprocal relationship between text and reader:

> We must not, in short, look only at mass-produced objects them-
> selves on the assumption that they bear all of their significances on
> their surface, as it were, and reveal them automatically to us. To do
> so would be to assume either that perceptible, tangible things alone
> are worth analyzing or that those commodified objects exert such
> pressure and influence on their consumers that they have no power
> as individuals to resist or alter the ways in which those objects mean
> or can be used. (221)

Radway, in effect, weds the Birmingham School's emphasis on audience
response and the institutional matrix of production to the detailed analysis associated with North American text-based criticism. And, while
Radway's study has been critiqued on a number of fronts since its first
publication in 1984 (see Brunt, as well as Radway's own reevaluation of
her work in the second edition of her book), *Reading the Romance* continues to be one of the most important and influential works in feminist
cultural studies.

The analysis of television has also complicated theoretical readings
of popular culture in recent years. The Birmingham School had made
that medium a prime focus of its analysis, but in North America, as
E. Ann Kaplan recounts in her introduction to *Regarding Television*, its
study was dominated by social science emphases and methodologies
until the early 1980s: "Little attention (as far as I can gather) was given

to television aesthetics, to how meaning is produced, or to television as an ideological institution functioning within a complex consumer circuit that allows only for the production of carefully constricted meanings" (xiii). In recent years, theorists such as Patricia Mellencamp, Jane Freuer, and Lynn Spigel have developed the possibilities Kaplan describes, thus both elaborating the subject matter and methodologies available to cultural criticism and expanding the readings suggested by the Birmingham School to incorporate questions of gender. In addition, cultural studies scholars—including Michelle Wallace, bell hooks, and Jacqueline Bobo, among others—directed feminist critiques at issues of race and class differences.

Negotiating Theory

In recent years some critics have stressed a distinction between studies that focus on scrupulously text-based analysis and more ethnographic or sociological approaches to popular culture texts. Jackie Stacey, for example, has taken issue with the earlier work of de Lauretis, Doane, and Mulvey, objecting to the poststructuralist and psychoanalytic approaches to popular films employed by such theorists. The distinction between studies of "textual" and "empirical" spectators, or audiences within and external to the film's narrative ("diegetic" and "cinematic" spectators), Stacey argues,

> is often used as a shorthand to characterise the difference between the psychoanalytic model in film studies and ethnographic approaches to female spectatorship which have characterised cultural studies work. . . . [T]he model of spectatorship predominantly employed within feminist film criticism is the psychoanalytic, "textual" one. . . . [F]ilm audiences have been of remarkably little interest to feminist film critics, who have remained sceptical about the empiricism of such studies. Such scepticism has resulted in a rather crude, blanket dismissal of women in the cinema audience, as if any study

which involves people who attend cinemas must necessarily fall into
the negative traps of empiricism. (23)

While Stacey's argument is not without merit, it generates a false schism
between text-oriented (North American) and audience-oriented (Euro-
pean) feminist cultural studies.[14] The pronounced distinction between
these two lines of inquiry gives rise to questions about how the two
might be related, how the dynamics of spectatorship are played out in
relation to particular texts and contexts. In Ien Ang's largely ethnographic work on television, for example, audience studies are read *as*
texts (see Brunt). Moreover, as documentary filmmaker Barri Cohen has
suggested, even so-called text-based critics of popular films (e.g., de
Lauretis and Doane) are also "readers" or audiences of the texts they discuss and thus incorporate audience responses, even if they do so implicitly and unconsciously.

    Christine Gledhill's articulation of the idea of "negotiation" is one
place to begin to reconcile some of the conflicts Stacey identifies. Gledhill argues for a theory of texts that both has the power to explain the
psychodynamics of cinema's female representations and can at the same
time accommodate the existence of social audiences (66–67). Negotiation, she contends, is a concept that could be central "in rethinking the
relations between media products, ideologies and audiences," and might
even bridge the gap between so-called textual and social subjects:

> As a model of meaning production, negotiation conceives cultural
> exchange as the intersection of processes of production and recep-
> tion in which overlapping but non-matching determinations operate.
> Meaning is neither imposed, nor passively imbibed, but arises out of
> a struggle or negotiation between competing frames of reference,
> motivation and experience. This can be analysed at three different
> levels: institutions, texts and audiences—although distinctions be-
> tween levels are ones of emphasis, rather than of rigid separation. . . .
> [Consequently, one can argue that] ideologies are not simply im-
> posed—although this possibility always remains an institutional op-

tion through mechanisms such as censorship—but are subject to
continuous (re-)negotiation. (68)

Negotiation is important in part because it enables a discussion of the
social—and as such frequently conflicted—ways meaning is produced
not just within texts but *among* texts, authors, audiences, and institutional structures. The concept is thus particularly suited to the analysis
of popular genres—and the popular genre of detective fiction especially—as regulating, contradictory, and transformable discursive sites,
generating the intersection of a complex set of institutional, (inter)tex-
tual, authorial, and audience engagements.

Gledhill's analysis also suggests ways in which popular genres are
practiced by publishers, authors, and audiences. "Practice" is an important word because it presupposes that genre exists not simply as an abstract, complete, and unchanging set of rules for behavior, but rather as
a set of related performances through which agency is possible. Here, it
is worth noting, practice does not make perfect: there is no such thing
as the "whole," "perfect" generic work that exists outside of its relationships with other texts and its context. These ideas are essential to our
analysis because we are calling attention to important analogies between
genre and gender. Like genre, gender is socially generated, but it is not
a simple set of rules, nor is it established on an uncomplicated model of
production and consumption. It is, rather, a regulating, contradictory,
and transformable set of discursive practices that may be negotiated and
renegotiated by different people in different contexts. Gender is, in addition, "practiced"—but never perfected—in the everyday lives of individuals in ways that are central to their sense of who they are and what
they can (and are allowed to) do. It, too, constitutes spaces of negotiation where change can be effected.

Finally, Gledhill's association of negotiation with ambivalence provides for a consideration of *popular* (as opposed to politically "radical" or
aesthetically "avant-garde") texts as possible sites of feminist agency. As
she remarks,

> Clearly, the ambivalence of textual negotiation produces a wider ad-
> dress—more serviceable to a capitalist industry—than a more
> purely feminist text, or counter-text could. . . . On the other hand,
> if we accept the role of the mass media in making cultural defini-
> tions—and also post-structural theory's exposure of the ideologi-
> cally "pure" and full representation, whether feminist or dominant,
> as an illusory goal—perhaps we may take a more positive stance to-
> wards the spaces of negotiation in mainstream production (87).

The notion of ambivalence is crucial for our purposes because we want
to examine women's appropriation of the traditionally masculine hard-
boiled generic mode. Genres do not "belong" to individuals or groups,
but they are conventionally associated with—and attractive to—certain
kinds of authors and audiences. As Janice Radway asserts at the end of her
1991 introduction to *Reading the Romance,* "A theory in which genre is
conceived as a set of rules for the production of meaning, operable both
through writing and reading, might . . . be able to explain why certain
sets of texts are especially interesting to particular groups of people (and
not to others) because it would draw one's attention to the question of
how and where a given set of generic rules had been created, learned, and
used" (10). Women's adaptation of the rules of hard-boiled fiction results
in a necessarily ambivalent generic permutation: a "woman's genre" that
is defined by its status as a "man's genre," too. In the next chapter, we
begin to negotiate the problematics of this ambivalent intersection.

Chapter 3

DOES SHE OR DOESN'T SHE?

The Problematics of Feminist Detection

> If feminism is now an uncomfortable part of the thriller's
> cultural repertoire, it is one which necessarily calls the
> achievements of Hammett and Chandler into question.
> Down these mean streets no easy male/female transposi-
> tions are possible.
> David Glover, "The Stuff That Dreams Are Made Of"

NEGOTIATING THE GENERIC CONTRACT

Many feminist scholars of detective fiction have been skeptical about the potential of women's practice of the hard-boiled detective novel to negotiate resistance, critique, or change within in a literary genre typically aligned with oppressive masculinity. While some critics applaud the feminist potential of the form in the hands of women writers, many others contend that any such potential gets lost in translation—that feminist political aims are necessarily negated by the inherently conservative demands of the genre. These scholars see "detective agency" as a contradiction in terms. We argue, on the contrary, that feminist agency

is possible not just within the confines of or despite t
the genre, but *through* those very conventions. The fe
tion of the hard-boiled mode can redefine textual an(
aries precisely because it comes into intimate contact wi
words, such practices make it possible to renegotiate tne "generic contract" between industry, authors, audiences, and texts. The ability of
women's hard-boiled fiction to perform this task is made possible by
its threefold character: it is a *practical* application of *political* tenets expressed through a *popular* form. This chapter looks at the critical controversy over women's appropriation of the hard-boiled novel in order
to address the ways in which feminist politics and fictive practice may be
brought together in the reading and writing of the genre.

In *The Woman Detective*, the most extensive study of female detectives
to date, Kathleen Gregory Klein outlines her interpretation of the
"woman questions" at issue when women take up the conventions of the
professional investigator novel. She sees such novels as a struggle between gender and genre in which the conventional private eye formula
inevitably achieves primacy over feminist ideology:

> The predictable formula of detective fiction is based on a world
> whose sex/gender valuations reinforce male hegemony. Taking male
> behavior as the norm, the genre defines its parameters to exclude fe-
> male characters, confidently rejecting them as inadequate women or
> inadequate detectives. A detective novel with a professional woman
> detective is, then, a contradiction in terms. The existence of the one
> effectively eliminates the other. (223)

The use of the hard-boiled mode by contemporary authors like Sue
Grafton, Marcia Muller, and Susan Steiner, she contends, "falsely seems
to signal a change in the genre," for such works simply reproduce patterns Klein sees as repeating themselves over and over since the first female sleuths appeared in the nineteenth century (221). Klein argues that
because mass-mediated culture in general, and the detective genre in particular, serves the interests of a relatively small elite power structure, it

necessarily confronts authors with a compromise in which "either feminism or the formula is at risk" (202). Thus, while Klein's most recent work suggests that some versions of women's crime writing do successfully challenge and reformulate both the detective formula and gender norms, she does not find these innovations in mainstream popular fiction (see "*Habeas Corpus*").

Rosalind Coward and Linda Semple, in their article "Tracking Down the Past," also see the conventions of hard-boiled writing as inhospitable to feminism. Like Klein, these critics do praise some mystery novels written by women as explicitly feminist in their aims and effects (especially those published by alternative presses), but they see the hard-boiled mode as particularly unaccommodating: "Given the extreme individualism, violence and outrageous social attitudes towards women and other minority groups which writers like Mickey Spillane, Dashiell Hammett and Raymond Chandler often display, it is hard to imagine a form less susceptible to a feminist interpretation." Despite "the sympathetic, independent heroines and politically satisfying plots" (46) in the work of such writers as Paretsky and Grafton, the genre is highly problematic, they argue, particularly because it offers little or no criticism of the violence of the traditional gumshoe novels. We take up the question of violence and the female body in chapter 5; here we note only that for Coward and Semple, as for Klein, gender and genre are necessarily at odds, and feminist intentions (however well-placed and sympathetic) simply cannot resist the hard-boiled genre's traditional power as a misogynist mode.[1] Australian fiction writer Finola Moorehead echoes this judgment when she insists that her book *Still Murder* "is not a genre novel. It can't be, because it has a women-identified central reality" (99). To gain the acceptance that is necessary for popularity, she submits, "the formula must be fundamentally male—even though it is written by women" (102).

Like popular culture itself, however, genres are neither simply subversive nor intrinsically conservative. Genre, rather, serves as a relational, conventional, and contradictory location that tends to complicate in practice any simple either/or categorization. For example, the original exemplars of the hard-boiled detective mode reconsidered some of the class constructions that had become a conventional element of the British mystery story, and thus have often been seen (particularly in light of their American origins) as revolutionizing the genre, both politically and linguistically. At the same time, the genre dramatized some of the conservative fears and anxieties arising from changes in traditional class and gender structures in the United States during the 1920s and 1930s. Thus the iconic characterization of the femme fatale in these stories dramatized the powerful allure (and mystery) of a refractory woman in control of her own desires, at the same time as the conventional narrative structure of hard-boiled novels regulated the legitimacy of that power in her inevitable incrimination, death, or confinement at the end of the story. In his discussion of the possibility of "Radical Thrillers," Stephen Knight asks, "Is the genre completely tainted with conservatism?" (186). He answers, in part, by offering a historical argument demonstrating that the political orientations of writers within the traditional genre, including Hammett and Chandler, differ substantially (179). Knight argues that if popular culture is a significant site of ideological production, then it is "a crucial force-field into which the left must enter" (186). We argue, similarly, that if the popular hard-boiled genre is a significant regulatory site for gender roles and behaviors, then co-opting such a form is an extremely important revisionary gesture that may work to alter the paradigms of both genre and gender.

In their introduction to *Killing Women*, a collection of essays by Australian women detective writers and critics, Delys Bird and Brenda Walker acknowledge the heterogeneity of the "mainstream" audience, as well as the potential agency of writers and readers to produce culturally resistant readings through popular culture itself:

> That popular writing is not simply (or at all) an opiate, but represents the tastes and values of many and is capable itself of political activity, means it can no longer be regarded as always innocently and conventionally reproducing dominant mass-consumer-directed ideologies.

Women writers of crime fiction, then, working in a male preserve
with a genre always considered definitively masculine despite its
numerous very well-known female practitioners, might now use the
genre in a way that confronted and challenged its maleness. Women
readers too could identify with these challenges, or construct their
own through re-readings of earlier "pre-feminist" writers. (12)

Bird and Walker configure a compelling legal scenario regarding feminist crime fiction when they observe that there is more than one way of
responding to the misogyny of conventional crime writing: "Crime fiction invites classification and investigation not from the point of view of
a narrow feminist prosecution, as a kind of class action, but rather as part
of the forensics of sexuality and narrative structure" (11).

Their point is well taken. The notion of a "class action" is, nevertheless, an appealing one, for it can represent the collective challenge posed
by the development of a sub*genre* (as opposed to a singular challenge
from any individual author), as well as the audience's participation in
that development. The term also evokes the popular "democratization"
of American literature essayed by the original hard-boiled writers (a *class*
action), now including women in that democracy. And it suggests the
possibility of both authorial and readerly response (a class *action*), in the
sense not just of legal action *against* but of agency *through* prescribed
generic conditions. Bird and Walker's choice of words implies that the
writing of the novel itself might be a "forensic" gesture, producing writing that goes beyond *describing* a legal case to, at some level, effectively
making a case for or against some set of principles.

Like Bird and Walker, Barbara Godard recognizes that the rewriting
of genre "reveals women's engagement with narrative as a critical strategy." Godard suggests the radical potential of such generic "border/
play," since it works "to expose the positioning of woman as silent other
on whose mutilated body the narrative is constructed in dominant discourse and to posit alternative positionings for women as subjects producing themselves in/by language" (45). Godard also underscores the
importance of the popular audience to the political value of crime fic-

tion. Indeed, Godard argues that feminist detective fiction is effective precisely because it constructs as criminal (and thus questions) the ideological formations in which readers are implicated, effecting a "double transformation" in which "the text is transformed from a work of suspense fiction to a political fiction and the practice of the novel is changed from one of mystification and revelation to one of investigation and transformation" (49). In Godard's analysis, both mainstream and avant-garde fiction fall on a continuum of generic practices that "turn dominant discourses inside out" (45).

Maureen Reddy's work, in her book *Sisters in Crime* and elsewhere, begins to account for the dialogic, responsive qualities of formula fiction previously left largely unaddressed. Reddy situates the development of the genre as coincident and analogous with the modern women's movement: "Feminist literary criticism, feminism as a social movement, and feminist crime novels have grown up together, so to speak. Just as feminist literary criticism challenges the traditional assumptions of the discipline of literary studies, so too does the feminist crime novel challenge the conventions of crime fiction" ("Feminist Counter-Tradition" 174). She concludes, "Feminist crime novels are best understood as constituting a new genre, less part of an existing tradition than a distinct counter-tradition" (174). Reddy's parallels between feminist literary criticism and literary practice are insightful, but her notion of "a distinct counter-tradition" might be interpreted as a strategic evasion of the problematics of generic revision, one that defuses important questions of reversal and resistance. It also ignores the ways in which women's writings are not "caught" in the prescriptions of genre but are necessarily always already inscribed in its discursive formulations, just as subjects are always already inscribed in the discursive formulations of gender.

Although Reddy conceives of the dialogic potential of the feminist countertradition she identifies, she still insists on labeling the genre itself (as distinguished from its feminist practice) as "basically monologic in form" (*Sisters in Crime* 6). For Klein, similarly, it is only feminist (mainstream) detective fiction that offers a "double-voiced discourse"

(*Woman Detective* 57). That is, it offers two sets of contradictory meanings to readers differentiated by gender: Women, she submits, are offered the fantasy of freedom and independence, while "men's fear of a
reality in which women can become the dominant group is assuaged by
the persistent fantasy of women who fail. . . . Reading the same novels,
they can read altogether different stories" (*Woman Detective* 170). While
the insight that readers may read the same texts in conflicting ways is essential, the conservative and progressive elements of generic conflict are
unlikely simply to split readers into separate gendered camps. Rather,
generic texts function much more equivocally for any given reader, offering both reassurances and reformative possibilities—in this case, potential for both identification and difference, as we noted in the reader
responses cited in chapter 2. Moreover, Klein's theory fails to explain
why certain readers prefer certain generic types and how readers distinguish among subgenres of detective fiction with some skill: those who
harbor genuine fears about women's power, or who are uncomfortable
exploring a subjectivity or ideology *significantly* different from their
own, are likely to choose to read a variant of the genre that does not
challenge their preconceptions.

REVISING THE SCRIPT

Klein's observations about the way genre can accommodate conflict
might be modified and extended by taking into account an effect of what
Michel Foucault refers to as "reverse discourse," or a discourse that repeats and inverts the ideological imperatives of the dominant discourse
in order to authorize those marginalized by it.[2] If the feminist hard-
boiled novel is perceived as a reverse rather than a double discourse,
then it can be read as producing a critique of the formula by reproducing it with strategic differences, thus redirecting the trajectory of dominant discourse. In isolation, a reverse discourse does not change or reconfigure anything; its efficacy depends on the reader's recognition of
differential intertextual relationships. It also depends on genre's ability

to signify in alternative ways, to accommodate ideologically contradictory practices without ceasing to be recognizable. The reverse discourse employed by gay rights activists provides an example outside genre: the pink triangle (originally used to identify gay men in Nazi concentration camps) has been co-opted to symbolize gay pride.

As Linda Grant puts it of her own practice as a detective writer, "I thought, 'Gee, the private investigator is such a male archetype, wouldn't it be fun to see what would happen if you put a woman in that role?' because when you take an archetype and stand it on its head, interesting stuff drops out." *Simple* gender role reversal, however, is not effective— or even possible: Sara Paretsky has described her initial experiments with the genre as a parody of the "Raymond Chandler–type" novel: "I had my detective, her name was Minerva Daniels, and she was in this sleazy office, down to her last two dollars, and this guy comes in—slim hips, broad shoulders—and he was going to be my main bad guy. But it wasn't working: there are too many things you have to keep in mind if you're doing role reversal" (qtd. in Shapiro, "Sara Paretsky" 67). "It occurred to me," Paretsky adds elsewhere, "that what I really wanted was not a stereotype, but someone who was like me and my friends" (qtd. in Shepherdson 38).

Feminist detective fiction constitutes a reverse discourse exploring positions of resistance and agency that were offered by previous practices but that were inaccessible to women. Reinscribing those discourses refuses stereotypical structures at the same time as it reveals their contradictions. For example, in Paretsky's experiment the hard-boiled convention of female sexuality as dangerous and even evil conflicts with the heroic status of the detective, and simple parody doesn't quite work. However, reinscribing and revising prior discourses does, potentially, allow a space for *differential* practice—this, perhaps, is the "interesting stuff" that drops out when you turn an archetype on its head. As Foucault has argued, a reverse discourse is an alternative discourse of power:

> Discourses are not once and for all subservient to power or raised up
> against it, any more than silences are. We must make allowance for

and unstable process whereby discourse can be both an
~~nd~~ an effect of power, but also a hindrance, a stumbling-
~~point~~ of resistance and a starting point for an opposing strategy. Discourse transmits and produces power; it reinforces it, but it
also undermines and exposes it, renders it fragile and makes it possible to thwart it. (100–101)

The power of the reverse movement is apparent in the ways in which it
employs the constructions of the dominant discourse in order to foreground (and transpose) the ideological imperatives that motivate it. To
invert Klein's assertion: with reverse discourse, neither feminism nor the
formula is necessarily at risk.

Reverse discourse is not in itself a subversive gesture—it can also be
used strategically to suppress marginal voices. As Susan Faludi demonstrates in her study *Backlash*, the rhetoric of "women's liberation" has
been used by its detractors during the 1980s and 1990s to discredit the
movement (e.g., in "backlash films" such as *Fatal Attraction* and *Disclosure*). Indeed, in chapter 7 we read the "adaptation" of Sara Paretsky's
detective V. I. Warshawski novels to film as one instance of this backlash
strategy. Because discourses are not stable or simple, their cultural contexts and effects need to be analyzed. As Foucault argues, "Discourses
are tactical elements or blocks operating in the field of force relations;
there can exist different and even contradictory discourses within the
same strategy; they can, on the contrary, circulate without changing
their form from one strategy to another, opposing strategy" (101–2).

"MARLOWE'S KISS MEANT EITHER DEATH OR JAIL"

Women writers of detective fiction strategically talk back to a genre that
has often demeaned, trivialized, and even demonized women. The genre
itself, however, offers an attractive position from which to investigate
agency. Equally important, even traditional examples of the hard-boiled
genre have recognized the power of female subjectivity and desire in the

figure of the femme fatale. Both Katherine V. Forrest and Sparkle Hayter have commented on the complex female characterizations developed by hard-boiled novels as one of the features of the genre they find most appealing. Hayter affirms that while she loves to read classic hard-boiled fiction, "I always wish I could also read the story as told by one of its women characters." In some ways Hayter's Robin Hudson novels undertake this reading by telling a (comic) story in which the central role of subjectivity and agency is female. Linda Grant identifies the importance of the figure somewhat differently. The femme fatale is, in effect, the victim of the hard-boiled detective's struggle to achieve a kind of macho independence by criminalizing feminine influences: "The tradition," she comments, "emphasized autonomy at the cost of intimacy. Marlowe's kiss meant either death or jail. Think about it: any time he got involved with a women she's either dead or off to jail. These were guys for whom any sign of emotional intimacy was dangerous. And the Lone Wolf is just the far end of autonomy." In her character Catherine Sayler, Grant capitalizes on the generic autonomy of the detective character because women, "at least in my generation, we're not raised to be very autonomous"; but she reverses the genre in her characterization of intimacy.

Female detective writers routinely draw attention to the ways they have used the conventions of the hard-boiled mode to engender agency in their female characters. Linda Barnes, author of the Carlotta Carlyle series, lists male hard-boiled writers of the past and their male descendants of the present among her literary influences, and points to the ways in which these authors function for her as a negative example:

> [T]he Dashiell Hammett, Ross Macdonald group [are among the authors who influenced my writings]. I mean even John D. [MacDonald] has been an influence on me, in that I don't kill all the women in my books, as he infuriated me by using a woman in each book, and disposing of her as easily as he possibly could so his hero could spend the rest of the book avenging this disposable female. And the "disposable female syndrome" is one of the things that I really get after the current guys for.

Barnes's description actually casts such narrative strategies as criminal: "no one ever kept a body count on John D. MacDonald as he killed them all, after [his character had finished] sleeping with them. I mean, that man was a serial killer."

Sara Paretsky diagnoses an extreme version of this very convention as it extends to contemporary crime fiction, reading it as a symptom of fears about women's social power:

> Since the passage of the initial Civil Rights Act, the emergence of women in significant numbers into the professions that had previously been mostly closed to them is resolved and OK for some men, but for others, it's a terrifying, emasculating experience. And when you feel terrified and helpless, your response is great anger toward the people you perceive as causing it. And this is being played out in what has become increasingly more graphic and furious material about the destruction of women—through rape, dismemberment, snuff films, etc. ("What Do Women Really Want?" 13)

Paretsky sees her own writing and that of others like her as a version of the crime genre that is in competition for audience sympathy: "I don't know which trend will come out on top in the end" (13). Far from being passive victims trapped in generic conventions, writers such as Paretsky, Grafton, Barnes, and the others under study here engage with them in order to counter them, and thus are able to exercise agency not in spite of their status as genre writers, but because of it.

The effects of reverse discourse depend on the reader's ability to recognize difference between *this* particular performance of the genre and those it both repeats and counters. Women writers frequently reflexively play on that recognition by alluding to hard-boiled conventions and writers. In Marele Day's *Case of the Chinese Boxes*, for instance, her detective Claudia Valentine encounters a man whose name is Joel Cairo: "If you're looking for the Maltese Falcon, you've come to the wrong place," she quips (43). The remark might also be read as directed to the reader of *The Case of the Chinese Boxes:* if you're looking for *The Maltese Falcon,* you'll find this place familiar—but also recognize its strategic difference from that literary norm. Lesley Grant-Adamson alludes to and mocks the individualistic heroism characteristic of hard-boiled novels through her characterization of detective Laura Flynn. Laura relaxes by reading a novel about a detective hero who succeeds where the police fail, addressing the reader with this aside: "You know the type: a courageous figure, a lone ranger operating outside society, untrammelled by friends and family and any consideration but Getting His Man and Seeing Justice Done. I like a little fantasy before I fall asleep" (14). Similarly, Sarah Dunant often writes self-consciously about hard-boiled iconography, both defining her character by it and distancing her from it. In *Fatlands,* for example, Hannah Wolfe comments that the clients who come into the office aren't "glamorous women with skirts slit to the thighs who tell their story through lazy curls of cigarette smoke while the light casts film noir shadows on the wall" (43). In *Under My Skin,* Hannah is surprised by a suspect's reference to *The Big Sleep:* "I mean for me Raymond Chandler is just part of the myth, the kind of thing PI's read instead of fairy-tales, but I don't expect others to be so well versed" (89).

When Wendi Lee's Angela Matelli decides to leave the military to become a professional investigator, she muses, "I had no illusions about the private eye business. I'd read a few detective novels and had really enjoyed them, but my reasons for being in the investigation field had more to do with my limited job skills than with romantic fantasies involving tough guys with names like Spade, Marlowe, or Hammer" (*Good Daughter* 3). Val McDermid's Kate Brannigan also reminds readers of the fictional "text books" on which her role is based—and her difference from them: "It's a piece of cake, being a lawyer or a doctor or a computer systems analyst or an accountant. Libraries are full of books telling you how to do it. The only text books for private eyes are on the fiction shelves, and I don't remember ever reading one that told me how to interrogate an eight-year-old without feeling like I was auditioning for the Gestapo"

(*Crack Down* 120). In Sue Grafton's novels, Kinsey Millhone frequently points to the differences between the actions of her hero and those of her male counterparts. In *"F" Is for Fugitive*, the PI laments: "I felt like I'd spent half my time on this case washing dirty dishes. How come Magnum, PI, never had to do stuff like this?" (159). The distinction is just as great between her and her "real" male peers; when Kinsey discovers, in *"I" Is for Innocent*, that the male PI on the case before her had charged $50 an hour, she queries wryly, "Morley was getting fifty? I couldn't believe it. Either men are outrageous or women are fools. Guess which, I thought. My standard fee has always been thirty bucks an hour plus mileage" (23). S. J. Rozan's Chinese American PI Lydia Chin makes a similar comment in *China Trade* about a male PI with whom she occasionally works, in an ironic addendum on the contingencies of economic (and iconic) difference: "He's a solo p.i., a one-person shop with a varied caseload, just like me. Only he's older, taller, and tougher looking—oh, and a male white person—which means he doesn't go as long between cases as I sometimes do" (13).

Grafton further shifts the mode's conventions by suggesting that the job of the detective was always one suited to women, but that those "feminine" aspects of detection have been strategically elided in traditional conceptions of the tough guy PI. Kinsey's comments, for example, often recuperate the domestic sphere into professional space, a gesture that makes women central to (rather than alienated from) the investigative process: "It had not been a very satisfying day but then most of my days are the same: checking and cross-checking, filling in blanks, detail work that was absolutely essential to the job but scarcely dramatic stuff. The basic characteristics of any good investigator are a plodding nature and infinite patience. Society has inadvertently been grooming women to this end for years" (*"A" Is for Alibi* 27). The author makes a similar gesture in *"B" Is for Burglar* when Kinsey emphasizes the importance of detail work again: "I was going to have to check it out item by item. . . . There's no place in a PI's life for impatience, faintheartedness, or sloppiness. I understand the same qualifications apply for housewives" (33).

RECASTING THE DICK

Despite such practical subversions of gender roles, critiques of women's practices of hard-boiled writing often condemn these novels as "drag performances," in effect using the language of "queerness" to discredit them. Susan Geeson, for example, sums up her criticism of writers such as Paretsky, Grafton, Barbara Wilson, and Liza Cody with the line, "You could say that the feminist PI's are Philip Marlowe in drag" (116). Ann Wilson is more moderate, suggesting that "drag" is a tactical problem involved in negotiating gender and genre performance: "The problem is one of having the heroine occupy a male subject position—the role of the hard-boiled detective—without making her seem as if she is a man in drag. The negotiations of gender and sexuality in Grafton, Muller, and Paretsky are deft attempts to remain faithful to the tradition of tough-guy detective fiction while disrupting its gender codes" (148). Alison Littler raises important questions about the "tactical production" of the hard-boiled mode—or the types of knowledge and power it promotes. In condemning its practices she inadvertently indicates its political potential:

> How the term "feminist" is defined, of course, will be crucial to the kind of answers that are offered. If, for example, "feminist" is used in a liberal-humanist-independent-career-woman-in-control-of-her-own-life sense, then most certainly the recent series of women private eyes are feminist. If, however, "feminist" refers to a woman deconstructing phallocentric ideologies wherever they are naturalized and structured into social, cultural and political practices, then a feminist private eye is a contradiction in terms. She is a man in woman's clothing—or is it a woman in man's clothing? (133)

Littler's final unresolved question—is she a man in woman's clothing or a woman in man's clothing?—points to the ways that feminist hard-boiled novels, conceived as a complex performance of gender and genre, may destabilize and denaturalize the very gender categories inherent to

the phallocentric ideologies. The "liberal humanist" and "deconstruc-
tive" feminist modes, while theoretically in conflict, may operate simultaneously in practice.

As Littler suggests, how the term "feminist" is defined is an important criterion of assessment. In *Murder by the Book?* Sally Munt organizes
women's detective fiction into categories that correspond to different
schools of feminism. She sees hard-boiled writing correlating with liberal feminist theory, an association made by Littler as well. And also like
Littler, Munt resorts to conventionalized gender positions in her analyses of the form. While Munt does point out that different readers might
respond to characters in different ways, she also reverts to gender stereo-
typing when she comments at some length on V. I. Warshawski's frequent clothing changes in Paretsky's novels:

> for the heterosexual male reader, or the lesbian reader, she may
> function as a glamorous spectacle (the outfits are often silk and al-
> most always are expensive); for the heterosexual female reader the
> function may be more aspirational, her style metonymically suggest-
> ing a bourgeois fantasy of empowerment. As a fantasy of empower-
> ment, Warshawski's style reassures the female reader that "dressing
> up" enables you to do the job. (47)

Offering several interpretations of this "curious feature," Munt contends: "The fetishization of clothes in Paretsky's work implies the 'drag-
gish' imperative of femininity, signalling its artifice" (47). Munt closes
off the radical potential of gender-bending in such novels, implicitly
aligning the clothing changes with eating disorders ("female excess always exacts a price"; 47). While she does draw attention elsewhere in her
study to the possibility of gender play she restricts that play to lesbian
practice, thus failing to take into account the ways in which gender is
"performed" by heterosexual subjects too.

The references to drag in these critical assessments point to the ways
in which gender is subtly rehearsed in feminist hard-boiled novels. As
B. Ruby Rich notes in "The Lady Dicks," feminist hard-boiled protag-

onists are involved in "crisscrossing the borders of sex and gender" (24). Theorist Teresa de Lauretis's argument, in *The Practice of Love*, foregrounds how the operation of clothing and fantasy contributes to political agency: "Foucault's term *'reverse' discourse* actually suggests something of the process by which a representation in the external world is subjectively assumed, reworked through fantasy, in the internal world and then returned to the external world resignified, rearticulated discursively and/or performatively in the subject's self-representation—in speech, gesture, costume, body stance, and so forth." Expanding on her point, de Lauretis stresses "the importance that fashion and social performance have, in all cultures and cultural (self-)representations, for the normative sexual identity of their subjects" (308). Thus fantasy and costume can disrupt normative gender and sexual representations. In Sue Grafton's novels, for example, clothing is often the subject of the narrator's ironic commentary. Kinsey, who wears jeans and turtleneck sweaters, has an "all-purpose black dress," adaptable to any situation requiring more conventionally feminine attire: "black with long sleeves, in some exotic blend of polyester you could bury for a year without generating a crease" (*"I" Is for Innocent* 216). The dress, in fact, becomes a kind of running joke in the series that may even signify the embattled status of conventions of femininity in Grafton's novels: it has survived immersion in an irrigation ditch (*"G" Is for Gumshoe*) and a bomb explosion (*"E" Is for Evidence*). The large frame of Linda Barnes's Carlotta Carlyle also resists feminine norms, literally prohibiting her from fitting into most female fashions: "I go barefoot a lot because I'm six one and I wear size 11 shoes. You may not realize this, but for all practical purposes, women's shoes stop dead at size 10," she confides to the reader (*A Trouble of Fools* 4).

Grafton actually makes a point of representing—and making a comic spectacle of—garments "unmentionable" in polite discourse. Trapped in a hotel room in *"G" Is for Gumshoe*, Kinsey is forced to listen to the avid lovemaking of her neighbors through the wall. Ever adaptable, the detective "stuffed a sock in each cup of my bra and tied it across my head like earmuffs, with the ends knotted under my chin. Didn't help much. I lay there, a cone over each ear like an alien, wondering at the peculiarities of human sex practices. I would have much to report when I returned to my planet" (87). Indeed, the bra itself might be seen as one of the peculiarities of human sex practices, and Grafton here defamiliarizes—and de-eroticizes—its use, employing at the same time a turn on the trope of the detective as (alien) outsider. Sparkle Hayter effects a slightly different process of comic defamiliarization in her parody of the iconic image of the pistol-packing male investigator. Hayter deliberately feminizes not just her protagonist, but her protagonist's weapons: Robin carries not a gun but "a bottle of cheap spray cologne spiked with cayenne pepper to approximate Mace and a battery-operated Epilady, which I realized after one use was a better offensive weapon than feminine aid" (*What's a Girl Gotta Do?* 22). Hayter thus also highlights the masochist devices that are conventionally used by women against themselves, in order to "produce" femininity.

The play on/with/of gender that is manifested by a female character assuming a conventionally male position works to destabilize and denaturalize norms established through behavior and dress. By shifting the signification of clothing and the bodies that clothing mediates, the feminist hard-boiled genre *performs* gender. And as Judith Butler's work demonstrates, performative gender can intervene in the reproduction of power relations. It complements reverse discourse, since it too depends on repetition with difference: "Performativity," Butler argues, "cannot be understood outside of a process of iterability, a regularized and constrained repetition of norms. And this repetition is not performed *by* a subject; this repetition is what enables a subject and constitutes the temporal condition for the subject. This iterability implies that 'performance' is not a singular 'act' or event, but a ritualized production" (*Bodies That Matter* 95). And it is a ritualized production analogous with genre itself. Butler's analysis applies well to the problematics of female hard-boiled writers, who work within—and against—a patriarchal literary and cultural tradition. These writers counter the utopian notion that one can work outside the patriarchal structure of Western society, at the same time that they make possible an understanding of gender as a set of regulating discourses that can be disrupted in practice. As Butler puts it, such performativity establishes "a kind of political contestation that is not a 'pure' opposition,' a 'transcendence' of contemporary relations of power, but a difficult labor of forging a future from resources inevitably impure" (241).

Reverse discourse and the notion of performative gender are concepts more frequently used by queer theorists than by theorists of heterosexuality, perhaps because the potential of the reverse most obviously speaks to the refashioning of gender enacted by gay and lesbian discourse. Yet it is in the interest of all gender critics to problematize and shift conventional gender constructions. Here, too, Butler's work is extremely useful. As Dennis W. Allen points out in "Mistaken Identities," "Although Butler's point is precisely that heterosexual identities are also constituted in the same way [as other identities], the tendency in the culture at large to dematerialize the heterosexual into a transcendental ground for discussion strongly counters a recognition of Butler's point while at the same time overdetermining the materiality of lesbians and gays." Allen asserts the need for a popular recognition of the fact that "the gender and sexuality of straight men such as Jesse Helms are also performative" (138–39). Butler's theories help to conceptualize heterosexual femininity as itself an "impure," unstable category.

REORIENTATIONS

Rebecca Pope sees Paretsky's novels evoking the possibility of deep, affectionate bonds between women outside the heterosexual romance plot, most notably in their development of the ongoing relationship between V.I. and her friend Dr. Lotty Herschel (159). To Pope, this and other explorations of lesbian themes suggest that V.I.'s "desire is more various and fluid than her practice" (166). Such desires are difficult to name in the terms available to conventional hard-boiled narratives in the masculine tradition. Their representation in Paretsky's novels is thus fore-grounded, not least because her work does not simply recapitulate the homosocial unease characteristic of those earlier narratives. Gender role instability is even more overtly thematized in Nevada Barr's *Track of the Cat*, Mercedes Lambert's *Dogtown*, and Sarah Dunant's *Under My Skin*, all novels in which ostensibly heterosexual detectives reflect on their sexual orientation, thereby making an investigation of the nature of sexual desire a central component of the narrative.

In Barr's novel, park ranger Anna Pigeon finds herself powerfully attracted to a lesbian colleague. When Anna articulates her feelings to her psychiatrist sister Molly, Molly considers alternate ways of explaining Anna's situation: "Maybe you're overwhelmed that this woman was warm and kind and female. Maybe you're gun-shy of attachment since Zach left you. . . . Maybe you are turning gay. That's well and good. I just wanted to give you some other things to think about. Powerful need for affection, identification—all that underrated and over-exploited sisterhood stuff—is visceral. Feels almost sexual to those not in touch with themselves" (83–84). While Anna finally decides that she is heterosexual, the text highlights the permeability of heterosexual-homosexual desires. Lambert's novel confronts the theme more overtly, when investigating attorney Whitney Logan's attraction to another woman leads her to question her sexual orientation; the text implies that with the solving of the mystery, a dis-solving of rigid heterosexuality has taken place.

In *Under My Skin*, Dunant links lesbian desire to the resistant reading by women of the film noir figure of the femme fatale, a reading that reconfigures the vicious trajectory of heterosexual desire in such films. In an interview, Hannah Wolfe is told about a woman who was in love with Lauren Bacall's character in the film *The Big Sleep*: "In love with Lauren Bacall, eh?" Hannah muses to herself, "She wasn't the only one" (89). In the course of an assignment at a women's health club, Hannah discovers the pleasure of another woman's sexual touch, an extension of a health massage:

"Oh, that's good," I said slightly breathlessly. Because I wanted her to feel secure and because it was. Flesh. This story was all about flesh and how important it was to make sure somebody else loves it. And when you come to think of it, I had something to learn from that too.

So I let her play around my upper thighs for a while, caressing, suggesting, exciting, until with an expert little flick her fingers slid under and in, into the mouth of me, where no one had been for what felt like such a long time. (234)

Though this pleasure is ultimately regulated by Hannah's role as an investigator of the club and the masseuse, and though Hannah's desire is finally recovered into a heterosexual dynamic at the end of the novel by a possible relationship with a man, these pat solutions do not fully recuperate either the language of pleasure or the fact that another woman has literally and figuratively gotten under her skin.

The female dick, in effect, signifies difference. This in-between locus can counter dominant constructions of gender and sexuality by placing in question the clear-cut and essentialized character of the norms established by previous practices of the hard-boiled mode. And mainstream formula fiction offers a controlled space that enables a wide audience to explore the borders of established categories and conventions. Thus, as John Cawelti contends, formula narratives may assist in the process of altering cultural norms on a broad scale, absorbing new possibilities while contributing to cultural continuity ("Study of Literary Formulas" 143).

This power of a popular genre is perhaps most evident in the recent growth of the lesbian detective novel, a development we identified in chapter 1. Until recently, however, Sandra Scoppettone, who features an "out" lesbian investigator in her Lauren Laurano series (the first, *Everything You Have Is Mine*, was published by Ballantine in 1991), was alone in her exploration of lesbian detection in the mainstream.[3] Almost all lesbian novels appeared in alternative press publications: since the 1970s, feminist presses such as Naiad, Seal, and Virago offered their readers lesbian investigators, including Sarah Dreher's Stoner McTavish, Katherine V. Forrest's Kate Delafield, J. M. Redmann's Mickey Knight, Mary Wings's Emma Victor, and Barbara Wilson's Pam Nilsen (in the United States); Eve Zaremba's Helen Keremos and Lauren Wright Douglas's Caitlin Reece (in Canada); Claire McNab's Carol Ashton (in Australia); and Val McDermid's Lindsay Gordon (in the United Kingdom). Such alternative publishing houses can produce novels that fall outside the purview of purely profit-driven mainstream publishers (presumably because they were perceived as "small-market" texts). For example, Susan Brown argues that

> [Barbara] Wilson, unlike say, Grafton or Sara Paretsky, who publish with major publishers, has much greater freedom to the extent that, as co-publisher of Seal Press, she controls her immediate mode of literary production. The fact that Seal is an avowedly feminist press which views books not solely as means to create profits but as "essential tools in stirring up debate and contributing much-needed facts and analysis," and is committed to "publishing books that are fun as well as empowering" (catalogue blurb), means that Wilson writes within a much different set of constraints than more mainstream detective novelists. (8)

While Brown's point is an important one, the crossover of a number of lesbian writers from small press to mainstream is evidence of the potential continuity of the two markets—that lesbian readers may be "mainstream readers" too. It also points to the possibility that once small press authors have adapted mainstream genres, they can gain access to other publishing outlets and audiences through the appeal of genre. As Scoppettone comments of her lesbian detective series, her readers "are predominantly lesbian but there are some gay men and a lot more heterosexuals than you, than I, ever expected. It does seem to have crossed over in the mystery field. I don't think there are a lot of . . . non-mystery readers, reading it. But there are a lot of heterosexuals that don't have a problem with it, or more than *do* have a problem." Since the early 1990s, it has become much more common for narratives featuring openly lesbian detectives to be published by mainstream presses.

It is worth recalling Cawelti's argument that "allowing for a certain degree of inertia in the process, the production of formulas is largely dependent on audience response" ("Study of Literary Formulas" 34). According to Katherine V. Forrest (who, as well as being a writer, is also an editor for Naiad Press), it was reader demand for her novels that generated a shift in publishers' conception of the mainstream audience itself:

> Initially, most of us [lesbian writers] went to small presses because the major presses simply wouldn't publish us. They had no notion of any sort of audience out there. There just wasn't that much interest in the kind of books we wrote, and so that gave rise to all of these small lesbian and feminist presses, which are still flourishing. And I think that what the small presses have proven is that there *is* an audience out there for these books, that it's sizable, it's literate, it's affluent, and it's significant.

Forrest perceives her novels as "crossover" texts; in them, genre makes possible the convergence of different readerships. While affirming that she writes for a lesbian audience, Forrest observes: "A wider audience has found these books. But I think they're finding them because people who like good mysteries like good mysteries." One of the reasons she decided to shift from Naiad to Putnam is that reviewers tend to overlook small press publications, which results in less audience awareness. Forrest affirms the importance of being "heard" by lesbian and straight readers, reiterating Dutton editor Carole DeSanti's observation that lesbians' "are the only untold stories." Thus, for Forrest, moving to a mainstream press is a "dream . . . come true." Her character, Kate Delafield "is in a high-visibility, high-profile, very high-pressure job," which allows the author to explore "how that impacted on her as a lesbian and her lesbian identity." The relationship between professional and sexual identity has become "a crucial dynamic in the series." And Forrest adamantly asserts that she has not been asked by Putnam to downplay or soften her character's lesbianism. Forrest's *Murder at the Nightwood Bar* is now gaining further public exposure: it is being made into a Hollywood film.[4]

Both Phyllis Knight and Laurie R. King began publishing their lesbian detective series with mainstream houses, and a number of other authors have shifted from alternative to commercial publishing houses, including J. M. Redmann and Mary Wings. The change in mainstream publishers' responses to lesbian authors is evident in Knight's explanation of how her lesbian detective Lil Ritchie's "coming out" evolved as part of a process that involved author, agent and editor:

> I hadn't made it at all obvious that Lil was a gay woman and the
> agent that I sent it to said, "you know, obviously, Lil's a gay woman."
> I was just going to try to ignore it because I thought I'd never get
> published by a mainstream press, and then when my agent sent it to
> St. Martin's, the editor there . . . said to me, "I'm going to take it
> anyway, but, you know she's obviously a gay woman." So when he
> sent me back my manuscript the first time with changes, at the end
> I had her dancing with a stranger and he said, "I put a woman in
> there, tell me if it's not all right." I didn't have the courage to do it,
> and so to have a publisher insist was sort of interesting.

COLORING OUTSIDE THE LINES

Racial and ethnic boundaries have been similarly challenged through the agency of genre convention. This is not simply, as Sally Munt would argue, a "literary equal opportunity" approach or a "positive images" strategy engineered by mainstream white feminist authors in which the traditional alignment of white skin with good and black skin with bad is reversed, and in which (as Munt argues of Sara Paretsky's novels) all conflicts and differences are effaced (90). While Munt accurately observes that alternative presses have made and continue to make efforts to publish female detectives of color, her argument assumes that race and racism are concerns that can be addressed only from marginal positions of literary production (i.e., works having non-"mainstream" authors, publishers, and audiences). She overlooks the ways that mainstream presses may extend the process she attributes to small presses, making the perspectives they offer accessible to a wide audience. Mass audience publications can and do work both to complicate racial categories and to subvert (rather than merely inverting) the racially linked moral absolutes of traditional detective fiction. They may also use the marginal position of the private detective and the popular genre itself to interpellate a heterogeneous audience that other publishing venues cannot reach.

A number of mainstream press writers—including Valerie Wilson Wesley, Eleanor Taylor Bland, and Chassie West, who feature African American protagonists; Dana Stabenow, whose central character is an Aleut; and Gloria White, whose detective is half-Latina—have made racial issues central to their narratives of investigation. These writers use the generic figure of the detective as outsider to explore the subjectivity of racial categories that fall "outside the law," a strategy we will examine at further length in chapter 6. In so doing, they use the rules of genre to explore the cultural regulations that define outsider status.

For example, Valerie Wilson Wesley uses the detective novel to expose the crimes of racism within law enforcement. Wesley's protagonist Tamara Hayle is a former cop who quits the force. In *When Death Comes Stealing*, she inquires into the death of a young African American man whom the police have routinely written off as a junkie. The victim of crime has been elided with the criminal, a situation Tamara aims to rectify: "Some lazy cop, tired at the end of the day or late for lunch, had proclaimed that Terrence Curtis had lived and died a junkie, and there was no more to be said about it. But I know different now. If he'd died of crack, he hadn't been an addict, and I was hot for a minute, angry again at the bullshit so many cops put down when it comes to black folks—the official incompetence, the easy way out" (36).

In Gloria White's novels, her half-Latina protagonist, Ronnie Ventana, often confronts racism. In *Charged with Guilt*, Ronnie's inquiries lead her to San Francisco's Hispanic underworld, an underworld that has erected its own system of justice because it has been written off by the police. Ronnie must request assistance from an old friend of her father's, and her ability to "translate" between the cultures is central to her ability to open doors literally and figuratively to the information that circulates in different communities:

> Santiago Rosales had decided to set up his bar on Ellis Street. Not that it was really a bar. It was an exchange. People went to El Ratón Podrido for information, to make connections, to score goods and weapons. They went there for things they couldn't get anyplace else. And Santiago never turned anybody away. . . .
>
> I reached the bar and, when the bartender ambled over, I said, "I need to see Santiago."
>
> He raised his eyebrows and lowered his eyelids. He didn't need to say a word. It was obvious he needed to hear more before he'd consider letting me through.
>
> "Ronnie Ventana," I said.
>
> His surly face broke into an unexpected grin. "Ah, *sí*. 'Cisco's daughter. *Cómo no! Pase, pase. Por aquí*." (283–85)

In Chassie West's *Sunrise*, police detective Leigh Ann Warren is so tired of the pressures placed on her by the Washington police force that she returns to her hometown in North Carolina for respite. While there she helps ensure that a proposed mall does not recklessly destroy an old African American cemetery. Eleanor Taylor Bland's *Dead Time* dramatizes the way the signifiers "black," "woman," and "police detective" can be read in contradictory ways, thus compromising Marti MacAlister's ability to be recognized as "representative" of official law enforcement. Called to a crime scene, Marti overhears how onlookers respond to her presence:

> "Well, *she* certainly isn't a police officer. I thought they were only letting in people on official business."
>
> A tiny dark-skinned woman with at least five slips hanging below a short, fuzzy blue robe answered.

"Hah. Got cop written all over her. Now ain't that a sight, Betty? Black and a woman and not wearin' a uniform." (21)

Novelists often use the detective narrative and the subjectivity that focalizes it to investigate race and ethnicity—including white authors, who complicate the concept of homogeneous whiteness. For example, in Rochelle Majer Krich's *Angel of Death* and April Smith's *North of Montana*, a narrative of identity parallels the narrative of investigation, and the protagonist of each novel learns that her ethnicity is not as homogeneous as she thought it was. As these novels demonstrate, the texts of white writers as well as those of writers of color can serve as sites from which dominant perceptions of race and ethnicity may be interrogated. One of the earliest exemplars of the female PI, Marcia Muller's Sharon McCone is part Shoshone, a feature often overlooked in critical discussions of Muller's work. Linda Barnes's novels almost invariably begin by establishing her character's ethnic and religious hybridity (she is Irish-Jewish). Consider, for example, the opening paragraph of *Snapshot:*

> Every April my mother used to host her own version of the traditional Passover seder. A mishmash of Hebrew, Yiddish, English, and Russian, it involved all Mom's union pals—Jews, Christians, Muslims, and pagans—who'd give rapid-fire thanks for the release of the ancient Hebrews from Egyptian bondage, and then launch into pre-chicken-soup tirades against General Motors, J. Edgar Hoover, and the FBI. I grew up thinking they were part of the religion. (1)

Even Paretsky's mainstream hero, whom Munt cites as a perpetrator of simplistic "liberalist pluralism," has complex class and ethnic identifications. The child of a Polish father and an Italian immigrant mother, V.I.'s first-generation, "new" world status is central to her position as investigator, and the character frequently calls attention to her cultural background and the dis/position it establishes: "I guess my ideals died the hardest. It's often that way with the children of immigrants. We need to buy the dream so bad we sometimes can't wake up" (*Killing Orders*

86–87). Her comment here also calls attention to the attraction of the liberal humanist democratic ideal as one possible (though not the only) source of agency. V.I.'s position creates a potential point of identification in the novels with more marginalized positions, one also opened up to readers. For instance, in *Bitter Medicine* V.I. perceives the institutional marginalization of Philippa Barnes, an African American woman who works for the Department of Environment and Human Resources. Barnes tells V.I., "The bureaucracy in a place like this just about kills you. If I had charge of the whole program, instead of just a piece of it—' She folded her lips, cutting off the sentence." In a moment of recognition that the reader shares, V.I. realizes, "We all . . . knew that having a sex-change operation—and perhaps dyeing her skin—was the only way that would happen" (165–66).

Feminist hard-boiled detective novels provide their readers with fictional narratives that have repercussions beyond their immediate textual performances. It is therefore important not to belittle the liberal feminist "fantasy of empowerment" that Sally Munt describes so disparagingly; writers and readers may use this fantasy as a point of departure, a site of agency and change. As we saw in chapter 2, letters to Sara Paretsky demonstrate that a fictional problem-solving heroine sometimes helps readers feel as if they can solve their own problems. In "Surviving Rape," an essay in *Theorizing Black Feminisms*, Andrea Rushing describes the pleasure and affirmation she experienced in reading "books about new-style U.S. women detectives" after she had been sexually assaulted:

> Week after week I gulp, as if drowningly desperate for air, their
> plain-spoken stories about acid-tongued, fast-thinking, single and
> self-employed women who not only dare to live alone, but scoff,
> sneer, seethe when men try to put them in their "weaker sex" place.
> Parched and starved, I read and reread Sue Grafton's alphabet adven-
> tures, but Sara Paretsky's books became my favourites because her
> Chicago-based private investigator is even more bodacious and sassy
> than my pre-rape self. And, in stark contrast to television and movie
> renditions of women as powerless victims of men, she both with-

stands and metes out physical violence in every single book. Murder
mysteries restore order to worlds thrown out of balance. (137)

Murder mysteries also offer alternative readings about just what constitutes "order" and "balance." And even if they do not always fully restore
order, they repeatedly dramatize, address, and renegotiate fantasies,
fears, and conflicts in the lives of their readers. Through reverse discourse, with its performative gender possibilities, these texts can both
inscribe an empowered female subject and rework the conventions of
subjectivity that make that position problematic.

"WELCOME TO MASS CULTURE"

Some novels even address explicitly their status as popular culture fantasies, offering a version of reverse discourse that relates to their own
fictional practice. Lia Matera's *Face Value* and Mary Willis Walker's *Red
Scream* both thematize the very system of popular culture that makes
them possible. Matera's *Face Value* is, among other things, an unusually
self-conscious example of the apparently contradictory way an author
can use the popular cultural form of the detective novel to look beyond
the "face value" of popular culture itself, foregrounding how its discourses (popular fiction, film, television, journalism) construct a sense
of "the real" that embodies powerful ideological messages. Matera's detective, lawyer Laura Di Palma, explains how she rose to fame on a defense tactic, used in a murder case, that came to be known as the "television syndrome" defense: she argued "that television creates a reality
more powerful than personal experience" (14). The defendant shot two
U.S. senators, under the influence of Clint Eastwood and Charles Bronson movies: he "had been inundated with television images of lone-wolf,
take-the-law-in-their-own-hands good guys" (155). Those images might
well be related to the tough guy detectives of the hard-boiled literary tradition; and in evoking the extreme example of a man who kills because
of the models they provide, Matera's novel dramatizes how rhetorically

powerful such fictional representations can be. On a less extreme note, the novel may also make readers more self-conscious about the ways in which popular cultural forms shape our sense of reality, even as it *uses* the popular form of the novel of private investigation to posit alternative possibilities for being and acting. The novel repeatedly suggests the ways in which "real" identities are repeatedly performed—for example, in the fashion, grooming, and (profitable) public spectacles of the high-powered female lawyer, the stripper, the New Age guru, and even Miss America. Contemplating the pervasive societal need for "something real," Laura wryly comments, "Welcome to mass culture" (16).

The narrative of *Face Value* involves Laura's investigation of a quasi-religious cult's practice of taping, visually modifying, and then marketing—without permission of the participants—the sexual consciousness-raising sessions that are part of its "therapy." Having viewed some of these tapes, Laura comments, "Like other 'erotic' films I'd seen, these tracked lowest-common-denominator fantasies featuring people who, for the most part, might have stepped off a television set. They left me feeling as if I'd watched a particularly embarrassing episode of 'The Newlywed Game.' They made me want to distance myself from mass culture, to flee into the artistic refinement of classical novels and old jazz" (30). Laura does not retreat, however. Indeed, she has no choice, since she is already implicated in the performances that make her own subjectivity and sexuality possible. Nor does Matera attempt to escape mass culture, though she does appropriate and redirect it in order to investigate the implications of different forms of popular "visual manipulation," both of images and audiences.

Walker's *Red Scream* uses the narrative of investigation to inquire into the ways in which crime writing controls the legitimating discourses that make "truths" about crime and criminality public currency. *Red Scream*'s investigative reporter Molly Cates has published a "true crime" book, *Sweating Blood*, that focuses on the motivations and actions of convicted serial killer Louie Bronk. During the writing of the book, Molly "had wrestled with the problem inherent in writing a book for entertainment which was based on other people's private disasters" (4). Yet as a writer she also gets a great deal of satisfaction from the way the final product lives up to the generic—and profit-generating—standards of the "true crime" genre:

> From the minute her publisher had first showed her the cover art, she had loved it because it was so attention-grabbing. The painting depicted a lonely stretch of highway with a woman's body lying in a ditch alongside; from the body blood flowed and surrounded the entire cover, front and back, with a shiny vivid red. She had recognized immediately that it would sell books. It was commercial, yes, sensational even. But that was the nature of true crime books and she wasn't going to apologize for it. (4)

Molly must confront her own complicity in sensationalizing the murders when *Sweating Blood* focuses unwanted attention on the family of Tiny McFarland, for whose murder Bronk has received the death penalty. Molly is also forced to consider the possibility that her book might be responsible for generating a copycat murder, reenacting its representation: "what if some maniac read her account of Tiny McFarland's murder and decided to do the same thing? . . . She felt a flush of hot confusion, like waking panicked from a nightmare not knowing what was real and what wasn't" (69).

Questions of what is "real" and what is "fiction" pervade this narrative, since Molly's "true crime" account is thrown into doubt when she visits Bronk on death row and is informed by the convict that in their initial interviews, his representation of events was not true but was what he believed she wanted to hear. At this meeting, Bronk contends that he is not responsible for Tiny's murder (though there is no question that he committed the others for which he has been jailed), and Molly must now deal with her own conflicting inclinations. Her first response is to disbelieve Bronk, because his latest statement threatens the generic claims of her "true crime" book: "If Louis didn't do it, then *Sweating Blood* was largely fiction" (191). Molly's second response is to conduct a supplementary investigation of the killings, over the course of which she becomes convinced that Louie's new narrative may be the "real" narrative—a narrative that is now impossible to verify, because much of the evidence has disappeared. When Molly realizes that she cannot sufficiently establish that Louis is not guilty of Tiny's murder, she tries to obtain a stay of execution by convincing the governor that Louie is now telling the truth.

Although the governor denies Molly's request, she does offer Molly advice about an alternative (legitimate) perspective for crime writing: "'I have a suggestion for you: how about writing more about crime from the victim's point of view? I reckon serial murderers sell books, but where are the stories of the [victims] of the world? People who survive the unimaginable and go on cheerfully—the stuff of real heroes'" (274). The "true crime" account of *Sweating Blood* has left the stories of the murder victims untold. And it has also potentially made Louie Bronk both criminal in and victim of its narrative, since it has shaped public opinion of him. Unable to stop the legal proceedings, Molly attends the execution and watches Bronk die for a murder he did not commit. *Red Scream* concludes with yet another story, an article in the *Lone Star Monthly* in which Molly corrects previous accounts and expresses her anger at the justice system and at herself for her complicity in Bronk's death:

> No one tried to stop [the execution]. Not one of us. I knew he was innocent, but I did nothing. I didn't object or cry bloody murder, or give in to the red scream—that shriek of terror and rage death-row inmates talk about. I just stood and watched—a passive witness.
>
> But no more.
>
> Here is my red scream. . . . (324, her ellipsis)

Molly's "true crime" account is embedded in a crime *fiction* that allows Walker to leave the reader with questions about how stories are constructed and what kinds of truths they produce, as well as about the legitimating power of the crime writer.

There are no easy answers to such questions—indeed, in a characteristic gesture, the narrative of *Red Scream* produces structural closure (we learn whodunit) but leaves its readers with a profound sense that other issues remain to be resolved. These include the legitimating function of the popular culture text itself—its ability to mediate alternative and often contradictory constructions of the real—and the related question of the connection between language, genre, and power. In chapter 4, we turn to the conventional language of hard-boiled fiction, which its American innovators saw as a uniquely truthful and powerful way of representing the sensational world of crime and criminals. Women writing in the hard-boiled tradition question their progenitors by drawing on the interrogative power of tough talk itself.

Chapter 4

THE TEXT AS EVIDENCE

Linguistic Subversions

"If it's that delicate," I said, "maybe you need a lady detective."

"Goodness, I didn't know there were any." Pause. "But I don't think a lady detective would do at all. You see, Orrin was living in a very tough neighborhood, Mr. Marlowe. At least, I thought it was tough. The manager of the rooming house is a most unpleasant person. He smelled of liquor. Do you drink, Mr. Marlowe?"

"Well, now that you mention it—"

"I don't think I'd care to employ a detective that uses liquor in any form. I don't even approve of tobacco."

"Would it be all right if I peeled an orange?"

I caught the sharp intake of breath at the far end of the line. "You might at least talk like a gentleman," she said.

"Better try the University Club," I told her. "I heard they had a couple left over there, but I'm not sure they'll let you handle them." I hung up.

Raymond Chandler, *The Little Sister*

TOUGH GUYS/TOUGH TALK

Ross Macdonald once observed, "The Chandler-Marlowe prose is a highly charged blend of laconic wit and imagistic poetry set to breakneck rhythms. Its strong colloquial vein reaffirms the fact that the *Black Mask* revolution was a revolution in language as well as in subject matter" ("The Writer" 183). Chandler himself read the innovations of his predecessor Dashiell Hammett as part of a "rather revolutionary debunking" not just of the material of fiction, but of its *language;* he traces this movement back to poet Walt Whitman and to novelists of the naturalist school, associating it with an American vernacular strain of literary practice ("Simple Art" 233). Hard-boiled writers saw their work as part of a revolution that made it possible to represent a more authentic version of reality with a different kind of literary "lingo." More specifically, they launched a rebellion against what they thought of as the artificial formal restrictions of the popular British cozy tradition, with its stylized techniques of characterization, its confining ratiocinative plot structures and modes of narration, and, perhaps most important, its conventionalized literary language. The Golden Age mystery was popular precisely because of its ingeniousness and artificiality: as one critic put it, "the charm of the pure detective story is its utter un-reality" (Nicolson 117–18). Hard-boiled writers such as Chandler were clearly unmoved by this charm, judging it phony and pretentious. Chandler concludes in "The Simple Art of Murder" that the kind of writing practiced by Dorothy L. Sayers "was an arid formula which could not even satisfy its own implications" (232), and Macdonald affirms that the *Black Mask* writers felt the formula "had lost contact with contemporary life and language" ("The Writer" 181).

The Golden Age murder mystery of the interwar period was stereotypically identified not just with the British, but especially with the female novelists who established its popularity, including Sayers, Agatha Christie, Marjorie Allingham, Josephine Tey, and Ngaio Marsh. As Alice Yaeger Kaplan perceives (27), it is both a British and a feminized current in mystery writing that Chandler denounces in "The Simple Art of Murder." Moreover, it is a tradition frequently associated with its extensive audience of female *readers*, whom Chandler's famous essay parodies as old ladies jostling at the mystery bookshelf for titles like *The Triple Petunia Murder Case* or *Inspector Pinchbottle to the Rescue* (224). The vulgarity of wisecracking hard-boiled speech was indeed shocking and subversive of conventional literary decorum; it was precisely the kind of language not to be used in the company of ladies, much less be used by the ladies themselves. In describing the present-day version of the classical mystery (the mystery that features an amateur detective), novelist Nancy Pickard once again relates this sense of decorum to a feminine audience of delicate sensibility, advising aspiring writers that in composing such mysteries "you generally can't use as much *bad language*, violence, sex or gore as you could in some other types of mysteries. And isn't *that* a relief? And isn't your mother grateful?" (65, first emphasis added). Sue Grafton, incidentally, wittily revises this stereotype of the fragile sensitive old woman reader of cozies in her novel *"B" Is for Burglar*. When Grafton's detective conscripts an elderly woman to help with her investigation, the woman eagerly responds by offering to learn the language of hard-boiled detection: "I'm going to start reading Mickey Spillane just to get in shape," she says; "I don't know a lot of rude words, you know" (103).[1] The character creates an analogy between her active participation in the case (she has to "get in shape") and a repertoire of hard-boiled linguistic "moves."

The hard-boiled stylistic revolution should also be read as running counter to the "high literary" avant-garde antirealist experimentations of modernist writers such as James Joyce and Virginia Woolf; in particular, detective fiction is in part defined by its mass-market appeal, while this form of literary modernism, typically characterized as elitist and academic "high culture," is seen as somehow exempt from the exigencies of the literary marketplace (see chapter 2). Such definition by contrast occurred during the Golden Age of detective fiction itself. In a 1929 article, for example, Marjorie Nicolson remarked on the academic reader's fondness for formal mysteries, which she claimed had developed as a kind of reader "revolt" against the "formlessness" and general decadence of contemporary literature (113, 114). Writing before women writers of Golden Age fiction had achieved their ascendancy Nicolson saw the detective genre not simply as "a man's novel" but as a more generally masculine endeavor, since its writers were able to engineer an "escape from a school of fiction which is becoming too feminized" (123).[2]

JUST THE FACTS, MA'AM

Hard-boiled writing was, as Julian Symons notes, an "American revolution" (153) in crime fiction, and this was specifically a stylistic revolution in that it validated the vernacular of the urban United States as its legitimate linguistic territory. It was at the same time a self-consciously populist "democratic" revolution that countered the inaccessible, anti-realist prose of modernism with its new brand of popular "vernacular realism." It is no coincidence that the forms of writing against which the hard-boiled style is defined are routinely constructed as simultaneously artificial, elitist, and *feminine*. As Dennis Porter puts it, "the new ethos of hard-boiled detective fiction was not only anti-English and anti-elitist, it was also antifeminist" (184). Intimately related to the popular, realist, and American "revolution" in novelistic language is hard-boiled writing's development of a self-consciously masculine style, a style that would act as an antidote to the perceived effeminacy of other approaches. When Chandler considered how Hammett's writing recovers and reshapes "the speech of common men," the gender specificity of his noun needed no emphasis ("Simple Art" 234). It is not surprising, therefore, that the modern literary stylist with whom hard-boiled writing is most often associated is Ernest Hemingway. Although critics have never really decided whether Hemingway was an influence on Hammett, or vice versa (see Chandler, "Simple Art" 233; Symons 157; Worpole 36), critics of both writers almost always use terms associated with masculinity to describe their innovations in narrative style (Worpole 39). Porter extends this notion of a masculine vernacular style to the formal innovations of a whole line of canonical American literature:

> Those stylists who from Mark Twain to Hemingway, Faulkner, and Norman Mailer created the idiom of the American literary mainstream also conspired to ensure that the voice of American fiction should be an aggressively male voice. At least until Erica Jong there has been no vernacular for women outside quotation marks. Bad grammar, slang, and even a strong regional accent, like cussing, blaspheming, hard drinking, and tomcatting, were the prerogatives of men and boys, defensive reactions against the encroachments of civilizing womankind and the tyranny of hearth and home. A linguistic double standard operated, making such language in a female mouth the sign of a bumpkin or a fallen woman. (184)[3]

The stylistic originality of hard-boiled writing included what Walker Gibson identifies as the rhetorical strategies of "tough talk." His description of these strategies, based on an analysis of the opening paragraph of Hemingway's *Farewell to Arms* (1929) (and later extended in a modified form to the discussion of Chandler's work), makes clear the degree to which the efficacy of the tough-talking narrator depends on his "plain-spoken" demeanor, on his anti-"literary" idiom, and on an implicit, fraternal bond with the reader. Gibson's use of gender pronouns stipulates that the narrator—and by extension the author—and assumed reader are by definition male:

> [The tough talker's] rhetoric, like his personality, shows his limitations openly: short sentences, "crude" repetitions of words, simple grammatical structures with little subordinating (I have no use for elegant variation, for the worn-out gentilities of traditional prose). His tense intimacy with his assumed reader, another man who has been around, is implied by colloquial patterns from oral speech and by a high frequency of the definite article. He lets his reader make logical and other connections between elements (You know what I mean; I don't have to spell it all out for *you*). He prefers

naming things to describing them, and avoids modification, especially when he is self-conscious about his language—even about
language generally. (41)

Despite the almost exclusive use of the "subjective" point of view in
hard-boiled stories and the implicit intimacy between narrative speaker
and reader, the flat, tough-talking voice denotes a certain sense of distance from its subject matter; its bluntness and often cynical tone give
a feeling of straightforwardness and authenticity. The tough-talker's
language tells us that he shoots straight from the hip, both literally and
figuratively. And taciturn narrators such as Philip Marlowe or Mike
Hammer give the impression of objectivity—their reticence implies a
refusal to engage with and thus become implicated in the corrupt world
that surrounds them. Hammett's description of Sam Spade as observing
a room with the "detached air of a disinterested spectator" well characterizes the hard-boiled narrative voice (*Maltese Falcon* 74).

David Glover identifies another rhetorical effect of the tough-talking
narrator: the repositioning of women as readers, which, he contends,
contributed to a gendered segregation of the popular fiction market
from the 1930s onward. As Tania Modleski points out, a second "Gothic
revival" of fiction marketed to women occurred at the same time that
hard-boiled detective novels were generating an unprecedented audience of male readers (*Loving with a Vengeance* 21).[4] Glover argues in addition that the hard-boiled "masculinization of crime fiction" reposi-
tions women as fictional characters as it simultaneously excludes them
as authors (74). The estrangement of women as readers, authors, and
characters is thus a product of what Bethany Ogodon calls the "'hard-
boiled' collectivity (readers, writers, detective-heroes)," a closed masculine circle formed by the genre that encourages an antagonistic "us
against them" structure (84).

We need to extend these observations in order also to recognize the
way the "vernacular style" validated the common *man*'s language and experience, universalizing the masculine perspective and in effect alienat-

ing women from the very language it designates as realistic, despite its self-styled democratic aims. For example, Ross Macdonald commented in an interview, "I think the American 'hard-boiled' detective novel was invented to reflect American society, which is essentially an equalitarian [*sic*] society" ("Interview" 183). It is perhaps no coincidence that at a moment in American history when women had just been accorded full voting rights (the Nineteenth Amendment was passed in 1920), they were implicitly excepted from the development of this uniquely American, "democratic" revolutionary literary genre. Although hard-boiled authors relied on a formulaic narrative of investigation, and although they developed their own easily recognizable (and highly artificial) protocols of style, these writers affirmed again and again their privileged access to the average American's real life (see, for example, Chandler, "Simple Art"; Macdonald, "Interview").

Kenneth Worpole recognizes how the kind of life they represent might alienate women readers, but he insists that "it is still important to defend, critically, vernacular realism because of its narrative strength and popular accessibility to the language of everyday life" (47). Yet it is also important to understand that the language of vernacular realism suggested that "everyday life"—in effect, reality itself—was a masculine space. Contemporary women writers in the hard-boiled mode seem to be acting on Worpole's injunction: they implicitly defend vernacular realism by employing recognizable (if modified) versions of hard-boiled "tough talk" and by self-consciously appropriating strategies of narrative and description from the hard-boiled repertoire. In so doing they gesture toward a reclamation of the territory of "the real" from which such writing had tacitly estranged women writers and readers. At the same time, they also draw on the strength of the hard-boiled detective narrative in order to be recognizable and accessible to a popular audience of both men and women. But they defend that reclaimed territory *critically*, appropriating popular culture as a viable (if limited) locus of feminist analysis and making the hard-boiled narrative of investigation available as an instrument of literary and social critique. And the formal and stylistic characteristics of their fiction are themselves elements of that critique. In fact, in appropriating and reversing the discourse of earlier novels, these works may be read as an investigation of the nature and power of hard-boiled language itself.

TALKING BACK

Peter Rabinowitz's analysis of the conclusion of Sue Grafton's first novel, *"A" Is for Alibi*, helps to illuminate how this early work cleverly forecasts the subversive potential of women's appropriation of hard-boiled generic conventions. Grafton's detective narrative reaches its climax when her detective, Kinsey Millhone, chased by the killer, Charlie, conceals herself in a large metal garbage container, clutching her gun. Charlie tracks her to this hiding place. Grafton ends the main narrative:

> He lifted the lid. The beams from his headlights shone against his golden cheek. He glanced over at me. In his right hand was a butcher knife with a ten-inch blade.
> I blew him away. (214)

As Rabinowitz argues, ultimately Kinsey's position "serves to remind us that even the trashiest literature can, if taken over and remade, serve as a site of empowerment" ("Reader, I Blew Him Away" 333). Grafton's language in this passage and elsewhere self-consciously evokes the attributes of the tough-talking hard-boiled narrator: the direct matter-of-fact descriptive voice; the short, simple words and sentences; the repetitive structures; the use of the definite article and material details; and an understated concluding punch line. That language becomes a point of departure for Grafton, a kind of sanction for her own ability to speak as a popular writer and a way of designating the tradition which she both emulates and contradicts. Thus, Scott Christianson observes, "Grafton appropriates hard-boiled language for feminist purposes as an exercise of language as power; in Foucauldian terms, she seizes the 'rules of formation' for the 'discourse' of hard-boiled fiction, thereby occupying a space or 'subject position,' formerly reserved for men only, from which she may speak with power as a woman" ("Talkin' Trash" 136). It enables her, in other words, to talk back to the masculine tradition on—or in—its own terms.

The ending of *"A" Is for Alibi* is also an implicit reconsideration of the formulaic narrative structure of many hard-boiled novels. As Kinsey's lover-turned-betrayer, Charlie is a male version of the hard-boiled femme fatale—he is an *homme fatal,* if we may coin a term. The final paragraph is therefore a self-conscious gender reversal of the hard-boiled narrative convention—one almost wants to call it the literary cleansing ritual—that involves achieving a sense of closure by violently eliminating (and in doing so silencing) the betraying woman, who epitomizes the threat to the narrator's moral authority.[5] In particular, it echoes the language and violent finales of many Mickey Spillane novels. Grafton's "I blew him away" evokes the blunt, pithy ending of Spillane's *I, the Jury* in which Hammer remorselessly guns down the femme fatale as he recounts, "The roar of the .45 shook the room": "How c-could you?" she gasps, realizing she is mortally wounded, and Hammer responds, "I only had a moment before talking to a corpse, but I got it in. 'It was easy,' I said."[6] Grafton's novel allows much more ambivalent readings. For example, unlike *I, the Jury, "A" Is for Alibi* ends with an epilogue that cannot quite contain the implications of the final killing. Kinsey's ambivalence about it is especially pronounced since she must acknowledge that her actions were part of a job from which she profited and which she continues to practice: "All together, I was paid $2978.25 for services rendered in the course of the sixteen days and I suppose it was fair enough. The shooting disturbs me still. It has moved me into the same camp with soldiers and maniacs. . . . I'll recover, of course. I'll be ready for business again in a week or two, but I'll never be the same" (214). Read at another level, Kinsey's admission might also cue readers to the necessarily ambivalent position in which Grafton too is placed, as one who uses her hard-boiled series to capitalize professionally on the powerful conservative conventions of the hard-boiled tradition (a choice that moves her, after all, into the same camp with the likes of Spillane), at the same time that she turns them to revisionist ends.

"YOU KNOW WHAT I MEAN; I DON'T HAVE TO SPELL IT OUT FOR *YOU*" (WALKER GIBSON)

One of the central rhetorical strategies of "tough talk" involves its interpellation of readers; it cements a familiar bond with them. From their inception, hard-boiled stories used a direct appeal to the audience in the style of the dramatic aside to reinforce an identification between narrator and reader. In fact, what is arguably the first hard-boiled story, "Three Gun Terry," published in *Black Mask* on May 15, 1923, and featuring Carroll John Daly's detective Terry Mack, began:

> My life is my own, and the opinions of others don't interest me; so don't form any, or if you do, keep them to yourself. If you want to sneer at my tactics, why go ahead; but do it behind the pages—you'll find that healthier.
>
> So for my line. I have a little office which says "Terry Mack, Private Investigator," on the door; which means whatever you wish to think it. I ain't a crook, and I ain't a dick; I play the game on the level, in my own way. I'm in the center of a triangle; between the crook and the police and the victim. The police have had an eye on me for some time, but only an eye, never a hand; they don't get my lay at all. The crooks; well, some is on, and some ain't; most of them don't know what to think, until I've put the hooks in them. Sometimes they gun for me, but that ain't a one-sided affair. When it comes to shooting, I don't have to waste time cleaning my gun. A little windy that; but you get my game. (43–44)

Detective novels authored by women, using a similar formal strategy, often both call attention to and frustrate the exclusive nature of the male bonding that such asides manufacture. The gesture accomplishes at least two functions in this context: it develops an intimate bond of identification between the narrator and a differently constituted readership, and it throws the techniques of male hard-boiled fiction into (often comic) relief.

Whether explicitly or implicitly, narratives *always* construct a "you" that is addressed by the narration. Women's hard-boiled novels tend to highlight women's traditional alienation from that "you," offering the woman reader a privileged, self-conscious place in the narrative. For example, Carlotta Carlyle's initial address to her readers in the opening pages of Barnes's *Trouble of Fools* stands in stark contrast with the adventure-style beginning of Daly's story: "The vacuum cleaner hummed pleasantly. If you've ever considered your Hoover's voice soothing, you've probably been shoving it across a high-pile carpet. From the right distance, propelled by other hands—in this case the paint-smeared hands of Roz, my tenant cum new-wave artist cum sometime assistant—vacuum cleaner buzz could make the lullaby obsolete" (1). As noted in chapter 3, Kinsey Millhone contrasts her routines with those of male counterparts in interrogative asides to the reader that, like Carlotta's aside, de-romanticize the macho myth of the detective through associations with women's domestic work. Sara Dunant's Hannah Wolfe mysteries often directly address the reader, and sometimes humorously develop a sly kind of female bonding through that address. For instance, in *Fatlands*, after having consumed too much coffee, the detective remarks, "Of course, feminism has given us girls the confidence to pee anywhere, but it had been a long time since breakfast and if I was going to stop I might as well make it work for me" (100). When she admits to having to ask for directions twice in one day, she solicits the reader to take her side and keep the information from her male partner: "I won't tell Frank if you don't" (100).

DISRUPTING THE GAG ORDER

Strategies that encourage an identification between narrator and reader are central to how tough talk and especially wisecracks function in women's hard-boiled writing. The narrator of hard-boiled stories speaks not just *to* but *for* the reader. In his article on detective fiction and the discourses of modernity, Scott Christianson recognizes the ways traditional hard-boiled wisecracks are defined against acceptable codes of literary and social decorum. The acting out represented by the wisecrack offers a vicarious thrill for the reader: "Against the good taste and breeding of hegemonic, dominant culture, the hard-boiled private eye is scandalous, indecorous, vulgar, offensive—and violent" ("Heap of Broken Images" 146). J. M. Redmann's detective Micky Knight uses the scandalous, indecorous, vulgar, and offensive nature of the wisecrack as a defensive device against a man who uses sexual obscenities to threaten her over the telephone. Micky puts the phone down until he is done speaking, then picks it up again and responds: "Sorry, Joey, my tampon was bleeding over and I could feel the blood running down my legs. I had to pull it out—it was covered with big, dripping clots. What were you saying?" (104). Her remark draws attention to the socially constructed nature of women's bodies as excessive, "monstrous," and even obscene— when they are not subject to masculine sexual control: Micky's uncontrollable status as a lesbian in her relationship to Joey has "provoked" his attempt to subordinate her by evoking a pornographic verbal scenario.

A similarly defensive "vulgar" gesture is enacted by Karen Kijewski's detective Kat Colorado, who casually picks her nose when she is taken captive, in defiance of her male captor's sense of propriety and, significantly, as a means of verbally shifting the balance of power between them:

> Picking one's nose is a small, but a crude and disgusting thing. It is repellent to most of us, to our sense of manners and presumably to our romantic and sexual sensibilities. Blackford looked astounded and repulsed. I smiled.
>
> "How very unladylike!"
>
> "I don't pretend to be a lady."
>
> "Just a private investigator," he said scornfully as he handed me my wine. I wiped my hand on the chair arm before I took the wine and watched him wince.
>
> "Exactly."

> The control had shifted. I no longer felt remotely like a captive
> or a whore and he no longer saw me as one. (*Katwalk* 212)

Kat's "unladylike" demeanor resists subordination. Through it, she refuses to be captive to rules that govern the role of "lady"—a role that
here is antithetical to Kat's performance as a private investigator.

D. B. Borton's private eye Cat Caliban is a grandmother who, on the
first page of the first novel in the series, explains both her genre-altering
difference from the stereotype of the detective and her penchant for
swearing as a means of making herself heard:

> "You don't look like no 'tectives on TV, Granny," Ben had an-
> nounced at his first opportunity to comment on my new career.
> He'd stuck one pudgy digit up his nose and pointed another one at
> me accusingly. "None o' them gots white hair."
> "Stick around for a few seasons, kid. They will," I'd answered.
> What the hell. I was used to skepticism. Any veteran mother that
> isn't has her goddam ears stuffed with kumquats.
> Swearing was a habit I'd picked up when Fred was alive. One
> day I got the impression that Fred hadn't been listening to me for a
> while. Say, twenty years. So I thought I'd try a little verbal variety
> to see if he'd notice. (*One for the Money* 1)

Above all, the wisecrack provides the potential for discursive resistance. When in Chandler's *Big Sleep* General Sternwood suggests that
detective Philip Marlowe disliked working for the district attorney, Marlowe replies, "I was fired. For insubordination. I test very high on insubordination, General" (10). Wisecracks are a method of wittily scor-
ing through language; they are an instance of verbal insubordination.
Lew Archer, for example, uses the wisecrack both as an insult and as a
way of verbally resisting a police officer. Indeed, his remarks jokingly
call attention to the disruption of his very patterns of language when he
is mistreated by authority. Asked "who the hell are you, anyway," he provides identification and adds, "Now ask me what the hell I'm doing here.
Unfortunately my chronic aphasia has taken a bad turn for the worse. It

always goes like that when a dumb cop takes a shot at me" (Macdonald, *Drowning Pool* 59). This dynamic of insubordination is extended and developed in significant ways in private eye novels in which the investigator is a woman. These works often emphasize the role of gender in the relationship between language and power.

In Sandra West Prowell's *By Evil Means*, the sexual power dynamic of the verbal response is made obvious when private detective Phoebe Siegel is leered at by Crank, a character who was bitten in the crotch by dogs. Her response to his aggressive visual advance draws attention, and, metaphorically at least, contributes to his (sexual) impotence:

> As soon as I approached, he looked me up and down with one of those looks that made me wish I was wearing a shroud. His eyes settled on my chest.
> "I hear you're a dick," he said.
> "I hear you're not."
> His mouth dropped open, and his face turned a deep crimson. (110).

For female private eyes, the wisecrack is a means of opposing conventional codes of feminine conduct. Such deflection takes place when characters "crack wise" within such novels; it also occurs when authors use tough talk to respond to the hard-boiled tradition itself. Talking back to masculine authority traditionally has been viewed as inappropriate behavior for women: it is a mode of resistance more plausible and ethical—and potentially subversive—than, say, physical violence. As a *Newsweek* reviewer once quipped of "the new breed of mystery heroines," "they're more apt to shoot from the lip than the hip" (Ames and Sawhill 66). Indeed, when Dunant's Hannah Wolfe faces a physical assault, she uses language: "My words were my weapons, sharp little knives slicing through the air, whistling ever closer to that smooth skin" (*Fatlands* 198).

Liza Cody's second Anna Lee mystery, *Bad Company*, is a particularly interesting example of the use of tough talk as resistance. The novel is, in an odd way, a hard-boiled version of the classic "locked room" mystery—but here it is the detective herself who is abducted by motorcycle gang members and locked in a tiny room with Verity, the young girl she tries to protect. The problem of the novel is one of agency: what does the detective do when the physical limitations are so constricted that she is denied almost all possibilities of action? As far as her movements are concerned, the plot is extraordinarily static: Anna is locked in the room for 185 of the novel's 287 pages. While her co-captive remains fearful and submissive, Anna resists their three male captors in the only way she can—verbally. Greeting them with such comments as, "Well, if it isn't Shake, Rattle, and Roll. . . . What kept you?" (109), she incessantly mocks them and cajoles them into providing adequate conditions for the captives. For example, when one of them grabs Verity, Anna comments "Oh, very clever. . . . Gestapo tactics on little girls. Pity there aren't any kittens for you to drown. You'd like that too" (110).

Verity worries that Anna is only provoking the men, who have all the power: "It isn't safe to talk back and cheek to them," she says. Anna replies, however, that the authority of their captors is the very thing that makes her verbal resistance necessary: "It might be even more dangerous to let them walk all over us. They've got too much of an edge already. We can't let them take more" (135). The child's compliance results in her perverse identification with her assailants and against Anna. At one point, Anna explains to Verity the principle behind her own antagonism, significantly incorporating an explanation of the way little girls are culturally conditioned to submission: "Listen, I know you're a well-brought-up girl, and you probably do what you're told at school too, but there are times when you've got to make trouble. It may be hard for you to believe, but some people don't deserve respect or good manners. And there are times when being polite and passive and timid only gets your rear-end kicked" (134). Anna feels "the danger of acquiescing very keenly indeed," but her resistance holds off her captors from "further liberties" (210).

The exercise of tough talk as reverse discourse is framed comically in

Linda Grant's *Woman's Place* when Catherine Sayler is patted on the behind by a male co-worker at the office. She responds in kind: "I'd reached over and returned the compliment, commenting, 'Not bad. A little time at the gym would tone that right up'" (7). Her gesture, of course, repeats and parodies that of her male "admirer," revealing that his presumptuous touch was anything but a compliment. In Sandra West Prowell's *Killing of Monday Brown*, private investigator Phoebe Siegel admonishes a police officer for cruelly lifting a young Native American boy by the belt loops on his pants; "I love seeing law enforcement at work, and that snuggie hold is nothing short of brilliant. Glad to see you guys have been trained in testicle tactics," she whispers ironically in his ear (35). After smart-mouthing a police officer, Val McDermid's private detective Kate Brannigan muses to herself and readers that her insubordination seems to be provoked by the authority of the police (much like Lew Archer's): "I can't help myself, I swear. Every time I run up against a copper who thinks he's in the last days of his apprenticeship to God, I get one on me" (*Dead Beat* 157).

STAND-UP COMEDY

An *Entertainment Weekly* reviewer put his finger on Karen Kijewski's character's combination of hard-boiled cynicism and comedic feminist fractiousness, as well as that of her generic counterparts, when he described Kat Colorado as "tough, single, beautiful, early 30s, hard-bitten, and, in prose style, the illegitimate child of Raymond Chandler and Roseanne Arnold (check the mystery shelves of your local bookstore—she has half a dozen identical sisters who practice under different names)" (Harris 58). Margaret Atwood expressed similar sentiments, observing that Eve Zaremba's lesbian detective Helen Keremos is "a cross between Lily Tomlin and Philip Marlowe" (qtd. in Skene-Melvin 18). Sparkle Hayter, author of the Robin Hudson series, is herself both a stand-up comedian and an experienced journalist. Her television journalist character's career is on the downslide because of her literal inability to keep her mouth shut: she belched during a live broadcast of a White House news conference, sometimes asks indelicate questions of interviewees, and often makes infelicitous comments to co-workers: "I always say," says Robin, "it takes seven major muscle groups just to hold my tongue" (*Nice Girls Finish Last* 4). When one of her companions reminds her that "as the old saying goes, you get more flies with honey than with vinegar," Robin responds, "Well, if you *really* want flies, you ought to try bullshit. . . . It's an old folk remedy" (*What's a Girl Gotta Do?* 52). Hayter's writing is a veritable *tour de farce* of comedic hard-boiled conceits.[7] At a network cocktail party, for example, she uses a version of the hard-boiled simile to describe one of her senior colleagues whose routine sexual harassment she describes wryly as "this little problem relating to women": "When he's sober and he comes face to face with a woman in a social setting, he tends to become focused on her breasts and can't look her in the eye. If she moves from side to side, his head moves from side to side too, *like a dog watching a tennis ball*" (*What's a Girl Gotta Do?* 16, emphasis added).[8]

The role of humor is crucial for several reasons. First, it allows the expression of sentiments that in any other form would be socially unacceptable, even "unspeakable"—or at the very least unpalatable in an entertainment genre. Sandra Scoppettone, like many of these authors, recognizes its utility: "I try not to preach. . . . Anything I do that is connected to a social issue or a comment on society I try to do with humor." Second, the detective's wisecracking use of humor represents the appropriation both of a certain kind of language and of the dominant speaking position. It thereby epitomizes the author's appropriation of the hard-boiled mode itself, which uses tough talk in order to talk back to and alter the ideological trajectory of traditional literature. As Susan Purdie remarks in her study of the power politics of humor, "Because discourse is potent, its control yields power; because joking intrinsically constructs a mastery of discourse, it always has unambiguous political effects which are produced on the back of its psychic operations" (125).

The detective is thus "the figure for the reader in the text"—not just in the classical sense, to which Glenn Most points, that both are intellectually engaged in solving the mystery (349), or even in the sense that the reader gets a vicarious thrill from the detective's exploration of the borders between the permitted and the forbidden, as John Cawelti argues (*Adventure* 35–36), but in her discursive positioning as one who is both able and permitted (in the space of the novel) to talk back to authority. This sense of vindication is clearly represented in J. M. Redmann's *Intersection of Law and Desire* when lesbian detective Micky Knight verbally lashes out at one of her interrogators for his homophobia during a police interview: though he is a criminologist, he confuses homosexuality with criminal child abuse. Micky's friend, a lesbian assistant district attorney who remains in the closet to protect her career, later approaches Micky, hugs her, and says, "You do give the best fireworks show. . . . I wanted to say something, but I get so caught up in what it'll cost me and what'll I gain." Micky responds, "He wouldn't hire me and I wouldn't work for him, so I have nothing to lose. As long as you've got me to mouth off, you don't have to" (299).

THE PRIVATE EAR: LISTENING IN ON LANGUAGE

Sandra Scoppettone engages in a more generalized version of reverse discourse in her novel *I'll Be Leaving You Always* by having her detective effectively talk back to language itself. The inquiry of Scoppettone's private detective Lauren Laurano into the death of her oldest friend Meg is as much an investigation into the social signification of everyday realist language as it is the investigation of a murder. Lauren, whose friends jokingly call her "Lobes Laurano, private dick" (5), is in fact identified as a kind of "private ear" who solves her cases by forcing herself to *listen* to words—not just because she is an obsessive eavesdropper (though she is), but because she is attentive to the voices of others and their linguistic subtleties. The epigraph to the novel, "My lifetime listens to yours" ([vii]), identifies issues of receptivity as a central concern of *I'll Be Leaving You Always*, though they are often developed obliquely. At one point in the story, for example, having been subjected to the "sonorous soliloquy" of a long-winded taxi driver, Lauren comments, "I confess, I don't understand people who love to hear the sound of their own voice. I already know what *I* know, so I find it much more interesting to hear what others think" (69). This attentiveness to other voices is presumably what makes her an effective detective. Perhaps it is also what makes Scoppettone an effective detective writer.

Lauren listens not just to what people say but to how they say it, and to what their linguistic choices signify. In one sense, *I'll Be Leaving You Always* is an investigation into the language of death, a language that is *always* at the center of detective fiction. Nevertheless, it is very seldom taken up as a subject of discussion—partly because the genre is to some extent realist, and realist language by definition is language that does not call attention to its own functioning: it pretends to be neutral and transparent. This is a rule that Scoppettone's work creatively bends by making language the frequent subject of her narrator's contemplation, setting realism against reflexivity. The metalinguistic commentary is integrated into the narrative, troubling—without actually breaking—its realist surface and placing the "real world" of the story in question. For example, in a gesture often used in her work, Scoppettone uses italics and the rhetorical strategy of reification—the figurative depiction of an abstraction as if it were a concrete thing—to transform ordinary language into something that the reader must reexamine. Indeed, Scoppettone makes words into clues in the investigation: "*Dead, murdered, killed, death.* The words rattle round in my head like alien beings" (16). This novel is at some level about coming to *terms* with death, and as such it is not just a "private" but a personal investigation that conflates the narrative of detection with the process of mourning.

As part of both processes, Scoppettone evokes and violates the kind of narratorial distance that is a convention of hard-boiled writing. For example, Lauren must confront the reality that her formerly vital, living, breathing friend has been reduced to a corpse, and that confrontation is represented as mediated through language. When a police officer, Cecchi, tells her that the authorities will release the body, she responds:

> *Body.* It takes me by surprise. This is Meg's body Cecchi is referring to and I'm not ready to accept her as a body.
> "You made the arrangements?"
> "No." I remind him about Blythe's not showing up.
> "So where's it gonna go?"
> *It.* I have the impulse to ask Cecchi to stop talking about Meg this way, but I curb that because I don't want to appear timorous or he might stop confiding in me. (85)

The violent narratives of hard-boiled fiction rely precisely on the treatment of death as a flat, material, unemotional fact and the representation of the body—particularly the female body—as an object. The original hard-boiled writers may have taken the body out of the library and put it onto the mean streets, but the voice of the tough-talking narrator ensured that it was invested with little emotional weight. For instance, having viewed the murdered body of his partner Miles Archer, Sam Spade is clearly unmoved. Even when a police officer offers the sympathetic observation that "Miles had his faults same as the rest of us, but I guess he must've had some good points too," the detective's reaction is curt: "'I guess so,' Spade agreed in a tone that was utterly meaningless, and went out of the alley" (Hammett, *Maltese Falcon* 16).

Lauren, in contrast, attends to the material details of her friend's death, arranging for the transfer of the body and for the funeral. In the course of these activities, she meditates on the way polite euphemisms can be used in an effort to distance a speaker and defamiliarize—or perhaps even disguise—distressing subjects. When the funeral director refers to the casket as a "container," Lauren muses, "No one says what anything really is anymore. Missions become *sorties*, handicapped are *physically challenged*, pets are *animal companions*, instead of a mistake, *friendly fire*. And now a coffin is a goddamn *container*. It's as if sanitizing the language will ease the pain of reality. It doesn't work" (*I'll Be Leaving You Always* 35). Everyday language is thus denaturalized, its shaping of reality exposed. Later in Scoppettone's novel, Lauren catches herself practicing the euphemistic tactic when she refers to the grim task of looking through the dead woman's apartment after her death as "the business at hand:" "*The business at hand?*" she repeats to herself, "Have I become a master at euphemisms? Am I such a coward I can no longer be direct, honest, candid even with myself? I'm disgusted" (115). Part of the detective's heroism involves facing up to the realities of language itself.

It is not just the polite language of euphemism that is emphasized by the prose of the novel but the more vulgar, hard-boiled terminology surrounding death. While tough talk may *seem* to confront reality more directly than more "refined" language, Scoppettone's novel recognizes both as capable of their own varieties of euphemism. In response to Lauren's questions, a suspect explodes, "You think *I* wasted Meg?" and Lauren is prompted to muse, "Here it is again. The only thing that ever changes is the verb: wasted; murdered; killed; offed; punched her/his ticket" (101). S. J. Rozan's detective Lydia Chin similarly observes how much it bothers her when cops talk about death using "words like stiff, whacked, burned. It always throws me, but I try not to show it" (66). Scoppettone's character realizes how thoroughly she has absorbed this kind of language as a tool of the private investigation trade when she is caught using it in order to detach herself from her emotions. Lauren speculates to her lover Kip on why Meg was killed: "Here's the thing: if Meg was about to blow the whistle, whoever dealt with the store owners probably knew about it and had some mechanic take her out" (239). Her language here draws on the very kind of slang that became a signature of hard-boiled writing. One example is Lew Archer's report in Ross Macdonald's *Drowning Pool* of a character's assassination and immolation: "They knocked me out. Then they ventilated Reavis with a dozen slugs and gave him a gasoline barbecue" (132). In Scoppettone's novel, however, the distancing effect of such elaborate figurative language is countered when Kip reprimands Lauren for offhandedly referring to a professional killing as being "taken out" by a "mechanic." Lauren responds,

> "That's what hit men are called."
> "You do it so you don't have to feel anything."
> I ignore this because it's true. (238)

Paretsky's V. I. Warshawski has a similar illuminating moment regarding hard-boiled language when she responds to a friend's inquiries "with a Sam Spade toughness I was far from feeling. . . . It sounded good, but it didn't mean anything" (*Bitter Medicine* 69). Such gestures in *I'll Be Leaving You Always* and elsewhere offer a kind of illocutionary analysis of vernacular realism, a critique of its functions and effects. At the same time, this analysis is delivered in the realistic manner that readers demand.

The narrative of Scoppettone's novel also documents Lauren's experience as a lesbian, not only because it is a central issue of the character's identity but also because the murder victim was a childhood friend who helped Lauren come to recognize and name her sexual orientation (Meg herself was heterosexual). When, as a teenager, Meg confronts Lauren with the idea that Lauren is not sexually attracted to men, Lauren denies it, as she has always denied it to herself, but Meg insists on the truth of her observation and assures her friend that it makes no difference to their relationship. "But Meg, I'm a freak," Lauren says. Meg replies,

> "No you're not. You're just a lesbian."
> The word ricocheted round the room, puncturing me in several places while it made its tour. *Lesbian.* It was ugly, degrading, and embarrassing.
> "I hate that word," I whispered, staring at the flowered carpet in her room.
> "You like *dyke* better?"
> "Ugh." I started to cry. (11)

Once again, a word is figuratively represented as if it were a substantial object—in this case a stock object of crime fiction violence, the ricocheting bullet. This description subtly brings the reader's attention to bear not just on the language of violence (which is an iconic element of hard-boiled narratives) but on the *violence of language itself,* the power of words to do harm. Valerie Wilson Wesley makes just this point in *When Death Comes Stealing* when a suspect being interviewed by private investigator Tamara Hayle uses the word "nigger":

> I couldn't believe what she'd just said! *Who you calling a nigger, white girl?* I hadn't heard a white person say that word since I'd left the [Police] Department and heard it every day. My reaction was pure reflex: I pushed the anger down to that place inside me where I'd always put it when I'd been on the force. Nigger bitch. Nigger whore. Nigger bastard. Nigger son of a bitch. I'd heard it so much it had lost its meaning. Just another word. (87)

Tamara's theory that the word has lost its meaning is belied, however, both by her initial reaction and by her realization that the woman who spoke the word with such contempt actually feels it applies to herself and her son, both of whose lives and self-esteem are in a shambles: "*Maybe that's your problem. Maybe that's why your son is so messed up*, I thought, but didn't say" (87).

Whereas in traditional hard-boiled novels language's force often originates in its referential and promissory power, in the guaranteed correspondence between spoken threat and physical action (the hard-boiled private eye is, in this sense, "a man of his word"), it is here and elsewhere exposed as powerful in itself. In *I'll Be Leaving You Always*, the young Lauren and her friend consider "queer" as an alternative to other homophobic labels for homosexuality, but finally arrive at the conclusion that "there's no good word" (12). The available names are not transparent, neutral terms; they constitute a kind of social value judgment. Using them, nevertheless, becomes a significant act of recognition for Lauren: it constitutes the first stage in her coming out.

Later in *I'll Be Leaving You Always*, when an altercation breaks out in the line of a New York delicatessen, Lauren hears the language of homosexuality used as a form of vicious insult: "Listen, fag," says the man at the counter to the customer who has angered him, "'I ain't givin' you nothin'. Get outta here" (90). The exchange deteriorates into a succession of jibes that vilify homosexual sex and that figuratively dismember and objectify the body. The novel creates an analogy between insult and assault; and as violent linguistic exchange mirrors a physical struggle, aggressive masculine sexuality is parodied: "There ensues a scuffle, and the words *cock* and *dick* are thrown back and forth as if there are no two other words in the language" (91). Lauren's own confrontation with the man behind the counter, interestingly, deals with the issue first in decorous, elevated "literary" language, and then in a wisecracking hard-boiled response that proudly reappropriates and affirms the term "dyke" as a defensive tactic. Lauren realizes that she cannot order from a man who has used such "distasteful" language:

> I say to him, "Sir, you have a childlike grasp of the English language, you're homophobic and one of the dumbest people I've ever encountered." I turn to leave.
> "Fucking dyke," he yells after me.
> "Absolutely," I say. "As much as I can." (91)

On the one hand, this is a retake of the hard-boiled smart-ass retort. On the other, it is a far cry from Sam Spade's snide references to "the gooseberry lay" or Mike Hammer's virulent homophobic rhetoric. Scoppettone's novel even emphasizes the offensiveness of the language of prejudice by associating it with criminal offenses. In the course of her investigation, Lauren discovers that she may not have known her friend Meg as well as she thought, for Meg may have been involved in criminal activity. She is also wounded to learn that Meg had referred to Lauren disparagingly as a "dyke" behind her back: "Which is worse," Lauren reflects, "that Meg might have been involved in something illegal, that she called me a dyke, or that she wasn't who I thought she was?" (77).

I'll Be Leaving You Always is remarkable for its extended, self-conscious investigation of language as a clue to a broader social text, but it is certainly not unique in making the power of words the subject of investigation. Indeed, a key strategy of feminist detective fiction in general is to incorporate metalinguistic implications into the texture of the realistic narrative. Nancy Baker Jacobs's detective Devon MacDonald, for example, often gets into linguistic wrangles with her older, more traditional partner Sam, who sometimes baits her by using language that might be seen as a misogynist relic of his hard-boiled professional role. Their friendly sparring—which Jacobs refers to as a "loving battle"—is often used to evoke the political aspects of language. "It's sort of a game that they play," says Jacobs, "and yet I'm hoping that through the game there are some points that might be made to the reader about the conditions women live in." When Sam makes an offensive reference, Devon thinks to herself, "If I could simply ignore Sam's bigoted terminology, he'd probably clean it up. I tried that technique often with third graders who used profanity to get my attention and it worked on them. But Sam isn't a third grader and he usually manages to push just past the point where I can hold my tongue. He needs to liberalize this thinking; I need more patience" (*Turquoise Tattoo* 16). Earlier, she explains that "One of Sam's favorite ways of needling me is to call me a 'girl,' but today I refused to rise to his bait. Sometimes dealing with Sam Sherman feels like being back in my third grade classroom" (10). Devon's musings strikingly reverse the symbolic age difference constructed by the word "girl," making *his* behavior seem infantile.

It has become what might be seen as a generic tic for detectives to flag the use of the diminutive word "girls" (and similar terms) to describe women, whether designating a detective or a victim. These may seem like small linguistic gestures, but Sara Paretsky offers insight into the importance of such offhand references in colloquial language:

the way that we [women] are defined is part of this insisting on a
system of subordination, and calling a woman a girl is fundamental

to it, because a girl *is* a child. A girl is not a fully realized human being. And the fact that it's integral to the culture and the use of language doesn't mean that that isn't the case. It means that it's so very
much the case that we now have internalized the idea that we are not
fully adult human beings. (interview by Richler)

Surely one of the central effects of the private "I" of the female detective is the representation of a woman's performance of an empowering speaking position made available by the genre. The subjective point
of view of the traditional hard-boiled detective novel is thus supple-
mented by an insistence on language that constructs and reinforces that
position. For example, Paretsky's own V. I. Warshawski, asked by her
host, "Now, you're not one of those modern girls who only drinks white
wine, are you?" asserts her hard-boiled persona, insisting on a tough
guy's iconic drink and a tough *woman's* appellation: "No, I'm a modern
woman, and I drink neat whisky. Black Label, if you have it" (*Guardian
Angel* 195). Sarah Dunant's detective Hannah Wolfe expresses sentiments very like V.I.'s when she corrects a character who has called her
"a very smart girl": "'Woman, please,' I said. 'It's deeply patronizing to
be called a girl'" (*Fatlands* 200). In an interview with a Chinese gang
boss, S. J. Rozan's Asian American detective Lydia Chin is identified by
her ethnicity and gender: the man snidely remarks, "you smart for ABC
girl." Lydia implicitly accepts the ethnic identification but strategically
rejects the designation "girl": "ABC, that's American-Born Chinese.
Girl, that's not me" (29). In a conversation in Judith Van Gieson's *North
of the Border*, investigator Neil Hamel anticipates the resolution of a sexual joke that a man is in the course of telling, thus disturbing the verbal
power dynamic implicit in the joke's rhetoric. Instead of feigning ignorance, she supplies the punch line, *literally* punching her interlocutor
in the shoulder and adopting the masculine voice (7). The stranger responds, "Not bad. . . . Not bad for a girl," but Neil insists on her adult
professional status: "I'm not a girl; I'm a lawyer" (7). When an acquaintance flippantly addresses Karen Kijewski's detective as "baby," Kat

Colorado muses, "Baby? I thought about it as I hung up. Baby? What kind of a name was that for a thirty-three-year-old PI? Dumb, that's what" (*Kat's Cradle* 189).

The analysis is not restricted to references to the private eye herself; it is often extended in order to call attention to the ways victim positions are *verbally* constructed and reinforced. In Lia Matera's *Face Value*, Laura Di Palma interviews a man who had been acquainted with several murder victims, to whom he refers offhandedly as "girls," and Laura detects in this diminutive term a sign of his lack of respect: "There was little sympathy in his manner," she observes, "little acknowledgment that people—not just 'girls'—had died" (122). In Michelle Spring's *Every Breath You Take*, detective Laura Principal makes a similar gesture, responding to police officer Neill's reference to "the dead girl" with an insistence on her proper name (65). This refusal to "have her reduced by Neill to 'that dead girl'" is part of the humanizing function of her investigation, which, her partner observes, is "to breathe life into 'this dead girl.' . . . I understand: you're going to make her real" (80). In a sense, Spring's realist narrative reverses the male murderer's sexual assault, linguistically reviving the victim by asserting her humanity. Similarly, Wendy Hornsby's Maggie MacGowan, in conversation with her police detective lover, catches him offhandedly using the word "girls" in a dismissive story about police "groupies." Maggie insists that he call them "women," but Mike responds, "Back then, we were pigs, they were girls. You gotta know the language of the times or you're not going to get this story at all" (*Bad Intent* 267). Nevertheless, Maggie later corrects him again: "She wasn't a *girl*, for chrissake, Mike, she was a human being with a big problem" (268).

THE SEMANTICS OF CRIME

Many works integrate an extended linguistic analysis into the texture of their narratives. In Karen Kijewski's *Copy Kat*, for instance, Kat must convince another character of the criminal nature of his sexual behavior, engaging in what amounts to a "semantic" argument that "I took her" and "I *made* her love me" or "I gave her 'payback'" all function as synonyms—or, rather, as euphemisms—for "rape" (306–8). The title of Sara Paretsky's *Bitter Medicine* might well be read as referring to the damaging linguistic "prescriptions" of patriarchal discourse, in particular those that underpin the American privatized corporate medical institution and the right-wing Christian antiabortion movement, which are linked in the novel's narrative. Paretsky's book is a particularly interesting example because it, like Scoppettone's *I'll Be Leaving You Always*, implicitly inquires into the language of mortality, the language on which detective fiction is founded but which it must generally naturalize in order to sustain its realistic effects. As Barbara Godard observes, while conventional murder mysteries ignore "the sexual politics of death," the feminist detective novel evinces a commitment to "the spying out of ideological discourses and the social practices they define" (49). For Paretsky, the definition of "murder" often becomes a profoundly political semantic issue. For instance, the death that propels the narrative of *Bitter Medicine* is that of a family friend of V.I., Consuelo Hernandez, who dies during childbirth at a private health care facility. This death, while not technically a murder, is the result of medical mismanagement, which originates in racial prejudice as well as the for-profit medical establishment's greater concern for protecting revenues than for attending to the needs of its patients—especially, it is implied, its female patients.

Although Consuelo's death results from medical malpractice rather than legally defined murderous intent, the narrative of the novel involves the "solution" of her death as if it were a murder—a process that entails attributing responsibility not simply to an individual but to a medical system that in various ways made proper treatment inaccessible to Consuelo. From the start, the hospital staff's use of language demonstrates little concern for Consuelo's humanity. The nurses refer to her as "number 108," transforming her linguistically from a person to a "case" (8). Because Consuelo is Hispanic, she is almost instantly stereotyped as indigent by the hospital staff, and the quality of her care is thus compromised: "She's some Mexican girl who got sick on the premises," says the nurse, "We do not run a charity ward here. We're going to have to move this girl to a public hospital" (10). Because of this misidentification, her treatment is delayed. When V.I. discovers the form the nurse had been completing, she comments cynically on its description—or rather construction—of Consuelo: "The only items completed were sex—they'd hazarded a guess there—and source of payment, which a second guess had led them to list as 'Indigent'—euphemism for the dirty four-letter word poor. Americans have never been very understanding of poverty, but since Reagan was elected it's become a crime almost as bad as child-molesting" (11). V.I.'s sardonic commentary is a good example of Paretsky's signature use of the detached hard-boiled narrative voice to provide offhand political and linguistic commentary: the character's observations highlight how language is used to categorize and evaluate—in a way that is ultimately implicated in Consuelo's death. In this case, the pregnant woman is deprived of all identity save her sex and the prejudicial label "Indigent," which is based on her racial appearance. The degree to which the novel judges such categorizations as both political and perverse is suggested in the last sentence of the quotation above, in which the government under Reagan is shown to have inverted the distinction between victim and crime. The narrator insinuates that language that effects such an inversion is itself, despite—or rather because of—its euphemisms, obscene.

Much of the narrative of *Bitter Medicine* centers on the Chicago women's health clinic that V.I.'s friend Dr. Lotty Herschel helps operate. The clinic is targeted by an antiabortion group whose demonstration against it finally erupts into a riot. The protesters are so threatening in part because of their appropriation of the language of crime to describe activities at the clinic, which include therapeutic abortions: they call the doctor "a murderer" (93). Once again, the definition of "murder" is a matter of interpretation, and the body in question, the novel emphasizes, is the female body as a site of contested power. Murder, it suggests, is a women's health issue. The antiabortion protesters borrow from the lexicon not just of crime but of crimes against humanity. They invoke the Holocaust, shouting "Murderers! Nazis!" (94); their newsletter calls the clinic "a DEATH camp more hideous than Auschwitz" (129). This perspective, however, is reversed by the novel's structure, which opposes Lotty's cooperative women's health clinic to the unhealthy practices of mainstream patriarchal medicine and religion. It is also resituated by Lotty, a Jewish woman, who reinvokes the language used by the protesters in order to tell V.I. how much their mentality frightens her, and how it threatens the American democratic ethos: "There was a night in Vienna when a Nazi mob gathered in front of our house. They looked just like this—animals, oozing hate. They broke all the windows. My parents and my brother and I fled through the garden and hid at a neighbor's and watched them burn our house to the ground. Never did I expect to feel that same fear in America" (95). Evoking the language of fascism is one of the ways that *Bitter Medicine* suggests the political operations of language. It also implicitly contrasts the conventionally individualized murders of mystery fiction with a historical instance of genocide. It is a book as much concerned with uncovering the institutional discourses—legal, medical, political—that have the power to define and control women's bodies as it is with the individualized bodies of the murder victims that are part of its more conventional detective plot. Or rather, it portrays the life-and-death fate of any individual body *as* a political body.

In so doing, the novel provides a discursive diagnosis, a forensic inquiry into the language of crime and the crimes of language. When women writers renegotiate the conventions of the hard-boiled tradition, they engage in a dialogue with detective novels of the past, interpreting them collectively as a body of evidence. Consequently, the (legal, medical, political) discourses that constitute them are subject to investigation. In his analysis of "tough talk," Walker Gibson describes the tough-talking narrator as taciturn and self-conscious about his use of language:

"He is close-lipped, he watches his words" (41). Like the traditional terse hard-boiled narrator, the woman detective also carefully watches her words, using them strategically to readdress and redress power imbalances. Equally important, the woman writer of detective fiction engages with both patriarchal language and the masculine hard-boiled tradition, appropriating and shifting their formal strategies. In other words, she watches *his* words too. Her text is evidence of this.

Chapter 5

PRIVATE I

Viewing (through) the (Female) Body

> I was brought up at a time when men were interested
> in men, and women were interested in men, and no one
> was interested in women. You know, you had to read
> Tom Sawyer in school, but you didn't have to read *The
> Little House on the Prairie*. And the literary voice was call
> me Ishmael, it was not call me Mary-Margaret.
>
> Linda Barnes

THE RULES AND HOW TO *BEND* THEM

When asked about why she adopted a woman's point of view in her
novels, Janet Dawson, author of the Jeri Howard private investigator series, replied, "I think it was just logical. I was writing in the first person,
which is common for private eye novels, and I feel more comfortable
writing as a woman than I do as a man. So it was logical to write a first-
person female point of view. In the initial stages I actually did try Jeri in
the third person, and I tried Jeri as an amateur detective, and neither approach worked." The hard-boiled detective novel is conventionally differentiated from other variants of the mystery story not just by its vernacular style, its professional investigator, and its broadly individualist

149

and subjective perspective, but, perhaps most strikingly, by its distinctive (though not exclusive) use of the first-person narrative voice of the investigator: the first-person narration formally unites these other elements, producing a "signature effect" of the genre. Dawson demonstrates an astute awareness of generic differences in her early experiments in which she tries on and rejects other possible voices and occupations for her series character.[1] The logic of Dawson's final generic decision is based on the intersection—a perceived fit—between the typical formal characteristics of the private eye literary genre and her own "comfortable" position writing as a woman; the result is, as she puts it, "a first-person female point of view," which unites the generic case with a gendered subjectivity.

In the Mystery Writers of America guide, *Writing Mysteries*, novelist Jeremiah Healy establishes guidelines for prospective writers in the private eye genre. His second rule—after "The Plot is Everything"—apparently contradicts Dawson's reasoning, for he proclaims, "The Hero Must be Male" (10). As a writer himself, however, Healy is sensitive to the possibility that genres-in-practice might operate differently in light of changing circumstances, authors, and audience expectations: the title of his essay is, after all, "The Rules and How to *Bend* Them" (emphasis his). He adds under Rule II that changes in society and its perceptions have allowed this dictum to be creatively violated by contemporary writers such as Sue Grafton, Linda Barnes, and Sara Paretsky (10). Dawson's comments on her use of point of view naturalize this infraction by calling it "logical," and this may well be because she writes her novels in relation to the generic precedents not just of Hammett, Chandler, and MacDonald but also of Grafton, Barnes, and Paretsky (her first book, *Kindred Crimes*, appeared in 1990).

Healy does not elaborate on the implications for the kind of gender/genre bending opened up when Rule II is combined with Rule VI, "Write in the First Person Narrative." While the private eye novel is typically oriented around a subjective perspective, this perspective may be conveyed either through the use of a first-person or third-person narration "focalized" through the character of the detective, who provides the perspective and literary style through which the story is told. As Healy points out, however, the eye that sees and the voice that speaks are most conventionally united in the first-person voice of the detective:

> [T]here is a sense that the private investigator novel must be written in the first person narrative style rather than the third-person narrative because that's the way both Hammett and Chandler did it. By way of comeback, both Hammett and Chandler wrote detective stories in both the first and third person styles, so this "rule" was never really a rule. However, the reason behind it is instructive: when the narrator speaks to the reader as "I," the reader comes to identify with the narrator and accepts the limitations of information that the typically chronological progression of first-person imposes on the structure of the book. (12)

These observations are pertinent here for several reasons. In pointing to the importance of the first-person narration, Healy highlights how narrative voice offers an important functional site of identification for the reader. He also draws attention to how it not only orients narration but also structures the narrative form of the detective story itself, predicated as that account is on a chronological unfolding (albeit almost always a retrospective one), a limited point of view, and a developmental accumulation of information. In short, the private eye novel has all the basic stylistic characteristics of the autobiographical narrative, which is also told in the first person; is linear, chronological, progressive, and cumulative; and offers an individualist presentation of an exemplary life. These are all characteristics of "the dominant current in autobiography" (Stanley 12). The hard-boiled novel tells the life story of the fictional professional detective, or "private eye," in the subjective voice of the private "I," and its autobiographical form offers a unique space for developing questions of character, conduct, and perspective as they relate to the rules of gender and genre, making it possible to revise the identity of the PI. In one sense, at the center of the female private eye novel is not the corpse but the living, speaking, and specifically *gendered* body of the detective. This body is not presented as object, as are the dead bodies of many mystery stories, or as the eroticized "to-be-looked-at" body of the femme fatale. Instead, readers are offered through the conventions of the private eye novel a position of subjectivity embodied in the feminine autobiographical voice.

CHARACTER BUILDING

The detective novel has always been a form of what might be called "life writing." Glenn Most, for instance, has urged historians of the genre to explore the historical coincidence between the rise of detective fiction and that of the modern biography. He also draws attention to the role of series fiction in extenuating the biographical form, thus ensuring a committed readership because the individual stories function as "installments in the fragmentary biographies of their [readers'] heroes" (345). This biographical impetus remains central for detective fiction. Works in a series are routinely marketed by appealing to the reader's investment in a character and continuing interest in his or her life story: they are, for example, regularly labeled on the dust jacket "a Spenser novel," "a Matthew Scudder mystery," or "a Sharon McCone novel." This appeal is especially important to stories that include a strong dimension of ongoing character development, which creates the feel of a life *in process* largely absent both from classic mysteries and from the traditional hard-boiled novel. Novelist Wendy Hornsby, discussing her series heroine, remarks that "The function of the traditional hard-boiled guy is to serve as a dispassionate guide through the underworld, and to come out unscathed (if not unscarred). I want Maggie MacGowen to develop in the course of each book, to be changed by the dramatic events of her life. I want her to be more human and less heroic in the classical sense than Sam Spade." Maxine O'Callaghan, author of the Delilah West series, confirms that her readers are as interested in developments in the personal story of her novels as they are in the mystery: "Yesterday's series

characters tended to stay the same age, stuck in a time warp. Today's series is really an ongoing story about the character's life. And believe me,
readers want that. The comments I get from fans are about what's happening to Delilah personally, not often about plot."

Jean Hager (author of the Molly Bearpaw series, which features a Native American civil rights investigator) observes that characters in many
contemporary female detective series "change and evolve from book to
book so that, in reality, there are two stories going on—the detective's
personal story which starts in the first book of a series and continues
through the last book in that series and the individual mystery story
which begins and ends in each book." In this formulation, the detective
story is both the story of a death and the story of a life. The first story
is a case that may be (at least provisionally) solved and "closed"; the second is a more attenuated mystery that remains open. The lack of closure
in the personal narrative is one of the major draws for readers who are
loyal to a series, ensuring their continuing emotional, ethical, and economic investment in the character. Sue Grafton's Kinsey Millhone
seems to acknowledge this doubled economy of narrative desire when at
the end of "D" Is for Deadbeat she muses on how closing the case involves
settling both financial debts and "debts of the human soul." She concludes her epilogue with an ironic reminder that no such sense of closure is achieved at the personal level: "Perhaps in this case all of the accounts are paid in full . . . except mine" (229, her ellipsis).

Autobiographical style orients the reader's engagement in ways that
are important for women's appropriation of the private eye form. Like
traditional biographies, most autobiographies presuppose both the historical reality of the subject and some sort of truth-claim for their story.
Even in its most apparently "factual" forms, however, the "I" of autobiography never simply and unproblematically *reproduces* the experiences
of an individual; it *constructs* a life story and in so doing participates in a
more general linguistic *production* of possibilities for subjectivity and
agency. Obviously, the private investigator novel is not autobiographical
in fact; but it does rely on the form. As in autobiography, the effect of the

private eye novel is predicated on complex relationships of identification, analogy, and even contradiction among author, fictional character, and reader. Shifting the gender of the private "I" is a potentially significant rhetorical and political gesture that reshapes the nature of those relationships, since the refashioned narrative both reflects and resists inherited models of subjectivity.

Jeremiah Healy's comments on the rules that govern the private eye genre are important to understanding the implications of this shift because he emphasizes the instability of inherited norms ("this 'rule' was never really a rule," he writes, reinforcing the heterogeneity of *practice* within a genre) and the notion that generic codes are open to interpretation—to *bending* without breaking. As the work of Judith Butler has demonstrated, agency is made possible by the potential for variation in repetition of rule-bound discourses. And both gender and genre qualify as rule-bound discourses whose performance in the private eye novel suggests that each is implicated in the other. When women writers practice the genre, the "I" of the private eye novel is both re-cited and re-sighted.

CROSSED I'S

Healy asserts that the rule about male heroes can simply be "abandoned" (10) when women take up private eye writing, but because of the way genre functions, such iconic elements are never fully erased in the minds of writers and readers. The practice of genre relies on remembering the rules, even when they are bent; and when women take up the subjective position offered by the detective novel, their writings always bear at least the traces of difference, of their departure from previous practices in the masculine tradition. As a generic gesture, then, the "I" of the detective novel always also signifies by its differential relation to "they" (its prior uses)—and, because genre is driven by communities of readers and writers, by its role of correspondence in a corporate "we." One of the ways difference from prior practice is often marked in detective novels that feature a professional woman investigator is their frequent use of male-identified names or nicknames for the detective hero: consider Janet Dawson's "Jeri" Howard, Julie Smith's "Skip" Langdon, Catherine Dain's "Freddie" O'Neal, Gloria White's "Ronnie" Ventana, Jean Femling's "Moz" Brant, Judith Van Gieson's Neil Hamel, Eleanor Taylor Bland's "Marti" McAllister, Ruby Horansky's "Nikki" Trakos, J. M. Redmann's "Micky" Knight, and Meg O'Brien's "Jesse" James.[2] The use of these names reveals that their identification with the male subject is—like the rules of both gender and genre—conventional and, therefore, subject to change, just as the nature of subjectivity itself is produced and altered in language. It is at just such points of conflict that the possibility of agency is revealed. The female character reinhabits and exploits the potential of the masculine subject position through the proper noun, a gesture that foregrounds contradiction and plays with audience expectations, creating pleasure by disrupting and revising both gender and genre codes.

In fact, the use of masculine names for female characters is one of the ways readers initiated in the genre can easily identify female revisions of the hard-boiled tradition, since jacket blurbs often highlight the incongruity. For example, the back cover of Horansky's *Dead Ahead* reads: "Nikki Trakos isn't 'one of the guys,'" and the promotional material on the back of Dain's *Walk a Crooked Mile* begins with a sentence in which proper noun and pronoun seem to conflict: "*Freddie*'s been hired—by *her* mother" (emphasis added). A similar contradiction is humorously played out in the frequently used epithet for the woman investigator, "female dick," a phrase that might also be read as a burlesquing of Freudian penis envy as it simultaneously draws attention to the performative body of the female detective—what she does defines her role as a "dick"; she hasn't got one. Irene Lin-Chandler parodies the naïveté of the biological determinism suggested in the term (not to mention differentials of desire) when she has a character call her female private eye a "self-appointed private clit" (177).

A related process takes place at the site of the "I." In their discussion of typical autobiographical practices, Julia Watson and Sidonie Smith stress the conservative, generic nature of the traditional autobiographical "I," which has often been taken to represent Man—the universal, rational, "agentive," and unitary subject (xvii)—though it formally marks individuality. Their argument applies particularly well to the autobiographical conventions of the hard-boiled genre, which are traditionally read as conveying both individuality and an Everyman quality: as Chandler himself describes the hard-boiled detective, "He must be a complete man and a common man and yet an unusual man" ("Simple Art" 237). Watson and Smith suggest, however, that the autobiographical form offers the possibility of asserting heterogeneity within hegemony, at the same time as it promises the potential for realizing an empowered subjectivity: "Participation in, through re/presentation of, privileged narratives can secure cultural recognition for the subject." According to these critics, autobiographical language makes available to the marginalized woman writer "a coinage that purchases entry into the social and discursive economy. . . . Deploying autobiographical practices that go against the grain, she may constitute an 'I' that becomes a place of creative and, by implication, political intervention" (xix). The economic metaphor used by Watson and Smith is particularly germane to our discussion, since mainstream private eye fiction relies on the popular market to culturally validate and to reproduce the subjectivity it posits. Such reproduction takes place within individual series (in each installment) and within the genre, whose conventions by definition must be reproduced by multiple authors.

The "I" narration is crucial because it enables the central fictional character to be both the subject who tells the story and the object of the narration: she narrates herself. This scenario is epitomized in visual terms in Carolyn Wheat's novel *Dead Man's Thoughts*, whose lawyer-investigator Cass Jameson is also an amateur photographer. After her lover is killed, she finds a book he meant to give her in which he has written, "For Cass. You are the Photographer / You are the Photograph" (57). It has become a commonplace of discussions about detective fiction to theorize both the process of investigation and the differentials of knowledge it involves in visual terms. The first psychoanalytic analysis of the detective narrative saw voyeurism as analogous not simply to the investigative narrative but to the repeated process of *reading* such narratives: "The voyeur is never entirely satisfied with his peeping which he has the compulsion endlessly to repeat like the detective story addict who rereads the same basic mystery tale without tedium," wrote Geraldine Pederson-Krag in 1949; "In the gradual revelation of clues that make up the bulk of the narrative, the reader is presented with one significant detail after another, a protracted visual forepleasure" (18–19). The detective's investigations do typically provide for reader and character alike a voyeuristic pleasure in the narrative's violation of the distinction between public and private scenes of knowledge: as Dennis Porter recognizes, "the secret of its power resides to a large degree in the trick that makes voyeurism a duty" (241). This "trick" is evoked, for example, in S. J. Rozan's *China Trade* when private eye Lydia Chin's friend observes that Lydia loves her job, "Because in the course of finding out what happened in whatever case you're investigating, you get to find out what everyone is up to" (82). When he adds that he finds that idea depressing she replies, "But not as depressing . . . as being in the dark" (83).

Lydia's response implies that the voyeuristic eye/I of the private eye's investigation is a site of power too—the power of knowledge, the power of articulation, and the power of the gaze. As Maggie Humm suggests, "The question of who sees what is at the heart of detective fiction. Traditionally, the detective is able to see as much as the criminal and cognitively much more. This differential of knowledge crystallises that hegemonic set which in her analysis of Hollywood films Laura Mulvey has called the scopic gaze. The detective is traditionally an 'eye' in a fiction about seeing" (203). In traditional private eye stories, as in traditional voyeuristic paradigms, the object of the gaze is typically female or feminized. The detective's scrutiny of the female form seems to literalize the voyeuristic nature of the private eye's inquiry. In Chandler's *Big*

Sleep, for example, Marlowe's first meeting with Mrs. Regan is centered on the visual: "I sat down on the edge of a deep soft chair and looked at Mrs. Regan. She was worth a stare. She was trouble. She was stretched out on a modernistic chaise-longue with her slippers off, so I stared at her legs in the sheerest silk stockings. They seemed to be arranged to stare at. They were visible to the knee and one of them well beyond" (17). Marlowe's investigation is driven by his (and the reader's) desire to see "well beyond" what it is forbidden to see. His gaze suggests the role of a female body that supplements the corpse at the center of the mystery—and both these bodies simultaneously attract and repulse him.

The voyeuristic gaze of traditional hard-boiled fiction is thus often intimately associated with sadistic violence against women. In a famous scene in *The Big Sleep*, for example, after having ejected a naked Carmen Sternwood from his bed, Marlowe perceives "the imprint . . . of her small corrupt body still on the sheets" and proceeds savagely to tear the bed to pieces (159). A pornographic scenario (nude pictures of Carmen Sternwood) is not only an element of that novel's plot, it is to a large degree representative of the way the private eye of the investigator functions as the site of an erotic, powerful, and by implication violent gaze—especially given that it is Carmen who is finally "exposed" as the guilty party at the end of the novel. In Mickey Spillane's work, the eroticized (and sadistic) power dynamic of the investigation is even more obvious. At the finale of *I, the Jury*, for example, as Mike Hammer articulates his solution to the series of murders he has been investigating, the femme fatale slowly strips naked before him, a gesture that equates his linguistic exposure of the guilty truth with the literal exposure of her corrupt sexual body; sexual and narrative tension is resolved with her violent death at Hammer's hands.

Laura Mulvey's theories of the male gaze as orienting filmic spectatorship have been contested—or at least complicated—in recent years by theorists (including Mulvey herself) who have envisioned an active and resistant female spectatorship of popular culture and by advocates of women's participation in popular cultural production.[3] Private eye novels featuring women investigators, by self-consciously reversing the male gaze of character, author, and reader, stage alternative practices of spectatorship and, significantly, produce corresponding theories of agency. Because of the conventional gendered power dynamic of the gaze, the appropriation of the narrative "I" of the private eye novel by women is always an ideologically loaded move.[4] Sarah Lacey, for example, seems aware that returning the gaze can be a deliberate gesture of reversal by which her character Leah Hunter resists being made the object of an implicitly pornographic scenario. In an interview in *File Under: Missing* with a suspect who calls her "a local bimbo" and tries to intimidate her, Leah responds by looking and talking back. Indeed, there is an important correlation between the returned gaze, tough talk (in the form both of dialogue and narration), and reverse discourse in general: "I ran my eyes all the way down him and back up again, and decided that outside of his business affairs whatever brains he had stayed in his dance support. He didn't like being eyed up any more than I had and that was tough" (16). Her gesture demonstrates the degree to which looking constructs, rather than only reflects, a position of control.

Many private investigation novels written by women place the power dynamics of the gaze itself under surveillance. They use the reflexive possibilities of the "I" narration either explicitly or implicitly to subject the gaze to investigation and reformulation. In Linda Grant's *Woman's Place*, investigator Catherine Sayler at several points during the course of her inquiries faces visual intimidation. Catherine, for example, describes an interview with a male executive in which "he very slowly and very obviously let his eye move down my body and back up. There was nothing subtle or furtive about it, and his smile said that he enjoyed immensely any discomfort that it caused" (66). As she wryly puts it at one point, in a meeting with male colleagues, "It's hard to carry on a conversation with a man who's staring at your breasts. Harder when there are three—men, not breasts." Catherine, however, resists and returns the gaze, both *within* the narrative and *in the process of narration itself*, which establishes her perspective as central: "I resisted the temptation to check my blouse for a broken button or large catsup stain. This was round two at the OK Corral, and I wasn't about to blink" (7).

Nor are the power dynamics here interrogated limited to the sexual. Sally Munt notes that "the politics of the gaze is openly explored in feminist crime fiction, showing how it is not just sexed and gendered, but also implicated within racial paradigms. Because this genre is so crucially concerned with perception, this allows for a degree of reflective interrogation as to the mechanisms of scrutiny" (198). Even—or perhaps especially—taking into account the limitations of mainstream detective fiction's mostly middle-class audience, autobiographical narration is a significant example of how the genre may make less politically engaged readers (both women and men) aware of issues of race, gender, and power through the intersections of potentially conflicting interests and identifications that take place at the site of the narrating "I."

The functioning of this site is most evident in the case of so-called minority writers, though the potential for intersections of subjectivity also exist for straight white writers. As we have seen, lesbian novelist Katherine V. Forrest has commented that the mystery genre provides for "a crossover [heterosexual] audience." In genre fiction, differing interests may find common subjective ground. This process of finding figurative common ground is reinforced by the literal "crossing over" of minority writers—including Forrest herself—to mainstream presses. Phyllis Knight, whose private investigator character, Lil Ritchie, is lesbian, has said that she likes the idea that her character "could be a little bit of a bridge builder" between gay and straight readers, appealing to both, though perhaps for different reasons.

Valerie Wilson Wesley, creator of the African American investigator Tamara Hayle, is even more explicit about the way her novels establish the possibility of crossover via the reader's identification with the subjectivity of her private eye. She contends that mystery books "cross over" barriers between black and white, male and female audiences, gay and straight, because they appeal at the level of genre to "people who like good mysteries." This crossover, however, involves *both* identification and an awareness of differences:

> [In mysteries] we learn the differences and the similarities [between people]. And the certain things that touch you no matter who you are. And I think that's a good thing, that mysteries teach you that. They teach you that consciousness, *and you learn it because the book is in the first person and you can't help but identify.* . . . And . . . I like to be a part of that. I like opening the world. (emphasis added)

Wesley suggests that this effect is tied to the fantasy element of mystery fiction: "part of a mystery is escaping anyway." Once readers occupy the character's shoes, they may be compelled to recognize their position of cultural or racial or gender conflict with that site, a recognition that enables the negotiation of differing subjectivities. This "I" may be a site of identification, but it is not constructed as the universal subject of conventional autobiography. Autobiographical practice here thus subtly "goes against the grain" (to use Watson and Smith's phrase, xix) and offers points of resistance, moments of differential awareness that make it possible to change—and not simply reenact and reinforce—the reader's conditioned ways of seeing the world. Indeed, it dramatizes what Nancy Hartsock calls a "standpoint epistemology": "an account of the world as seen from the margins, an account which can expose the falseness of the view from the top and can transform the margins as well as the center" (qtd. in Watson and Smith xx). The women detective's "failure" to fit the stereotype of the typical traditional detective may thus function for readers as a creative space of resistance and critique, a point of departure rather than a deficiency.

It is possible, as in Wesley's novels, for the established point of identification with the autobiographical narrator to render conspicuous the culturally produced "invisibility" of black women (playing ironically on the notion of the "visible" minority). In the second Tamara Hayle mystery, *Devil's Gonna Get Him*, the detective pauses while describing a surveillance operation, turning the private eye inward to comment on her own social invisibility as an African American woman—and the resulting efficacy of her viewpoint—which allows her to see without properly being seen as a subject:

> It's easy to follow somebody who doesn't know you from nothing, especially if you're black and a woman. The world takes you for granted then, and you're always somebody's something else—sister-lady ringing up the groceries or sweeping up the floor. I do my best work when people are limited by their own expectations. I smile a lot. Flash my toothiest grin. I've even been known to bend my head slightly and nod a bit to the left. A pleasant young Negress. A dependable, unassuming presence. And while I'm doing my act, I can follow some all-assuming fool to the ends of the earth, making all the notes I please. I love it when they realize that all the while I was bowing and scraping I was steadily kicking ass. (28–29)

In the situations Tamara describes, she strategically reverses the discursive position of the compliant black woman, taking advantage of a reproduced cultural norm in order to turn perceived passivity ("bowing and scraping") into agency ("kicking ass"); but in reading the story the white reader can no longer adopt the position of ignorance that the narrator describes. And while Tamara is invisible to audiences *in* the novel, her comments foreground her position for readers *of* the novel—her performance even takes on a parodic dimension. Moreover, at the same time as her narrating "I" provides a point of identification for nonwhite readers, the character's meditation underscores points of difference.

Similarly, in Kathy Hogan Trocheck's novels, private investigations are affiliated with detective Callahan Garrity's maid service, "House Mouse." Encouraging her daughter to start the private investigations business up again as an adjunct to her cleaning service, Callahan's mother draws attention to the usefulness of the viewpoint of women cleaners (many of whom are African American) as eyes that see but are themselves overlooked: "think of the kind of undercover work we could do if you got the detective agency going again. Nobody ever pays attention to the cleaning lady. Most of these people act like we're part of the woodwork. Why, we could collect evidence and do surveillance and all that stuff" (*Every Crooked Nanny* 36). Of course, the reader's enjoyment of "undercover work" involves appreciating the illusion of innocuousness that the "cover" creates.

LOOKING AGAIN

As Maggie Humm perceives, structures of looking have different resonances for lesbian sexuality, which collapse the "spectator/consumer practices" and breach conventionally constructed subjectivities (211). In fact, the autobiographical "I" of the private eye novel is the site for a "coming out" of lesbian sexuality. In *Everything You Have Is Mine*, Sandra Scoppettone subtly evokes the difference between the lesbian erotic look and conventional hard-boiled heterosexual dominance simply by having Lauren Laurano describe her longtime lover in a manner that recalls film noir–style iconography: "I look at Kip. The street light streams through the half-opened Levolor blinds, creating stripes across her naked body. Her nipples are erect, her mouth slightly open" (59). The hard-boiled convention that allows descriptions of sexual encounters is adapted to accommodate the representation of lesbian eroticism. It is also used to provoke a self-consciousness about the power dynamics of the heterosexual erotic look. In J. M. Redmann's *Intersection of Law and Desire*, lesbian detective Micky Knight visits a strip bar and watches the female stripper's dance, but she finds herself unaroused. She recognizes the economic roots of the eroticism associated with the audience's gaze: "I watched her struts and juts dispassionately. I know I'm supposed to be attracted to women, but none of this appealed to me. I wondered if some of the appeal for the cheering men, fully clothed on the sidelines watching, wasn't the power of their money to buy this show of big tits. The power imbalance that attracted them repelled me" (135).

One of the most subtle manipulations of the autobiographical narra-

tive of the private eye is developed by Trocheck. Readers are allowed intimate access to Callahan Garrity's body—specifically to her breasts, one
of the conventional sites of the obsessive male gaze and by extension the
gaze of the traditional male private eye (Mickey Spillane's Mike Hammer is virtually obsessed with breasts). The subjective voice of the detective in Trocheck's novel, however, makes voyeurism impossible, in part
because it refuses to eroticize the vulnerable, naked body of the narrating subject. In the first novel in the series, *Every Crooked Nanny*, Callahan discovers a lump in her breast:

> A month ago, in the shower, I'd been shaving my underarms when
> I encountered a bump in my right breast that I hadn't remembered
> being there before. At first, I'd thought it was an ingrown hair or
> something. It was the size of a small pearl when I found it. Two
> weeks later it was a bigger pearl. . . . My grandmother died of cancer
> when Edna [Callahan's mother] was a teenager. Edna had had a radi-
> cal mastectomy when she was forty. My own breasts weren't State
> Fair winners or anything, but I'd grown attached to them. (128)

The level of intimacy and emotional immediacy represented here would
be anathema to the hard-boiled narrator, although the passage does wittily both evoke and deflect the hard-boiled tone in its last sentence. The
story of Callahan's battle with cancer parallels her murder investigations,
insisting on the detective as an embodied subject (without eroticizing
her) and persistently evoking the question of mortality as a woman's issue. Trocheck's novel *To Live and Die in Dixie* complicates matters by jux-
taposing Callahan's illness with that of Jocelyn Dougherty, an anorexic
teenager. Callahan, whose own life is in jeopardy from cancer, has difficulty comprehending what she perceives as Jocelyn's suicidal behavior,
but the correlation of the two diseases points to threats to women's bodies that exceed the categories provided in traditional detective fiction.

Novels that address prostitution or pornography most obviously develop the capacity of the narrating "I" to examine and reposition the
power dynamics of the gaze, though in a sense this theme is simply an

extension of the private eye novel's reflexivity about looking and its implications. Wendy Hornsby's novel *Midnight Baby*, for example, begins
with a description of a visual image: a video portrait of a child prostitute
whom freelance documentarist Maggie MacGowan tapes for use in a
documentary on the varieties of child rearing. The description is initially
narrated with a sense of aesthetic distance, without the obvious intru-
sion of the first-person narrator, and in a way that generalizes the object
of the camera's gaze: "Under a full moon and sodium-vapor streetlights,
the girl was all silver: her pale cropped hair, her face with its heavy trow-
elling of matte makeup. The parts below her face, small, pushed-up bo-
som, narrow hips, muscled, serviceable legs, were banded in stretch jer-
sey and black mesh and could have belonged to any undernourished,
overused hooker between puberty and menopause" (9). The second
paragraph of the novel locates an aestheticized, anesthetized eye *behind*
the camera, an eye for whom the prostitute is of no more than formal
interest: "At first, I had no attitude about her. Through the viewfinder
of my video camera, she was no more than a photogenic image, good
filmic contrast to the fat toddlers I had spent the day recording in En-
cino" (9). But a shift in this static perspective marks the beginning of the
investigation that drives the narrative of the novel: it is not the dynamic
of voyeuristic desire that propels the story, but a recognition and rejection of that dynamic. With the third paragraph the subject position of
the narrator changes yet again, and this shift involves not just reflexivity
but a perceived implication of the narrative's/camera's gaze in its object:
"Guilt, or maybe the impulse of universal motherhood, I don't know
what, took over when I learned the girl was only six months older than
my own daughter, Casey. That made her fourteen and a half. My documentary project was nearly in the can, until I met her. Over-budget and
overdue as always, but under control. Until I met her" (9). The initial investigation into child rearing becomes both a criminal investigation and
an inquiry into the identity and motivations of the young woman herself, when she is found murdered. As so frequently happens in such novels, the murder investigation/documentary becomes a reconstruction of

the previously unremarked on, undervalued life story of the female victim of crime.

Barbara D'Amato's fourth Cat Marsala novel, *Hard Women*, also uses a journalistic investigator and explores the implications of the observing "I"/eye by using visual themes. In that novel Cat is asked to film a documentary television series on prostitution in Chicago, a project with visual emphasis unusual for a freelance print journalist. Her journalistic endeavor becomes part of a murder investigation when Sandra, a prostitute interviewee with whom she has become friendly, is found dead. Cat's videographic investigation of prostitutes in general and Sandra's death in particular are contrasted to the static, generic police photographs (and by implication their investigation) of the dead woman's body. Cat watches the police photographers at work documenting the death: "A lab man approached the body with his camera and started briskly snapping photos from several sides. A detective in plain clothes said a word or two to one of the uniforms, shrugged, and turned away. I know they see death all the time. I know they can't become emotionally involved. But it looked to me as if the unspoken message was 'This woman isn't a valuable member of society'" (9). In fact, readers ultimately learn that a police officer is responsible for the prostitute's death.

At the same time that it attempts to counter the police approach, however, Cat's investigating gaze is itself also placed under scrutiny. This gesture is made possible by the reflexive possibilities of the first-person narration. For instance, Cat begins her investigations by looking up escort services in the Yellow Pages directory under "Entertainment," and she finds herself snickering at the euphemisms for prostitution ("Rent a Dream," "Sophisticated Companions"). But then, she observes, "I caught myself at it. My behavior was no better than that of all the high school boys I had known years back with their own snickering and whore jokes" (85–86). The investigator, who conventionally catches criminals, catches herself. In doing so, she also "catches out" the observing gaze of the reader, which is also implicated in an economy of voyeurism. As Cat recognizes her own identification with the masculine eye of pornography, she resolves to resist this position in her investigation. To do so, she must surrender journalistic "objectivity" in favor of a position of identification with those she is investigating, intentionally blurring the distinctions between subject and object in her interviews:

> Going into this project, I'd thought a lot about my attitude toward this subject. As long as I kept that barricade between the hookers and me, as long as I thought of them as "them" and of myself as a different species, this investigation wasn't going to work, or at least it wouldn't really take off. . . . I was going to have to listen, not just hear. However incomprehensible a hooker's life seemed to me now, I was going to have to understand. (86)

Cat, interestingly, here abjures the gaze in favor of the listening ear, a gesture that explains the emphasis of this and other novels on dialogue and testimony rather than simply titillating, visual descriptions. Removed from her position of objectivity, Cat is ethically implicated in the investigation in several ways. She acknowledges a feeling of guilt because she recognizes that by including the prostitute in her study, she may have had some part in provoking her murder. More generally, she recognizes that her use of prostitutes as subjects for her documentary, despite her good intentions (or perhaps alongside them), may necessarily reproduce aspects of the exploitative prostitute-client relationship: Cat perceives that Sandra gives her an interview because she feels indebted to Cat for giving her a place to stay, musing, "I was buying her, too, wasn't I, just as other people did. I felt guilty" (105). Finally, Cat—like the novel's reader—is involved because her subjectivity is not immune to or removed from the subject matter she examines: "This entire investigation had undermined something in me, and I was feeling vulnerable. . . . Knowing two prostitutes, however briefly, had altered the way I viewed prostitution and even sexuality. I began to realize how much difference it made that we were all starting from different places, psychologically speaking" (224). The autobiographical narration of the detective story thus becomes a form of confessional narrative, drawing the reader into the detective's various forms of implication and elaborating her subjective, often emotional responses. In fact, in the course of the story, the narrator (and potentially the reader too) is changed by those responses.

A similar narrative of self-investigation and confession is one of the subtexts of Lia Matera's complex investigation of the politics, economics, and ethics of the pornographic gaze in her fourth Laura Di Palma novel, *Face Value*. That novel begins when Laura is asked to represent a woman who appears in erotic videotapes that were ostensibly made as a form of psycho-spiritual therapy but whose images were subsequently electronically manipulated and then released as a consumer product to video stores by Brother Mike, the woman's spiritual guru. As she investigates the case, Laura necessarily explores the world of pornography in its various forms. She finds herself at several points—to her dismay— interpellated in the pornographic scenario, responding to the images with which she is presented, and unable to separate her body's visceral response from her professional demeanor: "As an attorney, I was supposed to be safe from certain intimacies. Yes, I had cared about some of my clients. . . . My pity and my conscience were sometimes vulnerable. But my business suit and my sexual feelings had never been part of the same package" (131). The problematic erotics of the gaze are thus both evoked and critiqued from the detective's point of view.

The novel elaborates many of the implications of the pornographic gaze, one of them being the extension of its male-female/active-passive power imbalance to literal violence against women. At one point, for example, Laura witnesses a murder scene in a strip club theater in which the victims' mouths have been taped shut: "Immobilized in provocative lingerie and gleaming facelessness, the dancers might have been performance art: The Interchangeable Women" (81). The scenario draws attention to the literal objectification and depersonalization of the women as well as to their final silencing. It also implies that videotape (and by extension other forms of exploitative representation) and the suffocating adhesive tape accomplish different versions of victimization, figurative and literal. Laura flees to her apartment, hoping for a momentary refuge from memories of the scene of the crime, but finds that she cannot restore her safe, objective distance from it, because she too is subject to that gaze: "In the dark, for a tiny interval, I tried to reerect the wall of aloof voyeurism that had protected me from three days of sensory overload. But when I turned the light back on, the impossible scene was still before me" (133). She discovers that her apartment has been vandalized. Both Laura and the reader occupy a relatively safe position in relation to the murder itself, but they are not immune from its broader social/symbolic implications, from the connections between "art" and "performance."

One of the most interesting formal aspects of *Face Value* is its use of extended passages of dialogue to present various points of view from women on the complexities of the pornography question, from the erotic dancer who wants to reclaim erotica, to the antipornography crusader who insists on the direct connection between pornographic images and violence against women, to the feminist lawyer who advocates that women take responsibility for their own objectification, to the former prostitute who speaks on behalf of the labor rights of sex workers. This strategy offers what approaches a genuinely dialogic form, in which the narrating "I" shares the subjective perspective with other viewpoints, not all of which can be reconciled. The strategy, by insisting on multiple perspectives, also refuses simply to present the "woman's point of view." This technique is especially engaging because the investigating lawyer must, like the reader, negotiate her way through these various positions: her first-person narrative voice does not in any obvious way overwhelm the other voices in the novel or arrive at an authoritative resolution of the issue, although the murder plot of the novel is resolved. The power of the gaze is, however, dramatically confirmed in the novel's climactic scene of confrontation and violence when it is revealed that Brother Mike, in a position to prevent much injury and another death, has instead adopted the position of the voyeur, quietly videotaping the scene from just outside the room. In this case, detached viewership amounts to murder.

IMPLICATING BODIES

The "I" of the female investigator may be ethically implicated in the crime scenario in other important ways. Because of women's traditional position of vulnerability in patriarchal society, the figure of the female detective is often subject to threat in a way her male counterparts are not. In drawing out the potential parallel between victim and detective, novelists may evoke the larger social dynamic of subjection from which even the generic role of the tough guy detective does not make her immune. At the same time, they may capitalize on the reader's pleasure in seeing the victim role countered by the investigation itself. When the detective acts, she acts not just to satisfy a client but also to vindicate herself and, vicariously, the reader. As Glenwood Irons notes (recasting Tania Modleski's description of romance writing), "the newer women detectives" respond to inherited social structures by "detecting with a vengeance": "The 'mass produced fantasies' of women speak to our collective nightmares over the marauding, bullying, Rambo-style heroes of the mass media in the 1970s and 1980s. The obvious subversion of order which the woman detective represents perhaps addresses our collective desire to undercut or at least question the institutions which inform our daily lives" ("Introduction" xii).

Like Matera, Linda Grant both represents and reverses the oppressive effects of the patriarchal gaze in her narrative of investigation. Grant develops both the autobiographical and confessional potential of the first-person narrator in order to imply a continuity between the detective and victims of crime, thus destabilizing the "external," "objective" orientation of the private eye's observations and also attributing to her a unique insight into the crime itself. In *A Woman's Place*, Catherine Sayler's investigation into a sexual harassment case resurrects memories of her own harassment at the hands of a law school professor, a series of incidents that precipitated her decision to abandon a legal career. She makes a connection between her involvement in the current case and her own experience early in the narrative of the novel, commenting, "Because I'm a woman in a man's field, I have to put up with a certain amount of poor behavior [from men]. But I'm my own boss, so I don't put up with a whole lot. Like most women my age, I have some scars. Which was why this job appealed to me so much. And why I shouldn't have been so quick to take it. Scar tissue can dim the vision" (7). But "scar tissue" can also (at least figuratively) refocus the vision of character and reader alike. In this case, it enables Catherine to identify with the victims of intimidation; she admits, "I knew how it felt to sit in that chair next to a man who could promote or destroy your career and feel yourself completely powerless" (45). Catherine's comments thus establish a sympathetic link with women both inside and outside the novel who have experienced "poor behavior" of one sort or another; yet Catherine, unlike many women, is in a position to act, to be *subject of* both action and articulation. A similar dynamic is developed in J. M. Redmann's *Intersection of Law and Desire*, when Micky Knight's investigation into a child pornography ring recalls memories of her own abuse as a child.

The vulnerability of the detective and the correlation between victim and investigator are central to the narratives of Sharon Gwynn Short's *Past Pretense*, Ruth Furie's *If Looks Could Kill*, and Elisabeth Bowers's *Ladies' Night*. In each of these novels, the central character's shift from being the object of the masculine gaze to subject of action is paralleled by her initiation as a private investigator. This parallel suggests that the role of the female private eye may embody the desire for such self-possession of voice and body. Short's novel, for instance, in retrospective passages revisits Patricia Delaney's earlier life as a stripper and her rise to being the strip club's bouncer, having demonstrated her abilities by physically flipping the male club owner (72). She later takes up a job as a private investigator. The trajectory of her career is an obvious version of the shift (or flip) from object of the male gaze to active subject. Furie's novel is a virtual catalogue of the varieties and repercussions of the power of the gaze (both creative and destructive), as her title implies. At several points the detective is subject to the unwanted patronizing surveillance of a male police officer, which she compares with the look of that prototypical noir hero, the classic film private eye:[5] "'You know I'll go the extra mile for you, Fran.' He gave me a look that was straight out of an old Humphrey Bogart movie. I wanted to laugh. He was turning it on. He gave me the creeps" (139). The comparison highlights the equivocal position of the female private eye, both subject of and subjected to the male gaze. The sinister implications of her subjected status are played out when it is revealed the eyes of the police officer are behind the face mask of her stalker.

Furie's series begins with Fran's near murder by her physically abusive ex-husband, and the issue of wife abuse weaves itself into the story in a variety of ways. As she both emerges from the abusive relationship and emerges as an investigator, the narrative chronicles her professionalization and growing economic independence together with her evolution as the subject of the narration and investigation. Becoming a private eye thus for her epitomizes the surmounting of her submissive, self-effacing position as an abused wife. The job she takes as a "gal Friday" (from which she graduates into a position as a professional investigator) becomes what one of her friends calls a "lifeline" (17), a term with double resonance: the autobiographical life narrative of the private investigator is also a lifeline that charts the protagonist's development and acts as a counterpoint to the murder investigation.

Ladies' Night, the first installment in Elisabeth Bowers's short-lived Meg Lacey private investigator series, includes a long autobiographical flashback that describes Meg's transformation from complacent middle-class housewife to private detective. This embedded narrative (62–69) begins with Meg's rape at knife point in a supermarket parking lot. Looking back on the incident, Meg realizes: "That rape marked a turning point, but it couldn't have been the beginning. Yet when people ask me to explain myself I always start there because up to that time, I'd raised no eyebrows, rocked no boats. Like everyone, I had my peculiarities; like everyone, I'd harbored rebellious thoughts. . . . But the rape tipped the balance, was like a rock thrown through my window. It let the rest of the world in" (63). Meg lets the rest of the world in in several important and connected ways. She increases her sense of physical self-sufficiency by taking martial arts classes, thereby altering her point of view:

> Women are taught that the world is dangerous, that to fear it is only common sense. They are encouraged to keep their interests confined to their family and immediate neighborhood; they are encouraged to be unadventurous, both physically and psychologically. Therefore, as I became better able to defend myself physically, I changed psychologically; I become braver, more outward-looking. I began wanting to know things about things that had never interested me before. (63)

The detective's point of view is thus not abstracted; it is intimately linked with her physical nature, reinforcing the notion of an embodied subject. The character's initiation as a private eye becomes the culmination of the "outward-looking" impulse she describes. It also leads to an awareness of her own position of subjectivity—a self-consciousness about the grounding of the private eye's racial, cultural, and gender perspective. The private "I" of the narrator becomes a point of identification through which the reader can investigate both internal self-positionings and externalized alternative realities; each of these elements is central to the investigation.

While Bowers, like most writers in the genre, does not exceed the middle-class sensibility of her audience, she does use it in order to reveal the first-person narrative perspective of the private eye as positioned. In her work as a detective, Meg becomes aware of the conditions that produce her perceptions and experience, gradually realizing that "globally-speaking, I was a member of a minority. A very privileged, powerful minority—but a minority nonetheless. For the first time, I was getting to know people that did not share my assumptions and values, was seeing my class, my culture, my race from the point of view of those outside it" (64). The "outsider" status of the detective is thus used to reposition the white, middle-class role away from the center. Meg's occupation affords her the opportunity to explore (if not occupy) places and points of view other than her own. The narrative perspective of the novel makes it possible for readers, through their identification with the character, similarly to recognize and reflect on their positioned subjectivity in a manner that was never possible in traditional hard-boiled novels. Though it is certainly not a radical text, the narrative of *Ladies' Night* does subtly critique the universal subject of liberal humanism rather than simply reproducing it.

ENGENDERING VIOLENCE?

Women's detective novels frequently call attention to the subject of the narration as an embodied subject, as the narratives of *Past Pretense, Ladies' Night,* and *If Looks Could Kill* demonstrate, and therefore the reader is often aware that the female investigator is vulnerable to physical violence. This vulnerability is in one sense an attribute of the hard-boiled genre, which Tzvetan Todorov calls "the story of the vulnerable detective": "the detective loses his immunity, gets beaten up, badly hurt, constantly risks his life, in short, he is integrated into the universe of the other characters, instead of being an independent observer" (51). But violence signifies differently in women's detective novels, partly because it signifies differently for women outside the novels. As Sarah Dunant puts it, "female private eyes are fighting a much bigger battle, coping with the physical, emotional and sexual ramifications of violence" ("Rewriting the Detectives" 28). Dunant's detective Hannah Wolfe, confronted with a killer's threatening advance, thinks to herself: "So all those tired old film directors were right. Men and women. Violence and sex. It comes with the territory, an inevitable function of power" (*Fatlands* 206). The female detective is, like the male PI, integrated into the universe of the other characters in the novel, but that universe is often self-consciously represented as one ordered by sexual difference.

Delys Bird and Brenda Walker observe that "the question of whether it is possible to write crime fiction that satisfies the necessities of the genre for suspense and fear, for excitingly cathartic resolutions and so on, yet remains subversive or at least questioning of the genre's typical positioning of women is a necessary preoccupation for feminist crime writers" (14–15). This preoccupation is developed in the first-person narrative's self-consciousness about the embodied and gendered nature of the narrating "I," as well as its relation to the subjectivity central to masculine exemplars of the genre. In an essay in the *Guardian*, Dunant considers the problem of negotiating violence when the detective is a woman:

> The solution lies partly in how you write the violence itself and partly in how you deal with its aftermath. When it comes to the first, the genre offers you some help. The most classic private eyes are first person narrations. Make that first person a woman and your heroine already has one big thing going for her: she is the subject as well as the object of violence. Like everything else in the story, it is seen through her eyes. That simple but radical transference of vision means that, whatever happens to her in the dark alley, voyeurism isn't such an easy option on the part of the reader. Unlike so many women in this genre, she is not just a body. She also has a voice and one to which you have to listen. ("Rewriting the Detectives" 28)

It is important to recognize the iconic value of violence in hard-boiled writing. As Sue Grafton puts it, "detective fiction is the stuff of violence, so you'll always be dealing with some form of it" ("G Is for (Sue) Grafton" 12), but her own work often both uses and explores the public and private repercussions of hard-boiled violence. So does the work of Valerie Wilson Wesley. Her detective Tamara Hayle says, "They never tell you how hard it is to kill another person, how it messes with you. . . . It was a blot on my soul, and I knew it" (287). The equivocal "they" of Tamara's soliloquy might well refer to traditional detective novels.

Part of the "simple but radical transference of vision" that Dunant describes involves the pleasure readers experience in perceiving what is gained in the generic translation from male to female point of view. In Val McDermid's novel *Kick Back*, for instance, detective Kate Brannigan, having been run off the road in her car, finds herself in the hospital. She is insistent about calling for a ride home, and her comments deliberately distance her persona from the masculine hard-boiled response to violence: "I simply didn't feel up to walking the half-mile home or coping with a taxi. Yes, all right, I admit it, I was shaken up. To hell with the tough guy private eye image" (69). Dunant's PI suffers from nightmares following her assault, confessing that "it's a cause of some shame for a private eye to be waking crippled by nightmares so long after the event. Do the boys suffer this, I wonder, finding the hangover from the violence nastier than the one from the booze? Sometimes I think I'm in the wrong job, trying to fit the myth to the reality. But only sometimes" (*Under My Skin* 35). Her comments draw attention not just to the slippage between male and female performances of the tough guy "myth" but also to problems central to the myth itself. Similarly, when Janice Law's detective Anna Peters finds herself imprisoned and in imminent danger of being killed, she imagines herself being shot—but then realizes that her experience will not match the aesthetic conventions of Hollywood adventure films, and the glamour of violence is deflated: "Before I could stop myself, my mind framed the scene: birch trees, figures moving in the sunlight, a close-up of faces, then a long shot, frozen by the sound of the gun. Of course, it never happened that way except on the screen. I was certain it didn't feel that way. It felt the way I felt: cold, sore, frightened, and prey to sudden regrets" (*Big Payoff* 158).

It has become a cliché to observe that women's recasting of hard-boiled violence sometimes plays out for readers a kind of revenge fantasy against threatening or patriarchal figures (Irons, "New Women Detectives" 128; A. Kaplan 28; Munt 98–99, 198; Rabinowitz, "Reader, I Blew Him Away" 332; Turnbull, "Bodies of Knowledge" 40). There is something particularly satisfying for readers in seeing a woman in a physically active role, taking symbolic action against representatives of the forces that normally threaten women and of which they are often fearful. The revenge fantasy is almost parodically acted out in the climax of Sandra West Prowell's *By Evil Means* when PI Phoebe Siegel defends herself against her male assailant with a cane made from a petrified walrus penis (350). The revenge scenario is approached with critical self-consciousness in Furie's *If Looks Could Kill*, when a battered women's support group jokingly speculates on the possibility that they could band together and beat up their abusive husbands. "Instead of a support group," Fran comments, "we would be a terrorist group." "And," another of the women observes, "the violence would continue" (236).

The female private detective's confidence on the "mean streets" is part of a fantasy that negotiates the territory between the fear of vulnerability and an ideal of physical integrity and self-protection. Linda Barnes, for instance, asked about how she hopes her books affect her readers, referred (somewhat wryly) to the "role model" function of her PI Carlotta Carlyle:

> sometimes I talk about her as a one woman take-back-the-night movement. She is not afraid to walk around her neighborhood at night, and she doesn't believe that any woman should be afraid to walk around her neighborhood at night, she doesn't think that it's a stupid thing to do. She thinks that the stupid thing is that anyone should be trapped in their household by fear. She doesn't go out shootin' up the neighborhood, but she makes sure that she can defend herself. Now, I wish there were not such a need for defense, "I wish there were not so many guns out, and so few brains," I think is a quote from Dashiell Hammett.

Linda Grant also discusses her detective in terms of the limitations conventionally placed on women's ability to move and act ("Don't take risks," "You can't go there," "You can't do that"): "I wanted to create a woman—and that also goes to why I created a woman detective—I wanted her to be someone who confronted those limitations and went beyond them and wasn't warped by them." This aspect of the detective's role is illustrated in Dunant's *Fatlands*, when the PI Hannah Wolfe recalls her fear of going out at night during the time when the Notting Hill rapist was active (she was then a student), adding wryly, "But then now it's my job not to be so scared of everything" (26). Alice Yeager Kaplan theorizes this situation when she asks, "How can a woman take possession of the city when she is—in poetics as in the annoying encounters of everyday life—the symbol that the universal male must disrobe in his quest for knowledge?" (27). She suggests that writers such as Sara Paretsky have found one answer: use fiction to transform the symbol into a resistant speaking subject who is, thereby, able symbolically to reclaim the masculine mean streets.

David Glover argues that in the traditional hard-boiled novel the original violence of the murder is reenacted and compounded in its investigation. "What is at stake, then," he concludes, "is a refiguring of the physicality of violence and symbolic possession of the means of violence" (77). In his view, these narratives place a premium on "the endurance and integrity of the male body as the condition of narrative movement" (78). Glover's comments illuminate one of the most conventionalized features of the female private eye novel: the hero's persistent concern with her own physical fitness and well-being. Nancy Pickard directly alludes to this as she distinguishes the professional detective from the amateur: most amateur detectives "aren't even trained in self-defense. By and large, they don't jog five miles a day, wear a Black Belt, or work out down at Gold's Gym three times a week. (Can you imagine Miss Marple lifting weights?)" (64). As Pickard implies, it has become an iconic element of the female private investigation novel for detectives to work out or jog regularly, and especially to practice some form of self-defense training. Of course, this is an important practical part of the detective's professionalized role; as V. I. Warshawski often points out, her body is a tool of her trade and thus must always be fit for action. The obsession with self-defense and physical fitness is also, however, a symbolic possession of the object of violence, making it an active subject—taking control of the gendered body itself, vulnerable as it has traditionally been to being (literally and figuratively) overpowered by patriarchal figures.

The resistant female body does not always replace the gun as an icon of crime fiction violence, but it is an important supplementary signifier. Marele Day's Claudia Valentine draws attention to the role of the body as her primary instrument of self-defense, observing in *The Life and Crimes of Harry Lavender*: "My legs are my best weapon. If I'm close enough I can do a karate kick that knocks them flat. If I'm far enough away I run. That's what they mean in the profession by 'using your legs as a weapon.' And I don't carry a gun like some of my more cowboy colleagues. 'Why don't you, Claudia? Can't fit it in your handbag?' If I don't have one then I can't use it and conversely it can't be used on me" (37). Even when a character like Dunant's Hannah Wolfe eschews using her body as a weapon, she calls attention to the way her gun functions as a practical substitute for it and protector of it. In a moment of crisis she reaches into her handbag for her weapon, addressing the reader ironically: "You find it corny, no doubt, that I should resort to such girlie aids, that I shouldn't be able to fell a grown man at ten paces with flying feet? Myself, I prefer to see it as the triumph of technology over muscle. I did try martial arts once but do you realize how long you have to study to get your foot as effective as a squirt of tear gas? It would leave a girl no time to make a living" (*Fatlands* 137).

Representing the defensive body is a way of gendering the abstract narrative voice. It is also often a way of evoking the larger social dynamic around violence against women. In Janet Dawson's *Take a Number*, for example, detective Jeri Howard investigates the murder of an abusive ex-husband; but its autobiographical narrative also investigates another site of violence, the domestic violence done *by* the murder victim to his wife (who has unjustly been accused of the murder). This aspect of the story is emphasized in Jeri's ongoing attempt to understand how and why the victim's wife coped with her abuse and its aftereffects. The violence of the murder is countered by the domestic violence of which the husband is guilty, and the book attempts perhaps not to "solve" domestic violence but to understand it as a social "mystery." At the climax of the novel, the detective's identification with victims of violence against women is suggested, as is her professional ability to resist it: "I hate to admit it, but I'm afraid of being beaten up. I've encountered physical violence before. I've come to blows several times during my tenure as an investigator, though I usually rely on a quick tongue and quick reflexes to avoid getting punched out. But sometimes that isn't enough" (337).

Sarah Lacey's detective Leah Hunter often calls attention to the importance of martial arts training when she needs to defend herself. In *File Under: Missing*, Leah is ambushed. In the course of fending off her attacker, she adds another dimension to individual self-defense by drawing an analogy between her own defensive posture and that of battered women: "It's hard to follow the action when every instinct is to roll into a ball and hide away someplace. I wondered how some women managed to put up with this kind of treatment on a regular basis" (123). Lacey's book, significantly, also describes an episode in which the detective and her friend take on a male opponent, bloodying his nose. During the melee, her friend hits the man with a notably domestic weapon, a milk bottle. Similarly, during the climax of Kathy Hogan Trocheck's *Every Crooked Nanny*, one of the staff of Callahan Garrity's cleaning business stops the killer with a vacuum cleaner hose.

In a number of books, the questions of violence and the safety of the body are connected with the myth of the lone wolf, apparently "independent" figure of the detective in order to introduce questions of *social* security, thereby revealing that the integrity of the individual body is tied not just to individual self-defense but also to social and economic networks that extend well beyond its physical borders. In Michelle Spring's *Every Breath You Take*, for instance, when private eye Laura Principal is hospitalized after an injury, she comments on the current shortage of hospital beds in Britain. She considers sneaking out of the hospital without her doctor's permission, but a nurse informs her that should she do so, she would lose her insurance coverage. Laura silently acquiesces, thinking, "Now any self-employed person needs to keep up-to-date with insurance against illness or injury; but to void your insurance in my job, where occasional injury is almost guaranteed, would itself be a sign of unfitness for work" (191). In Dunant's *Fatlands*, the detective enjoys some cholesterol-laden bacon, commenting ironically on her social security—or lack thereof: "Who wants to grow old, anyway, particularly if you're the only one you know who doesn't have a pension plan?" (7). In Janet Dawson's *Take a Number*, Jeri Howard's search for a key witness who is homeless leads her to contemplate the fate of the burgeoning population of homeless people in the Bay Area and the causes of their increase in numbers, such as the closure of mental hospitals, the decline in affordable housing, the economic and political climate, the widening gap between rich and poor, and the growing holes in the social safety net. A nun puts it in simpler terms—terms that implicate the detective herself: "[Sister Anne] says being homeless can result from an unlucky combination of factors, such as the loss of a job, with no savings or family to fall back on. That's a definition Jeri Howard, self-employed with a little money in the bank and family in the area, can understand and appreciate. My safety net is intact. But it wouldn't take much to rip a hole in what I often take for granted" (194). The detective's physical capabilities are thus always challenged by the risks she undertakes, and her defenses against them, for these defenses are constituted by physical, intellectual, emotional, social, and economic resources.

"I WASN'T ARCHER, EXACTLY, BUT ARCHER WAS ME" (ROSS MACDONALD)

The *linguistic* resources of the detective are reflected in her position as narrator, a stance that becomes self-defensive in relation to generic precedents. The narrating "I" is the pivotal theoretical site where *telling* and *doing* become one, where it becomes clear that enunciation is an *act*—both a fictional performance and an action in itself that produces important effects. One way of answering the question, What does the private eye do in a private eye novel? is: She tells her story; she speaks for herself; she acts as an author. The "I" is thus a locus that draws out a key analogy between the female author of the novel and its central female character: both characters and authors are represented in the fiction of the narrating "I." Clearly, this is *not* to say that private eye novels are literally or necessarily *about* the lives or specific experiences of their writers; however, the autobiographical form produces a rhetoric of identification, not just between the reader and the detective character but also between the novelist and the detective.

For example, the detective story is a kind of fantasy site for writers as well as readers. As Sara Paretsky acknowledges, the V. I. Warshawski series fulfilled her fantasies of creativity: "I had had a fantasy about writing a book for a long time. In fact, I wrote my first story when I was six, but I grew up in a family where girls became secretaries and wives, and boys became professionals. I wasn't expected to have talents" (qtd. in Shapiro, "Sara Paretsky" 67). J. A. Jance, who writes the Sheriff Joanna Brady series, describes her love of detective fiction as a child and concludes that "I always wanted to be a writer, but I was not allowed in the creative writing programs at the university when I got there in the early sixties because creative writing classes were not open to girls. I was told that girls become teachers, boys become writers." But she adds that "the wonderful thing about writing is that there's more than one way over the mountain to yon." Anne Wingate, who writes the Deb Ralston police series under the pseudonym Lee Martin, avers that she made her mind up as a child to be a Texas Ranger but was told by her grandmother that she couldn't be—though she could be a Rangerette: "When I found out that meant a baton twirler I was completely outraged."[6] Sandra Scoppettone jokingly draws attention to the autobiographical nature of her detective in her remark that "I've never written the obligatory autobiographic novel and my Laurano series comes closest to that. . . . I can have her eat everything I'd like to eat and not gain weight" (interview by Sorrells).

It is important to note that both authors and characters are working women.[7] When Sue Grafton described her motivation for relinquishing her job as a television scriptwriter to begin the Kinsey Millhone alphabet novels, she echoed the sentiments often expressed by fictional private detectives: "I wanted to be my own boss again, to struggle with material that mattered to me" ("G Is for (Sue) Grafton" 5). Wendi Lee's series character gives virtually the same reason for leaving the military to become a private eye: "I was tired of everyone telling me what to do. I wanted to be my own boss. So I became a private investigator" (*Good Daughter* 4). "I'm my own boss," says Linda Grant's detective (*Woman's Place* 7). Both women writers and female detectives are economically compensated and empowered (to one degree or another) by their ability to draw on and bend generic/social rules to their own advantage. There is, then, at least a theoretical analogy between the generic agency of women authors who have developed a revisionist form and audience and the physically and intellectually active investigations of the fictional female private detective.

The correspondence between author and character is certainly nothing new: Stephen Knight has observed that Chandler's Marlowe "has much in common with the archetypal spokesman of that figure, the lonely writer" (*Form and Ideology* 159). Perhaps the most notorious example of the exploitation of this identification is Mickey Spillane's self-promotion as the prototype for Mike Hammer, which included making publicity appearances costumed as the detective and playing him in the 1963 film *The Girl Hunters* (see Van Dover 151–52). Such identification, however, works differently for women writers. The identification of author and detective clearly has sound commercial motivations here too, but it involves less the "ethical solipsism" of which Kenneth Van Dover accuses Spillane (152) than the literal embodiment of the female hero. It is a way of visually representing the fictional detective associated with a real woman's body. The gesture of insisting on female authorship and even glamorizing it is most frequently associated with widely successful and recognizable authors. Sue Grafton, for instance, has often been pictured in magazine profiles holding a gun, or leaning against a Volkswagen Beetle (her hero's vehicle of choice) emblazoned with the vanity plates "KINSEY." Linda Barnes, similarly, appears on her dust jackets leaning against a taxi, evoking her cabbie detective Carlotta Carlyle. Sara Paretsky is sometimes pictured with a golden retriever, a canine pet she "shares" with her fictional protagonist V. I. Warshawski. Janet Dawson has appeared sporting that icon of the hard-boiled detective, a fedora hat. When such photographs are used to market women's detective novels, the association between author and private eye becomes an important way of reinforcing the author's role as active *subject*, a way of resisting efforts to make the female author the passive object of an erotic gaze.

It also affirms the private eye/I as the site of the kind of women's role-playing fantasy and identification described above. The detective hero is, in other words, not the object of the reader's fantasy but the subject of her projection. Sue Grafton has commented on the autobiographical character of her novels, stressing that the private eye is a kind of idealized projection of herself: Kinsey, she remarks, is "a stripped-down version of me. She's the person I would have been had I not married young and had children. She'll always be thinner and younger and braver, the lucky so-and-so. . . . Because of Kinsey, I get to lead two lives—hers and mine. Sometimes I'm not sure which I prefer" ("G Is for (Sue) Grafton" 10). Marcia Muller has similarly commented that Sharon McCone is "more like me than I intended at the start. I wanted to put some distance between us by giving her some of the courageous attributes I don't think I have" (qtd. in Isaac, "Situation, Motivation, Resolution" 23). "In some ways," Linda Barnes remarks of her series character, "I think of Carlotta as the good part of me, the part that takes action when it would be easier not to take action, the part that rights wrong."

Peter Rabinowitz's analysis of Grafton's *"A" Is for Alibi* extends this rhetoric of identification; he suggests that Grafton plays with the hard-boiled genre, transforming it into "a vehicle to express women's rage" ("Reader, I Blew Him Away" 332). He connects this impulse in the novel with Grafton's half-joking autobiographical comment in an *Armchair Detective* interview that the novel "is partly based on a little scheme I came up with to kill an ex-husband of mine. . . . Of course I knew I'd get caught at it and I'd have to spend the rest of my life in a shapeless prison dress. . . . So I decided to put the murder plot in a book and get paid for it, and thus have the best of all possible worlds. It launched a whole new career for me" ("G Is for (Sue) Grafton" 8). Rabinowitz concludes that "since men have used the genre as a way of venting antifeminism in a socially acceptable manner, Grafton writes *Alibi* to make space for her rage against at least one man in her life" (332).

Such tensions between autobiography and the fiction are often important to both writers and readers of women's writing in the hard-boiled tradition. For example, Barbara D'Amato calls attention to the continuity between the kind of active research in which she was routinely engaged as a writer and the investigations of her character, investigative journalist Cat Marsala: "One of the great benefits of having an investigative reporter is that I get a chance to investigate issues I'm interested in finding out more about. My reactions become hers. . . . [As a true crime writer] I was a female investigator, and she became a female investigator." Linda Barnes affirms of Carlotta Carlyle that "her family is not my family, but many of her causes are my causes." Sue Grafton remarks of Kinsey Millhone that "Her biography is different, but our sensibilities are identical" ("G Is for (Sue) Grafton" 10). Nancy Baker Jacobs comments, in turn, that "the things that I tend to get my blood boiling about . . . do find their way into my fiction"; she identifies many of these specifically as feminist issues that have relevance outside the fictional narrative of the novel.

In fact, authors frequently comment that their novels offer a place creatively to voice social and political issues near and dear to their hearts.

Sandra Scoppettone argues that the combination of a personal, intimate subjectivity and the possibility of social commentary is a signature of women's appropriation of the hard-boiled narrative:

> One of the major differences [between the traditional practitioners of hard-boiled writing and contemporary female writers of detective fiction] is that those men did not really deal with feelings or with personal lives that much and I certainly do, so many of the women seem to do. That's the difference between us, right? Here's how it's alike: the private eye is first person and it's able to comment on society, it's one of the reasons I chose the form.

Nevertheless, most authors are intensely aware of the danger of allowing their own personal voice to disturb the realist surface of the novel and produce a didactic effect. Authors almost inevitably invoke the metaphor of "speaking from a soapbox" or "sermonizing" to convey the danger of letting an authorial presence obtrude into the fictional reality of the novel.[8] As Wendy Hornsby puts it, "I am always mindful of the advice of the old movie mogul who warned a screenwriter, 'If you want to send a message, call Western Union.' I work very hard not to hammer the reader with polemic." But what holds the links of the various installments of series fiction together is a combination of constant formal features, consistent values, and the continuing character—in short, the sense of an ongoing narrative unified by a *single sensibility*.

The association of author's and character's voice has another effect: though not implying a direct one-to-one referentiality, it does reinforce a continuity between the world inside and the world outside the novel. The "I" of the detective is the pivot point that defines the boundary between the fictional world and the real world. One of the places this marginal position is made evident is in the reflexive commentaries—or, as Marcia Muller calls them, "philosophical asides"—made possible by the first-person narration. For example, in Muller's *Trophies and Dead Things*, while Sharon McCone tracks down the heirs of the founder of the Berkeley Free Speech Movement in the 1960s, she at the same time mentally revisits her own past. Coming across her twenty-year-old love beads, she reflects, "They glimmered in the day's fading light—opalescent blue and pink and green and yellow symbols of an era that perhaps was never as joyful or innocent as some of us remember it" (27). Such asides are ambivalent in their voice as well as audience: they are an internalized meditation on the detective's fictional world, but at the same time they interpellate the reader and her world. As Glenn Most has observed, the literary detective defines and is defined by the margin between text and reader, both "facing inward to the other characters in the story and facing outward to the reader, with whom only he is in contact" (341).

The private eye/I of the narrative is thus *both* private and public and speaks from an individual point of view; but it identifies the contingencies and investments that orient its position. In so doing, it dramatizes in fictional form the old feminist adage that the personal is the political. The women authors who appropriate the narrating "I" of the private eye novel modify it in ways that are necessarily *self*-conscious. They evince an awareness that the body in question in the detective story is a gendered body, whether it is the body of the detective-narrator; the body of the victim; the generic corpus of texts, a body of stylistic, formal, and ideological practices that compose the hard-boiled detective novel; or the body of the reader. In each case, the private eye and what it sees are subject to re-vision, and in each case, the body performs.

Chapter 6

PLOTTING
AGAINST THE LAW

Outlaw Agency

"You're a cop, Pat. You're tied down by rules and regulations. There's someone over you. I'm alone. I can slap someone in the puss and they can't do a damn thing. No one can kick me out of my job. Maybe there's nobody to put up a fuss if I get gunned down, but then I still have a private cop's license with the privilege to pack a rod, and they're afraid of me. I hate hard, Pat."

Mickey Spillane, *I, the Jury*

CRISIS INTERVENTION

In his study of the detective genre, Dennis Porter points out that the hard-boiled story in its earliest days was a response to the turbulent American city of the 1920s and reflected a deep unease with the threats that this milieu posed to law and order: "Along with the reemergence of xenophobia, immigration curbs, and a 'Red Scare,' an unprecedented crime wave also occurred that caught the public imagination because it was 'spectacularly innovative' in its tactics, weaponry, and mobility. . . .

The result was that 'the eastern metropolis came to resemble the west-ern cowtown, with its daylight holdups, gun battles in the streets, and cross-country pursuits'" (196–97).[1] Porter also draws attention to the coincidence in 1929 of the inauguration of Herbert Hoover, an avowed conservative; the stock market crash; and the publication of Dashiell Hammett's *Red Harvest*, which he designates the first full-length hard-boiled novel:

> The irony is in the circumstance that the private eye began to flour-ish in popular literature at a time that coincided with a major crisis of American individualism as the political philosophy of industrial capitalism. In the fiction, if no longer in life, the myth of heroic in-dividualism persists. The Continental Op [Hammett's hero] reaf-firms his mastery over a city out of control in a way that the presi-dent signally failed to do for American society at large. (176–77)

The historical parallel between Hoover's election and that of Ronald Reagan in 1980, another Republican president committed to American political conservatism (together with the election of long-lived Conser-vative governments in Britain in 1979 and Canada in 1984), is one worth noting. The change in political climate in the early 1980s arose at least in part from a nationalistic reaction to the Vietnam War, a loss of faith in government following the crimes of Watergate, and an economic decline that had begun in the early 1970s. One of the by-products of this con-servative reentrenchment was an escalating antifeminist backlash, mani-fested by the rise of the right-wing Moral Majority, the founding of the conservative Heritage Foundation, the well-publicized activism of Phyl-lis Schlafly, and the landmark failure of the Equal Rights Amendment in 1982 (Ryan 101). The conservative governments that persisted into the 1990s sponsored a *renewed* rhetoric of individualism whose familiar and powerful model of individual agency (directed and motivated by the "free" market entrepreneurial capitalist system) detracted from social programs; at the same time, they promoted a "law-and-order" agenda that required increased funding both to domestic enforcement agencies (especially for the "war on drugs") and to the military as part of the early 1980s revival of the cold war (the equivalent, perhaps, of Hoover's "Red Scare"), undertaken so that America might once again "stand tall." These platforms, however, posed a fundamental *threat* to freedom and security—especially from the point of view of women (as well as the poor, the aged, and racial and other minority groups), who were arguably victims of both its rhetorical and economic assaults. Such developments ran strikingly counter to the discourse of equality and democratic access that liberal feminist activism had made current in the 1970s, creating what might well be seen as another kind of crisis in American individualism, one that strongly affected women.

The female private eye novel begins to flourish in popular literature at the moment of this crisis. The new subgenre mediates its most pressing contradictions, playing out some of the fantasies and fears that constitute the crisis and working through in an entertaining fictional context some of the contradictions that fuel it—contradictions rarely so easily resolved in real life. In doing so, the female private eye novel reproduces and renegotiates some of the central elements of the original hard-boiled novel. The traditional novel posits a condition of (at least relative) freedom for the detective. It demands that he act outside and often against the authorized centers of power, in a modernized version of the American tradition that values acting out against the institutional centers of government and big business. As Dennis Porter wrote in 1981, "the strength of the hostility felt by many Americans toward the institutions of government is, of course, as old as the Republic and as new as the 1980 presidential campaign" (176).

VIRGINIA WOOLF MEETS THE LONE WOLF

The hard-boiled novel draws extensively on the enduring American myth of the cowboy or outlaw hero: the detective represents an alternative form of justice. In the absence of reliable and authentic systems of law and order, the heroic individual of the old West had to act *as* an individual, taking the law into his own hands. In introducing a story (significantly titled "Rough Justice") by one of the early *Black Mask* private eye writers, William F. Nolan even describes its detective hero as "John Wayne without the horse" (157). In "The Hard-Boiled Detective Story: From the Open Range to the Mean Streets," Richard Slotkin traces the evolution in the dime novels of the late nineteenth and early twentieth century from depicting the Indian-fighters of the Wild West to portraying detective characters. The wild "frontier" is thus transferred to the streets of the urban metropolis (96). For Slotkin, the combination in a single figure of the outlaw and the detective is the defining feature of the modern hard-boiled detective story:

> The inner life of the figure is that of the outlaw, whose perspective
> is that of a victim of social injustice. He has seen the underside of
> American democracy and capitalism and can tell the difference be-
> tween law and justice, and he knows that society lives more by law
> than by justice. Yet he also embodies the politics of the police detec-
> tive, the belief that we need order, some kind of code to live by if we
> are to keep from degenerating into a government of pure muscle
> and money. (99)

The detective is, in other words, a marginal figure who for readers explores in fantasy the border between the law and unlawfulness, between social norms and deviancy, between social security and individual risk. When Carroll John Daly introduced his private eye Race Williams in 1927 in *The Snarl of the Beast*, he established the convention that the detective have a distinctively marginal status: "My position is not exactly a healthy one," the detective tells the reader; "The police don't like me. The crooks don't like me. I'm just a halfway house between the law and crime; sort of working both ends against the middle" (qtd. in Nolan 35).

As Jane S. Bakerman perceives, however, the "fact of their maleness" significantly mitigates both the marginal position of such hard-boiled detective heroes and their isolation as individuals: "Though they are not widely respected members of 'the system,' they are obviously members of the male power structure. . . . [H]ard-boiled protagonists enact patriarchal roles. . . . [T]he investigator behaves as a stern father who temporarily replaces social disorder with propriety by punishing these criminally disobedient and dangerous perpetual children" (128–29). And these "perpetual children" are frequently female—or feminized[2] — characters. They are epitomized, perhaps, in *The Big Sleep*'s giggling, thumb-sucking, baby-talking—and murderously insane—femme fatale Carmen Sternwood, "a pretty, spoiled and not very bright little girl who had gone very, very wrong" (Chandler, *Big Sleep* 64).[3] Richard Slotkin argues that the relocation of the Western genre from open range to mean streets also shifts the basis of the struggle over the "frontier" from race (white cowboys against Indians) to class. It might equally be argued that the equivalent of the threatening Native American presence (also often characterized as childlike) of the western novel's "wild West" is, in the hard-boiled novel, the wild woman. In *The Big Sleep*, the private eye takes on the punitive role abdicated by erstwhile patriarch General Sternwood, whose negligence and invalid status—his metaphoric and literal paralysis—have allowed his daughters to run wild; Sternwood's debility functions as a synecdoche for a larger patriarchal system of social control (his military title designates his leadership role) now weak and corrupt, necessitating the private eye's symbolic individualist intervention as a society-rescuing knight errant.

In his analysis of Chandler's *Farewell, My Lovely*, Stephen Knight insists that the novel's "outer, socially-attuned story" that concerns itself with gangsters and civic corruption in effect camouflages the more personalized "inner story," which poses the more significant threat to the detective. The corrupt center of that plot is "a malicious but resourceful and seductive woman," Mrs. Grayle, whose name should cue the reader to her role as the primary object of the detective-hero's ironic quest (*Form and Ideology* 153). Rather than functioning merely as a personal antagonist, however, the malicious and resourceful woman seems to be associated in the hard-boiled genre with the degenerative forces at work in the social system. She is not just a criminal; she poses a larger danger, outside of and threatening to the social order itself. Therefore, according to the conventions of the hard-boiled story, she must be killed, imprisoned, or otherwise punished by the detective in order for the plot to be resolved. Her desire (usually represented as both sexual and materialistic) is both attractive and threatening, because it exceeds the structures of social control. Slavoj Žižek's psychoanalytic analysis of the hard-boiled narrative affirms that the femme fatale is the character who represents "not ceding to one's desire" (63).

But "excess" must be seen in historical terms as well: the femme fatale also marks a reaction against the changes in women's social roles that threatened their traditional domestic function as moral guardian. As Cynthia Hamilton argues, the suffrage advocates had succeeded in gaining the vote for women in 1920, making public involvement a political tool:

> Women had sinned in other ways as well. They had been active in the trade-union movement, and now public sentiment had shifted away from the unions. Having joined the workforce in increasing numbers, entering new fields of employment during the war, women were now viewed as usurpers. Women's organizations had been active in pushing for reforms during the Progressive era, but with the campaign for Prohibition successfully concluded, reform was in disrepute. The increased personal freedom enjoyed by women, including the much announced new sexual freedom of the 1920s, also stirred resentment; their search for personal fulfillment socially, sexually and intellectually was seen as a direct abdication of their guardianship of Christian humanism. (32–33)

The femme fatale embodies resentment of the active, competitive woman who would take advantage of newly won freedoms (Hamilton 34), representing female power in the social and economic realm as inappropriate, deviant, . . . and unlawful.

The hard-boiled mode thus offers contemporary women writers a highly conflicted generic prototype for feminine agency, especially when

it comes to women's relation to law and order. But it is precisely the contradictions that arise between the masculine outlaw-hero and the femme
fatale that make women's appropriation of the genre so interesting. We
should again note that as the product of mainstream popular fiction, the
male hard-boiled hero is the center of attention for a population of readers whose desires and anxieties his story dramatizes, making him a far
from marginal figure in this regard. The hard-boiled novel achieves its
popularity at least in part by positing the tantalizing possibility that one
can speak and act outside of pervasive and defective institutional structures—a possibility even more tantalizing to and meaningful for women,
who have often been systematically excluded from and routinely oppressed by such structures. As Porter observes, "in the disciplinary society of the United States the ideal unseen seer of law enforcement was
conceived to be an independent business man, who in his most memorable fictional incarnations is strictly free-lance" (179).

The subtle social surveillance made possible by the private eye may
be quite desirable to women writers, as is the detective's affirmation of
the hard-won position of the independent business*woman* in the working world, as we argued in chapter 1. The hard-boiled genre inscribes a
contestatory position for its hero, offering the precedent—indeed, the
necessity, as far as the genre is concerned—for representing not just an
eye that sees but a voice that speaks from the margins, a voice originating in a character who both talks and behaves in an insubordinate manner. It offers the imaginative possibilities of a folk-hero protagonist who
functions as a vehicle of social protest, or, rather, it revives this protagonist from its incarnation in the private investigator of the 1920s and
1930s (Porter 180). Women's appropriation of the ambivalent figure of
the hard-boiled detective opens up a site of discursive power that provides a unique space for self-conscious reflection on/of the laws of gender and genre. The hard-boiled hero is a figure who refuses (or is pre-
vented from) acting on (or within) the "orders" of many aspects of the
existing (legal, social, moral) system, even if his investigation and solution do ultimately reproduce aspects of that system (especially its im-

plicitly and explicitly gendered power dynamic). For women writers, it may not be so easy or heroic to simply refuse established sites of discursive power. By taking up the position of the detective, they can deploy for their own ends a popular—and politically engaged—generic "code." And women writers have a great deal at stake in using the heroic female agency made available by the detective genre to analyze and even subvert the misogynist power of law enforcement agencies of various stripes.

Women who take advantage of a typically masculine genre like hard-boiled detective fiction are, in a sense, generic outlaws who, in appropriating powerful linguistic conventions, resituate and redirect power. When they adapt the generic character of the detective hero, for example, they not only recast the role of the outlaw but also destabilize the codes of the genre itself. At the same time, they work to suggest the inadequacy and perhaps even the constructedness of the heroic model they employ. While the traditional hard-boiled novel demonized and punished the female character who contravened conventional ideas about feminine submissiveness by desiring and acting, the feminist hard-boiled novel makes that role a heroic one, a gesture that would have been inconceivable to the early practitioners of the genre. Working through the conventions of the genre to subvert some of its most powerful traditions, both authors and characters of the "tough gal" novels make a kind of feminist "outlaw agency" possible.

Kathleen Gregory Klein questions the possibility of such agency, asking, "Can or should a feminist detective operate professionally to bolster the patriarchal system? Should she remain part of Virginia Woolf's 'society of outsiders' instead?" (*Woman Detective* 5). Klein's questions are presented as "serious ideological problems" posed by revisionist feminist approaches to the detective genre. She implies that in most novels of this kind, membership in the sorority of private eyes and the society of feminist outsiders is mutually exclusive. But to novelist Shelley Singer (author of the Barrett Lake series), it appears that the two roles may well be related: "A woman, I think, tends to look at the world from the outside, because it hasn't been our world. So there's a slight shift [offered by the female detective] in that respect." Maggie Humm hints at a similar response to Klein when she cites Woolf in her discussion of feminist detectives:

> In the celebrated quotation from *A Room of One's Own* Virginia
> Woolf described the role of women in patriarchal society: 'if one is
> a woman one is often surprised by a sudden splitting off of con-
> sciousness, say in walking down Whitehall, when from being the
> natural inheritor of that civilisation, she becomes, on the contrary,
> outside of it, alien and critical' (Woolf, 1929, p. 101). Some sixty
> years before Warshowski [*sic*], Woolf's account foreshadows the way
> in which feminist detectives might walk their mean streets. (185)

The "mean streets" Woolf describes, interestingly, are no crime-ridden back alley but rather the site of Britain's legislative buildings, the place where laws are made and where, to borrow from Humm's title, women are often constituted as "legal aliens."[4] Paradoxically, by their very compliance with the "laws" of the traditional hard-boiled genre, women writers can make use of the alienated—but powerfully contestatory and insightful—position inscribed in those codes, creating a position from which it is possible to explore and respond to not just the genre's but society's masculinist imperatives.

RIDING SIDESADDLE

One way "tough gal" novels call attention to this process is by evoking the mythical figure of the "outlaw" hero essential to their generic prototypes. For example, in *A Woman's Place*, Linda Grant's detective Catherine Sayler directly alludes to the analogy between the detective and the cowboy. While discussing a new client, Catherine's African American business partner Jesse compares the new generation of computer entrepreneurs with "the gamblers, gunslingers and prospectors" of the old West. Catherine, however, evinces some discomfort with the comparison—though she is quite willing to play with it in passing:

I'm less than enthusiastic about this metaphor. When you're in the corporate security business and your clients include high-tech companies, it's unnerving to realize that your partner thinks he's working at the OK Corral. "And just who are you—Wyatt Earp or Doc Holliday?" I asked.

"Just Wyatt Earp's trusty sidekick," he said in a phony accent with a mocking grin.

I tried to imagine Wyatt Earp in high heels with a black sidekick carrying a laptop and a six-gun and couldn't suppress my laughter. (3)

Catherine's imaginative send-up of the cowboy figure comically underscores the alignment of (white) race and (masculine) gender that generally goes without saying in the traditional western's version of the hero. Nevertheless, the figure of the heroic outsider that is central to the western does also suggest the powerful possibilities of Catherine's outsider position in the high-tech company she infiltrates in order to investigate a campaign of sexual harassment.

The name of Meg O'Brien's serial character—a hard-drinking, wise-cracking journalist for the Rochester *Herald*—similarly evokes the solitary hero of westerns: she is called Jessica James, or "Jesse" for short. The name calls attention to her ambivalent position as "outlaw": her situation in the business for which she works is precarious, not just because she is, as her boss puts it in *Salmon in the Soup*, lacking in "team spirit" (8), but also because she is an alcoholic. This borderline position is exacerbated by her romantic attachment to a male mobster, which she calls "my obsession for a man who lived outside the law" (6).[5] The attachment, in turn, evokes and contradicts yet another set of conventions (those of the gangster genre), since her attachment to the mob boss is decidedly un-moll-like. Another investigative journalist, Wendy Hornsby's Maggie MacGowen, also comically mixes generic conventions, slyly calling attention in a passing remark to the western origins as well as to the "revolutionary" nature of her hero. In preparation for a late-night excursion into a dangerous Los Angeles neighborhood, she accepts a weapon: "Feeling like Annie Oakley, or maybe Che Guevara, I took out the clip, zipped it inside my bag, and stowed the pistol under my seat" (*Bad Intent* 86). Interestingly, Maggie feels this sense of revolutionary power on *disarming* the gun. The most effective weapon she carries with her into East L.A. is not the pistol but the tools of her journalistic trade, a camera and tape recorder—and these tools have their equivalent in the representational skills wielded by her author. In *The Good Daughter*, Wendi Lee's private eye Angela Matelli distances herself from the cowboy image, deciding not to carry a gun with her everywhere because "I would feel a little too much like a gunfighter in the old west" (5). In April Smith's first novel featuring Ana Grey, *North of Montana*, an FBI coworker flirts with the investigator, adding eroticism to the image of the female gunslinger by jokingly calling her "Annie Oakley in black lace" (67). Catherine Dain's private eye Freddie O'Neal harbors a notable private obsession for cowboy movies.

Dana Stabenow's third Kate Shugak novel, *Dead in the Water*, also alludes to a tradition of outlaw folk-heroism. Stabenow's Alaskan investigator is conscripted into the crew of the *Avilda*, a deep-sea crab boat, in order to investigate secretly the suspicious disappearance of two crew members. With difficulty, Kate carves out a place for herself in the exclusively masculine, highly isolated, and physically punishing environment of the ocean crabber. At the conclusion of the novel, when Kate's efforts have solved the mystery and brought the criminals to justice, we finally learn the origins of the name of the craft on which she has been serving. Kate asks Nordensen, the owner, about his ships: "'What's the latest one's name?' Kate said. 'The *Mary Lovell*, wasn't it? The *Avilda*, the *Madam Ching*, the *Anne Bonney*. And now the *Mary Lovell*. Beautiful names. You have plans for a *Grace O'Malley* in the future?" (192). To the amazement of her male crewmates, Kate reveals that all the ships in the fleet have been named for female pirates:

> "I went over to the library at the Unalaska School this morning and looked them up in the encyclopedia. Avilda was some kind of Viking, Grace and Lady Killigrew terrorized the English Channel, Mary

and Anne shot up the Caribbean with Morgan and Blackbeard, and Madame Ching thought the south China Sea was her own private lake. Alaska Venture's boats are all named after lady pirates."

"Some of them not so much the lady," Nordensen reminded her. (193)

Again, the private eye is implicitly aligned with outlaw figures, in this case historical characters who are in violation of both the laws of the sea and the laws of gender-appropriate behavior. The analogy also suggests that Kate's subordinate, outsider role in the crew is retrospectively belied by her ultimate "command" of the situation on the ship—and indeed her protection of the entire fleet. Stabenow, like other women authors of revisionist detective novels, "pirates" the male adventure story as well as the detective plot, turning them to highly successful "illegitimate" ends by substituting a female hero. The argument Richard Goodkin makes about Paretsky's detective hero applies more generally to the outlaw status of the hero of the feminist private eye novel: "From the perspective of a conformist social order, her heroism, or difference, is itself a crime" (89). From the perspective of the rewritten genre, however, it is an extraordinary achievement.

In a more recent novel, *A Cold-Blooded Business,* Stabenow further complicates the scenario. In this novel Kate is hired to investigate drug use at an oil company's remote northern pumping station. Stabenow exploits the clichéd characterization of the "cowboy" nature of the oil business. Her heroine, however, is no cowboy but quite literally an Indian. The novel explores the conflicted position in which Kate finds herself as an Aleut working for an industry responsible for the exploitation of the northern environment and its aboriginal peoples (an environmental disaster much like the grounding of the *Exxon Valdez* figures in the story). It also characterizes her as both a gendered and racial "other" in relation to the CEO of the Alaskan division of the oil company: "He removed his cowboy hat, smoothed back his hair and reseated the hat with the air of a trail driver ready to ship the herd out to Abilene in the teeth of rustlers, tornadoes and hostile Indians. He looked across at Kate, yet another hostile Indian" (145).

Such gestures exemplify the multivalent subject position established in feminist detective novels. Stabenow creates, in effect, an Indian cow-girl (cow-woman?). Similarly, in Judith Van Gieson's recent novel *Parrot Blues*, investigator Neil Hamel contemplates with her boyfriend what Indians they might have been had they lived in the days before the conquest. "I'd like to have been Dextrous Horse Thief Woman," Neil speculates, naming an Apache woman. The analogy draws attention to a shared violation of the rules of legal and gendered behavior: "'She could ride, shoot and steal horses as well as any man.' Mythmaking for sure. The truth was, I hate riding, and I don't like horses. But I do like doing things as well as a man" (36). Another equivocal racialized outsider position is established in Marcia Muller's Sharon McCone series, in which her heroine is part Shoshone Indian; her gender and racial marginality are, in effect, conflated. In a 1984 interview, Muller described how she arrived at this aspect of Sharon's character: "In one of the early manuscripts . . . I hit on the idea of making Sharon part Indian. One of my old friends was a sort of throwback. The rest of the family were the proverbial 'tow-headed kids' with blonde hair and blue eyes—and there was this dark-haired, dark-skinned outsider of a sister. So I included it in Sharon" (qtd. in Isaac, "Situation, Motivation, Resolution" 22–23). In the early novels, Sharon develops a relationship with a police officer who sometimes addresses her with the nickname "papoose," explaining, "That's what they call little Indians, isn't it? Or would you rather I called you 'squaw.'" Sharon replies in a fury, "You have no business calling me either. I don't have to listen to your comments on my ancestry or on the way I look" (*Edwin of the Iron Shoes* 84). As Frederick Isaac observes, the character's persistent use of the demeaning name implies his feeling of superiority, as a police officer and as a man—more particularly, as a *white* man ("Situation, Motivation, Resolution" 25). The "joking" slurs become an increasing source of friction in the relationship.

FORCIBLE EXITS

It is, of course, conventional for the outlaw status of the hard-boiled hero to be established by his history as a former police officer, whether he has quit because of disaffection with (or contravention of) the restrictive power structures of the force, or the breakdown of the legal bureaucracy, or the corruption of its various aspects. Women practitioners of the private eye genre have also often created characters who have become disillusioned with a law enforcement career. Sue Grafton's Kinsey Millhone, for example, is an ex–police officer. In *"B" Is for Burglar*, Kinsey describes how her alienation from the occupation grew:

> I went through the police academy when I was twenty, joining Santa
> Teresa Police Department on graduation. I don't even remember
> now how I pictured the job before I took it on. I must have had
> vague, idealistic notions of law and order, the good guys versus the
> bad, with occasional court appearances in which I'd be asked to tes-
> tify as to which was which. In my view, the bad guys would all go to
> jail, thus making it safe for the rest of us to carry on. After a while, I
> realized how naïve I was. I was frustrated at the restrictions and frus-
> trated because back then, policewomen were viewed with a mixture
> of curiosity and scorn. I didn't want to spend my days defending my-
> self against "good-natured" insults, or having to prove how tough I
> was again and again. I wasn't getting paid enough to deal with all
> that grief, so I got out. (1)

Added to the conventional cynicism about the ability of the law to mete out a moral code of justice ethically and efficiently, Kinsey also perceives injustices in the law enforcement system itself—in this case not corruption but enforcement of a stereotypical and misogynist gender code. Grafton thus creates what Sandra Tomc calls the "adversarial space," key to the feminist detective's position (47).

Kathy Hogan Trocheck's Callahan Garrity, Linda Barnes's Carlotta Carlyle, Liza Cody's Anna Lee, Sandra West Prowell's Phoebe Siegel, and Valerie Wilson Wesley's Tamara Hayle are all also former police officers. Their point of view enables these characters to see both inside and outside the law. They are in a position to observe the functioning of legal institutions and the very nature of institutional authority. They also sometimes comment on the way such institutions routinely exclude women, or fail to serve and protect women's interests or those of other marginalized groups. Perhaps the most striking example of the latter involves Wesley's African American detective Tamara Hayle, now owner-operative of Hayle Investigative Services, Inc. In the first novel in the series, Tamara is spurred on in her investigation of the death of her ex-husband's son because she recognizes from her experience as a police officer the racism behind the force's inadequate action on the case. The reader eventually learns that Tamara resigned her position when police racism came home to roost in what she calls her young son's "initiation into black manhood" (111). Tamara describes one evening when Jamal, a nine-year-old, accompanies his baby-sitter Marvin and several other teenage friends on a trip to the mall, driving a little faster that they should:

> They, my brethren in blue, pulled them over because of the speed, they said, to a side street off the road, and got nasty when Marvin gave them some lip. They bloodied his nose for being a "smart-ass nigger" then knocked him around for good measure and asked if "anybody else wanted some." Jamal peed his pants. When he started to cry, they knew he was a kid, "big for his age," got scared and let them go. (*When Death Comes Stealing* 112)

In the eyes of the law the boys were "a car full of young black men cruising through Belvington Heights after dark in a late-model car, and that meant trouble" (112), but Tamara obviously sees the situation differently. In *Devil's Gonna Get Him*, the second book in the series, Tamara is asked by a prospective client why she left the force and she tells him she got "Sick of being called a nigger bitch every day of my beat" (6). Her use of the cliché "brethren in blue" is painfully ironic, for it describes a broth-

erhood that does not include her. The irony is underscored by her colloquial use of the word "sister" to describe and address her female black
friends. Although her superior officer is furious at the incident involving Tamara's son, and promises to punish the offending officers, Tamara
concludes her account, "I quit two weeks later, and everybody except Jamal thought I was crazy, but he was the one who counted" (*When Death
Comes Stealing* 112). "Going private," or leaving the force, is for Tamara
a way of acknowledging—and perhaps even redressing in some way—
the injustice done to her son and, by implication, the more widespread
injustices of the police.

And leaving the force more generally for women operatives involves
rejecting the gender codes it represents and enforces. One exception is
Eleanor Taylor Bland's character Marti MacAlister, who remains on the
police force despite the different codes of "legitimacy" it enforces on her,
based on her gender and race (she is African American). She stays because the job gives her a position of power, and this argument might also
be applied to Bland's own use of the police procedural mode. In *Slow
Burn*, for example, Marti considers another character's attitude that policing was "men's work," remarking that

> [This attitude] wasn't out of line with unofficial departmental policy.
> There were special rules for her: Be twice as good, twice as smart,
> and work twice as hard. She was no longer certain whether those
> rules existed because she was black, or because she was female. She
> accepted it because nobody would understand what she was talking
> about if she complained. She had never cared about wearing a uni-
> form or carrying a shield and a weapon, but valued the authority
> they represented. She hoped she wouldn't abuse what power she had,
> but she refused to be excluded from the exercise of power. (69)

Another obvious way of configuring an ambivalent relationship to the
institutions of the law is by making the professional investigator a lawyer
or former lawyer. Taffy Cannon's Nan Robinson, for example, is an investigator for the California State Bar, and Judith Van Gieson's Neil Hamel

is a lawyer/investigator. Stabenow's Kate Shugak is a former member of the Anchorage district attorney's investigative staff. Julie Smith's Rebecca Schwartz is a self-identified feminist attorney who, in *Death Turns a Trick*, represents an organization for the rights of prostitutes, women conventionally designated by the law as "criminals." Carolyn Wheat's investigator Cass Jameson, according to one of her friends, "went to law school to be a more effective rebel" (12), and the phrase is an apt one to describe the ambivalent role of the detective who uses legal, generic, and gender rules in order to counter them.

Sara Paretsky's V. I. Warshawski, a former legal aid lawyer who loses faith in the profession and becomes a private investigator, is perhaps the most prominent example of the lawyer-turned-investigator. In *Bitter Medicine* she meets police detective Conrad Rawlings, who notices that she has been wounded, and asks about her professional status:

> "Guess I've seen too many knife wounds in my time. I don't fool so easy—at least not over them. Now over the difference between a private eye and a lawyer, that stumps me sometimes. Which are you, Ms. W.—lawyer or detective?". . . .
>
> "Both, Detective. I'm a member of the Illinois bar in good standing. And I'm a licensed private investigator. Also in good standing. At least with the State of Illinois." (65)

The move from public to private sector affords a position of good standing from which to make observations on the legal system, a position now located outside the centers of power. And in a series, an elaborated analysis of various kinds of legal issues from novel to novel is possible. In *Guardian Angel*, V.I. explains to Detective Rawlings why her role conflicts with his:

> Conrad, I know there are good cops; my dad was one. But cops are like any other group of people—when they get together they act clannish. They like to show their collective muscle to people outside their clique. And society gives you guys a lot of power to bulk up your muscle. Sometimes I think my whole job consists of standing

outside different cliques—of cops or businessmen or whatever—
with a yellow flag to remind you that your outlook isn't the only
one. (260)

As Paretsky herself comments of her protagonist, "I find that she gives
me the opportunity to look in depth, and over time, at issues of law, society and justice" ("Writing a Series Character" 60). Sue Grafton makes
a similar point about the viability of the private eye genre as a whole: "I
think the private eye has always functioned literally as a private eye—as
an observer and as someone who comments on society and on family relationships and on the state of justice" (qtd. in Herbert 32).

Paretsky and Grafton are certainly not alone in this. In Michelle
Spring's *Running for Shelter*, PI Laura Principal is hired to find a missing Filipino maid and exposes in the process of her investigation the British justice system's inability to protect the most basic welfare of foreign
domestic servants. In Elisabeth Bowers's *No Forwarding Address*, Meg
Lacey also takes on a missing persons case—indeed, "missing persons"
might function as a synecdoche for those people who have been bypassed
or ignored by conventional systems of justice. Meg ultimately acts on behalf of the missing woman, a battered wife, who has good reason for going missing, since friends, family, and legal system cannot perceive the
peril in which she and her child live their daily lives. The community cannot, in other words, identify the domestic milieu as the scene of a crime.
In Marcia Muller's *Wild and Lonely Place*, Sharon McCone chooses to
neglect some of the responsibilities of her assignment to protect an em-
bassy so that she may be an advocate on behalf of an endangered child
who lives there. The novel's plot turns on the question of diplomatic immunity—the inability of the law to bring to account the illegal behavior of diplomatic personnel. In Linda Barnes's *Coyote*, Carlotta Carlyle
works to help a woman whose status the law does not recognize, an illegal immigrant. The case leads her to a series of unpublicized murders
of immigrant women: "Why isn't it in the papers?" she asks. "Because
they're poor women? Because they're illegals, Hispanics, nobodies?

Somebody kills off a bunch of rich white Brahmin ladies, I bet it makes the morning news" (82). Lia Matera's two series, which both feature lawyers, often negotiate the ambivalent legal terrain between licit and illicit, moral and immoral behavior. In *Designer Crimes*, Laura di Palma suspects that someone is designing crimes for wronged employees who have no legal recourse against employers who have acted against them in ways morally unacceptable but technically legal. The book thus introduces questions about moral versus legal fairness and about who gets to decide what is a crime.

Barbara D'Amato's novels also often turn on definitions and perceptions of crime itself: in *Hardball*, for instance, Cat Marsala investigates an organization campaigning to decriminalize drugs and treat drug addiction as a medical rather than a legal problem. In *Hard Luck*, Cat inquires into a proposal to create a giant lottery corporation; in *Hard Women*, prostitution is the subject of her scrutiny. D'Amato herself stresses the ambiguities surrounding such issues and makes clear that her novels turn on a distinction between individual practice and the systemic nature of the problems revealed by that practice: "Most of us are opposed to people damaging their minds with drugs, and yet we are the most medicated society the world has ever known. Most of us are opposed to people wasting their hard-earned money gambling, yet most Americans now live in lottery-legal states, where essentially public money goes into glossy ads convincing people to gamble. Most of us are opposed to prostitution, but where are all the customers coming from?" Such questions, implicit in D'Amato's novels, subtly interpellate the reader in defining the nature of criminality and its practice.

As the title of the opening chapter of Paretsky's *Tunnel Vision* implies, V. I. Warshawski's investigations almost always hinge on legal "power failure[s]" of one sort or another, and the roles of detective and legal advocate are at least theoretically conflated in Paretsky's novels (and many of the others listed above) as the investigations negotiate the intricacies of the legal system. Equally important, they develop the concept of advocacy on behalf of a client who, for one reason or another, has little or no conventional legal power to speak or act for him- or herself. In this sense, the detective acts as agent not just in her own right but also *for* the abjected "other." Her endeavors often represent by implication a fantasy that centers on an individualized version of (social) activism. And while the agency of the individual is key, this formula does not, as the originary hard-boiled novels did, discredit group action or define it as in itself criminal (Hamilton 31). The subgenre is different both because female private eyes often rely on social networks and because individual action on the part of the female character and her clients has *representational* value. It symbolizes the possibilities of women's agency—showing women's ability to act, even in a limiting social context. The female professional investigator novel thus offers a popular form of novelistic "legal representation," often for interests and issues that fall outside the law.

Examining writers such as Paretsky, Grafton, Katherine V. Forrest, and Barbara Wilson, Delys Bird and Brenda Walker note that the primary function of their female investigators is not simply to solve the crime and punish the criminals "but to attempt to heal those innocently involved in crimes. This derives from a recognition that both systems of justice and the concept of justice administered through patriarchal institutions and structures is deeply flawed and rarely recuperative for those people caught up in any criminal matter" (37). Interestingly, in speaking to her friend Dr. Lotty Herschel, V. I. Warshawski uses a similar medical metaphor to express the powerlessness she feels as an individual working against the systemic social problem of urban crime, and thus to explain her reluctance to investigate the violent death of one of Lotty's colleagues. The private eye, she claims, cannot combat crime in general, and solving one murder is as ineffectual as a doctor attending to a single patient in a cholera epidemic. Lotty responds: "Well, to use your analogy, if one friend I loved was dying in this epidemic, I would treat him, even if I couldn't stop the plague. And that's what I'm asking on Malcolm's behalf. Maybe you can't solve the crime, maybe the epidemic of gang violence is too big for anyone, even the state, to solve. But I am asking you, friend to friend, for a friend" (*Bitter Medicine* 38). This analogy highlights the way in which Paretsky's books in particular, and feminist detective novels in general, explore—and exploit—the possibilities of individual agency even as they expose the limitations of that agency. In the process they convey to their audience, especially women readers, both a sense of potential empowerment and a consciousness of systemic oppression.

"WHAT THE HELL WENT ON RATHER THAN WHO DONE IT"

While consciousness of oppression potentially impels agency, oppression itself obviously restricts it: this is a compelling and problematic combination for readers. Linda Grant's character Catherine Sayler alludes to just such an equivocal situation when she reflects, after an ineffectual interview with a known sexual harasser, "It's a very short jump from impotence to rage for me, and I made it as I walked back to my office" (*Woman's Place* 43). This kind of duality is reinforced in the narrative structure of feminist detective novels, as we will argue shortly. In *Bitter Medicine*, V.I. takes up Lotty's challenge to act as an individual, and by the end of that work the specific crimes introduced by the narrative have been solved: we discover the circumstances surrounding the murder of Dr. Malcolm Tregiere as well as the prior, related death of Consuelo, a young woman who dies in childbirth. This aspect of the case is therefore "closed" both in the legal sense that the individuals immediately responsible are exposed and in the literary sense that "the events of the story become fully intelligible to the reader" (Belsey 70). However, while the "criminal" elements of *the system* have been exposed by the narrative, those transgressions have not been *solved* in any significant way: the practice of medicine, as well as the complex extenuating multidimensional problematic of women's health, remains essentially the same at the end of the book as at the beginning—except, perhaps, that readers are made more aware of these issues than they were at the outset.

Raymond Chandler once drew attention to a similar kind of narrative complication when he characterized hard-boiled writing's rejection of the mechanical puzzle plots that define the traditional whodunit. Hard-boiled stories, he observed, are about a search "not for a specific criminal, but for a *raison d'être*, meaning in character and relationship, what the hell went on rather than who done it" (*Raymond Chandler Speaking* 57). For Paretsky and many other women writers of detective fiction, "what the hell went on" extends beyond even "meaning in character and relationship" to the ideological raison d'être of systemic crimes—"who done it" often turns out to be a societal entity. In Paretsky's novels, the narratives conventionalize a "doubled architecture,"[6] part of which works toward traditional closure but part of which *depends* on a lack of resolution. The traditional trajectory of Paretsky's plots satisfies the reader by solving individualized crimes against the person or property. These are the kind of crimes Marxist critics such as Ernst Kaemmel or Ernest Mandel would identify with the bourgeois individualist/capitalist tradition of the detective story. As Mandel puts it in *Delightful Murder*, "The detective story is the realm of the happy ending. The criminal is always caught. Justice is always done. Crime never pays. Bourgeois legality, bourgeois values, bourgeois society, always triumph in the end. It is soothing, socially integrating literature, despite its concern with crime, violence and murder" (47–48). The unresolved aspects of Paretsky's plots, however, tend to concern criminals who are not caught, justice that is not done, and crimes that do pay. These are often "corporate crimes," whether carried out by actual corporations (as is often the case) or committed by other institutionalized power groups, with communal victims; Paretsky's work therefore suggests a critique of the dominant social order. The narrative establishes the connection between individual and corporate crime in an interesting way: it frequently generates a recognition that the specific mystery that instigated the investigation is indexical of some larger wrongdoing. Through a process of metonymic displacement, the narrative reinterprets the initial crime as evidence of something else.

For example, as discussed above, *Bitter Medicine*'s investigation of the clearly defined murder of Malcolm Tregiere forces a reconsideration of Consuelo Hernandez's death in childbirth, which leads to questions about the practices of institutionalized corporate medicine and the "policing" of maternity. *Indemnity Only*, another of Paretsky's novels, begins as a missing persons case but leads to the exposure of a pension fraud that threatens the old age security—and thus the very lives—of workers. This discovery redefines the "paternal" role of the corporate structure as patriarchal in a distinctly negative sense—thereby making the corporation guilty of a combination of capital and capitalist crime. Corporate crime is also revealed in *Blood Shot*, when an investigation into the paternity of an old friend of V.I.'s becomes the thread that unravels the corporate "paternity" of a crime involving the toxic contamination by a chemical company of its own workers and the environment. Traditional "murder-by-poison" is thus reworked into a scenario that challenges corporate authority. The title of *Guardian Angel* refers at one level to the role of the detective, but it also alludes to the exploitative legal guardianship arranged for an incapacitated elderly woman and, ironically, to the absence of a social support network to protect her interests. The narrative of *Deadlock* implicates the shipping industry not just in murder but in systemic corruption. *Burn Marks* begins with a bothersome visit by V.I.'s Aunt Elena, but the narrative leads to the exposure of unethical practices in low-income housing developments, city politics, and the police. This novel is not simply set in the conventional seedy urban setting; it investigates the institutional, economic, and social causes of urban decay. In *Tunnel Vision*, the detective plot proper, which begins with a murder in V.I.'s office, expands to "in-corporate" issues concerning homelessness, family violence, and financial fraud.

Richard Goodkin's statement about *Killing Orders* might well sum up the way Paretsky's narratives—and the narratives of other women in the genre—work toward a sense of resolution while simultaneously opening up new dimensions of both crime and the crime story. In solving the case, Goodkin argues, "V.I. recognizes that the social order is a killing, repressive force, a tyranny which bases its authority on combatting a disorder which it can neither tolerate nor do without" (104). In *Killing Orders*, the social, economic, legal, and religious orders are linked. Paretsky's narratives culminate in the exposure of the institutions that support the social order as *systemically* criminal.

The narrative of the traditional detective story is driven by the reader's desire to solve an enigma, to be fully informed (in the terms of the story) by its conclusion. The narrative thus rehearses a recuperative movement from ignorance, injustice, and weakness to knowledge, justice, and power.[7] However, in feminist hard-boiled novels, at the same time as the narrative forecloses on the enigmatic aspect of individual crimes in a traditional way, it is also structured according to the disclosure of less easily resolved endemic injustices and oppressions, making possible a level of social or psychological inconclusiveness and thus critique. Knowledge in such novels does not necessarily confer power or justice in any simple equation. In a televised interview, Paretsky identified this aspect of her novels' conclusions:

> In general, I think that you do not change or affect entrenched powerful institutions and my books make that clear, that I have no expectation that life is going to be made better in Chicago or America as the result of V.I.'s work. You know, the people who actually murder or do mayhem in my books are hired hands of the wealthy elite. The books make it clear that after the curtain falls these guys are going to be let off with fines or slaps on the hand or even nothing at all and that those systems will stay in place. (interview by Richler)

Thomas Schatz's study of Hollywood genre films underscores their importance as "social problem solving operations" (24). He assesses the way in which these films achieve popularity by "repeatedly confront[ing] the ideological conflicts (opposing value systems) within a certain cultural community, suggesting various solutions through the actions of the main characters" (24). In other words, they address social issues near and dear to their audience (sometimes in a disguised form) and resolve them in the course of telling an entertaining story—or, rather, they tell an entertaining story *because* they address such issues in a displaced, satisfying way. The catch, of course, is that the narrative demand for a happy ending is in conflict with the complexity and entrenchment of the ideological issues at stake; the actions of the characters cannot adequately address the kind of problems that the story raises. The "narrative rupture" (Schatz 32) produced by this conflict is usually repressed by popular formula fiction, which attempts to reinforce a pacifying feeling of closure by diverting the audience's attention from any unresolved levels of meaning.

In feminist detective novels, however, self-consciousness about such conflicts becomes part of the formula itself, creating an unsettling disruption of established norms. There is, evidently, something compelling to the readers of these works about the balance they achieve between an awareness of resolution and rupture, as well as between the feelings of passivity they provoke and the necessity for and possibility of active response. The narrative strategies involved represent an important development of the formal conventions of the detective plot, one that elaborates on the American hard-boiled story's tendency to represent crime as integrated into society rather than simply "detachable" from it, as crime had been depicted in the British cozy tradition (Mandel 46).

Women writers of serial detective fiction have often turned this tendency to feminist and analytical ends. In their writing, the world outside the novel tends to be implicated in the crimes within. Liza Cody, like Paretsky, draws attention to the ways in which her own plots often remain unresolved: "When I finish a book I very rarely finish on the note that a wrong has been righted and somebody brought to justice because quite frequently they aren't. A lot has been explained, but not a lot will be done about it" (interview by Richler). Here Cody identifies a significant disjunction in her narratives between knowledge ("a lot has been explained") and power ("but not a lot will be done about it"). The narrative interest in Cody's novel *Headcase*, for instance, like that of Bowers's *No Forwarding Address*, shifts from finding a missing young woman to finding out why she has run away and how she has been victimized. And, as Glenwood Irons and Joan Roberts perceive, while technically the narrative allows the reader knowledge of the crime and its solution, the knowledge that the origins of the crime remain unremedied is palpably unsettling: "As in life, where there are few simple solutions, the solution of the murder in *Headcase* leaves us with a sense of emptiness since it does not explain away the victimization of the central character, Thea Hahn. In fact, the prime victimizer, Thea's father, simply believes that his daughter's mind has been 'poisoned' against him by the use of drugs" (70). They observe, "Cody avoids the relatively straightforward solutions of the [P. D. James] Cordelia Gray novels, preferring to leave Anna with a sense of emptiness at the desperate future faced by her clients and even by herself. This kind of ending is indeed a Cody trademark" (71).

Linda Grant's novels also frequently evoke such disjunctions. Grant's detective Catherine Sayler specializes in investigations into corporate and financial operations. She often uncovers the corruption secreted in computer systems, which might well function as an extended metaphor for the idea of "systemic crime." In *A Woman's Place*, for instance, Catherine is hired to track down a hacker who has been using his skills to manipulate computer systems in order to sexually harass women employees of a male-dominated high-tech company. What begins as a series of distressing sexual pranks (the sending of obscene anonymous e-mail messages and photographs to women employees) escalates into a succession of violent sexual murders of women, highlighting the destructive potential of the word "hacker." The narrative suggests a continuity between figural and literal assaults on women, as both are intended to eradicate them from positions of power in the workplace. When her male business partner insists on the distinction between depictions and enactments of men's violent sexual fantasies, Catherine stresses the dynamic of power at stake in representation and the deployment of power in the "real" world: "You think this is about sex?" she says; "I think it's about the same thing the Klan's about. It's just a different set of victims" (47).

Furthermore, the aggressive acts presented in the novel stand in for the phenomenon of sexual harassment at large, in both its subtle and obvious forms. The novel may thereby hint at the potential of popular fictional representations to voice the power inequities of the real world, even if it can't solve them. At the same time, the investigation exposes an unsettled—and unsettling—dysfunction (sexual harassment) that is a routine aspect of the working world. For instance, during an interview with the corporation's vice president, Catherine pointedly asks him about "larger patterns of harassment," tacitly accusing him of the sexual intimidation for which he is well known in the company. He responds by directing her back to the specific case at hand: "The pranks are the problem here" (42). Catherine's narration, however, muses on the relationship between her own role in the case she has undertaken and the harassment scenario: "Just as the hand on the thigh wasn't about sex, this wasn't about the prankster. It was about power, pure and simple. Seeing who blinked first" (42–43).

This aspect of the novel highlights one of the features of the female private investigator potentially most attractive to readers—working (to some degree) outside the entrenched power structure, she is able to act effectively against it: this is the feminist version of Chandler's detective as redemptive knight errant, who walks the "mean streets" but "is neither tarnished nor afraid" ("Simple Art" 237). Julie Smith, author of the Skip Langdon and Rebecca Schwartz mysteries, has called attention to her own appropriation and displacement of Chandler's metaphor:

> I think about my work now as "mean rooms," a twist on Chandler's concept of the "Mean Streets." The concept of evil I'm trying to describe relates to ordinary but horribly cruel things in life, what happens in your own house, where you ought to feel safe and comfortable. That is what fascinates me these days. I also think of this as related to women and our issues. Men battle other men for power in obvious ways, while women struggle with emotional traumas and more intimate but terrifying sources of terror. (qtd. in Isaac, "Investigator of Mean Rooms" 9)

Smith's comments help explain the feminist detective story's frequent interest in domestic crimes, especially domestic violence, but they are clearly applicable to other sorts of "mean rooms" too. In *No Forwarding Address*, Elisabeth Bowers makes it clear that the scene of the crime is not always an obviously "criminal" external, urban locale. The interiors of suburbia can be mean, too: "When you grow up as I did, in a middle-class Canadian home, you are taught that evil exists elsewhere, in other neighborhoods, other countries. You see it on television; it stays on the other side of the glass. Now, of course, I know that behind those closed suburban doors of my childhood the usual atrocities were being committed: wife battering, child abuse, murder, rape" (3).

KNIGHTS AND PAWNS

As Chandler's "Simple Art of Murder" makes clear, the quest motif is a topos of traditional hard-boiled narratives.[8] This is a narrative in which a lone hero pursues a lofty moral goal, though the hard-boiled novel's secular version often materializes and ironizes the quest. For example, in Hammett's *Maltese Falcon* Sam Spade embarks on an overtly materialist quest for a valuable religious icon associated with the Crusades (123). In *The Big Sleep* Philip Marlowe's quest to "save" Carmen Sternwood is ironically foreshadowed in a stained-glass panel in the Sternwood home that shows

> a knight in dark armor rescuing a lady who was tied to a tree and
> didn't have any clothes on but some very long and convenient hair.
> The knight had pushed the visor of his helmet back to be sociable,
> and he was fiddling with the knots on the ropes that tied the lady to
> the tree and not getting anywhere. I stood there and thought that if
> I lived in the house, I would sooner or later have to climb up there
> and help him. He didn't seem to be really trying. (3–4)

The quest narrative of *The Big Sleep*, it turns out, is not really about "freeing" a damsel in distress; but in identifying the feminine source

‿eing that the dangerous influence of the femme fatale is
‿olled—Marlowe, in other words, doesn't free the damsel—he ensures that she is restrained.

The same topos is central to women's detective fiction. As Linda
Grant comments, the American hard-boiled novel is "a quest, in which
the detective encounters something and is tested, defines himself
through his actions. . . . I wanted to explore that test within the female
context." The story of the investigation does propose a comforting "solution" to the problem *within* the narrative, and in doing so it offers a
sense of vicarious vindication to readers: the plot of Grant's *Woman's
Place*, for example, culminates with Catherine's confrontation of the
murderer after he has taken her prisoner. This is a variant on the "mor-
tal conflict" that is the culmination of many quest stories. She decides,
"I could play into his fantasy—weep and beg, dissolve into hysterics so
completely that he'd have to slap me to regain control. Or I could play
counter. I could challenge him, goad him to rage so strong that he'd
want to strike me" (242). Catherine "plays counter" in part by reversing
patriarchal discourse, talking back and talking tough. She calls attention
to the gendered dynamics of the situation by the mocking use of a
Freudian cliché: "They say men who like big guns have small dicks. Does
your gun make you feel powerful?" When the killer threatens to "make
you so sorry. I'll . . ." Catherine retorts with sarcasm, "You'll what? Shoot
me? Hit me with your big gun? I'm terrified" (243). Language itself becomes a defensive weapon—and perhaps even a parodically phallicized
one, since Catherine does verbally cut her opponent off, and she is, after
all, herself a "dick." At the same time, however, the narrative reminds
readers that patriarchal power, as it is embodied in corporate sexual harassment, remains intact.

Nancy Baker Jacobs's books are also striking examples of the way
feminist detective narratives often assign guilt to powerful conservative
structures and forces that exist in some recognizable form outside the
novel. Her novels tend to constitute those organizations and impulses as
"criminal" not just because they are responsible for specific crimes but

because of how they perpetuate various kinds of oppression. Again, the narrative opens up questions about criminality and its social contexts and causes even as it closes in on the particular crime's solution. *The Silver Scalpel*, for example, like Paretsky's *Bitter Medicine*, traces an investigation that uncovers the unethical, and ultimately murderous, activities of a religious antiabortion group. In *The Turquoise Tattoo*, private detective Devon McDonald is hired to search for a potential genetic match for a sick child who requires a bone marrow transplant, and this search develops into a murder investigation in which a white supremacist organization is implicated. The latter organization's obsession with racial purity is an indecent variation on the theme of genetic integrity with which Devon's inquiries humanely begin and end. *A Slash of Scarlet* investigates a "lonely hearts" ad scam. The case exposes women's passive imbrication in idealized notions of romantic love, which makes them susceptible to sexual and economic victimization by men. That novel ends with Devon making public, on a popular televised talk show, the scheme of the con man who had exploited a series of women by playing on their romantic illusions. "For now," the narrator comments, "all any of them could hope for was a chance to warn other lonely and gullible women against falling in love too quickly with a man who seems too good to be true" (246). In a sense this talk show finale epitomizes the way in which the narrative of the novel as a whole (and others like it) offers a popularized public venue for women (and men) to talk about such issues, opening them up as fare for discussion. The last lines of the novel indicate the beginning of the talk show: "I swallowed, took a deep breath and smiled at the camera. The red light went on" (246).

READING BEYOND RESOLUTION

The feminist detective novel manages a tense negotiation of conflicts internal and external to its story. The individualized crimes of detective fiction are comfortably contained within the fictional world, both because they are resolved and because they are limited to fictional characters in fictional situations, however realistically portrayed. The detective can solve the individual crime *in* the novel, but the reader knows from her or his own experience that the broader problems it raises extend beyond the borders of the book. Readers must thus recognize their own continuing involvement with, implication in, or oppression by the defective system that the novel has exposed. Grant, for example, calls attention to the continuity between "internal" and "external" crimes in the acknowledgments to *A Woman's Place* when she thanks "the many women who shared their stories of sexual harassment and intimidation with me. Many of the incidents in this book are drawn from their experiences" ([vii]). The continuity between the world inside and outside the novel is also affirmed by vernacular realism's tendency to set the narrative in a contemporaneous historical period, which is then often referred to directly—such as Paretsky's mention of Reagan's policies in *Bitter Medicine*. In the preface to *Guardian Angel*, Paretsky explicitly calls her character one "who exists in historical time," noting that her books take place in the year she writes them (x). Lia Matera grounds the labor-relations plot of *Designer Crimes* in historical reality by having her hero comment that "the skeleton of old labor laws, picked clean by the 'right-to-work' forces of the eighties, were rarely enforced by the National Labor Relations Board," as well as by having her mention the Reagan and Bush administrations by name (87). In *Running for Shelter*, Michelle Spring quotes from a 1994 issue of the *Guardian* newspaper that, in turn, cites a 1913 inquiry into the conditions of domestic service, ironically revealing how little things have changed in the intervening decades ([viii]). Dana Stabenow includes a mock disclaimer in the form of an author's note at the beginning of *A Cold-Blooded Business:*

> This book is a work of fiction. There's no such man as John King.
> There is no RPetCo. There were never any drugs at Prudhoe Bay.
> There wasn't any booze, either. Nobody ever wrapped duct tape
> around the TransAlaska Pipeline; turtles never raced at the Base
> Camp; two women never sold $20,000 worth of magazine subscrip-

tions in two days at Crazyhorse; nobody's ever sold Native American artifacts to the Detroit Institute of Arts for $55,000; no oil company ever spilled ten million gallons of oil into Prince William Sound; and I've got some land for sale in Wasilla, guaranteed swamp-free, beneath which Arco's about to find a natural gas field the size of the Sadlerochit. (viii)

Such gestures suggest a continuity between the social order portrayed in the book and the social order in the world in which the book is read, creating a dialogic relationship between the two. The satisfactions afforded the reader who vicariously experiences the exciting, heroic actions of the protagonist and the resolution of the mystery at the center of the plot are reinforced by the sense that the novel's narrative is both plotted by and may be plotted onto the world outside the borders of the book—that is, that the plot's resolution is somehow *meaningful* to the reader in more than simply a formal sense. Yet the degree to which the narrative is meaningful also depends on its *lack* of formal closure, on the lingering sense that it remains unresolved, that the narrative is engaged with ongoing social relations, and that the female private eye novel is therefore still challenging to—or able to plot against—the rules of gender and genre. The iterative character of the series form itself depends on this lack of closure and the need for continuing negotiations. Both character and narrative thus retain their potentially subversive position as (to borrow Carroll John Daly's metaphor) "a halfway house" of fiction, able to work both sides of the law.

Chapter 7

"SHE'S WATCHING THE DETECTIVES"

The Woman PI in Film and Television

[The femme fatale] is not the subject of feminism but a
symptom of male fears about feminism.

Mary Ann Doane, *Femmes Fatales*

CHERCHEZ LA FEMME

While the hypothetical woman viewer suggested in our chapter title may
watch any number of cinematic detectives detecting a surfeit of crimes,
very few of the detectives she watches will be women. Although the publishing industry has witnessed a virtual explosion in tough gal PIs since
the early 1980s, the mean streets of Hollywood have so far proved a dead
end for the female dick. Given the financial imperatives of feature films
and the obvious profit potential of the revisionary mode already demonstrated by the book business, it is curious that Hollywood has not capitalized on the woman detective, especially since television has demonstrated the value of this character: she has appeared in a number of
prime-time television series and episodic dramas. The presences and ab-
sences of the female PI in visual media raise interesting questions about

the ways generic change is produced differently in novels, films, and television. Traditional mysteries often take as part of their modus operandi the goal of "*cherchez la femme*," since the woman is typically represented as the object of mystery and desire from the point of view of male investigators and audiences. It now becomes important to turn that investigation to locating the position of the woman as a subject of visual representation.

Though the woman detective is absent as the prime subject (though not as the prime suspect) in most mainstream Hollywood productions, she has made some appearances—and disappearances—on both the silver and small screen. A number of films featuring active female investigators have been produced over the past decade, most notably Jonathan Demme's *Silence of the Lambs*, Kathryn Bigelow's *Blue Steel*, and Rod Holcomb's *Donato and Daughter*. These films all portray women agents who operate in the service of law enforcement agencies (the FBI and the New York and Los Angeles Police Departments, respectively). Each of these films conforms to the "police procedural" mode, tracking the female agent/officer's efforts to detect a criminal from her institutional position and detailing the step-by-step methodology of her investigation. To varying degrees, each also dramatizes the problems women encounter within institutional sites, thus providing some critique of conventionally male-defined (institutional and generic) spaces. However, because the female cop works on behalf of the law (and, hence, works in the "Name of the Father," in the Lacanian sense) her agency is also recuperated by the public institutions she represents. Consequently, she performs differently from the female PI, who works as a private operative peripheral to (if not actually outside) the law.

By and large, the woman PI represents a position more threatening to social norms than the female cop, since the latter is sworn to uphold and to protect the law of the state, and since the former is in part defined by her resistance to it. Interestingly, the adaptation of the female PI to film has been limited to Jeff Kanew's *V. I. Warshawski*, a work that, we will argue, strategically reverses the reversals produced by feminist versions of the hard-boiled detective novel and thus effectively undercuts the (detective) agency of its protagonist. Indeed, some feminist critics argue that the conventional structure of the Hollywood production system itself precludes this agency. As Jackie Byars intimates, changes to the concept "detective" and changes in gender definition are inextricably linked (128). It may be that the particular shift in gender definition required for the cinematic representation of the hard-boiled female investigator is simply too hot for Hollywood to handle, given the ways its modes of production and marketing as well as its audiences differ from even mass-market novels. Certainly, "gals with guns" who operate outside the law have been a staple of mainstream cinema's offerings,[1] but those gals have always been constructed as armed and *dangerous*.

The film noir of the 1940s and early 1950s attempted to reproduce the style of hard-boiled pulp novels by using an expressionistic representational method characterized by chiaroscuro lighting effects, claustrophobic interiors, dark urban exteriors, and dialogue that often borrowed from the tough cynical language of the written works.[2] Along with the conventions of narrative, verbal, and visual style, the film genre developed a set of sexually charged iconic characterizations. Thomas Schatz suggests that film noir "tinged Hollywood's traditional macho-redeemer hero and domesticating heroine with a certain ambiguity" (114). The noir hero resembled his textual predecessor in that he performed as a solitary agent who fought corruption according to his own individualistic moral code. That ethos was reflected in the film's morally and visually coded characterizations of women, which relegated them either to the role of "good girl," often a sexually neutral secretary, or to the figure of the femme fatale, a character whose seductive charms always concealed a deadly trap. As Jon Tuska writes, in the films noirs of the 1940s and 1950s the femme fatale, a powerful woman in possession of her own sexuality, "behaves as if she is independent of the patriarchal order. In the course of the film therefore, or at least by the end of it, the *femme fatale* must be punished for this attempt at independence, usually by her death, thus restoring the balance of the patriarchal system" (199).

Not surprisingly, the emergence of these noir character types coincided with the gender-role anxiety and the cultural depression that developed during and immediately after World War II. Schatz incisively correlates "this changing visual portrayal" with the cultural attitudes of the time:

> Hollywood's *noir* films documented the growing disillusionment with certain traditional American values in the face of complex and often contradictory social, political, scientific, and economic developments. On the one hand, big business and widespread urban growth offered Americans increased socioeconomic opportunity but on the other, it left them with a feeling of deepening alienation. Changing views of sexuality and marriage were generated by the millions of men overseas and by the millions of women pressed into the work force. The postwar "return to normalcy" never really materialized—the GI's triumphant homecoming only seemed to complicate matters and to bring out issues of urban anonymity and sexual confusion. Two fashionable intellectual and literary trends of the period were existentialism and Freudian psychology, both formally articulating the individual, familial, and mass-cultural concerns which were troubling postwar America. (113–14)

The cultural anxieties and sexual tensions arising during the war and postwar periods contributed to the ideological negotiations of film noir.

Another important element in its production and dissemination was the organization of the Hollywood studio system.[3] The 1940s were the heyday of the Hollywood production system, and in that decade more people went to the movies than ever before. Large and dependable audiences were drawn to the "double bill," which paired higher-budget "A" films with low-budget "B" genre offerings—usually westerns or gangster or detective films. These genre films were economically made and thus provided a larger reliable profit than did their more costly counterparts on the bill. The vertically integrated studio systems guaranteed the wide exposure of the B films, since studios owned chains of theaters in which to show their offerings. They also gathered together stables of stars, contract players, and directors to serve as the relatively cheap labor force that the demanding production schedules required. As is true of genre fiction, genre film was economical because of its standardized plots, characterizations, and styles; its industrial mode of production; and its mass audiences.

The late 1940s and the 1950s, however, saw the demise of the studio system. The successful enforcement of antitrust laws in 1948 gradually broke down the studios' integrated structure. Shortly thereafter, the increase in production costs arising from technological innovations such as Technicolor, together with the decrease in theater attendance resulting from the emergence of television, brought about changes in the Hollywood system. By the 1960s, mainstream production largely focused on the creation of blockbuster films—movies with high budgets and bankable stars, often produced by independent production companies and distributed under the remaining studios' auspices. At the same time, stars, no longer under continuing obligation to studios (which had contractually demanded their performance in low-budget offerings), were able to pick and choose their vehicles—and, to some extent, to name their price. This resulted in the performer's equivalent of the blockbuster film: the superstar actor.

As a result, although westerns and detective films were still produced, they were less frequent (no longer ensured by the double bill) and less economical. Noir as a generic style itself was largely lost, in part because of the dominance of color technology. The hard-boiled hero, nevertheless, outlived the film noir era, appearing in high-budget offerings including Roman Polanski's *Chinatown* (1974), Robert Altman's *Long Goodbye* (1973), and Lawrence Kasdan's *Body Heat* (1981). Traces of the noir femme fatale resurface significantly in a series of films made during the Reagan and Bush administrations, which, as Susan Faludi has argued, oversaw a backlash against feminism. The cultural panic produced by the emergence of strong independent (and often single) women as a cultural and economic force is played out in a series of films (e.g., *Fatal Attrac-*

tion, The Hand That Rocks the Cradle, Basic Instinct, and *Disclosure*) that demonize and punish a sexually threatening single woman who jeopardizes the integrity of the nuclear family. This figure, like both the femme fatale of film noir and her novelistic prototype, manifests great uneasiness about sexual roles.

The problematic nature of women's depiction in mainstream American cinema may be linked to the nature of the Hollywood production system and the conventions of style and technique it developed. Jackie Stacey, for example, in summarizing early feminist analyses of Hollywood film, details the ways in which conventional narrative films visually undercut the performance of an active female character: "In popular cinema point-of-view shots and shot/reverse-shot editing techniques are used to achieve the effect of seeing the female characters as objects of desire through the eyes of the male characters. The conventions of Hollywood narrative cinema construct a particular spectator position, then, whilst carefully covering up the ways in which this is achieved" (21). The gendered dynamic of visual spectatorship Stacey describes also extends to audio effects. Kaja Silverman offers a provocative analysis of the ways in which audio and visual effects work to exclude women both as authoritative subjects of representation and as spectators interpellated by the film text. Affirming that it "is by now axiomatic that the female subject is the object rather than the subject of the gaze in mainstream narrative cinema," Silverman argues that

> Classical cinema projects these [gender] differences at the formal as
> well as the thematic level. Not only does the male subject occupy
> positions of authority within the diegesis, but occasionally he also
> speaks extra-diegetically, from the privileged place of the Other.
> The female subject, on the contrary, is excluded from positions of
> discursive authority both inside and outside the diegesis, she is con-
> fined not only to safe places *within* the story (to positions, that is,
> which come within the eventual range of male vision or audition),
> but to the safe place *of* the story. Synchronization provides the
> means of that confinement. (131–32)

Silverman's comments are particularly apropos to the hard-boiled film persona, who is sometimes represented through voice-over narration and extradiegetically directed commentary.

Yet the workings of "classic" Hollywood production technique to undercut the discursive authority of female protagonists do not entirely prevent viewers from producing resistant readings. As feminist film critic and filmmaker Michelle Citron argues, "The potential for subversion in a mainstream context nonetheless does exist" (61), even though that potential is limited by the film industry's economic and gender power structures. Citron suggests that mainstream cinema has produced conventional representations of women in part because very few female directors work in that medium, and those that do often have little money at their disposal:

> Most women directors working in Hollywood have been confined to traditional women's genres such as melodrama—Lee Grant's *Tell Me a Riddle* (1980), Amy Jones's *Love Letters* (1983); or comedy—Amy Heckerling's *National Lampoon's European Vacation* (1983); Lis Gottlieb's *One of the Boys* (1985), Susan Seidelman's *Desperately Seeking Susan* (1985). Few have been allowed to direct detective films, thrillers, or science fiction, genres which are "male" as well as more expensive to produce. (61)

The assumption that female filmmakers will make feminist films and male filmmakers misogynist ones is overly simplistic, as Citron herself admits; moreover, "women's genres" are often venues for the exploration of strong women characters.

Ridley Scott's 1991 film *Thelma and Louise*, written by Callie Khouri, raises questions about the production of generically subversive films featuring female protagonists, especially in light of the critical controversy it generated. As the reviews compiled by the University of Minnesota's Women's Studies Department suggest,[4] the prospect of culturally "unlicensed" female characters with guns troubled many viewers, although the representation of men in a similar position has long been fully licensed by Hollywood genres like the gangster film, the detective film, the western, and even the male "buddy" caper/chase movies on which *Thelma and Louise* was modeled. The furor over *Thelma and Louise* offers some insights into why Hollywood has been reluctant to take up the female private eye. The dearth of female Hollywood writers, directors, producers, and studio executives certainly contrasts with the number of women writers, editors, and agents active in the publishing industry's decision-making processes. The publishing industry may well be more amenable to experimenting and developing alternative genre markets; after all, the production costs of generic experiments in novels are quite small when compared to the relatively large financial outlay needed for even a low-budget film. It may be that the publishing industry differs from Hollywood in that its female consumers have an established track record of supporting so-called women's genres such as romances, whereas filmmakers have traditionally tended to target male viewers, especially following the advent of the blockbuster phenomenon and the lucrative spin-off marketing associated with it (Francke 99).

Genre works are predicated on particular material conditions: they provide audiences with a cheap and readily available source of entertainment, and they draw on iconographies, narrative patterns, and conventions of characterization that become familiar through frequent repetition. Consistent exposure to formula fiction is crucial, since it functions *generically:* the works perform as a group, rather than as individual texts or single events. When, like the female private eye novels we have examined, works function as installments in a series, they repeat not just the conventions of the genre but those established for the series itself.[5] As John Ellis contends, however, contemporary film production demands that its products be single, "complete in themselves and distinct from other films" (30). Genre films are still produced today, but not in the same way as during Hollywood's classic era, in part because current films can no longer rely on the large and dependable audiences delivered to B films by the A features of the 1940s. Marketing strategies have also changed. Ellis claims that while generic codes continue to locate a film in relation to similar films, "the demands of marketing also dictate that the film should be able to function as a distinct entity. It cannot be simply the repetition of other films" (34). The individuality constructed by many current films distinguishes them from genre novels, which are experienced not as "special" events but as part of a continuing process of interacting with the genre in an intimate, informal, and often domestic reading setting. For the price of $5 to $7, paperbacks can be read, reread, traded, or resold; engagement with film generally consists of a single viewing that carries a higher price tag, especially because "going to the movies" comprises a whole set of consumer activities. As Ellis argues, the viewer's position among "an anonymous group of people . . . the crowd with its sense of belonging and loneliness" is central to the experience of watching a film (26). The very nature of the cinema renders it a viewing locale more obviously positioned in public space and thus, perhaps, a more inherently risky social locus for the performance of subversive generic acts. And the irregular nature of current moviegoing also works against the gradual and consistent exposure to generic conventions necessary for a formula to mediate alternative representations.[6]

IN LIKE A LION, OUT LIKE A LAMB

That Hollywood is more likely to integrate female characters into a conventional generic format without fundamentally threatening its norms than to reverse the ideological trajectory of the genre is one way of explaining the adaptation of the police film to accommodate female characters.[7] While the female character is assimilated into the institutions of law and order within the film, the role of female agency is controlled by the rules and restrictions of the police procedural genre. The character's potential as an outlaw figure is consequently diminished. Yet even though the female cop's agency may be strictly regulated, her appearance is a significant gesture that rescripts a historically male-identified genre. Jonathan Demme's *Silence of the Lambs* (1991) provides a case in point. The film portrays the contributions of an FBI trainee, Clarice

Starling (played by Jodie Foster), to apprehending a serial killer. Clarice's ambivalent position within the male milieu of the FBI academy and the scene of gendered film spectatorship is set up in the opening frames of the film, as Clarice runs through the woods. The camera follows her with a series of long shots and tracking shots that, when coupled with the audio track of her ragged breathing, presents a scenario familiar to viewers conditioned to expect trouble when they see women running through woods alone: the woman in jeopardy. As viewers expect, Clarice is accosted by a man, but when the camera zooms in on the FBI logo stitched to his hat, those expectations are both foregrounded and countered: he has interrupted her training to solicit her help in an investigation. Rather than being a victim, Clarice is quite literally an agent, though she is, it becomes clear, a subordinated agent-in-training. This opening dynamic is repeated through the course of the film, as Clarice's status teeters back and forth between the possibilities of female agency and the conventions associated with the voyeuristic appeal of female victimization.

Jack Crawford, the head of the FBI's behavioral sciences unit, asks Clarice to develop a psychobehavioral profile of convicted serial killer Hannibal "the Cannibal" Lecter. What he does not tell Clarice is that Lecter has information about the serial killer "Buffalo Bill" (who "skins his humps"), whom Crawford is investigating. Clarice is thus a part of Crawford's team, and yet not a part; she is both subject of the investigation and a lure for Lecter. Lecter's psychiatrist, for example, comments on Crawford's intelligence in sending "a pretty young woman to turn him [Lecter] on." He adds, "And are you ever to his taste," attaching a sexual element to the film's black humor about Lecter's trademark— eating his victims. As Clarice enters Lecter's ward, she is subjected to lewd comments from the other patients; one hisses, "I can smell your cunt." Clarice is thus sexually objectified by the doctor and his patients, as she struggles to assert her subjectivity as the interviewing agent. And her subordinate role as novice FBI agent is further developed in her role as the audience/pupil of Lecter's lectures.

It is, perhaps, precisely because Clarice's vulnerability renders her agency less intimidating that the film is able to address the patriarchal construction of the male domain she seeks to enter. For example, to ward off the psychiatrist's objectifying appraisals Clarice responds, "I graduated from U.Va., sir, it's not a charm school." More important, she rebels against Crawford's routinely sexist practices. At one point, Crawford singles out Clarice in order to clear a room of state troopers. Noticing that his action had upset her, he nevertheless dismisses it as "in the line of duty," and therefore of no matter. But Clarice insists, "It matters. Cops look at you to see how to act. It matters, sir." Her comments may also obliquely call attention to the ways audiences look to films as regulators of social behavior: it matters how that behavior is represented.

When her male colleagues leave her behind to follow a fruitless lead, Clarice decides to conduct her own investigation into the circumstances of Buffalo Bill's first murder. At the first victim's home, her gaze is arrested by pictures of the young woman, and she makes connections between the female body objectified by the camera's gaze and the objectified female form of a tailor's dummy. She then perceives the link between sewing patterns and the wounds she has seen on the victims, reading domestic clues in order to arrive at an insight that has escaped her male colleagues: Clarice realizes that Buffalo Bill is using women's skins as material with which to sew himself a new body. The bodies of the victims are for him the materials of his own sexual transformation. They are thus not just objectified victims—Buffalo Bill wants to steal their feminine body, and through it their subjectivity. This criminally insane scenario is in some ways a model for the film, which both objectifies Clarice and capitalizes on the perspective of the embodied female subject. It is no coincidence, therefore, that in the climax of the film Clarice herself becomes both Buffalo Bill's hunter and his prey. After a prolonged pursuit in which Clarice is literally in the dark and Bill views her through night-vision goggles, Clarice finally gets him in her sights and kills him.

The film concludes with Clarice's graduation from training school. While a woman agent cuts into a cake bearing the FBI logo, a symbolic act suggesting that women are now entitled to a piece of the institutional pie, Clarice remains poised between the inside and the outside of the law. After Crawford congratulates her and welcomes her into the force, Lecter, having escaped custody, telephones her from his hiding place to offer fatherly praise. Clarice's integration into law enforcement, and the vindication in her capture of one serial killer, is thus mediated by the release and praise of another, and Lecter is literally given the film's final word. He is also given an extradiegetic perspective on the narrative in whose conclusion the criminal oversees the law enforcement operative. Clarice's representation in this film is unquestionably equivocal and perplexing,[8] but *The Silence of the Lambs* does raise important questions about female agency in the institutional site within the film (the FBI) and in the generic site of the film (the thriller-police procedural).

BLUE STEEL, SILK STALKINGS

Kathryn Bigelow's 1990 film *Blue Steel* develops similar themes, though it met with less box-office success. Bigelow's film documents a female cadet's initiation into the New York Police Department. Megan Turner (played by Jamie Lee Curtis) is first seen in a training simulation based on a domestic conflict. In a scene echoed early in *Silence of the Lambs*, the female officer-in-training misjudges the situation and gets "shot." Her student status established, the film's pretitle sequence relays Megan's graduation into the police force. While she dons her police uniform, the camera lingeringly pans over Megan's body, emphasizing the conflation of sexuality and power that defines her role. The film, however, seems to read this conflation as both a contradiction and a threat. A friend tells Megan, "I can't believe you're a fucking cop. You're on the right side of the law!" But the power that role makes possible, ironically, also puts Megan outside the law. For example, when her partner asks why Megan has chosen to become a police officer, she responds, "I wanted to shoot people"; and when a would-be suitor repeats the question, "You're a good-looking woman, beautiful in fact, why would you want to become a cop?" Megan's violent nature again underscores her unmanageable, menacing potential: "I like to slam people's heads up against walls." Megan is posited as a woman whose agency, by definition, is unruly and even illicit. Her overzealousness is confirmed when she stops a grocery store robbery by killing the perpetrator, and the phallic nature of her actions is underlined in her superior's comment that "she emptied an entire load" into the suspect.

Megan performs simultaneously the contradictory generic roles of law enforcement agent and femme fatale. The provocative sexual nature of her position is suggested when Eugene Hunt (played by Ron Silver), a witness to the grocery store shooting, is driven over the edge by seeing her use the gun. The unstable Eugene becomes obsessed with Megan and goes on a killing spree in tribute to her, inscribing Megan's name on his bullets. The signature (not to mention her violent propensities) makes Megan a suspect in the crime, the object of the investigation as well as its subject. After Eugene engineers a "coincidental" meeting with Megan, they (improbably) begin to date; when the two are about to make love, Eugene's fascination with Megan's gun finally alerts her to his identity as the ".44 Magnum Killer."[9]

The film's climax dramatizes the gender conflicts that define Megan's role. When she tries to arrest Eugene, his lawyers cast Megan as a hysteric who is fatally attracted to their client. Since it is Eugene's word against hers, the onus shifts to Megan to prove Eugene's guilt; at the same time, she overtly shifts from agent to victim when Eugene begins to stalk her. This development is linked to the theme of spousal abuse woven throughout the film. Eugene proceeds to kill Megan's best friend, threaten her family, shoot her lover, and rape her. In the shoot-out with Eugene that follows these events, Eugene empties *his* chambers, but Megan does not take him into lawful custody. Rather, she carefully aims her weapon at him and shoots him repeatedly. In one sense, this reverses the violent judgment often visited on the femmes fatales of film noir and expresses Megan's rage at her subjection, but in another it attests to Megan's inability to perform within the confines of the law. It also, interestingly, reproduces her role as slasher film survivor, the "Final Girl" "who encounters the mutilated bodies of her friends and perceives the full extent of the preceding horror and of her own peril" (Clover 267). As film reviewer Roger Ebert notes, "*Blue Steel* is a sophisticated update of *Halloween*, the movie that first made Jamie Lee Curtis a star" (s.v. "*Blue Steel*"). It thus calls attention to how the serial killer film's use of a psychopathic monster creates a hybrid between the police procedural and the horror genres, one in which female characters are often ambiguously placed as retributive agents and eroticized victims of violence. The repeated association of the female agent with the investigation of serial killings and stalkings might also be read as a disturbing negotiation of female fears and of male fantasies. It certainly makes the permeability of the roles of victim and investigator central to narrative interest.

FATHERS AND DAUGHTERS

Donato and Daughter, a television film adapted from a "Jack Early" (a.k.a. Sandra Scoppettone) novel, is yet another version of the serial killer scenario. In it, Lieutenant Dina Donato of the Los Angeles Police Department (played by Dana Delany) is asked to lead an investigation into the serial murders of nuns. Dina's position as *female* head of the task force is reinforced and then undercut when she is asked to include her father, Sergeant Mike Donato, on the team. Dina's role of authority on the police team suggests a reversal of "natural" order, as a daughter is given a position over her father. The reversal also masks the patriarchal nature of the work environment itself. The casting of action-film tough guy Charles Bronson as Mike Donato further contributes to his role as powerful counter to Dina's authority,[10] and workplace sexism is dramatized but largely legitimized in *Donato and Daughter*. For instance, Dina's objections to her father's inclusion in the task force earn her a lecture on how "a professional can put aside *his* personal problems" (emphasis added), and Mike instructs her, "You can't expect to be a good cop if you're this thin-skinned." Dina must deal with a task force member who balks at being "partnered with a skirt," as well as with her father's tendency to "translate" her orders to the team. Although she warns Mike, "Don't act like my interpreter. You treat me like a child, don't explain me," she *is* literally his child, and she is characterized as overly sensitive, tentative, and vulnerable.

The alignment of Dina's vulnerability and her feminine domestic role is emphasized when her concerns for her young son and her child care problems intrude on the investigation. Distinctions between her personal and professional lives collapse. In one scene, Dina is depicted at home, crying over a photograph. When the camera pulls back, framing her in a window, a man's head intrudes into the filmic frame, outside the window frame. Dina is thus situated as the object of the peeper's intrusive gaze as well as the camera's: the female police officer is placed under surveillance by voyeur and viewer alike. As the object of the killer's desire, and the subject of the investigation into his criminal actions, Dina elides the boundaries between agent and eroticized victim. The climax of the film finally positions Dina as a victim in need of rescue by her father, a situation that reinforces both his literal paternal role and his role as the authentic representative of the paternal function of the police force. While *The Silence of the Lambs*, *Blue Steel*, and *Donato and Daughter* all dramatize the problem of gender equity in institutional settings, they also suggest that the police procedural is itself one of those enclaves, especially when its repeated conflation with the serial killer genre reinforces a visual dynamic in which the female investigator is victimized.[11]

SHOT/REVERSE SHOT

Though the police procedural has demonstrated the possibility of carving out a place (however ambivalent) for female protagonists in a traditionally masculine genre, the figure of the female private eye is virtually absent from Hollywood films, despite the subgenre's success in novels. Jeff Kanew's *V. I. Warshawski* (1991) is a significant exception. Kanew's film, starring Kathleen Turner, is an excellent example of Hollywood's attempt to use book trends to react to changes in American consumer attitudes and interests (Max, "'Warshawski's' Mysterious Journey" 71). Indeed, one reviewer called *V. I. Warshawski* "less a movie than a marketing concept, a pastiche stitched out of the best-seller lists" (Dargis 64). The film was, by all accounts, a box-office flop, though according to Glenwood Irons, "it has been a steady success at the video stores" ("Introduction" xxiii). Yet its aesthetic inadequacies and the ways in which it failed to gauge and engage the interest of its projected audience are instructive and revealing, dramatizing the ideological conflicts in its adaptation of Paretsky's winning formula.[12] *V. I. Warshawski*, perversely, represents an example of what Faludi calls a conservative "backlash" against the very trends that the film was optioned to exploit. Its efforts to attract a female audience by drawing on publishing trends end up reinscribing—indeed reifying—the voyeuristic male spectator as normative and even as constitutive of the female "private eye." Kanew's cinematic adaptation of Paretsky's novels strategically invokes and then revokes Paretsky's revisions of the hard-boiled tradition, systematically recuperating the figure of the feminist detective into a collection of conservative cultural norms. In other words, the film appropriates a subversive approach to a conservative genre in order to underwrite a new conservatism. Accordingly *V. I. Warshawski* may be read as the site of contradictory cultural codings of both gender and genre, a site that reveals anxieties within the Hollywood institution—not simply about the idea of a woman's detective agency but about detection as a figure for women's agency in general.

The conventions of the detective film genre as they are adapted in this movie seem unable to accommodate a woman detective who is the empowered subject of the investigation. Instead of being the subject of the cinematic gaze, the woman detective is here most frequently offered uncritically as its eroticized object, a process also played out in the addition of the visual conventions of the stalker film to the police procedural. *V. I. Warshawski*'s representation of its heroine often foregrounds this problem by (unintentionally) thematizing the centrality of the voyeuristic male gaze. The film's opening sequence, for example, concludes with V.I.'s ritual morning jog, in which she is shown in shots that fragment her body, framing Kathleen Turner from the waist down. This is virtually an establishing shot of Turner's body as the locus of the film's visual interest; it parallels the opening establishing shot of Chicago's skyline. A group of male runners draw attention to this objectifying look *within* the narrative, calling out *"Babe—look!"* and hooting as they pass her. The film then cuts to a rock video–like close-up of V.I.'s feet in high heels on pavement, followed by a close-up of her first client, and an eyeline match cut to a slow camera tilt up her body, mirroring his clearly lascivious look and offering an exaggerated version of the position that the camera routinely takes through the course of the film.

In a later sequence, V.I. reluctantly converses with her philandering lover Murray (played by Jay O. Sanders), a newspaper reporter who in the novels is a platonic friend; in this instance, he barges into her bathroom while she is taking a bath. The camera pans languidly up her body, again following her male admirer's gaze. Though he is not nominally the detective in the story, Murray's offscreen voice appropriates the role of the voice-over narration often used in detective films, or the role of fictional narrator as voyeuristic "private eye." Murray explicitly describes his own positioning—as well as his visceral response to V.I.: "He stood gazing as the steam rose gently from the water, knowing that just beneath this fragile blanket of bubbles lay her silken nubile body. He felt the stirring of a warm throbbing passion." In this instance, dialogue paradoxically positions the male character extradiegetically—or at least he speaks as if he occupied an extradiegetic position in relation to V.I. Moments later, the bathroom is invaded by a recent acquaintance and his daughter, turning private space into a public spectacle staged for the eye of the audience *in* the film, a scenario that replicates the situation of the audience *of* the film.

The power dynamics of this reorientation of subjectivity are made all the more disturbing in the film's gendered presentation of violence. While violent incidents in which V.I. prevails are shot primarily in neutral medium or long shot, we are offered lingering point-of-view close-ups of her when she must passively submit to being slapped by mobster Earl Smysen. V.I. responds to Smysen's blows by complaining, "Do you know how hard it is to get blood out of cashmere?" The film appears to play on an assumed audience pleasure in seeing Smysen get blood out of the cashmere-clad V.I., in seeing V.I. pay for her smart-mouthed challenges to men's authority. The visual pleasure of her punishment, in other words, overwhelms V.I.'s wisecracking verbal resistance. When V.I. is in a position to return Smysen's blows, the camera is positioned to identify with his pain and humiliation. Later in the film, violence against V.I. is overtly associated with both visual and sexual pleasure. When the villainous Trumble Grafalk threatens her in his office with a set of callipers, V.I. casually looks out the window, then down at his crotch (implying that he is aroused), and poses the double entendre, "Does everybody get this view?" to which he replies, "Only the females . . . You see, I fuck a lot."

Even if such language seems a little strong for a film originating with Disney's Hollywood Pictures, the underlying morality of *V. I. Warshawski* is firmly within the Disney tradition of family entertainment, fortified by the Reagan-Bush era's conservative notion of "family values." Despite its generic veneer of detection, the central impetus of the film's narrative is not the detective genre's characteristic gathering of clues and exposure of the criminal. In fact, the film jumbles the plots of Paretsky's first two novels, *Indemnity Only* and *Deadlock,* so badly that the detective narrative loses its urgency. *V. I. Warshawski* is impelled, rather, by the attempt to reconfigure a version of the "traditional" bourgeois family. While Paretsky's novels offer alternatives to the nuclear family and often document the defects of its patriarchal structure, Kanew's film works implicitly to transform the professional detective into a wife and mother.

The plot of the film is propelled by two signal events. First, prior to its beginning, V.I. discovers the unfaithful Murray in bed with "a redhead." This recounted sexual incident substitutes for the discovery of a body conventional to the beginning of mystery stories. In response, V.I. goes to a pickup bar and meets Boom Boom Grafalk, a hockey player to whom V.I. is immediately romantically attracted (though in *Deadlock* Boom Boom is V.I.'s cousin, not a love interest). The romantic, even domestic, trajectory of the plot is telegraphed in the early bar scene, when V.I. obsesses on her sequined red stiletto pumps, which she is convinced magically attract men. Right on cue, Boom Boom trips on the shoes, and as he gallantly slips one of them back on her foot, V.I. says, "Cinderella story," perhaps identifying a happily-ever-after salvation-by-marriage plot as a model for the movie as a whole. The shoes may also remind some viewers of *The Wizard of Oz*, another film in which ruby slippers work magic . . . when combined with the mantra, "There's no place like home." Dialogue calls attention to the way V.I.'s detective skills are centrally directed toward a romantic resolution. When Boom Boom promises to call her, V.I. says, "If you don't, I'll hunt you down. I'm a private eye, remember?"

Boom Boom is involved in a custody battle with his wife Paige, making the fragmentation of family relationships central to the plot. Paige was not only unfaithful to her husband during their marriage, but after the divorce she further disrupted the family by marrying her husband's brother. Now she claims custody of their child in order to further her business interests. Paige is the central criminal of the film, and her crime is not merely dishonest business practices or even conspiracy to commit murder (all aspects of the deflected detective plot of *Deadlock*, a story that focuses much more heavily on the Byzantine operations of the shipping industry and that presents the institutional locus as the true scene of the crime); rather, Paige's abdication of her role as mother constitutes the film's main transgression. As Faludi describes it, the conservative backlash in Hollywood is marked by portrayals of women's lives as "moralist tales in which the 'good mother' wins and the independent woman gets punished" (113). *V. I. Warshawski* goes through considerable generic contortions to demonstrate this thesis, for V.I., a single professional hard-boiled detective, must be portrayed as the "good mother" if she is to occupy the space prescribed for a female protagonist. The impetus of the film's opening credit sequence seems to be that V.I. is no homemaker: her apartment is a mess, and her refrigerator is full of unidentifiable smelly things. When Boom Boom hires her to baby-sit his twelve-year-old daughter Kat, she seems at a total loss. When he is promptly killed in a mysterious explosion, V.I. is left in charge of the youngster, with whom she teams up for the investigation.[13]

Perhaps the most obvious foregrounding of the motherhood motif in *V. I. Warshawski* is Kat's school project, a social science experiment in motherhood in which she must look after an egg as if it were her baby. By the time she meets V.I., she has already "killed" several eggs, and while at first it appears that there will be a humorous parallel between these failed attempts at motherhood and V.I.'s lack of maternal skills, it turns out that the film's narrative is dominated by *the detective's* progressive education as an adoptive mother, particularly the cultivation of her protective instincts and her progressive grooming of Murray to play the role of faithful husband and father.

At the beginning of the film, Murray had perversely pretended to be V.I.'s husband in order to thwart Boom Boom's interest in her, leaving the apartment with the line, "Don't forget couples therapy tomorrow." "Therapeutic" role-playing—an adult version of playing house and a kind of "play-within-a-film" device—becomes an important means of reinforcing the mother-daughter relationship between V.I. and Kat in *V. I. Warshawski*. They frequently pretend to be or are mistaken for mother and daughter, and the casting of Angela Goethals as Kat encourages the audience's identification of physical similarities between the two fair-haired actors. In one sequence, they use role-playing to establish Murray's projected part as husband and father. V.I. and Kat discover Murray in bed with yet another woman, this time "a blonde." Joining forces in order to protect the integrity of the Murray-V.I.-Kat conventional nuclear family they are in the process of constructing against the "other woman," V.I. and Kat pretend to be Murray's neglected wife and daughter, thereby shaming the interloper into a quick exit.

The climax of *V. I. Warshawski*, which is set on a ship at Chicago's docks, involves the ultimate custody battle: a symbolic shoot-out between Paige, the "bad mother," and V.I., the "good mother," that takes place over Kat's unconscious body, which is suspended in a lifeboat that suspiciously resembles a cradle. After having killed her second husband Trumble, ostensibly to save Kat, Paige's final dramatic gesture is becoming (to cite another backlash film) "the hand that rocks the cradle," in the sinister sense that she presses the button that drops the damaged lifeboat—not to protect but to kill her daughter. For this act, according to the logic of the film, she must not only die, but die violently and spectacularly. Nancy Paul, the actor who plays Paige, is costumed in this scene in a shawl-collared coat with very large padded shoulders, an outfit in which 1940s embodiments of the femme fatale such as Barbara Stanwyck or Joan Crawford would have been quite comfortable. In the closing scenes of *V. I. Warshawski*, scenes that are shot in a distinctly film noir visual style, V.I. acts both as a protective mother and as the enforcing, retributive agent of the patriarchal system. In one of the few violent acts identified with V.I.'s point of view, she shoots Paige point-blank, right between the eyes.

But V.I. is not simply a representative of the patriarchal order, since the film also seems to be responding to the challenge posed to that order by the role of the contemporary female hard-boiled detective as action hero. One form this response takes, oddly enough, is the coding of the detective herself according to the conventions of the cinematic femme fatale. As reviewer Manohia Dargis put it, Warshawski is "femmed up to box-office specs" (64)—and this is true in the sense both that she is painstakingly feminized as heterosexual and that she is femme fatale-d up. The problematic conflation of femme fatale and detective is perhaps instantiated most comically when V.I. conducts the preliminary part of her investigation at the shipyard clad in an elegant black evening dress, a dressing gown, and slippers. The outfit may be a symptom of the film's confusion about just how one dresses a woman detective for work at night within the limited iconography of the detective film genre.

Visual and verbal conventions associated with the femme fatale provide one way of understanding the representation of violence against the woman detective as it has already been described here. V.I. escapes the ultimate fate associated with the role because she is more or less "cured" of its most disruptive features by the end of the film: the family relationship between V.I., Murray, and Kat has been cemented, with V.I. hovering behind an ambulance, apparently poised to nurse the other two back to health after their ordeal. As discussed earlier, the classic femme fatale is often perceived as a manifestation of anxieties about the masculine roles and the social and financial power that accrued to women on the home front during World War II; in *V. I. Warshawski* the woman private eye embodies similar anxieties about the power of the independent, working women produced by post-1970s feminism. The visual representation of the femme fatale is also quite consistent with the conspicuous portrayal of V.I. as object of the erotic gaze, particularly the "*directed* glance" that focuses on spiked heels and silk stockings, as Janey Place has noted (45). *V. I. Warshawski* is littered with such shots of its heroine.

Tellingly, advertisements for *V. I. Warshawski* were accompanied by a caption that read, "Killer eyes. Killer legs. Killer instincts," conveying the deadly eroticism characteristic of the classic femme fatale. The sexual nature of the threat Paretsky's character posed in the eyes of *V. I. Warshawski*'s producers is epitomized in the film by V.I.'s use of a pornographic nutcracker in the shape of a woman's body as an instrument of torture with which she extracts information from a suspect. Her character literally becomes a "ball breaker." In the final line of the film, the device is turned to less menacing and more socially integrative ends: she threatens to use it to enforce Murray's fidelity, joking, "Have you ever seen what I can do with a nutcracker?" If the nutcracker or the femme fatale's appropriation of the phallic gun weren't obvious enough images of the castrating woman, V.I. foils her pursuers at one point with a borrowed fire hose, whose impressed owner comments, "She can handle my hose anytime." The female detective as femme fatale is here perceived as embodying a sexual energy that threatens to exceed patriarchal control and containment within the heterosexual economy.

One means of containing the potentially destructive sexual energy of the femme fatale is to represent it as a commodity in an economy controlled by male desire: in this case, to see the professional woman as a form of prostitute. Caryn James's review, in fact, compared *V. I. Warshawski* to Gary Marshall's prostitution fable, *Pretty Woman* (1990), another recent hit (H7). At the same time as Kanew's film markets motherhood, it offers a countermotif of prostitution, conveying the point that women's work outside the home is akin to sexual immorality. The pattern is first developed when the bar in which V.I. meets Boom Boom is referred to by Murray as a "meat market." It is no coincidence, then, that V.I.'s first client in the film is a meatpacker, and we later learn that she turns down the case because he offered her "$5,000 a week to look after his sausage." When V.I. must make a quick change of clothes in the back of a taxi, the audience is shown a close-up of the cabbie's fascinated eyes in the rearview mirror. Noticing his gaze, V.I. responds by saying, "Consider that your tip." Once again, the male gaze is not only foregrounded but thematized, and its object is constructed as a consumer product. V.I.'s promised trade of information about the Grafalk family with Murray is likened to an exchange of sexual favors, and when V.I. doesn't "come across" with her half of the bargain, she gloats to Murray that "you always did suffer from premature articulation." This kind of humor is a sexualization of the hard-boiled private eye's wisecracking style, one that symptomatizes an uneasiness with representing women's sexuality and, further, one that conflates agency with sexual threat. At a metafictional level, such remarks are also a (perhaps unconscious) way of representing the film actress as another kind of prostituted working woman, whose performance allows her to benefit economically from, but ensures that she remains subordinate to, a mode of production and reception governed by male desire. As it stands, then, Kanew's *V. I. Warshawski* provides an unfortunate object lesson in the problematic translation of a feminist "private eye" from novel to the Hollywood screen; in the difficulty of attracting a female audience while constructing a normative, eroticized, male-identified spectatorship; and in the contradictions involved in creating a women's "action film" without inscribing a position for female agency.

WE'LL BE BACK—AFTER THESE MESSAGES

While films with female investigating agents certainly contain conflicting elements, women viewers can, nonetheless, take pleasure in the portrayal of the strong woman investigator, viewing "against the grain" in much the same way as some women take pleasure in the strength and sexuality of the femme fatale.[14] Audience resistance is an important factor in media reception, although, as Robert H. Deming perceptively notes, "it is important not to confuse this kind of interpretive play with the absolute 'freedom to read oppositionally,' for in many cases the range of freedom is limited" (206). Indeed, Christine Gledhill points to the ways in which the representation of disenfranchised or minority groups in mainstream narratives must be seen as a means of making productive use of cultural contradictions and forging different subjectivities by "entering socio-economic, cultural and linguistic struggle to define and establish them in the media, which function as centres for the production and circulation of identity" (72). And broadcast television is an important site where the production and circulation of identity takes place.

Television is also a place that has represented the female investigator in a variety of different forms. This variety in itself suggests that television, in spite of its limitations, allows a process of renegotiating different subjectivities that diverges from Hollywood film. Jackie Byars goes so far as to contend that "challenge and resistance can be discovered where we might least expect it: in American prime-time network television . . . Prime-time television offers, in its many genres, a diversity even greater than that found in Hollywood at the height of the studio system" (124). Byars may seem to be waxing a bit rhapsodic, but she does call attention to the "gender gap" between Hollywood's lavish investments in blockbuster action films and the inevitably smaller budgets of films more overtly aimed at a female audience.[15] Lizzie Francke's analysis of women screenwriters in Hollywood concludes that by the late 1980s, "the type of product that the film industry was peddling seemed increasingly dictated by the desires and tastes of what the marketing departments identified as the core consumer: the twenty-five-year-old male" (99).

To a much greater degree than film, television has defined its audiences as female. The reasons for this are largely economic. Julie D'Acci observes:

> Although television, as an apparatus for producing consumers, has predictably marketed to upwardly mobile women, men, teens, and children, it has always, from the earliest days of its history, considered middle-class women—primarily white ones—to be the main consumers of the products it advertises. . . .
>
> Because they are seen as TV's main consumers (and, at least by some, as its major program selectors), women have been a consistent target audience for network prime time throughout the medium's life span. (65–66)

While the conception of women as consumers of both products and representations is undoubtedly an ambivalent one, it does enable them to have some power—even if it is traceable to buying power—in television programming, which ensures that female protagonists and "women's issues" get air time. Despite its homogenizing mass-market appeal and its accountability to corporate concerns—both features of mass culture at large—television has the potential to speak oppositionally from within mass culture and thus to help negotiate change. As Byars puts it,

> A minority discourse—a feminine voice—has been engaged in a long-standing, active, though not always explicit, opposition to the dominant, masculine discourses in popular American film and television. Drawing on and expanding theories that acknowledge a long overshadowed minority discourse allows us to see a tradition of chal-

lenge in the contested narrative spaces not only at the margins, but at the very centre, of American culture. (128–29)

Notably, television negotiates the middle ground between the public and private domestic realms. Suzanna Danuta Walters suggests that "Perhaps television narrative, combining a domestic environment with a relationship-based content and an ongoing, open structure allows for more space for a female viewer" (76). Television's episodic, serial form opens up some of the possibilities we identified in the serial form of popular novels, among them the balance between narrative resolution and openness. Television programs often resolve single episodes, but since the protagonists return week after week, viewers develop a familiarity with the program's central characters, its narrative strategies, and the kinds of themes it develops.

As Denise Mann argues in her analysis of the 1950s sitcom *The Martha Raye Show*, television operates in the gap between the Hollywood star and the "domestic" viewer. Mann contends that as a program encourages "women at home to identify with media celebrities whose lives mirror their own, a new form of celebrity worship is invoked and a new form of cultural hegemony is validated—one which constructs women as 'consumer allies' by aligning the values of home and family with popular media representations of celebrities" (60). The television star's appearance every week mitigates her position as outside and superior to "everyday life," bringing both character and series "home." Thus, like formula fiction, television may work to mediate and negotiate changes in representations of female agents and agency.

POLICING WOMAN

The female professional detective made her debut on prime-time TV at about the same time as in fiction, the 1970s. And as in the novels we examined in chapter 1, the TV detective was initially accommodated to the police procedural genre, a gesture that resonates with the focus of 1970s feminism on equal opportunity in the workplace. One of television's first women investigators was Angie Dickinson's Pepper Anderson of *Police Woman*, which aired between 1975 and 1978. Traditionally "feminine," but working in a male milieu, Dickinson's character was kittenish and sexually provocative, and her physical attractiveness was often central to her ability to do her job; sexual allure and agency were thus conflated. She often, for example, went undercover in order to place male criminals in a compromising position or to elicit confidences. And while her own position was thus compromised and highly ambiguous, the series did begin to open conventional male spaces to include women. Indeed, her ability to work effectively undercover was based on the criminals' mistaken belief that "police" and "woman" are contradictory categories.

More complicated representations of female agents followed, such as those in the ensemble drama *Hill Street Blues*. However, it was the CBS series *Cagney and Lacey* that moved most obviously to link feminist concerns, investigative agency, and the television series. The series, which began with a made-for-TV movie in 1981, focused on the professional partnership of two female police detectives who were often assigned to cases involving sensitive "women's" issues. *Cagney and Lacey* has occasioned a number of analyses by feminist critics. D'Acci, for example, engages in an extended reading of the series in her book *Defining Women: Television and the Case of "Cagney and Lacey,"* which concentrates on the ways in which this female-oriented cop show represented the cultural problem of defining "femininity." At one level, the series provided female viewers with an opportunity to identify with unglamorous, working women who also dealt with a number of social problems of current interest. D'Acci perceives some of the conflicts mediated by the series' specific attempt to focus episodes on "women's issues":

Although these women's-issues episodes were perceived as exploitation opportunities by some people involved with the series, and although they presented knotty problems for feminism (for example, by showing women, including the protagonists, as victims, or by implying that the problems had neat solutions and that everyday, "normal" life went on despite them), they also addressed such topics as social inequities, violence against women, and women's bonding in struggle. Furthermore, as the audience letters indicated, the episodes met important and deep-seated needs in a number of viewers. (160)

Moreover, as Gledhill argues in her analysis of the program, *Cagney and Lacey* exemplifies how television series may be defined as sites of textual negotiation: "Contradictory pressures towards programming that is both recognizably familiar (that conforms to tradition, to formal or generic convention) and also innovative and realistic (offering a twist on, or modernizing, traditional genres) leads to complex technical, formal and ideological negotiations in mainstream media texts" (69–70). The casting of women in the police procedural produced generic change that was, in many ways, beyond the control of its producers, since it made gender conflict in the police squad inevitable: "But the series could not evoke such gender conflict with any credibility if it did not acknowledge discourses about sexism already made public by the women's movement in America. Such discourses in their turn become an inevitable source of drama and ideological explanation" (70). *Cagney and Lacey*'s narratives were, accordingly, "made out of" a series of negotiations about gender roles, sexuality, heterosexual relations, and female friendships (Gledhill 70), and they performed this operation through the discourses of law and policing made available by the police procedural.

Television's serial possibilities, its appeal to female audiences, and its situation on the border between private and public worlds make it a particularly interesting medium in which to develop the figure of the female private eye. In the 1970s, for example, *Charlie's Angels* clearly exploited the glamorous and eroticized consumer spectacle of three beautiful women often both fashionably and scantily clothed. Indeed, Farrah Fawcett-Majors's career in advertising virtually constituted her as the site of cumulative consumer practices, and her persona sparked a hairstyle fad. The program also contained these female private investigators in a detective agency owned by an absent patriarch and run by his male representative. However, although the Angels worked for a man, they also worked together as women, and the investigative situation was predicated on the premise (replayed in the opening sequence of each episode) that each of the female operatives had left the police force because of the stereotypical and demeaning feminine roles that had been assigned her in law enforcement. The female action-adventure series (however campy and exploitative) thus positioned itself as a generic substitute for the limited possibilities of the police procedural. For Susan J. Douglas, these conflicting impulses were central to the program's success: "The reason *Charlie's Angels* was such a hit was that it exploited, perfectly, the tensions between antifeminism and feminism" (213). Explaining her own pleasure in watching the series, Douglas turns to the collective agency of the three central investigative roles:

> Once the angels were given the case and their undercover roles, they
> usually acted independently of Charlie. What we saw, as the case
> progressed, were three women working together, sharing informa-
> tion, tips, and hunches, using inductive and deductive reasoning to
> piece together the solution of the crime. They tested their percep-
> tions and ideas against one another, and if one fell too easily for
> some man's explanation of things, the others razzed her for being
> too soft. (213–14)

Douglas is certainly not alone in her appreciation of the series.[16] While viewers enjoyed the eroticized spectacle of the female investigator, her "appearance" (both her presence as star and her physical attractiveness) in the television private eye genre was also a source of pleasure.

A similar equivocality marks *Remington Steele*, which aired between 1982 and 1987. Like *Charlie's Angels*, the series was predicated on the problem of gender inequity: the female protagonist, Laura Holt (played by Stephanie Zimbalist), had to front her private investigative agency with an invented male figurehead in order to be taken seriously; and while the real man (played by Pierce Brosnan) who takes on the role conforms to the image of a private eye, he is an incompetent investigator. Laura is thus the competent woman behind the man, though she must remain behind the man. The romantic tension between the two characters, especially in the later episodes, also altered the generic effect of the private eye narrative by mixing it with the heterosexual romance plot. A similar shift from detection to romance takes place in *Moonlighting*, which ran from 1985 to 1989. In that program, Maddie Hayes (played by Cybill Shepherd) and her cohort David Addison (Bruce Willis) worked together to operate a detective agency. The series' experiments with postmodern reflexivity often made the artificial nature of both generic and gender roles apparent, though it has also been suggested that Maddie's extreme mannerisms and behavior, her patently "excessive" status, was one way of containing any threat she might pose.[17]

PRIME TIME/*PRIME SUSPECT*

While some critics have argued that the consumer basis of television tends to homogenize its audience, the changes of the industry in the 1990s (new networks, specialty channels, satellite broadcasting), international co-productions, and the alternative broadcast forum of public television have allowed North American television viewers access to several programs originating in Britain that develop the figure of the female investigator in interesting ways. The *Prime Suspect* (1991) miniseries and its sequels (co-produced by Granada Television and Boston's WGBH, and aired in North America on PBS) constitute one of the most significant depictions of a professional female investigator to be aired on prime-time television. The miniseries was written by Lynda La Plante and starred Helen Mirren as Jane Tennison, a deputy chief inspector leading her first murder investigation. According to Rebecca Eaton, executive producer of *Mystery!*, the anthology series on which *Prime Suspect* first appeared, it was "the highest-rated series in the five years we have records for" (qtd. in Max, "La Plante in Her 'Prime'" 79). Dell Publishing optioned a novel "tie in" by La Plante, and Hollywood bought the rights for an as-yet-unproduced film version—a rare media "triple crown" (Max, "La Plante in Her 'Prime'" 79). The success of the first installment led to subsequent *Prime Suspect* incarnations, all of which repeated with variations the generic formula established in the first series, and all of which featured Mirren in the lead role (though not all were written by La Plante): *Prime Suspect 2* was produced in 1992 and *Prime Suspect 3* in 1993. Three two-hour movies, *Prime Suspect: The Lost Child*, *Prime Suspect: Inner Circles* (which won an Emmy Award in 1996), and *Prime Suspect: The Scent of Darkness* have subsequently appeared on PBS's *Masterpiece Theatre* anthology.

The various *Prime Suspect* series were an essential part of an occurrence virtually unheard-of in the world of North American television: the development of a number of writer-driven and writer-identified series, and the simultaneous production of a woman writer as a recognizable name with star power in the (British) television industry. La Plante achieved her first major television success as a writer with her Euston Films/Thames Television miniseries *Widows* in 1983, a narrative starring Ann Mitchell that twisted the gender of the gangster/caper film formula by having the widows of an armed robbery team plan and carry out the crime in which their male partners had lost their lives. The series was followed several years later by two sequels, *Widows II* and *She's Out*, both of which reprised Mitchell's role as Dolly Rawlins—in the latter case, as the leader of a crew of female ex-convicts who live together in a decaying mansion while they organize a train robbery. The first *Prime Suspect* established a reputation for La Plante on both sides of the Atlantic, and during the early 1990s, she was responsible for a number of series that explored masculine enclaves: for example, the BBC1 program *Civvies* dealt with the lives of British ex-paratroopers; the BBC2 drama *Seconds Out* explored the world of boxing; the Anglia Television thriller *Framed* portrayed the growth of a police officer's identification with his male quarry; and the Channel 4 dark thriller *Comics* was situated, ironically, in the world of stand-up comedy. But La Plante was also strongly identified with her investigation of the power of women and especially women's relation to the law, themes that resulted in generic permutations new to television audiences. In addition to *Prime Suspect*, *Widows I* and *II*, and *She's Out*, La Plante wrote *Seekers*, an ITV miniseries starring Brenda Fricker as a middle-aged white housewife who, after the apparent death of her private eye husband, discovers that he has also left behind a young, black, and very pregnant mistress, played by Josette Simon. The two "survivors" team up to form an oddly matched private detective agency, which ultimately investigates the indiscretions of the male private eye himself. La Plante also wrote *The Governor*, starring Janet McTeer, a Granada Television miniseries that turned the conventional "prison film" on its head (and extended some of the themes and narrative structures of *Prime Suspect*) by following the career of a female warden whose job it is to maintain order among both inmates and guards in a volatile high security men's prison. La Plante was given featured billing—often above that of the main actors—as writer of each of these productions.

Such was La Plante's public identification (at least in Britain) with gritty, realistic stories exploring the relationships among women both inside and outside the law that it could be parodied by comedians Dawn French and Jennifer Saunders in their television series *French and Saunders*. In the 1996 episode titled "The Job," Mossie Smith (who played Police Constable Maureen Havers in several of the *Prime Suspect* series), Janet McTeer, Anne Mitchell, Helen Mirren, and even La Plante herself made guest appearances. In the spoof, La Plante plays the gang boss, and "The Job" is the top-secret script for her next blockbuster series, over which the various actors/gangsters squabble for prime female roles. As head of her own production company, La Plante was now literally "the governor," a creative force of considerable influence. La Plante's accomplishments suggest that changes in who controls an institution like television production may effect significant shifts in the perspective of its products, a possibility that echoes the sway in publishing of such writers as Grafton and Paretsky.

Prime Suspect opens up the critical potential of the television police procedural without diminishing its ability to entertain.[18] While Dianne L. Brooks argues that *Prime Suspect* "fails to significantly challenge conventional representations of race and gender" (93), her critique is based on the premise that television, as a popular culture medium, can offer only a certain restricted set of ideals and is thus necessarily limited in its presentation, even when it appears to be challenging conventions (94). For her, the "popular" and the "politically resistant" are mutually exclusive categories. Similarly, Sandra Tomc claims that

> While part of the telefilm . . . is concerned with elaborating the male-dominated system that traps and oppresses women, the final portions of it are governed by a compensatory effort to make sense of Tennison's heartfelt desire to be, in her own words, "one of the lads." How does the feminist detective's pursuit of acceptance as a police*man* mesh with her metaphoric status as a victim? It doesn't. *Prime Suspect* is one of a number of women's crime stories released or published in the early 1990s that bizarrely combine an aggressive critique of "patriarchy" with a narrative that highlights the virtues of submission and conformity. (47)

Both Brooks's reading and the subtler but also condemnatory (from a feminist standpoint) reading of Tomc fail to take into account a number of factors. These include the positioning and potential agency of the television spectator, the internal dynamics of the gaze established by *Prime Suspect*'s visual style, and the significant ways in which the series differed from its generic predecessors.

These readings also fail to account for what Lorraine Gamman sums up as the kind of generic destabilization, merging of fiction and nonfiction, and parodic effect accessible within the parameters—indeed, *made possible by* the parameters—of mainstream television to "'subvert' dominant meanings about women in popular culture and to create pleasure, surprise and interest in feminism" (24). The strategy of merging fiction and nonfiction applies particularly well to *Prime Suspect*, since, in addition to La Plante and Mirren, there was a third "woman behind the woman" of *Prime Suspect:* the real-life figure of Jackie Malton of London's Metropolitan Police Force, one of Britain's first and few woman DCIs (see Strong). The continuity between Jane Tennison's fictionalized and real-life experiences of workplace discrimination was reinforced by La Plante's extensive research techniques, which included spending a considerable period of time with Malton. It was also made clear to viewers by the presentation of an interview with Malton following one of the episodes (in the PBS airing, at least). Moreover, reviewers (and presumably audiences) did recognize the larger resonances of this particularized representation: a critic for the *New Statesman*, for instance, perceived that *"Prime Suspect* depicted a heightened version of the experience of career women in all professions" ("Intruder").

Brooks's and Tomc's criticisms of the feminist potential of *Prime Suspect* also overlook the powerful effect of the interpretation of the role of Jane Tennison by Helen Mirren, a classically trained British actor who has established a reputation for her intelligence, her intensity, and the diversity of the roles she has undertaken in both British and American films. One reviewer asked how it was possible for Tennison to be perceived as an underdog, given the power of Mirren's presence (Wolcott 26). The same writer, interestingly, commented that Mirren's "trim execution recalls the Humphrey Bogart of *The Maltese Falcon* and *The Big Sleep*" (29), suggesting that Mirren's distinctive hard-boiled performance exceeds the conventions of the police procedural, creating links back to the private eye tradition in film and literature.

Prime Suspect literally exposes a male conspiracy in sites of authority, and it does so by representing *conflict* within those sites—conflict introduced largely by the emergence of a female police deputy chief inspector. Such conflict is revealed when, for example, Tennison invokes the language of parliamentary protocol in a comment about DS Bill Otley.

Instead of supporting her in the investigation of a series of murders, Otley persistently conspires to undermine her authority, becoming an internal opposition party: "Next thing I know he'll be asking for a vote of
no confidence." Each of the three miniseries extends the figure of the
"boys' club" in order to suggest the misogynist power of male bonding.
The members of the police squad are collectively referred to as "the
lads" (despite the presence of women among them), but it becomes clear
that this group extends well beyond Tennison's subordinates. The first
Prime Suspect portrays a tribute party/boxing match for a police officer,
from which Tennison is conspicuously excluded; *Prime Suspect 2* takes
place against the backroom politics of a local by-election and secretive
meetings of senior officers ("old boys") who, in effect, place Tennison
under surveillance and determine her professional fate; and *Prime Suspect 3* establishes a parallel between several kinds of boys' clubs that have
overlapping memberships (while also reinforcing the boys' club trope by
representing Tennison's senior officer with a set of golf clubs positioned
immediately behind his desk): an all-male retirement dinner for a senior
officer, a drag club/pedophile ring frequented by respected male members of the legal establishment, and a drop-in center for (male) street
kids run by an apparently benign paternal figure, who is actually villain-
ously manipulative.

In each of the series, moreover, the narrative proceeds according to a
double structure in which Tennison is pitted both against the nominal
criminal and against the representatives of the law itself: her male colleagues, subordinates, and superiors. The criminal is almost always
guilty of violent sex crimes (rape-murder in *Prime Suspect*, rape-murder
and pornography in *Prime Suspect 2*, and pedophilia, murder, and arson
in *Prime Suspect 3*), and members of the second category are guilty of in-
sidious "gender crimes" involving discrimination. Indeed, in *Prime Suspect 3*, the two categories are collapsed when Tennison exposes a senior
officer's pedophilic practices and a police cover-up of them. Far from lo-
calizing violence against women (as Tomc argues), such narrative gestures reveal its systemic nature.

More specifically, the crime with which the first episode of *Prime Suspect* opens is not a murder (that act occurs prior to the narrative's beginning), but a crime committed by the police. The opening shows the arrival of police cars to the murder scene, tightly framed images of male police officers, and the furtive exchange of a "black book" taken from the crime scene. This is the book, viewers later learn, in which the murdered prostitute recorded the names of her clients, and it incriminates DCI John Shefford for taking favors from prostitutes. From the beginning, the audience is introduced to two related crimes—that *investigated* by the police and that *committed* by the police. One of the primary attractions for audiences of police procedurals is the interest in the cachet associated with specialized techniques of crime solving; here, this interest is redirected to an exploration of how these techniques are used strategically to misdirect and exclude Tennison, the woman inspector in charge of the murder case. For example, messages to Tennison are delayed; she is sent off to the country on a wild-goose chase; the evidence contained in the black book is hidden and altered; and police records are tampered with. Indeed, the "prime suspect" of the program's title is identified within the first ten minutes by DNA evidence involving his rare blood type, and this premature "solution" invites viewers to identify other crimes and suspects. Shefford, for example, is a probable murderer, though his colleagues do not consider him as such. In protecting him, police officers are, ironically, guilty of impeding a police investigation. Tennison herself is perceived by her squad with suspicion, and viewers might well ask themselves of what crime she is guilty—the answer, almost certainly, is being a woman in authority. In fact, at one point it becomes apparent that the police squad is busily investigating not the murders but Tennison's sexuality, in order to find out with whom she is sleeping and, presumably, to discover her sexual orientation (DS Otley makes a reference to her "skinny dyke ass").

The structure of police-criminal surveillance is reversed here, and Tennison (the leader of the criminal investigation) is subject to the incriminating gaze of the other police officers. The voyeuristic nature of this gaze is emphasized by the officers' interest in Tennison's sexuality and by a later incident in which Moyra Henson, the common-law wife of the prime murder suspect, flashes her breasts at the officers in disgust at their unrelenting surveillance. It is essential to note, however, that this development occurs *within* the narrative. The narrative itself is critical of that objectifying gaze, and the audience is positioned to identify not with *it* but with Tennison's subjection *to* it and with her alternative gaze. It is therefore problematic to conclude that "the viewer will ultimately objectify Jane, as she is made the object of the 'gaze' rather than the controller of it" (Brooks 95). On the contrary, the camera often literally takes Tennison's part, perhaps most strikingly during the excruciating first squad meeting, when, through camera movement, viewers follow Tennison's gaze across a sea of undifferentiated suits and unsympathetic male stares. Significantly, that sequence is reproduced with a difference in *Prime Suspect 2*, when the camera, positioned just behind his shoulder, invites the audience to identify with the subjection of Sgt. Bob Oswald (a black officer new to the investigative team) to the gaze of his all-white co-workers and to perceive his position as a racial minority as a parallel to Tennison's position as a woman in the first *Prime Suspect* miniseries. This perception is, of course, made ironic by Tennison's initially unfair treatment of the black officer.[19]

It becomes increasingly clear that Tennison is not viewed as a figure of authority by men within the narrative of *Prime Suspect*. Hence, during an interview, the father of a victim persistently addresses himself to the subordinate male officer who accompanies Tennison, assuming that the police*man* is in charge. DI Frank Jones is similarly mistaken for the commanding officer when he and Tennison visit Manchester to interview prostitutes at the scene of one of the killings. Certainly the male members of the police squad do not address Tennison as a commanding officer, yet this undermining of her authority is self-consciously offered by the narrative as an object of *criticism*. The narrative of *Prime Suspect*, then, is driven both by the accumulation of evidence against the suspect, George Marlow (as most police procedurals are), and by that evidence's performance in support of Tennison and her increasing credibility and empowerment in her investigative role. The program establishes this second dynamic visually by offering Mirren an increasingly dominant position in the frame—in its opening sequences, her petite figure is virtually overwhelmed by the bulk of male officers (for example, in a shot in the station house elevator, Tennison almost disappears behind three male colleagues); this is less and less the case as the narrative continues, since the use of close-ups of Mirren invites viewers to identify with her. In turn, the sympathies established by the narrative, the camera's position, and Mirren's performance work to affirm Tennison as a figure of authority and to discredit those officers who impede her.

Tennison's controlling gaze is not absent from the narrative but is represented differently. And it is this *difference* that makes possible her agency within the institutional structure of the police. Tennison's perceptions are not, as Brooks suggests, based on "feminine intuition" (91), but on seeing (and hearing) evidence differently than do her male colleagues. In one instance, Tennison discovers that the first murder victim's body has been misidentified when she recognizes the labels in the clothing and realizes that the garments' cost places them beyond the means of Della Mornay, the prostitute whom the male officers assume is the victim (because the body is found in Mornay's apartment).[20] In another, she identifies the shoe size of the body as inconsistent with that of Mornay, a detail the investigating officers had missed. When she articulates these discrepancies, the camera cuts to a reaction shot—a glance of recognition from WPC Maureen Havers, the junior female officer who often appears in the background of squad room scenes. It is WPC Havers who, at several points, supplies information crucial to the solution of the case. At a squad meeting she shyly offers a theory based on her observation of a murder victim's manicure and her recollection that Moyra is a trainee beautician, but she is drowned out by masculine voices until Tennison demands that she be heard. In *Prime Suspect 3*, Tennison's presence as the leader of the vice squad actually seems to license and solidify resistance to Otley's homophobia, making it possible for WPC Kathy Bibby to talk back to and laugh at Otley's snide announcement of the "Fairy of the Week Award" by responding, "We'll be awarding the Prick of the Week Award. Apparently you're not eligible, 'cause you've been one ever since you've arrived." In the climactic scene of the first series, Moyra Henson refuses to give essential evidence until the male officers leave the interview room: "I won't talk in front of them." Three rapidly edited close-ups follow, moving from Moyra to Tennison to WPC Havers, and thus triangulate the female gaze, the gaze that controls the solution of the crime. Indeed, there is a projected fourth "corner" of this visual figure: the gaze of the viewer, whose look, here, is interpellated as female.

A similar look between women takes place in the final episode of *Prime Suspect 2*. This look transforms Tennison's antagonistic relationship with a young black law student, Sara Allen, the sister of the man who has died in police custody. Despite the difference in their race, both women are struggling to gain access to power and justice through patriarchal legal institutions, and they are also visually victimized by the murderer. Outside the courthouse after the inquest, the camera lingers on a powerful look of recognition and identification between Sara and Jane. Each woman has been made the object of the murderer-pornographer's gaze, an appropriate visual metaphor for her disempowerment: the killer takes photographs (which are then published in a tabloid newspaper) of Tennison in a compromising embrace with Oswald; he also sends Allen intrusive photos of her emerging from a bath, another gesture of intimidation. Jane urges Sara to supply information key to the case, saying, "He can't turn us into victims as well," and when Allen tells the traumatic story of what she and her brother witnessed on the night of the murder, Tennison significantly gets up and walks around the table to hug her, shifting the oppositional structure of the interview room. Tennison makes a similar move during an interview with a transvestite in *Prime Suspect 3*. She is, notably, the only police representative who looks on Vernon as feminine, calling her by her preferred name, "Vera." And Vera is well aware of the difference, telling Tennison:

"You're not like the others . . . I've always appreciated the way you speak to me."

In the first *Prime Suspect*, Tennison is also linked to other female characters through the ways in which they are mutually objectified by the male gaze. Looks between women and the potential identification of the viewer counter and critique the conventional male gaze. "The lads" dismiss prostitutes (the prime targets of the serial killer) as subhuman: one prostitute tells Tennison, "They [the police] never give a shit about Jeannie [one of the killer's prostitute victims]," and this is confirmed when officers say that the murdered prostitutes were "bloody well asking for it," and "slags ain't the word for 'em." But Tennison insists on listening to the testimony of these women and on taking them seriously. When she interviews a group of prostitutes over a drink, she is rewarded with a description of a suspect's car, a better sense of the suspect's appearance, knowledge about the position of Jeannie's body when found and how it had been "unofficially" moved, and the incriminating information that DCI Shefford was not just a police officer but a john. She also learns the elided, humanizing story of the dead woman's life.

At one point during this interview, a passing man mistakes Tennison for a prostitute and propositions her. Tomc argues that "for a split second as Tennison sits in that pub, with all the power and authority she commands as the police detective suspended in misunderstanding, she and the dead girl are dangerously interchangeable. Mistaken for a hooker, Tennison can now be read as a candidate for the killer's urges" (46). Leaving aside her persistent references to the victims as "girls," Tomc's identification of this moment in the series as pivotal is quite just. However, because the diegesis itself is consistently affiliated with Tennison, the identification between the prostitutes and investigator *critically* suggests that as "working women," both Tennison and the prostitutes are routinely subject to violence and intimidation because of their sex—a recognition of shared female experience that crosses class lines (for a short time), just as the connection between Sara Allen and Tennison in *Prime Suspect* 2 crossed (without effacing) race lines. The prostitutes and Tennison are again linked by a look of vindication in the final sequence of *Prime Suspect* as Marlow is indicted.

Finally, *Prime Suspect* visually establishes a parallel between Tennison and Moyra Henson. Cross-cuts, for example, link the scene of Moyra leaving George to look at a police lineup and Tennison leaving her lover, Peter. Later, a shot of Moyra taking off her makeup in front of a mirror, with George reflected behind her, is paralleled by a shot of Tennison looking into the mirror in the locker room at the police station. Far from being a narcissistic gaze, in both cases this is a look of growing self-possession—particularly since the image of Moyra documents her dawning realization that the partner she has so vociferously defended may be guilty. The parallel between the two scenes also subtly implies that each woman is, in effect, "sleeping with the enemy"—Moyra, literally, and Tennison, figuratively (as "married" to her job)—and each must face up to her position in an abusive relationship.

While the plots of the three miniseries follow conventions that allow Tennison's triumph and vindication in the end, they are also always ambivalent—much like the plots of the private eye detective novels we have examined throughout. All imply that though small victories must be savored, the power of the system leaves a sour taste in the mouth. This lack of resolution foregrounds the contradictions central to the superficially satisfying resolutions of each. Hence, George Marlow's "not guilty" plea in the final shot of *Prime Suspect* leaves open the possibility that the legal system will acquit him (indeed, his case is reopened in *Prime Suspect: The Scent of Darkness*). By the end of *Prime Suspect 2*, although the murder of a mixed-race woman has been solved, the answer to the question with which the miniseries began—"Is it possible to expect justice in this country if you are a person of color?"—remains equivocal at best. In the final moments of *Prime Suspect 2*, Tennison is passed over for promotion, and her offer to celebrate with her squad is undercut by DCI Thorndike, who takes over the position she should have occupied. Tellingly, Tennison leaves the station house alone. While the police refuse to bring charges against the drop-in center adminis-trator who has abused his protégés, *Prime Suspect 3* concludes with Ten-nison "accidentally" leaving an incriminating file on her desk, giving a female reporter access to it. Her oblique suggestion of the headline that might accompany the resulting story suggests her role as subversive au-thor of a narrative that will incriminate the police as well.

Moreover, the miniseries are not absolute in their portrayal of Ten-nison herself, whose determination to succeed often reproduces some of the deficiencies of the system against which she is so often pitted. This is particularly true of *Prime Suspect 2*'s investigation of racial conflicts. The narrative of this miniseries invites an analysis of the *structurally* problematic nature of authority: Tennison is implicated in both sexual and racial discrimination against Sgt. Oswald, the black officer with whom she has had a brief affair and who later joins her squad. Tennison's subject position is thus represented at the interstices of conflicting asso-ciations of race, class, and gender, and the viewer's identification with her is likely to be partial and positioned. As the mixed race of the mur-der victim in the middle miniseries subtly suggests, the solutions it of-fers are not simply black or white, nor are any of the *Prime Suspect* series simply "radical" or "conservative." Rather, while the *Prime Suspect*s may differ from the female private eye genre, these police procedural televi-sion programs might well clear the way for other generic experimenta-tions, much as female police procedural novels did in the 1970s.[21]

SISTER, SISTER!

The first television adaptation of a feminist hard-boiled author can be found in a British production. London Weekend Television's *Anna Lee Mysteries*, the product of British commercial television, was based on the Liza Cody novels that feature PI Anna Lee.[22] The ambivalences em-bodied by the *Anna Lee Mysteries* exemplify Gledhill's contention that popular culture comprises a field of textual/cultural/media negotiations

(68–70). The series nevertheless makes possible an exploration of the agency and empowerment dramatized by the role of the female private eye, even as it places the legitimacy of that role in question.

Anne Dudley's signature song for the series introduces Cody's overtly feminist hero to TV viewers. The music track reverberates as the opening (and closing) credits roll and is accompanied by images of Anna undertaking a number of traditionally masculine jobs: welding, fixing her car, and testing an electronic alarm system. She is often depicted at home, wearing a T-shirt bearing a picture of Rosie the Riveter and the slogan "We Can Do It." This slogan is corroborated by Anna's actions. In one scene, for example, she comes to the aid of her large wrestler neighbor, Selwyn, and opens the jar with which he is struggling; in another, she offers to "have a look" at a male friend's car for him. But in spite of such gender reversals, the program also reneges on its promise of a capable female hero by situating Anna in a fluctuating mode of in/competence.

This is an effect developed throughout the series. Despite her investigative competence, Anna is often dramatized as capricious and overly enthusiastic, features absent from her portrayal in Cody's novels. The first episode, "Headcase," provides an example. It begins with a close-up of Anna, awakened by an alarm clock. As she reaches for a cigarette, she lifts a running shoe from the floor and sighs. The camera follows her on her morning jog, and then shifts to a scene that explains her actions. In the flashback, Anna interviews for a job at Brierly's Detective Agency. Mr. Brierly (or the "Commander," as he prefers to be called), asks Anna why she has left her job on the Metropolitan Police, after three years of service. Her response ("I had problems with bureaucracy") elicits his correction: "More like problems with authority." The Commander proceeds to read from Anna's file, noting her "tendency to get emotionally involved, [her] tendency to fly off the handle, and [her] tendency to use excessive force." When he adds, "I would not have thought you were capable of excessive force," he overtly flags her small size, and at the same time covertly questions her capacity for the job. Following up on his line of inquiry, the Commander asks Anna if she keeps fit. She assures him, "Oh yes, sir, four hours in the gym—and running sir," and in so doing, provides viewers with an explication of the opening sequence, to which, at this point, the camera returns. Anna is visualized panting and gasping, now, barely managing to finish her run, and about to face her first day as an employee of Brierly's. The viewer might well ask if she is "fit" for the job.

Anna's ambiguous position in the TV drama is emphasized when she arrives at the office. Scantily clothed in a thigh-high skirt, the camera angles afford the Commander and home viewers flashes of her panties, and the detective is constructed as a spectacle of sexual provocation. Brierly disapprovingly asks if she always wears her skirts so short (as do other characters throughout the narrative), and she replies that she believes her clothing appropriate to her scheduled undercover work in a record store. As she "un-covers" in order to go "undercover," then, Anna is figured in a manner similar to TV characters such as Pepper Anderson and Charlie's Angels. At the same time, this scene, in tandem with the opening sequence, underscores Anna's ingenuity as well as her misplaced enthusiasm—when the Commander informs her that she has been reassigned to a sensitive case, involving the disappearance of a high-ranking civil servant's daughter, the laugh is more *on* her than with her.

"Headcase" documents both Anna's excessive zeal and her inability to follow through on it. In a parodic recasting of Clint Eastwood's Dirty Harry films, Anna and a male colleague, Bernie Schiller, challenge a suspect, and Anna taunts: "Come on, punk, make my day." Yet, as the suspect lifts her off her feet, the parody is deflated, and Bernie is forced to come to her rescue. At the same time, however, Anna's vulnerability is an asset as well, since it allows her insights into the victims of the crimes she investigates. This aspect of her role is hinted at in the segment's title, "Headcase," which suggests a connection between Anna's investigation and the psychology of crime. At several points in the episode, sexual offenses involving the gaze are explored. When Anna checks into an Eastbourne hotel, she meets a Norman Bates–like hotel manager, who is obsessed with a police portrait of a dead man. The manager's necrophilia foreshadows the strange behavior of the bellboy who shows Anna to her room. In dialogue that recalls Hitchcock's *Psycho*, the bellboy leers, "It's a sticky day. I bet you can't wait to get under that shower." The intertextual reference is extended when the camera follows Anna as she undresses for the shower, and the unobserved bellboy peeps at her through a transom, replicating the watching of Marion Crane by Norman Bates. The narrative positions Anna as the object of the voyeur's gaze and aligns the viewer with the latter, generating sexual titillation through Anna's unintentional striptease. It also, however, calls viewers on this alignment when (unlike her filmic counterpart Marion Crane) Anna realizes that she is being watched, and takes control of the situation by chasing the bellboy into the hallway. Even so, her action does not diminish her sense of violation: her repeated insistence that she feels dirty dramatizes the response of the victim, and the audience itself is incriminated in this scenario.

The *Anna Lee Mysteries* draw attention at several other points to the mechanisms of representation and the gendering of the spectator's gaze, even as the episodes remain largely complicit in reproducing these processes. "Dupe," for instance, begins with a pretitle sequence established by a visual pan of Manhattan, accompanied by the sound of upbeat music. The camera cuts to a woman walking down a hallway to an elevator. She enters the elevator and the scene cuts again, to a cinema projection room, and then to a close-up of another woman. As the camera pulls back for a long shot, this second woman is framed as the spectator of a film, signaling to television viewers that they are part of a *mise en abyme*: the home audience is watching a TV character watching a woman in a film (a woman who, the audience learns shortly, is also being watched *within* the film). Through a series of parallel cuts, "Dupe" establishes that the actions of the spectator-character duplicate those of the woman in the film-within-the-television-show, both of whom, it develops, are being stalked. The *mise-en-abyme* structure suggests continuities between the represented and "real" worlds. The defamiliarizing effect of its use of reproduced images also reveals the conventional structures of viewing, implicating the television audience of "Dupe" in the exposed representational mechanisms that make a spectacle of women's victimization.

"Dupe" concentrates on Anna's efforts to solve the murder of the spectator/character Deirdre, a woman who has become so enamored with the dangerous and seductive images of women in movies that she leaves home to pursue a career in film. She is thus "duped" into a naive attempt to reproduce the glamorous spectacles of femininity she finds in the cinema. Deirdre's career dead-ends with her involvement in a crime syndicate that pirates Hollywood features. And Anna, who joins forces with an officer of the Motion Picture Association of America, is involved in policing both the way movies are illegally duplicated (in violation of copyright laws) and the powerful ways they engender duplications of themselves in their audience's sensibility. "Dupe" also calls attention to the impact of repeated representations of violated women, but it moves beyond a simple condemnation of "negative" feminine stereotypes: in the character of Anna Lee, it explicitly counters the images of victimization with which it began. The role of the female PI embodies a generic repetition with a difference.

While Anna identifies with the female victims in the narrative, she violates the filmic "script" for female behavior, performing as a female avenger. In "Headcase," her own experience with sexual violation (in the Eastbourne hotel room) motivates her to blackmail a father into providing the daughter he sexually molested with continued psychiatric treatment. In "Dupe," Anna's anger over Deirdre's fate compels her to pursue an investigation into film piracy. In "The Cook's Tale," Anna comes to the aid of an old school friend, Laura, who suspects her husband of having an affair. The "other woman" is found dead in Laura's home, and Laura is the obvious suspect, but Anna's belief in her friend's innocence prompts her to investigate the seemingly open-and-shut case. Indeed, female solidarity becomes an important motif in this episode, for Anna's support enables Laura to begin taking responsibility for her actions and to overcome her alcoholism.

Within the series, women's friendship and political commitment bring to the fore questions concerning the relationship between individual feminist agency and group action. In "Dupe," Anna seeks assistance from a former police associate and friend, Ros Russell. Ros, who feels betrayed by Anna's decision to leave the Met, initially refuses to help. She responds to Anna's plea, "Ah, come on—I thought we were friends," succinctly: "We were, but then you left," and the dialogue that follows highlights the intersection of the personal and the political, and the opposition between individualist responses to the status quo and attempts to produce institutional change:

ANNA: I wasn't getting anywhere. You, of all people, know what it's like for a woman in this throwback to the stone age.

ROS: Yes, and at the first sign of sexism, you throw it all in and run for cover in some tuppeny-ha'penny private investigation firm. That really struck a blow for equality in the Metropolitan Police, didn't it? And meanwhile, it's muggins like me who go on, on their own, trying to get things changed so other women won't have the same problems.

Ros relents, and to her "Ah, I'm sorry, but—" Anna adds, "You miss me," and the two reconcile. The reconciliation is uneasy, however, for while it identifies the tensions between the different forms of agency open to women, it does not gloss over the ways in which Anna's decision to strike out on her own is both a limited response and one that has effects on others.

As if to demonstrate the latter point, Anna's relentless individualist pursuit of criminals endangers her family and friends. In "Diversion," Anna decides to follow up on a clue while baby-sitting her nephew, and in so doing places the child's life in jeopardy. In "Requiem," Anna's neighbor Selwyn helps her on a case, only to be arrested for his pains. At the same time, Ros's charge that Anna has opted out of the collective she formed with the other female police officers further reinforces the ways

Anna's work as a private investigator individualizes her political commitment. The Commander draws attention to the problematics of Anna's economically defined position in his reminder: "You're for hire, like a taxi. You go where the client wants you to go." Yet, like the traditional male private investigator, Anna is not limited by institutionalized legal definitions in her pursuit of other possibilities of justice. For example, in "The Cook's Tale" she is able to prove Laura's innocence when the police have closed the file, and she often works with Ros to solve crimes since, from outside the law, she can follow up on clues that Ros, constrained by her official status, cannot.

In turn, Anna's performance as a private investigator does not isolate her. She frequently works with Brierly's other agents, Bernie (an aging investigator whose domestic ties often conflict with his performance of duty) and Stevie (a black man, whose affiliations with London's multicultural scene complicate some of the series' plots). And Anna's personal life often overlaps with her professional duties, breaking down the tradition of the loner detective. "Requiem" depicts Anna's investigation of a female rock star's apparent suicide and the PI's subsequent romantic involvement with a record producer, William Gilmore, who is the suspect in the case. While Brierly is certain that Gilmore has killed the singer, Anna remains convinced of his innocence. The Commander contends that her personal involvement with Gilmore has clouded her professional judgment. Anna gets angry, and charges: "I've worked for this company for nearly a year, I've solved case after case after case, and still you treat me with absolutely no respect. You treat me like a schoolgirl." At the Commander's retort, "All too often you act like one," Anna blows up. She accuses her employer of sexism and, in no uncertain terms, quits the agency: "I've had it. Your paternalistic chauvinistic behavior makes me feel sick."

Anna's involvement with Gilmore may complicate her involvement with the case, but the relationship also serves as a stage for a series of gender inversions. In one scene, Gilmore proposes to Anna on his yacht, and she ironically comments: "I should have known, sailing up the

Thames on a £10 million boat with a multimillionaire with a diamond ring—again." Fairy-tale gender stereotypes are also inverted when it is Anna who comes to Gilmore's rescue during a fight scene, and when she later refuses his proposal. Anna's acknowledgment of the attraction he holds for her, in conjunction with her discovery that he has used her, underscores her vulnerability, yet it leaves her in a position of strength. In the episode's concluding sequence, Brierly visits Anna to beg her to return to work. Although she responds, "I'll think about it," this scene reconfirms her confidence and credibility.

In "Diversion," Anna acts on behalf not of an individual but of a community. Working as a volunteer in the preparations for a multicultural Carnival parade, Anna is asked by the organizers to investigate a series of threatening letters they have received. Aligned with the people of color sponsoring Carnival and against the entrepreneur who seeks to appropriate the celebration for financial ends, Anna works with Stevie to protect the parade. And yet, this episode also relegates Carnival to a sideshow, for the ritual parade is used to mask the robbery of a Greek bank executed by two Turkish Cypriots. The crime is allegedly staged for nationalist reasons, and in opposing it with the Carnival parade, the episode might be read as pitting racial "others" (the Caribbean community) against ethnic "others" (Greeks and Turks)—especially since Anna, who saves the day, might be seen as the "white savior" of Carnival. Yet the narrative of "Diversion," like those of the other Anna Lee mysteries, demonstrates that (television) entertainment is not simply a "diversion" from the political world; it is itself politically constituted.

COPY CATS

In conclusion, it is worth remembering that the genres are not static. We have already pointed to the growing popularity of lesbian PIs and detectives of color as a significant development. Our analysis in this chapter has also hinted at another mutation of the genre: the serial killer murder mystery in which the investigator is a woman. The variant has

achieved remarkable popularity in Patricia Cornwell's Kay Scarpetta series, whose central character is a forensic pathologist. Cornwell's novels
have spawned a wealth of imitators, all of which focus on serial killers.
Linda Fairstein, Lisa Scottoline, Kathy Reichs, Christine McGuire, and
Nancy Taylor Rosenberg are among those who write within this new
subgenre; and, while many of them infuse their books with feminist
sympathies, the fact that the perpetrators of serial killings are inevitably
male, and the victims almost invariably female, counterpoints the agency
of the woman investigator by constantly reminding readers that she is a
potential (and often actual) victim of the serial killer's psychopathy. The
replication of the killing in each novel's narrative also suggests that a
fascination with victimization underlies interest in the investigator's
agency, and the forensic focus on the female victim's body posits an objectification that counters the investigator's subjectivity. We have already discussed several films in which the role of the female investigator
is conceived of in relation to a stalker or serial killer, examining how
these narratives tend to reproduce a gendered paradigm of spectatorship. Owing largely to Cornwell's success as a best-selling author, the
serial killer narrative featuring a female investigator is being further developed in big-budget films and in well-publicized recent television series, including *Profiler*.[23]

Jon Amiel's feature film *Copycat* (1995) suggests some possibilities for
a reading of the serial killer narrative's gendered scenarios that may put
reverse discourse into play. This film provides a twist on the familiar
trope of the female victim, and in doing so it both reproduces and challenges the conventions developed in popular serial killer films like *Man-
hunter* (1986), *Jennifer 8* (1992), *Blink* (1994), *Natural Born Killers* (1994),
Seven (1995), and *Jade* (1996).[24] *Copycat* features Holly Hunter and
Sigourney Weaver as co-investigators of a serial killer. Hunter plays
M. J. Monahan, a senior inspector with the San Francisco Police Department, who is partnered with a younger male colleague, Inspector
Reuben Goetz (played by Dermot Mulroney). An early scene in *Copycat*
reverses the scenario played out in both *The Silence of the Lambs* and *Blue*

Steel in which a novice female investigator is "killed" in a training simulation. In *Copycat*, M.J. runs Reuben through a remedial gun maneuver and corrects *his* firing technique. After Reuben has precipitously fired his gun, M.J. cautions: "The good news is that you're still alive. . . . Didn't anyone at the academy teach you to shoot conservatively? You shredded him." She then describes the correct procedure in which a carefully placed bullet to the shoulder forces the target to "drop the gun, and you read him his Mirandas." This way, she points out, "you haven't taken a human life." Later in the film, when Reuben is taken hostage, he performs in the manner she has outlined, but he relaxes too soon, fails to kick away the shooter's gun, and is killed in the process. M.J. blames herself, but her lieutenant consoles her: "You made a decision and it was the right decision—you just got the wrong result."

The opening sequences of *Copycat* focus on Dr. Helen Hudson (played by Weaver), a world-renowned expert on serial killers, delivering a lecture in a crowded amphitheater. In the middle of her speech, she asks all the men in the room to stand, and then asks all nonwhites and those outside the age range of twenty to thirty-five to be seated again. As she surveys the group of men who are left, Hudson informs her audience that "nine out of ten serial killers are white males between the ages of twenty and thirty-five—just like these." Reversing conventional expectations, in this scene Hudson breaks down the notion of the serial killer as the monstrous "other." After her lecture, however, Helen is attacked in the women's washroom by Darryll Lee Cullum (played by Harry Connick, Jr.), an escaped serial killer whom she had helped to convict. Although she survives the attack, she is plagued by a paralyzing case of agoraphobia. Given Weaver's reputation for strong female roles in films like the *Alien* series, her shift here to the role of victim is provocative.

Thirteen months later, a serial killer begins to stalk women in San Francisco, and Helen, almost despite herself, feels compelled to offer help to the police. Although she is dismissed as a hysteric by most of the force, M.J. and Reuben believe that Hudson may offer valuable advice.

Accordingly, with her help, they deduce that this particular murderer is systematically reproducing the modus operandi of earlier serial murderers: he is a copycat killer.

While M.J. and Helen initially have difficulty establishing a relationship, they eventually work together to trap the killer. It is the shared female gaze of the detective and psychiatrist that counters the voyeurism of the murderer. The two women jointly manipulate computer technology, survey the murder scenes, and ultimately rewrite the serial killer's script to assert their own agency. When Helen is targeted as the final victim of the killer (who is acting at the behest of the imprisoned Darryll Lee Cullum), she refuses to comply with the killer's attempt to reenact perfectly her earlier victimization in the washroom. Instead, though her life is in peril, she mocks him and asserts her position of knowledge and power: "You think I'm afraid of you? I know who you are. I know all about you. You're just a sad, second-rate, boring, impotent, little copycat." She spits at him, and manages to save M.J. by stabbing the killer with broken glass and spraying him in the face with a can of aerosol cleaner. As she bursts out onto the roof of the building, Helen overcomes her agoraphobia; and when the killer finds her there, she laughs at him. As he approaches her with a knife, M.J., who has followed the two to the roof, shoots him, once, in the shoulder (just as she had advised Reuben earlier). But when he proceeds toward her with a gun in his hand, she kills him in self-defense. As Helen walks toward M.J., she kicks away the killer's gun (as Reuben should have done in the earlier scene), and the two women smile at each other.

The film does not end here, however. Its conclusion is focalized through the perspective of Darryll Lee, who, like Hannibal Lecter in *The Silence of the Lambs*, oversees the film's conclusion. Darryll Lee is writing from prison to one of his psychopath disciples and wishing him "happy hunting"—the killer may be dead and Darryll Lee in prison, the film implies, but there are plenty of copycats out there to replace them. *Copycat* ends with the suggestion that Cullum will stalk Helen for as long as he lives, a suggestion that underlines the feature's promotional line:

"remember, *he*'s out there." Nonetheless, though this scene works to close off some of the revisionary possibilities offered in the roles occupied by the two women, *Copycat* does offer a reverse discourse in its revision of the victim paradigm and in its self-conscious thematization of the possibility of using repetition to differential ends. This film, and its literary and cinematic and television counterparts, indicates that the female detective genre is undergoing further twists and complications. The figure of the female investigator continues to reproduce itself. With new generic permutations, it also differs from itself in its continuing engagement with popular cultural fantasies and anxieties. In so doing, it raises provocative questions about the shifting nature, function, and potential of women's (detective) agency.

Appendix

The following reader survey was sent out on the electronic newsgroup "DorothyL," a forum intended for Internet discussions of detective fiction. The survey was used to assess the reading habits and preferences of detective fiction readers with access to the Internet. We received 112 responses; the majority of the respondents were women (97 as opposed to 15 men), and most were in their thirties or forties. The data illustrated that most respondents fell in the $50,000+ household-income bracket, and 59 out of the 112 were married (36 were single; 6 were divorced; 4 were separated or widowed). Most respondents had undertaken postgraduate studies (79) and only one had not finished primary school. Ninety-two of the respondents were American, 10 were Canadian, 4 Australian, and we received one response each from the Netherlands, Japan, Germany, and the United Kingdom. One respondent failed to answer this question. While, clearly, this is not a representative or quantitative survey, it does provide for interesting anecdotal information about those readers of detective fiction who have Internet access.

THE SURVEY

June 15, 1995

Dear Fellow DorothyLers,

I am an assistant professor in the Department of English at the University of Waterloo, Canada. I am conducting research on the reading habits and preferences of people who read mystery novels.

I would appreciate it very much if you would complete the attached, brief survey. The questions are quite general. Completion of the survey is voluntary and is expected to take about twenty minutes of your time. Although I would prefer if you answer all of the questionnaire items, please note that you may decline answering any questions you prefer not to answer. I ask that you please do not identify yourself in any way and that you understand that your participation is completely voluntary. On receiving your response, I will separate it from your e-mail address in order to preserve your anonymity.

Please reply to my e-mail address: mjones@watarts.uwaterloo.ca. PLEASE DO NOT REPLY TO DOROTHYL. Your response by July 1, 1995, would be greatly appreciated.

This project has been reviewed and approved through the Office of Human Research and Animal Care at the University of Waterloo. However, if you have any questions or concerns resulting from your participation in this study, please call this office at (519) 885–1211, extension 6005.

Thank you in advance for your assistance with this project. If after receiving this message you have any questions about this project, or would like information about the study results, please feel free to contact me by e-mail or telephone at (519) 885–1211, extension 5379.

Manina Jones, University of Waterloo
Waterloo, Ontario, Canada

THE QUESTIONNAIRE

1. Are you a regular reader of mystery novels? YES/NO
2. Who are your favourite authors? (List a maximum of five).
3. Do you regularly read mysteries by any of the authors listed below? YES/NO
   (Linda Barnes, Eleanor Taylor Bland, Elisabeth Bowers, Liza Cody,

Patricia Cornwell, Barbara D'Amato, Catherine Dain, Janet Dawson, Alison Drake, Susan Dunlap, Jean Femling, Katherine V. Forrest, Sue Grafton, Linda Grant, Sharon Gwyn Short, Joan Hess, Kathy Hogan Trocheck, Kay Hooper, Nancy Baker Jacobs, Karen Kijewski, Margaret Maron, Lee Martin, Lia Matera, Val McDermid, Marcia Muller, Meg O'Brien, Maxine O'Callaghan, Lillian O'Donnell, Sara Paretsky, Marissa Piesman, Sandra Scoppettone, Sarah Shankman, Gillian Slovo, April Smith, Julie Smith, Dana Stabenow, Elizabeth Atwood Taylor, Judith Van Gieson, Sandra West Prowell).

3a) If yes, which ones?

4. Who are your favourite female authors of detective fiction? (List a maximum of five).

5. Who are your favourite male authors of detective fiction? (List a maximum of five).

6. Do you enjoy detective novels with strong female heros? YES/NO

7. Do you prefer novels with amateur female detectives to those that feature professional women investigators (e.g., private detectives, lawyers, police officers)? YES/NO/I DON'T DISTINGUISH

7a) If you have a preference, why?

8. By and large, do you think of detective novels by women authors as feminist? YES/NO

8a) Why or why not?

9. Please add any further comments you may have.

10. What is your age?

11. What is your gender? M/F

12. What is your total household income?

(a) 0–$25,000 per year

(b) between $25,000 and 50,000 per year

(c) more than $50,000 per year

13. What is your current marital status?

(a) single

(b) married

(c) widowed

(d) separated

(e) divorced

14. What is your education level?

(a) less than grade 8 or equivalent

(b) primary school

(c) high school

(d) some college

(e) completed college

(f) post-graduate studies

15. In what country do you presently live?

Notes

1. THE PRIVATE EYE AND THE PUBLIC

1. Only Canadians Margaret Millar and L. R. Wright and Briton Ruth Rendell had won before.

2. Quotations attributed to authors, agents, and editors that are not followed by parenthetical citations refer to interviews by telephone, e-mail, or letter conducted specifically for this project. See the works cited for a full listing of these interviews and the dates on which they took place.

3. O'Callaghan describes her publishing history:

Death is Forever sold to Worldwide for their Raven House Mysteries in August of 1979 when the line was first being put together. *Death* was published in 1980 in the book club edition (the only ones marked as First Printing, identified as #28 and by the yellow frame around the cover photo); 1981 saw the mass market edition (identified as #14 with the yellow frame at the top, the photo bleeding off the bottom).

Raven House quickly bought two more titles—wonderful, until the ax fell. Accustomed to big romance market profits, sales were not up to expectations—although in today's market the figures look good. *Run from Nightmare* was just coming out; *Hit and Run* was in copy-editing. *Run* was virtually dumped; copies sold at Pick and Save for 39 cents. Rights to the three books were reassigned to me 1983 [*sic*]. . . .

By the time the rights reverted and my agent began to market *Hit and*

Run, I had other commitments [O'Callaghan also writes horror novels].
("Delilah, Then and Now" 3–4)

Hit and Run underwent extensive revisions, was bought by St. Martin's Press,
and was published in 1989. The series continues with *Set-Up* (1991), *Trade-Off*
(1994), and *Down for the Count* (1997).

4. Smith did create a male protagonist, Paul MacDonald, a soft-boiled private eye, but he appears in only two novels, *True Life Adventure* (1985) and
Huckleberry Fiend (1987).

5. We are borrowing from the PI Writers of America's definition of professional investigators: those characters who are paid for services rendered as part
of their investigative work. Thus not only private eyes but investigative report-
ers, attorneys who do their own investigating, insurance agents, and the like all
qualify.

6. It is difficult to be precise, since publishers do not generally make public
demographically based market surveys. More than half of the members of the
Mysterious Book Club (the Book-of-the-Month Club's mystery arm) are
women, and the same is true of the Mystery Guild (Carter 21).

2. GUMSHOE METAPHYSICS

1. Thrillers, westerns, and detective fiction, however, unlike romance fiction, have traditionally not been perceived as "women's genres" (see Modleski,
Loving with a Vengeance; Radway; Mumford). They thus tend to suffer rather less
at the hand of literary critics and in popular perception. In his article on detective fiction, for instance, W. H. Auden attempts to legitimize detective fiction
by masculinizing it in contrast with the feminine form of romance novels.

2. For example, it becomes particularly important to keep a serial writer's
backlist in print, as author J. A. Jance stresses: "people have gone back and read
all my backlist. So because all of the backlist is in print, they're all available. That's
the advantage of . . . series, from a marketing point of view, since as you pick
up new readers with expanded print runs of later books . . . people like what
you've done and go back and read those earlier jobs. [Unfortunately, sometimes
when] an author starts to hit it, the backlist has gone bye-bye because it's not in
print."

3. The only form that comes close to displaying this dynamic is the televi-

sion soap opera: viewers, through their letters, sometimes affect the fate of fictional characters and have direct influence on story lines.

4. Quotation used with permission of the author.

5. Eleanor Taylor Bland and Chassie West also feature female African American protagonists and are published by mainstream presses, but their heroes (respectively, Marti MacAlister and Leigh Ann Warren) are police officers, and thus their novels conform more to the conventions of the police procedural than to the hard-boiled detective novel.

6. Forty respondents said they thought of these novels as feminist, 63 said they did not, and 8 qualified their answers.

7. Indeed, one respondent felt cheated by what he concluded was the unannounced (feminist?) "agenda" of the survey itself: "When I started to respond to this survey I thought that it dealt with the reading habits and preferences of people who read mystery novels. As I have completed the survey I have realized that you really had another agenda in mind. It's too bad!" (respondent 15).

8. We should acknowledge once again our indebtedness to the bibliographical work undertaken by the authors of these volumes. They were invaluable in documenting the rise of the female professional investigator novel and its relation to the genre as a whole.

9. For example, in the eighteenth century the early English novel was often argued to possess little merit in relation to the "serious" pursuit of poetry. Notably, in this debate the novelistic threat was characterized as feminine.

10. Marshall McLuhan argues in *From Cliché to Archetype* that in the nineteenth century, "the speed with which the printed word now related public and the author turned the author into a corporate one, and this distressed people like John Stuart Mill, Carlyle, and Matthew Arnold, who saw the new situation as tragic" (38)

11. The class of consumers, as Terry Eagleton points out, was for the first time composed of significant numbers of women: "The working class was not the only oppressed layer of Victorian society at whom 'English' was specifically beamed. English literature, reflected a Royal Commission witness in 1877, might be considered a suitable subject for 'women . . . and the second- and third-rate men who [. . .] become schoolmasters.' . . . The rise of English in England ran parallel to the gradual, grudging admission of women to the institutions of higher education" (27–28; bracketed ellipsis his).

12. Cynthia Hamilton documents the explosion of the pulps in the early

twentieth century: "Barely two dozen pulps were being published at the close of the First World War, but by the middle years of the Depression over 200 pulp magazines reached 25 million readers" (56).

13. In her provocative article "Banality in Cultural Studies" (1990), Meaghan Morris contends that one strain of contemporary cultural studies has become repetitive in its insistence on the supposedly radical transformative potential of popular culture: "I get the feeling that somewhere in some English publisher's vault there is a master disk from which thousands of versions of the same article about pleasure, resistance, and the politics of consumption are being run off under different names with minor variations" (21). The flood of "sexy" critical texts, sometimes superficial and formulaic in their analyses, has been called "the Routledgization of the academic world" (although Routledge is certainly not the only offending publisher—nor, obviously, are all Routledge texts at fault). Even more provocatively, Michelle Wallace has labeled some current cultural studies work as "mind-fuck candy for the intellectually overendowed" (23). Such observations point to the "trendiness factor" that is an aspect of mass media studies. Among other things, Morris's observations about the standardization of critical work leads us to identify the industrial capitalist model within the academy itself, flourishing as a result of professionalization, the pressure to publish, and the competition for jobs and job advancement (see also Nelson). Such an identification is important because it foregrounds the economic motivation, conventional basis, and politically implicated nature of scholarship in general. Criticism of popular culture, it is important to remember, is subject to the same historical, economic, political, and social influences and conflicts that drive and define its object of study.

14. Much of the early work Stacey censures was produced in the 1970s and early 1980s, and thus could not draw on the breadth of scholarship available to her in 1994.

3. DOES SHE OR DOESN'T SHE?

1. The debate over contemporary avant-garde writing—postmodern theory and fiction—casts an interesting light on arguments over finding feminist agency in detective fiction. Because postmodern literature often undertakes a decentering of the individual subject, many of its critics doubt its ability to convey subversive messages. In her theoretical writings, Nancy K. Miller engages with the

postmodern celebration of subject fragmentation (or the critique of the self-contained and coherent thinking, knowing being) by asserting that "only those who have it [subjectivity] can play with not having it" (53). While postmodern novels are frequently attacked for fracturing the subject and thereby displacing political potential by abrogating boundaries, critics of the feminist hard-boiled novel often condemn the mode for insufficiently questioning traditional liberal formations of subjectivity. For example, in appraising Anna Lee, Liza Cody's character, Sally Munt notes that the professional PI functions as "the self-determining agent of liberal fantasy, reinstating the quintessentially liberal myth of independence" (52). Munt inadvertently draws attention to a catch-22 faced by the woman writer: to some extent she's damned if she does, and damned if she doesn't. For a more extended discussion of the debate over poststructuralist and postmodern theory, see Butler and Scott's collection, *Feminists Theorize the Political*, and Hutcheon's *Politics of Postmodernism*.

2. Munt notes in passing that lesbian fiction constitutes a reverse discourse in action (126), but she does not extend her argument to explore the ways in which feminist revisions of the hard-boiled mode function similarly.

3. As we observed in chapter 1, the first installment of Eve Zaremba's lesbian detective series was published by a mainstream press, but this was "an aberration" (Zaremba, "A Canadian Speaks" 45).

4. Sandra Scoppettone describes her sense that the film and television industry lags behind popular novels in its representation of lesbians by about ten years. Scoppettone had her own brief encounter with Hollywood when actress Cybill Shepherd optioned her books: "She approached all the networks. Nobody would do it." Perhaps in return for Shepherd's enthusiasm for the project, Scoppettone makes her a "guest" character in *My Sweet Untraceable You*. Scoppettone relates that she was contacted by a prospective film producer just after her Lauren Laurano series first appeared; "We love everything you have," he said, "We think it's great, but is the lesbian thing important?"

4. THE TEXT AS EVIDENCE

1. As an example of the broad age spectrum that female PI novels reach, one eighty-five-year-old reader responded to our inquiries by observing that Sara Paretsky is her favorite author and that she "regularly reads" Linda Barnes, Sue Grafton, and Karen Kijewski. Grafton herself commented in an interview that

"I get notes from little old ladies who complain about my language. I write back and we have chats about the F-word. It's fun" ("G Is for (Sue) Grafton" 12).

2. In granting permission to reprint her essay in *The Art of the Mystery Story*, Nicolson noted,

> I hope it may be possible for you to call the attention of your readers to the fact that this essay was published in 1929. The only part of the essay which I think is now seriously out-of-date is my statement that women do not write good detective stories. In 1929 Agatha Christie's *The Murder of Roger Ackroyd* was well known, but as I indicated in the essay, it was written as a tour de force. In 1929, Dorothy Sayers was comparatively little known in America. Ngaio Marsh was still in her (literary) cradle. Other women like Mignon Eberhart and Leslie Ford were just beginning to appear on the horizon. As a matter of fact, so many of the best detective stories of the last decade have been written by women that my statement sounds either naïve or uncritical. Since these women are among my favourite mystery authors, I should not like readers to feel that I do not admire their works. Therefore if you can call the readers' attention to the fact, you will relieve my conscience and I won't feel that I have sold the ladies down the river! (111)

3. It is important to note that hard-boiled language did not necessarily come "naturally" even to its male practitioners. As Fredric Jameson has observed, Chandler himself, because he was educated in England, came to the American idiom secondhand: "even those clichés and commonplaces which for the native speaker are not really words at all, but instant communication, take on outlandish resonance in his mouth, *are used between quotation marks*, as you would delicately expose some interesting specimen" (124, emphasis added); the same argument has been used of Ross Macdonald, whose origins were Canadian (Knight 141).

4. Modleski sees a similar split in film production occurring around the same time:

> In the forties, a new movie genre derived from Gothic novels appeared around the time that hard-boiled detective fiction was being transformed by the medium into what movie critics currently call "film noir." . . . Beginning with Alfred Hitchcock's 1940 movie version of *Rebecca* and continuing through and beyond George Cukor's *Gaslight* in 1944, the gaslight films may be seen to reflect *women's* fears about losing their unprecedented freedoms and being forced back into the homes after the men returned from fighting to take over the jobs and assume control of their families. (*Loving with a Vengeance* 21)

5. Catherine Belsey defines closure in the "classic realist" text:

Among the commonest sources of disorder at the level of plot in classic realism are murder, war, a journey or love. But the story moves inevitably towards *closure* which is also disclosure, the dissolution of enigma through the
re-establishment of order, recognizable as a reinstatement or development of
the order which is understood to have preceded the events of the story itself.

The moment of closure is the point at which the events of the story become fully intelligible to the reader. The most obvious instance is the detective story where, in the final pages, the murderer is revealed and the motive
made plain. (70)

6. Rabinowitz also notes this echo ("Reader, I Blew Him Away" 333).

7. Scott Christianson describes the hard-boiled conceit as "a particularly
pointed or extended metaphor or simile which is usually serious, and which is
spoken to the reader directly to convey the detective/narrator's complex sensibility" ("Talkin' Trash" 133).

8. Some writers, like Dana Stabenow, use the hard-boiled simile as a marker
not of gender but of cultural difference. Stabenow's Aleut investigator Kate Shugak describes an oil pipeline whose outer metal layer is peeling off: "big chunks
of the second, foamlike layer were gouged out seemingly at random and a green
plastic subderma hung in strips like velvet from a caribou rack" (*Cold-Blooded
Business* 56).

5. PRIVATE I

1. Marcia Muller and Sue Dunlap are both examples of novelists who have
engaged in similar, though more extensive, "experiments" with different subgenres of mystery writing. Each is the author of three series. Muller has written
three Elena Oliverez novels, which feature an amateur museum curator; the
three-novel Joanna Stark series, which stars an art investigator; and the twenty-
novel (at most recent count) Sharon McCone private investigator series. Dunlap
has written ten (at last count) police procedurals, which focus on Jill Smith, a
California homicide detective; three Vejay Haskell mysteries, which feature an
amateur protagonist who works as a meter reader; and three (at last count)
private eye novels, whose main character is Kiernan O'Shaughnessy, a former
medical examiner who becomes a private investigator.

2. Others use "generic" names that have the feel of the vernacular use of

the surname as a name for men, in place of the more intimate first name: for example, Sue Grafton's Kinsey Millhone, Sue Dunlap's Kiernan O'Shaughnessy, Shelley Singer's Barrett Lake, Bridget McKenna's Caley Burke, and Kathy Hogan Trocheck's Callahan Garrity. V. I. Warshawski's responses to inquiries about her use of difficult-to-categorize initials and the nature of her first name constitute what amounts to a running gag in Paretsky's series ("Veeyai!" one character exclaims, "What an unusual name. Is it African?"; *Indemnity Only* 47). At one point, Warshawski explains that she uses her initials because "I started out my working life as a lawyer, and I found it was harder for male colleagues and opponents to patronize me if they didn't know my first name" (*Indemnity Only* 161).

3. For discussions relating to popular culture forms, see, for example, the collections *Female Spectators*, ed. Pribram; *The Female Gaze*, ed. Gamman and Marshment; and Mulvey's own "Afterthoughts on 'Visual Pleasure and Narrative Cinema' inspired by *Duel in the Sun*," included in her *Visual and Other Pleasures*.

4. Kathleen Gregory Klein has analyzed several early instances of female private eye novels (largely written by men) that seem incapable of reformulating the female detective as the subject of the gaze. These works evince what Klein calls a "*Playboy* ethos" glamorizing sexual liberation as a lifestyle—but from a male point of view (*Woman Detective* 175) that confuses the detective's role as subject of the investigation and her "necessary" role as object of the erotic gaze of the implicitly male reader. This confusion is perhaps best expressed in the title of Henry Kane's 1959 novel *Private Eyeful*, featuring detective Marla Trent. According to Klein, characters such as Kane's Marla Trent, G. G. Fickling's (a pseudonym for Gloria and Forrest E. Fickling) Honey West, and Arthur Kaplan's Charity Bay sexualize the detective's body, and these writings regularly make the association between her profession and prostitution. As Klein says of Fickling's character, she manages to lose her clothes in the course of most investigations, and

> Regular puns on "private eye" and "private parts" are enhanced for a Broadway production about her life:
>
>> I'm a private eye,
>> With a private list of parts,
>> That you cannot buy
>> In any stores or supermarts.
>> My equipment is expensive,

And sometimes quite recompensive,
As you can see!

([Fickling,] *Blood and Honey* 25)

(qtd. 132)

According to Willeta Heisling, the Honey West series was "a big success, and [she] ended up with her own television series starring Anne Francis" (*Detecting Women* 2 67).

Klein's analysis is particularly interesting given that the *Playboy* ethos she identifies is reproduced in the adaptation of Sara Paretsky's V. I. Warshawski's character from fiction to the film *V. I. Warshawski* (see chapter 7).

5. Bogart played both Sam Spade and Philip Marlowe.

6. Wingate did go on to become a reporter and a Georgia police sergeant, as well as a novelist.

7. This is certainly not to say that writers of mysteries featuring amateur detectives are not professionals in their own right. Their professional status, however, is a less prominent feature of the reception of the novels, and the functions of professionally telling and doing come together in the "private eye" novel in particularly significant ways.

8. Janet Dawson remarks, "It's not that I set out to find a particular soapbox with each book." Linda Grant comments that "a soapbox is a pretty boring place." Sara Paretsky notes that "I don't want to be on a soapbox as a writer, because I think the quickest way to kill your fiction is to be writing sermons with it" (qtd. in Shapiro 93). Maxine O'Callaghan writes, "I don't believe in soapboxes." Nancy Baker Jacobs says that her character "deals with feminist issues all the time, though I'm hoping that she's not up on her soapbox." Laurie R. King asserts that she avoids making "a conscious choice of axes to grind or soap boxes to stand upon. . . . [I]t takes a great deal of skill to remove the whiff of the pulpit from the pages." Shelley Singer observes that in teaching mystery writing, "I try to convince people not to make speeches in their books. It's a very difficult thing to keep from lecturing in fiction."

6. PLOTTING AGAINST THE LAW

1. Porter quotes Lee Kennett and James La Verne Anderson's *Gun in America* (187–88). Cynthia S. Hamilton argues that the problems of corruption and

criminal conspiracy were to some extent a creation of the national press's lurid reporting of the time (30).

2. Bethany Ogodon suggests that "the 'destroying woman' is as much a localisation or symbolization of the degenerate, corrupt, soft-boiled and always dangerous masses (who, in America, are perceived as immigrants, a word which has a dirty flavour in this culture) as she is an exemplar of the treacherous nature of 'Woman'" (82). The dangerous "other" of hard-boiled fiction, Ogodon argues, frequently incorporates nonwhite men, women, and homosexual and impotent white men (76).

3. Liza Cody calls this "the giggling bimbo syndrome" in hard-boiled fiction and cites it as a part of the "negative" influence on her work by writers such as Hammett and Chandler: "I find their women . . . poisonous" (interview by Richler).

4. British author Sarah Dunant may even be calling attention to a connection with Woolf by naming her private eye "Hannah Wolfe"—which of course also resonates with the detective's role as "lone wolf."

5. Linda Barnes's Carlotta Carlyle also finds herself attracted to a man on the wrong side of the law: Sam Giannelli, son of a mobster. Her friend Mooney, a police officer who would like a romantic relationship with her, chides her for being "attracted to outlaws, not cops" (*Snapshot* 34).

6. Tzvetan Todorov's famous work on detective fiction describes the narrative "architecture" of the murder mystery as composed of a doubled structure in which two stories gradually converge: the story of the crime, which is initially an unknown quantity (and often transpires prior to the narrative of the novel), and the story of the investigation whose purpose it is to reconstruct the true story of the crime, thereby allowing the identification and punishment of the perpetrator (44).

7. Literary critic Roland Barthes argues that narratives in general are structured by the deciphering of an enigma: an unknown principle or missing element is gradually elaborated by the story's telling. The reader's desire to be fully informed (in the terms of the story), which drives her or his relationship with the narrative, is ultimately satisfied by the work's conclusion (76). Barthes's observations have often been taken as a particularly good description of the traditional detective story's narrative unfolding. For example, an excerpt from Barthes' book *S/Z* is included in Most and Stowe's *Poetics of Murder* under the title "Delay and the Hermeneutic Sentence," though it (unlike the other essays in the volume) does not explicitly deal with detective fiction.

8. Northrop Frye describes the quest as an essential aspect of the literary romance plot: "The essential element of plot in romance is adventure, which means that romance is naturally a sequential and processional form. . . . The complete form of the romance is clearly the successful quest, and such a completed form has three main stages: the stage of the perilous journey and the preliminary minor adventures; the crucial struggle, usually some kind of battle in which either the hero or his foe, or both, must die; and the exaltation of the hero" (186–87). While the hero of the quest narrative may be a Messianic hero and redeemer of society, secular quest-romances may have "more obvious motives and rewards," like treasure (192–93).

7. "SHE'S WATCHING THE DETECTIVES"

1. We are indebted to Barri Cohen and Kevin Dowler for the phrase "gals with guns."

2. Films noirs were also often literally adapted from hard-boiled novels: for instance, John Huston's *The Maltese Falcon* (1941), Howard Hawks's *The Big Sleep* (1946), Billy Wilder's *Double Indemnity* (1944), Edward Dmytryk's *Murder, My Sweet* (1944, based on Chandler's *Farewell, My Lovely*), Irving Reis's *The Falcon Takes Over* (1942, based on Chandler's *Farewell, My Lovely*), Stuart Heister's *The Glass Key* (1942), Robert Montgomery's *Lady in the Lake* (1946), and Robert Aldrich's *Kiss Me Deadly* (1955). Both Hammett and Chandler worked in Hollywood as screenwriters.

3. This historical overview of the Hollywood studio system and its collapse is indebted to work such as Bordwell, Staiger, and Thompson's *Classical Hollywood Cinema* and Schatz's *Hollywood Genres*.

4. The collection produced by the Women's Studies Department at the University of Minnesota contains some 150 pages of reviews published over an approximately six-month period. Reviews bear titles such as "Women Who Kill Too Much: Is 'Thelma and Louise' Feminism or Fascism?," "The Deadlier of the Species," "Toxic Feminism on the Big Screen," etc.

5. The popularity of series film, in contrast, declined with the studio system after World War II, although it is showing signs of resurgence.

6. The advent of easily accessible home videos and perhaps more regular viewing may develop a different dynamic.

7. *Thelma and Louise* demonstrates that generic reversals are possible, but the

film shows few signs of having produced spin-offs operating similarly in the genre.

8. Foster was awarded an Oscar for her performance during the Motion Picture Academy's designated "Year of the Woman"—a year marked, ironically, by a dearth of strong female roles. Anthony Hopkins also received an Oscar for his role.

9. In "Making the Call," Peter J. Rabinowitz discusses the generic refusal performed by the film when Megan resists the urge to call in the police.

10. Sandra Scoppettone has remarked, referring to Bronson's star status, "My idea of Mike Donato was not Charles Bronson. But of course that's why it [the film] got made."

11. Bob Rafelson's 1986 film *Black Widow*, which features a female investigator for the Justice Department played by Debra Winger, is another interesting exploration of the paradigm; here, the object of the investigation is another woman (played by Theresa Russell). Essays by Valerie Traub and Cherry Smyth explore the lesbian subtext generated by this relationship.

12. As *Time* magazine's Richard Corliss perceived, the film was a conspicuous manifestation of the Hollywood machine's efforts to address a "lingering dilemma: how to get women into the summer movie mainstream" (66), a market dominated by male action films. Based on the popularity of the early Paretsky novels, and on growing sales of the "tough gal private eye" genre, in 1985 Tri-Star Pictures optioned lifetime character rights on Paretsky's Warshawski series for what *Variety* estimates as a "modest amount—probably a low six-figure pickup" (Max, "'Warshawski's' Mysterious Journey" 71). Paretsky's explanation of her decision to sell the rights to her character is an economic one: she has argued that the initial sale allowed her to quit her day job with an insurance company in order to pursue a career as a full-time novelist (interview by Gzowski). She has, however, been notably circumspect about her response to the film, and it appears she was given little opportunity to participate in its production.

13. It should be noted that in the novel, while V.I. professionally represents Kat, she leaves the child safe with a male caregiver in order to pursue the case.

14. Mary Doyle has argued for the V. I. Warshawski film character as "one small step for womankind."

15. The Arnold Schwarzenegger extravaganza *The Last Action Hero* had a budget of more than $70 million, whereas even a lavish historical romance like

The Portrait of a Lady had a budget of only $12 million. *The Piano* cost $8 million; *Four Weddings and a Funeral*, $4 million; *Little Women*, $6 million; and *Waiting to Exhale*, $15 million.

16. Douglas notes that according to the Nielsen ratings, at one time 59 percent of all TV sets were tuned to *Charlie's Angels* (212).

17. We are indebted to Kevin Dowler for this insight about Maddie's "excess." Alison Lee argues that *Moonlighting*'s postmodern gestures were firmly contained within a realist frame (134). Nonetheless, the series is a precursor of such experimental television programs as David Lynch's *Twin Peaks*.

18. It should be noted that before *Prime Suspect*, the *Mystery!* anthology program had been dominated by adaptations of traditional British literary mysteries, such as those featuring Doyle's Sherlock Holmes, Christie's Miss Marple and Hercule Poirot, Dorothy L. Sayers's Peter Wimsey, and Margery Allingham's Albert Campion stories. Though it also included more contemporary police procedurals based on the work of P. D. James (featuring Inspector Dalgleish) and Colin Dexter (featuring Inspector Morse), these did not tend to focus in a self-conscious way on urban settings as the *Prime Suspect* series did. And the anthology had also been lily white in its racial constitution—a feature thrown into relief by *Prime Suspect 2*, which focused on racial tensions on the police squad and in the neighborhoods of contemporary London.

19. The parallel between Tennison's and Oswald's positions is brought forward in a later scene when Tennison accuses Oswald of trying too hard at his job: "What are you trying to prove?" Oswald replies, "Well, you're no different. I watched you on the [training] course [where Oswald and Tennison met and had a brief affair]. You know they're all lined up wanting to see you fall flat on your face. So you want to be the best, come out on top. And I'm the same as you. Which is why, when I calmed down and thought about it, I understood why you've been treating me like the office boy." When Tennison reminds him that he is part of a team, his reply—"Am I?"—reflects his exclusion both by "the lads" and by Tennison.

20. A similar strategy is employed in Linda Fairstein's novel *Final Jeopardy*. In that novel, the female protagonist is able to identify a suspect by his distinctive shirt cuff (139).

21. Interestingly, when Helen Mirren accepted her Emmy Award for *Prime Suspect: Inner Circles*, she thanked *Cagney and Lacey* for paving the way.

22. Of the five segments aired to date, two ("Headcase" and "Dupe") closely

follow Liza Cody's novels of the same name. The other three episodes are merely "based on characters developed by Liza Cody."

23. Patricia Cornwell has been commissioned as executive producer and screenwriter of a film version of her novel *From Potter's Field*. She has also signed a $27 million, three-book deal with the Putnam publishing house (E. Bennett).

24. The darkly comic Cohen brothers movie *Fargo* (1996), too, suggests challenges to genre conventions, especially in its portrayal of a pregnant police chief, as does John Waters's satiric *Serial Mom* (1994).

Works Cited

PRIMARY TEXTS

Barr, Nevada. *Track of the Cat*. New York: Putnam, 1993.

Barnes, Linda. *Coyote*. New York: Dell, 1990.

———. *Snapshot*. New York: Dell, 1994.

———. *A Trouble of Fools*. New York: Fawcett Crest, 1987.

Beal, M. F. *Angel Dance*. New York: Daughters, 1977.

Bland, Eleanor Taylor. *Dead Time*. New York: Signet, 1993.

———. *Slow Burn*. New York: Signet, 1993.

Blue Steel. Directed by Kathryn Bigelow. MGM, 1990.

Borton, D. B. *One for the Money*. New York: Diamond, 1993.

Bowers, Elisabeth. *Ladies Night*. Seattle: Seal, 1988.

———. *No Forwarding Address*. Seattle: Seal, 1991.

Cannon, Taffy. *A Pocketful of Karma*. New York: Fawcett Crest, 1993.

Chandler, Raymond. *The Big Sleep*. New York: Vintage, 1976.

———. *The Little Sister*. New York: Ballantine, 1949.

Cody, Liza. *Bad Company*. 1982. London: Arrow, 1993.

———. *Bucket Nut*. London: Arrow, 1992.

———. *Headcase*. 1985. London: Arrow, 1992.

———. *Monkey Wrench*. London: Arrow, 1995.

———. *Musclebound*. New York: Mysterious, 1997.

"The Cook's Tale." *Anna Lee Mysteries*. Based on characters by Liza Cody. London Weekend Television, 1994. Arts & Entertainment Network, 1995.

Copycat. Directed by Jon Amiel. Starring Holly Hunter and Sigourney Weaver. Warner Brothers, 1995.

Dain, Catherine. *Bet Against the House*. New York: Berkley, 1995.

———. *Walk a Crooked Mile*. New York: Jove, 1994.

D'Amato, Barbara. *Hardball*. New York: Worldwide, 1991.

———. *Hard Luck*. New York: Worldwide, 1992.

———. *Hard Women*. New York: Scribner, 1993.

Dawson, Janet. *Kindred Crimes*. New York: Fawcett Crest, 1990.

———. *Take a Number*. New York: Fawcett Crest, 1993.

Day, Marele. *The Case of the Chinese Boxes*. London: Coronet, 1994.

———. *The Life and Crimes of Harry Lavender*. London: Coronet, 1988.

"Diversion." *Anna Lee Mysteries*. Based on characters by Liza Cody. Granada Television, 1993. Arts & Entertainment Network, 1995.

Donato and Daughter. Directed by Rod Holcomb. Starring Charles Bronson and Dana Delany. CBS, 1990.

Dunant, Sarah. *Fatlands*. London: Penguin, 1993.

———. *Under My Skin*. London: Penguin, 1996.

"Dupe." *Anna Lee Mysteries*. Based on the novel by Liza Cody. London Weekend Television, 1994. Arts & Entertainment Network, 1995.

Fairstein, Linda. *Final Jeopardy*. New York: Scribner, 1996.

Forrest, Katherine V. *Murder at the Nightwood Bar*. Tallahassee, Fla.: Naiad, 1991.

———. *Murder by Tradition*. Tallahassee, Fla.: Naiad, 1991.

Furie, Ruth. *If Looks Could Kill*. New York: Avon, 1995.

Grafton, Sue. *"A" Is for Alibi*. New York: Bantam, 1987.

———. *"B" Is for Burglar*. New York: Bantam, 1986.

———. *"C" Is for Corpse*. New York: Bantam, 1987.

———. *"D" Is for Deadbeat*. New York: Bantam, 1988.

———. *"E" Is for Evidence*. New York: Bantam, 1989.

———. *"F" Is for Fugitive*. New York: Bantam, 1990.

———. *"G" Is for Gumshoe*. New York: Fawcett Crest, 1990.

———. *"H" Is for Homicide*. New York: Fawcett Crest, 1991.

———. *"I" Is for Innocent*. New York: Holt, 1992.

———. *"J" Is for Judgment*. New York: Holt, 1993.

Grant, Linda. *A Woman's Place*. New York: Scribner, 1994.

Grant-Adamson, Lesley. *Flynn*. London: Faber and Faber, 1991.

Hammett, Dashiell. *The Maltese Falcon*. 1929. New York: Vintage, 1992.

Hayter, Sparkle. *Nice Girls Finish Last*. New York: Viking, 1995.

———. *What's a Girl Gotta Do?* New York: Penguin, 1994.

"Headcase." *Anna Lee Mysteries*. Based on the novel by Liza Cody. London Weekend Television, 1993. Arts & Entertainment Network, 1995.

Horansky, Ruby. *Dead Ahead*. New York: Avon, 1990.

Hornsby, Wendy. *Bad Intent*. New York: Penguin, 1995.

———. *Midnight Baby*. New York: Signet, 1994.

Jacobs, Nancy Baker. *The Silver Scalpel*. New York: Putnam, 1993.

———. *A Slash of Scarlet*. New York: Pocket Books, 1992.

———. *The Turquoise Tattoo*. New York: Pocket Books, 1991.

James, P. D. *The Skull Beneath the Skin*. Harmondsworth: Penguin, 1982.

———. *An Unsuitable Job for a Woman*. London: Faber and Faber, 1972.

Kijewski, Karen. *Copy Kat*. New York: Bantam, 1992.

———. *Kat's Cradle*. New York: Bantam, 1992.

———. *Katwalk*. New York: Avon, 1990.

Komo, Dolores. *Clio Browne: Private Investigator*. Freedom, Calif.: Crossing, 1988.

Krich, Rochelle Majer. *Angel of Death*. New York: Mysterious, 1994.

Lacey, Sarah. *File Under: Missing*. London: Coronet, 1993.

Lambert, Mercedes. *Dogtown*. New York: Penguin, 1991.

Law, Janice. *Backfire*. New York: Worldwide, 1994.

———. *The Big Payoff*. Boston: Houghton Mifflin, 1976.

———. *Cross-check*. New York: St. Martin's, 1997.

Lee, Wendi. *The Good Daughter*. New York: St. Martin's, 1994.

Lin-Chandler, Irene. *The Healing of Holly-Jean*. London: Headline, 1995.

Macdonald, Ross. *The Drowning Pool*. New York: Warner, 1977.

Matera, Lia. *Designer Crimes*. New York: Pocket, 1995.

———. *Face Value*. New York: Pocket, 1995.

———. *A Radical Departure*. New York: Ballantine, 1988.

———. *The Smart Money*. New York: Ballantine, 1988.

———. *Where Lawyers Fear to Tread*. New York: Ballantine, 1987.

McDermid, Val. *Crack Down*. New York: Scribner, 1994.

———. *Dead Beat*. London: Gollancz, 1992.

———. *Kick Back*. London: Gollancz, 1993.

Muller, Marcia. *Edwin of the Iron Shoes.* New York: Mysterious, 1977.

———. *Trophies and Dead Things.* New York: Mysterious, 1990.

———. *A Wild and Lonely Place.* New York: Mysterious, 1995.

Muller, Marcia, and Bill Pronzini. *Double.* New York: Mysterious, 1984.

O'Brien, Meg. *Salmon in the Soup.* New York: Bantam, 1990.

O'Callaghan, Maxine. "A Change of Clients." *Alfred Hitchcock's Mystery Magazine*, January 1974, 23–39.

———. *Death Is Forever.* Raven House Mysteries. Toronto: Worldwide, 1980.

O'Donnell, Lillian. *The Phone Calls.* New York: Putnam, 1972.

Papazoglou, Orania. *Wicked, Loving Murder.* New York: Penguin, 1985.

Paretsky, Sara. *Bitter Medicine.* New York: Ballantine, 1987.

———. *Blood Shot.* New York: Dell, 1988.

———. *Burn Marks.* New York: Delacorte, 1990.

———. *Deadlock.* New York: Ballantine, 1984.

———. *Guardian Angel.* New York: Delacorte, 1992.

———. *Indemnity Only.* New York: Ballantine, 1982.

———. *Killing Orders.* New York: Ballantine, 1985.

———. *Tunnel Vision.* New York: Delacorte, 1994.

Pincus, Elizabeth. *The Two-Bit Tango.* San Francisco: Spinsters, 1992.

Prime Suspect. Written by Lynda La Plante. Starring Helen Mirren. Granada Television/WGBH. *Mystery!* PBS, 1991.

Prime Suspect 2. Written by Alan Cubitt. Starring Helen Mirren. Granada Television/WGBH. *Mystery!* PBS, 1992.

Prime Suspect 3. Written by Lynda La Plante. Starring Helen Mirren. Granada Television/WGBH. *Mystery!* PBS, 1993.

Prowell, Sandra West. *By Evil Means.* New York: Bantam, 1993.

———. *The Killing of Monday Brown.* New York: Walker, 1994.

Redmann, J. M. *The Intersection of Law and Desire.* New York: Norton, 1995.

"Requiem." *Anna Lee Mysteries.* Based on characters by Liza Cody. London Weekend Television, 1994. Arts & Entertainment Network, 1996.

Rozan, S. J. *China Trade.* New York: St. Martin's, 1994.

Scoppettone, Sandra. *Everything You Have Is Mine.* New York: Ballantine, 1991.

———. *I'll Be Leaving You Always.* New York: Little, Brown, 1993.

———. *My Sweet Untraceable You.* New York: Ballantine, 1994.

Short, Sharon Gwyn. *Past Pretense.* New York: Ballantine, 1994.

The Silence of the Lambs. Directed by Jonathan Demme. Orion, 1991.

Smith, April. *North of Montana*. New York: Knopf, 1994.

Smith, Julie. *Death Turns a Trick*. New York: Ivy, 1982.

———. *New Orleans Mourning*. New York: Ivy, 1990.

Spillane, Mickey. *I, the Jury*. 1947. Reprint, New York: Signet, 1975.

Spring, Michelle. *Every Breath You Take*. New York: Pocket, 1994.

———. *Running for Shelter*. London: Orion, 1996.

Stabenow, Dana. *A Cold-Blooded Business*. New York: Berkley, 1994.

———. *Dead in the Water*. New York: Berkley, 1993.

Trocheck, Kathy Hogan. *Every Crooked Nanny*. New York: HarperCollins, 1992.

———. *To Live and Die in Dixie*. New York: HarperCollins, 1993.

Uhnak, Dorothy. *The Bait*. New York: Simon and Schuster, 1968.

———. *The Ledger*. New York: Simon and Schuster, 1970.

———. *Policewoman: A Young Woman's Initiation into the Realities of Justice*. New York: Simon and Schuster, 1964.

———. *The Witness*. New York: Simon and Schuster, 1969.

V. I. Warshawski. Directed by Jeff Kanew. Starring Kathleen Turner. A Buena Vista release of a Hollywood Pictures presentation in association with Silver Screen Partners IV of a Jeffrey Lurie and Chestnut Hill production, 1991.

Van Gieson, Judith. *North of the Border*. New York: Pocket, 1988.

———. *Parrot Blues*. New York: HarperCollins, 1995.

Walker, Mary Willis. *Red Scream*. New York: Doubleday, 1994.

Wesley, Valerie Wilson. *Devil's Gonna Get Him*. New York: Putnam, 1995.

———. *When Death Comes Stealing*. New York: Putnam, 1994.

West, Chassie. *Sunrise*. New York: HarperCollins, 1994.

Wheat, Carolyn. *Dead Man's Thoughts*. New York: Dell, 1983.

White, Gloria. *Charged with Guilt*. New York: Dell, 1995.

Wilson, Barbara. *Sisters of the Road*. Seattle: Seal, 1986.

Wings, Mary. *She Came by the Book*. New York: Berkley, 1996.

Zaremba, Eve. *A Reason to Kill*. Toronto: Amanita, 1978.

CRITICAL WORKS

Adorno, Theodor W. *The Culture Industry: Selected Essays on Mass Culture*. Edited by J. M. Bernstein. London: Routledge, 1991.

Allen, Dennis W. "Mistaken Identities: Re-Defining Lesbian and Gay Studies." *Canadian Review of Comparative Literature* 21 (1994): 133–48.

Ames, Katrine, and Ray Sawhill. "Murder Most Foul and Fair." *Newsweek*, May 14, 1990, 66–69.

Annichiarico, Mark, Eric Bryant, Amy Boaz Nugent, Wilda Williams, and Barbara Hoffert. "Backed by Popular Demand." *Library Journal*, February 15, 1994, 120–23.

Anthony, Carolyn. "Many Ways to Mayhem." *Publishers Weekly*, October 17, 1994, 43–44, 50, 52, 54.

———. "Mystery Books: Crime Marches On." *Publishers Weekly*, April 13, 1990, 24–29.

Arnold, Matthew. *Culture and Anarchy* (1869). Edited by J. Dover Wilson. London: Cambridge University Press, 1984.

Auden, W. H. "The Guilty Vicarage." In *The Dyer's Hand and Other Essays*, 146–58. London: Faber, 1963.

Bakerman, Jane S. "Living 'Openly and with Dignity': Sara Paretsky's New-Boiled Feminist Fiction." *Midamerica: The Yearbook of the Society for the Study of Midwestern Literature* 12 (1985): 120–35.

Barthes, Roland. *S/Z: An Essay* (1974). Translated by Richard Miller. New York: Hill and Wang, 1985.

Belsey, Catherine. *Critical Practice*. London: Methuen, 1980.

Bennett, Eugene. "Stranger Than Fiction." *People*, July 22, 1996, 44–45.

Bennett, Tony. *Formalism and Marxism*. London: Methuen, 1979.

———. "Putting Policy into Cultural Studies." In Grossberg, Nelson, and Treichler, *Cultural Studies* 23–37.

Benstock, Shari. *Textualizing the Feminine: On the Limits of Genre*. Norman: University of Oklahoma Press, 1991.

Berger, Arthur Asa. *Popular Culture Genres*. London: Sage, 1992.

Bird, Delys, ed. *Killing Women: Rewriting Detective Fiction*. Sydney: Angus and Robertson, 1993.

Bird, Delys, and Brenda Walker. Introduction to Bird, *Killing Women* 1–61.

Bordwell, David, Janet Staiger, and Kristen Thompson. *The Classical Hollywood Cinema: Film Style and Mode of Production to 1960*. New York: Columbia University Press, 1985.

Bourdieu, Pierre. *The Field of Cultural Production: Essays on Art and Literature*. Edited by Randal Johnson. New York: Columbia University Press, 1993.

Brainard, Dulcy. "Marcia Muller: 'The Time Was Ripe.'" *Publishers Weekly*, August 8, 1994, 361–62.

Brooks, Dianne L. "Television and Legal Identity in *Prime Suspect.*" *Studies in Law, Politics, and Society* 14 (1994): 89–104.

Brown, Susan. "Violating Conventions: Barbara Wilson's *Sisters of the Road* and the Feminist Detective Novel." Paper delivered at the Learned Societies Conference, Charlottetown, Prince Edward Island, May 1993. Photocopy.

Brunt, Rosalind. "Engaging with the Popular: Audiences for Mass Culture and What to Say about Them." In Grossberg, Nelson, and Treichler, *Cultural Studies* 69–80.

Butler, Judith. *Bodies That Matter: On the Discursive Limits of "Sex."* New York: Routledge, 1993.

———. *Gender Trouble: Feminism and the Subversion of Identity.* New York: Routledge, 1990.

Butler, Judith, and Joan W. Scott, eds. *Feminists Theorize the Political.* New York: Routledge, 1992.

Byars, Jackie. "Gazes/Voices/Power: Expanding Psychoanalysis for Feminist Film and Television Theory." In Pribram, *Female Spectators* 110–31.

Callendar, Newgate [pseud.]. Review of *"A" Is for Alibi,* by Sue Grafton. *New York Times Book Review,* May 23, 1982, 41.

———. Review of *Edwin of the Iron Shoes,* by Marcia Muller. *New York Times Book Review,* November 27, 1977, 36.

———. Review of *Indemnity Only,* by Sara Paretsky. *New York Times Book Review,* April 25, 1982, 21.

Carcaterra, Lorenzo. "B Is for Bestseller." *Writer's Digest,* January 1991, 43–45.

Carter, Robert A. "Scene of the Crime." *Publisher's Weekly,* March 29, 1991, 17–21.

Cawelti, John. *Adventure, Mystery, and Romance: Formula Stories as Art and Popular Culture.* Chicago: University of Chicago Press, 1976.

———. "The Study of Literary Formulas." In *Detective Fiction: A Collection of Critical Essays,* edited by Robin W. Winks, 121–43. Englewood Cliffs, N.J.: Prentice-Hall, 1980.

Chambers, Andrea, and David Hutchings. "Make No Bones about It, Sue Grafton's Detective Heroine Is a Real Pistol." *People,* July 10, 1989, 81–82.

Chandler, Raymond. *Raymond Chandler Speaking.* Edited by Dorothy Gardiner and Kathrine Sorley Walker. London: Hamish Hamilton, 1962.

———. "The Simple Art of Murder." In *The Art of the Mystery Story,* edited by Howard Haycraft, 222–37. New York: Grosset and Dunlap, 1946.

Christianson, Scott R. "A Heap of Broken Images: Hardboiled Detective Fiction and the Discourse(s) of Modernity." In *The Cunning Craft: Original Essays on Detective Fiction and Contemporary Literary Theory*, edited by Ronald G. Walker and June M. Frazer, 135–48. Macomb: Western Illinois University Press, 1990.

———. "Talkin' Trash and Kickin' Butt: Sue Grafton's Hard-boiled Feminism." In Irons, *Feminism in Women's Detective Fiction* 127–47.

Citron, Michelle. "Women's Film Production: Going Mainstream." In Pribram, *Female Spectators* 45–63.

Clover, Carol. "Her Body, Himself: Gender in the Slasher Film." In *Fantasy and the Cinema*, edited by James Donald, 91–133. London: British Film Institute, 1989.

Cody, Liza. Interview by Daniel Richler. *Imprint*. Toronto: TVOntario, May 1992.

Corliss, Richard. Review of *V. I. Warshawski*. *Time*, May 8, 1991, 66.

Costello, Elvis. "Watching the Detectives." By Elvis Costello. *My Aim Is True*. London, 1977. Demon Records 20271. Audiocassette.

Coward, Rosalind, and Linda Semple. "Tracking Down the Past: Women and Detective Fiction." In *Genre and Women's Writing in the Postmodern World*, edited by Helen Carr, 39–57. London: Pandora, 1989.

Cranny-Francis, Anne. *Feminist Fiction*. Cambridge: Polity, 1990.

D'Acci, Julie. *Defining Women: Television and the Case of "Cagney and Lacey."* Chapel Hill: University of North Carolina Press, 1994.

D'Amato, Barbara. "Welcome to Sisters in Crime!" Promotional letter for Sisters in Crime. November 1994.

Dahlin, Robert. "Expanding the Scene of the Crime: Judging from the Body of Evidence, the Basic Whodunit Now Spills Over into Thrillers, Even General Fiction." *Publishers Weekly*, April 22, 1996, 38–47.

Daly, Carroll John. "Three Gun Terry." In Nolan, *Black Mask Boys* 43–72.

Dargis, Manohia. Review of *V. I. Warshawski*. *Village Voice*, August 6, 1991, 64.

Davie, Donald. "Ezra Pound's *Hugh Selwyn Mauberley*." In *The Pelican Guide to English Literature: The Modern Age*, edited by Boris Ford, 315–29. Harmondsworth: Penguin, 1964.

De Lauretis, Teresa. *The Practice of Love: Lesbian Sexuality and Perverse Desire*. Bloomington: Indiana University Press, 1994.

Décuré, Nicole. "V. I. Warshawski, a 'Lady with Guts': Feminist Crime Fiction by Sara Paretsky." *Women's Studies International Forum* 12 (1989): 227–38.

Deming, Robert H. *"Kate and Allie:* 'New Women' and the Audience's Television Archives." In Spigel and Mann, *Private Screenings* 203–16.

Doane, Mary Ann. *Femmes Fatales: Feminism, Film Theory, Psychoanalysis.* New York: Routledge, 1991.

Doane, Mary Ann, Patricia Mellencamp, and Linda Williams, eds. *Re-Vision: Essays in Feminist Film Criticism.* Los Angeles: American Film Institute, 1984.

Douglas, Susan J. *Where the Girls Are: Growing Up Female with the Mass Media.* New York: Random House, 1995.

Doyle, Mary. "Cross Currents." *Globe and Mail* (Toronto), August 2, 1991, A7.

Dunant, Sarah. "Rewriting the Detectives: For the Increasing Numbers of Women Entering the Crime Thriller Genre, One Question Is Paramount: How Do You Beat Up a Contemporary Heroine?" *Guardian,* June 29, 1993, Features sec., 28.

Eagleton, Terry. *Literary Theory: An Introduction.* Minneapolis: University of Minnesota Press, 1983.

Easthope, Antony. *Literary into Cultural Studies.* London: Routledge, 1991.

Ebert, Roger. *Roger Ebert's Video Companion.* Kansas City, Mo.: Andrews McMeel, 1994.

Eco, Umberto. "Innovation and Repetition: Between Modern and Post-Modern Aesthetics." *Daedalus* 114 (1985): 159–88.

Ellis, John. *Visible Fictions: Cinema, Television, Video.* London: Routledge and Kegan Paul, 1982.

Faludi, Susan. *Backlash: The Undeclared War against American Women.* New York: Crown, 1991.

Fiske, John. "Popular Discrimination." In *Modernity and Mass Culture,* edited by James Naremore and Patrick Brantlinger, 103–16. Bloomington: Indiana University Press, 1991.

Foucault, Michel. *The History of Sexuality: An Introduction.* Translated by Robert Hurley. New York: Vintage, 1990.

Francke, Lizzie. *Script Girls: Women Screenwriters in Hollywood.* London: British Film Institute, 1994.

Friedan, Betty. *The Feminine Mystique.* New York: Dell, 1964.

Frye, Northrop. *Anatomy of Criticism: Four Essays.* 1957. Reprint, Princeton: Princeton University Press, 1973.

Gamman, Lorraine. "Watching the Detectives: The Enigma of the Female

Gaze." In *The Female Gaze: Women as Viewers of Popular Culture*, edited by Lorraine Gamman and Margaret Marshment, 8–26. London: Women's Press, 1988.

Gamman, Lorraine, and Margaret Marshment, eds. *The Female Gaze: Women as Viewers of Popular Culture*. London: Women's Press, 1988.

Geeson, Susan. "Ain't Misbehavin'." In Bird, *Killing Women* 111–23.

Gibson, Edie. "The Sisterhood of Sleuths." *Publishers Weekly*, May 5, 1989, 27–39.

Gibson, Walker W. *Tough, Sweet, and Stuffy: An Essay on Modern American Prose Styles*. Bloomington: Indiana University Press, 1966.

Gledhill, Christine. "Pleasurable Negotiations." In Pribram, *Female Spectators* 64–89.

Glover, David. "The Stuff That Dreams Are Made Of: Masculinity, Femininity, and the Thriller." In *Gender, Genre, and Narrative Pleasure*, edited by Derek Longhurst, 67–83. London: Unwin Hyman, 1989.

Godard, Barbara. "Sleuthing: Feminist Re/writing the Detective Novel." *Signature* 1 (summer 1989): 45–70.

Goodkin, Richard E. *"Killing Order(s):* Iphigenia and the Detection of Tragic Intertextuality." *Yale French Studies* 76 (1989): 81–107.

Grafton, Sue. "G Is for (Sue) Grafton: An Interview with the Creator of Kinsey Millhone Private Eye Series Who Delights Mystery Fans As She Writes Her Way through the Alphabet." Interview by Bruce Taylor. *Armchair Detective* 22.1 (1989): 4–13.

———, ed. *Writing Mysteries: A Handbook by the Mystery Writers of America*. Cincinnati: Writer's Digest Books, 1992.

Grossberg, Lawrence, Cary Nelson, and Paula Treichler, eds. *Cultural Studies*. New York: Routledge, 1992.

Hall, Mary Bowen. "Editors Confirm: Women Are Hot." *Sisters in Crime Newsletter* 5.4 (1993): 5.

Hall, Stuart. "Encoding and Decoding in the Media Discourse." Stencil, Paper 7. Birmingham: Centre for Contemporary Cultural Studies, 1973.

Hamilton, Cynthia S. *Western and Hard-Boiled Detective Fiction in America: From High Noon to Midnight*. Iowa City: University of Iowa Press, 1987.

Harris, Mark. "Smooth Operator: The Return of Fiction's Feistiest Female Detective." Review of *Wild Kat*, by Karen Kijewski. *Entertainment Weekly*, March 4, 1994, 58.

Hartman, Geoffrey. "Literature High and Low: The Case of the Mystery Story." In Most and Stowe, *The Poetics of Murder* 210–29.

Healy, Jeremiah. "The Rules and How to *Bend* Them." In Grafton, *Writing Mysteries* 9–14.

Heising, Willetta L. *Detecting Women 2: A Readers' Guide and Checklist for Mystery Fiction Written by Women.* Chelsea, Mich.: Purple Moon, 1996.

Herbert, Rosemary. "Aiming Higher: Some of Today's Top Crime Writers Are Breaking New Ground in Terms of Setting, Sleuths, and Motivation." *Publishers Weekly*, April 13, 1990, 30–32.

Hornsby, Wendy. "Afterword: When the Walls Came Tumbling Down." In *Maxine O'Callaghan: Bibliography, 1974–1995*, 49–51. Royal Oak, Mich.: ASAP, 1994.

Humm, Maggie. "Legal Aliens: Feminist Detective Fiction." In *Border Traffic: Strategies of Contemporary Women Writers*, 185–211. Manchester: Manchester University Press, 1991.

Hutcheon, Linda. *The Politics of Postmodernism.* London: Routledge, 1989.

Huyssen, Andreas. "Mass Culture as Woman: Modernism's Other." In *Studies in Entertainment*, edited by Tania Modleski, 188–207. Bloomington: Indiana University Press, 1986.

"Intruder in a Man's World." *New Statesman*, December 11, 1992, 36.

Irons, Glenwood. "Introduction: Gender and Genre: The Woman Detective and the Diffusion of Generic Voices." In Irons, *Feminism in Women's Detective Fiction* ix–xxiv.

———. "New Women Detectives: G Is for Gender-Bending." In *Gender, Language, and Myth: Essays on Popular Narrative*, edited by Glenwood Irons, 127–41. Toronto: University of Toronto Press, 1992.

———, ed. *Feminism in Women's Detective Fiction.* Toronto: University of Toronto Press, 1995.

Irons, Glenwood, and Joan Warthling Roberts. "From Spinster to Hipster: The 'Suitability' of Miss Marple and Anna Lee." In Irons, *Feminism in Women's Detective Fiction* 64–73.

Isaac, Frederick. "Investigator of Mean Rooms: A Profile of Julie Smith." *Clues* 15.1 (1994): 1–11.

———. "Situation, Motivation, Resolution: An Afternoon with Marcia Muller." *Clues* 5.2 (1984): 20–34.

————. "What Do They Want Us to Read?" Paper presented at the Popular Culture Association Annual Conference, Las Vegas, March 1996.

James, Caryn. "These Heels Aren't Made For Stompin'." *New York Times*, August 4, 1991, H7.

Jameson, F. R. "On Raymond Chandler." In Most and Stowe, *The Poetics of Murder* 122–48.

Kaemmel, Ernst. "Literature under the Table: The Detective Novel and Its Social Mission." In Most and Stowe, *The Poetics of Murder* 55–60.

Kaminsky, Stuart M., and J. H. Mahan. *American Television Genres*. Chicago: Nelson-Hall, 1986.

Kaplan, Alice Yaegar. "Critical Fictions: Alice Yaeger Kaplan on the New Hard-boiled Woman." *Artforum* 28A (January 1990): 26–28.

Kaplan, Cora. "An Unsuitable Genre for a Feminist?" *Women's Review* 8 (July 1986): 18–19.

Kaplan, E. Ann. Introduction to *Regarding Television: Critical Approaches—An Anthology*, edited by E. Ann Kaplan, xi–xxiii. American Film Institute monograph series 2. [Frederick, Md.]: University Publications of America, 1983.

Kennett, Lee, and James La Verne Anderson. *The Gun in America: The Origins of a National Dilemma*. Westport, Conn.: Greenwood, 1975.

Klein, Kathleen Gregory. *Great Women Mystery Writers: A Biocritical Dictionary*. Westport, Conn.: Greenwood, 1994.

————. "*Habeas Corpus:* Feminism and Detective Fiction." In Irons, *Feminism in Women's Detective Fiction* 171–90.

————. *The Woman Detective: Gender and Genre*. Urbana: University of Illinois Press, 1988.

Knight, Stephen. *Form and Ideology in Crime Fiction*. Bloomington: Indiana University Press, 1980.

————. "Radical Thrillers." In *Watching the Detectives: Essays on Crime Fiction*, edited by Ian A. Bell and Graham Daldry, 172–86. London: Macmillan, 1990.

Lacan, Jacques. *The Four Fundamental Concepts of Psycho-Analysis*. Edited by Jacques-Alain Miller, translated by Alan Sheridan. New York: Norton, 1981.

Langstaff, Margaret. "Unravelling Puzzles, Gaily." *Publishers Weekly*, October 23, 1995, 43.

Lee, Alison. *Realism and Power: Postmodern British Fiction*. London: Routledge, 1990.

Lipsitz, George. *Time Passages: Collective Memory and American Popular Culture*. Minneapolis: University of Minnesota Press, 1990.

Littler, Alison. "Marele Day's 'Cold Hard Bitch': The Masculinist Imperatives of the Private-Eye Genre." *Journal of Narrative Technique* 21 (1991): 121–35.

MacCabe, Colin, ed. *High Theory/Low Culture: Analysing Popular Television and Film*. Manchester: Manchester University Press, 1986.

Macdonald, Ross. "Interview with Ross Macdonald," by Sam L. Grogg, Jr. In *Dimensions of Detective Fiction*, edited by Larry N. Dandrum, Pat Browne, and Ray B. Browne, 182–92. [Bowling Green, Ohio]: Popular Press, 1976.

———. "The Writer as Detective Hero." In *Detective Fiction: A Collection of Critical Essays*, edited by Robin W. Winks, 179–87. Englewood Cliffs, N.J.: Prentice-Hall, 1980.

Mandel, Ernest. *Delightful Murder: A Social History of the Crime Story*. London: Pluto, 1984.

Mandle, Joan D. *Women and Social Change in America*. Princeton: Princeton Book Company, 1979.

Mann, Denise. "The Spectacularization of Everyday Life: Recycling Hollywood Stars and Fans in Early Television Variety Shows." In Spigel and Mann, *Private Screenings* 41–70.

Max, Daniel. "La Plante in Her 'Prime': The Creator of TV's 'Prime Suspect' Mysteries Is on a Roll." *Variety*, March 8, 1993, 79.

———. "'Warshawski's' Mysterious Journey: How the Tough-Gal Private Eye Got the Shakers Moving in Hollywood." *Variety*, June 22, 1991, 71.

McGuigan, James. *Cultural Populisms*. London: Routledge, 1992.

McLuhan, Marshall. *From Cliché to Archetype*. New York: Pocket, 1971.

Mellencamp, Patricia, ed. *Logics of Television: Essays in Cultural Criticism*. Bloomington: Indiana University Press, 1990.

Miller, Nancy K. "The Text's Heroine: A Feminist Critic and Her Fictions." *Diacritics* 12.2 (1982): 53–74.

Modleski, Tania. *Loving with a Vengeance: Mass-Produced Fantasies for Women*. New York: Routledge, 1982.

———, ed. *Studies in Entertainment: Critical Approaches to Mass Culture*. Bloomington: Indiana University Press, 1986.

Moorehead, Finola. "Equal Writes." In Bird, *Killing Women* 99–108.

Morris, Meaghan. "Banality in Cultural Studies." In Mellencamp, *Logics of Television* 14–43.

Most, Glenn W. "The Hippocratic Smile: John le Carré and the Traditions of the Detective Novel." In Most and Stowe, *The Poetics of Murder* 341–65.

Most, Glenn W., and William W. Stowe, eds. *The Poetics of Murder: Detective Fiction and Literary Theory*. San Diego: Harcourt Brace Jovanovich, 1983.

Muller, Marcia. "Appreciation: As Delilah Would Say . . ." In *Maxine O'Callaghan: Bibliography, 1974–1995*, 9–12.Royal Oak, Mich.: ASAP, 1994.

———. "Creating a Female Sleuth." *The Writer*, October 1978, 20–22, 45.

Mulvey, Laura. *Visual and Other Pleasures*. Bloomington: Indiana University Press, 1989.

Mumford, Laura Stempel. *Love and Ideology in the Afternoon: Soap Opera, Women, and Television Genre*. Bloomington: Indiana University Press, 1995.

Munt, Sally R. *Murder by the Book?: Feminism and the Crime Novel*. London: Routledge, 1994.

Nelson, Cary. "Lessons from the Job Wars: Late Capitalism Arrives on Campus." *Social Text* 44.13 (1995): 119–34.

Nelson, Cary, Paula A. Treichler, and Lawrence Grossberg. Introduction to Grossberg, Nelson, and Treichler, *Cultural Studies* 1–26.

Nicolson, Marjorie. "The Professor and the Detective." In *The Art of the Mystery Story*, edited by Howard Haycraft, 110–27. New York: Grosset and Dunlap, 1946.

Nixon, Nicola. "Gray Areas: P. D. James's Unsuiting of Cordelia." In Irons, *Feminism in Women's Detective Fiction* 29–45.

Nolan, William F. *The Black Mask Boys: Masters in the Hard-Boiled School of Detective Fiction*. New York: Morrow, 1985.

O'Callaghan, Maxine. "Delilah, Then and Now." In *Maxine O'Callaghan: Bibliography, 1974-1995*, 1–5. Royal Oak, Mich.: ASAP, 1994.

O'Donnell, Lillian. "Norah Mulcahaney: New York's Finest." In *Murderess Ink: The Better Half of the Mystery*, edited by Dilys Winn, 118–20. New York: Workman, 1979.

Ogodon, Bethany. "Hard-boiled Ideology." *Critical Quarterly* 34.1 (1992): 71–87.

Paretsky, Sara. Interview by Peter Gzowski. *Morningside*. CBC Radio, Mary 27, 1992.

———. Interview by Daniel Richler. *Imprint*. TVOntario, May 1992.

———. "What Do Women Really Want?: An Interview with V.I.'s Creator." *Professional Communicator* 10.3 (1990): 12–13.

———. "Writing a Series Character." In Grafton, *Writing Mysteries* 55–60.

Pederson-Krag, Geraldine. "Detective Stories and the Primal Scene." In Most and Stowe, *The Poetics of Murder* 13–20.

Pickard, Nancy. "The Amateur Sleuth." In Grafton, *Writing Mysteries* 61–66.

Place, Janey. "Women in Film Noir." In *Women in Film Noir*, edited by E. Ann Kaplan, 35–67. London: British Film Institute, 1978.

Pope, Rebecca. "'Friends Is a Weak Work for It': Female Friendship and the Spectre of Lesbianism in Sara Paretsky." In Irons, *Feminism in Women's Detective Fiction* 157–70.

Porter, Dennis. *The Pursuit of Crime: Art and Ideology in Detective Fiction*. New Haven: Yale University Press, 1981.

Pribram, E. Deidre, ed. *Female Spectators: Looking at Film and Television*. London: Verso, 1988.

Purdie, Susan. *Comedy: The Mastery of Discourse*. Toronto: University of Toronto Press, 1993.

Pykett, Lyn. "Investigating Women: The Female Sleuth after Feminism." In *Watching the Detectives: Essays on Crime Fiction*, edited by Ian Bell and Graham Daldry, 48–67. London: Macmillan, 1990.

Rabinowitz, Peter J. "Making the Call: Generic Refusal in *Blue Steel*." Paper presented at the International Society for the Study of Narrative Literature Conference, Salt Lake City, Utah, April 1995.

———. "'Reader, I Blew Him Away': Convention and Transgression in Sue Grafton." In *Famous Last Words: Changes in Gender and Narrative Closure*, edited by Alison Booth, 326–46. Charlottesville: University Press of Virginia, 1993.

Radway, Janice A. *Reading the Romance: Women, Patriarchy, and Popular Literature*. 1984. Reprint, Chapel Hill: University of North Carolina Press, 1991.

Reddy, Maureen T. "The Feminist Counter-Tradition in Crime: Cross, Grafton, Paretsky, and Wilson." In *The Cunning Craft: Original Essays on Detective Fiction and Contemporary Literary Theory*, edited by Ronald G. Walker and June M. Frazer, 174–87. Macomb: Western Illinois University Press, 1990.

———. *Sisters in Crime: Feminism and the Crime Novel*. New York: Continuum, 1988.

Rich, B. Ruby. "The Lady Dicks: Genre Benders Take the Case." *Voice Literary Supplement*, June 1990, 24–27.

Rushing, Andrea. "Surviving Rape." In *Theorizing Black Feminisms*, edited by Stanlie M. James and Abena P. A. Busia, 129–42. London: Routledge, 1993.

Ryan, Barbara. *Feminism and the Women's Movement: Dynamics of Change in Social Movement, Ideology, and Activism*. New York: Routledge, 1992.

Schatz, Thomas. *Hollywood Genres*. New York: McGraw-Hill, 1981.

Scoppetone, Sandra. "'Always a Surprise . . .': An InterNet InterView with Sandra Scoppettone," by Walter Sorrels (http://www.mindspring.com/~walter/). Posted September 1997.

Shapiro, Laura. "The Lady Is a Gumshoe: V. I. Warshawski, Street Fighter Extraordinaire." *Newsweek*, July 13, 1987, 64.

———. "Sara Paretsky." *Ms.*, January 1988, 66–67, 92–93.

Shepherdson, Nancy. "The Writer behind Warshawski." *Writer's Digest*, September 1992, 38–41.

Silverman, Kaja. "Dis-Embodying the Female Voice." In *Re-Vision: Essays in Feminist Film Criticism*, edited by Mary Ann Doane, Patricia Mellencamp, and Linda Williams, 131–49. Los Angeles: American Film Institute, 1984.

Skene-Melvin, David. "Investigating Investigating Women." In *Investigating Women: Female Detectives by Canadian Writers, an Eclectic Sampler*, edited by David Skene-Melvin, 8–50. Toronto: Simon and Pierre, 1995.

Slotkin, Richard. "The Hard-Boiled Detective Story: From the Open Range to the Mean Streets." In *The Sleuth and the Scholar: Origins, Evolution, and Current Trends in Detective Fiction*, edited by Barbara A. Rader and Howard G. Zettler, 91–100. New York: Greenwood, 1988.

Smyth, Cherry. "The Transgressive Sexual Subject." In *A Queer Romance: Lesbians, Gay Men, and Popular Culture*, edited by Paul Burston and Colin Richardson, 123–43. Routledge: London, 1995.

Spigel, Lynn, and Denise Mann, eds. *Private Screenings: Television and the Female Consumer*. Minneapolis: University of Minnesota Press, 1992.

Stacey, Jackie. *Star Gazing: Hollywood Cinema and Female Spectatorship*. London: Routledge, 1994.

Stanbridge, Alan. "Cultural Policy/Cultural Theory: A Research 'Agenda.'" Paper presented at the Conference on Cultural Policy: State of the Art, Brisbane, June 1995.

Stanley, Liz. *The Auto/Biographical I: The Theory and Practice of Feminist Autobiography*. Manchester: Manchester University Press; New York: St. Martin's, 1992.

Strong, Merilee. "The Woman behind the Woman." In *Helen Mirren: Prime Suspect: A Celebration*, edited by Amy Rennert, 73–79. San Francisco: KQED Books, 1995.

Summer, Bob. "Getting Clued In: Series Are Serious." *Publishers Weekly*, October 25, 1995, 44–46.

Swanson, Jean, and Dean James. *By a Woman's Hand*. New York: Berkley, 1994.

Symons, Julian. *Bloody Murder: From the Detective Story to the Crime Novel: A History*. London: Pan, 1972.

Thompson, E. P. *The Making of the English Working Class*. London: Gollancz, 1963.

Todorov, Tzvetan. *The Poetics of Prose*. Translated by Richard Howard. Ithaca: Cornell University Press, 1977.

Tomc, Sandra. "Questing Women: The Feminist Mystery after Feminism." In Irons, *Feminism in Women's Detective Fiction* 46–63.

Traub, Valerie. "The Ambiguities of 'Lesbian' Viewing Pleasure: The (Dis)Articulations of *Black Widow*." In *Body Guards: The Cultural Politics of Gender Ambiguity*, edited by Julia Epstein and Kristina Straub, 305–28. New York: Routledge, 1991.

Turnbull, Sue. "Bodies of Knowledge: Pleasure and Anxiety in the Detective Fiction of Patricia D. Cornwell." *Australian Journal of Law and Society* 9 (1993): 19–41.

————. "Dying Beautifully: Crime, Aesthetics, and the Media." *Australian Journal of Communication* 22.1 (1995). 1–13.

Tuska, Jon. *Dark Cinema: American Film Noir in Cultural Perspective*. Westport, Conn.: Greenwood, 1984.

Van Dover, J. Kenneth. *Murder in the Millions: Erle Stanley Gardner, Mickey Spillane, Ian Fleming*. New York: Frederick Ungar, 1984.

Wallace, Michele. "For Whom the Bell Tolls: Why Americans Can't Deal with Black Feminist Intellectuals." *Voice Literary Supplement*, November 1995, 19–24.

Walters, Suzanna Danuta. *Material Girls: Making Sense of Feminist Cultural Theory*. Berkeley: University of California Press, 1995.

Walton, Priscilla L. "Paretsky's V.I. as P.I.: Revising the Script and Recasting the Dick." *Literature/Interpretation/Theory* 4 (1993): 203–13.

Watson, Julia, and Sidonie Smith. "De/Colonization and the Politics of Discourse in Women's Autobiographical Practices." In *De/Colonizing the Subject: The Politics of Gender in Women's Autobiography*, edited by Julia Watson and Sidonie Smith, xi–xxxi. Minneapolis: University of Minneapolis Press, 1992.

Watts, Ian. *The Rise of the Novel: Studies in Defoe, Richardson, and Fielding.* Berkeley: University of California Press, 1964.

Wilson, Ann. "The Female Dick and the Crisis of Heterosexuality." Irons, *Feminism in Women's Detective Fiction* 148–56.

Winston, Robert P., and Nancy C. Mellerski. *The Public Eye: Ideology and the Police Procedural.* New York: St. Martin's Press, 1992.

Wolcott, James. "An Appreciation." In *Helen Mirren: Prime Suspect: A Celebration,* edited by Amy Rennert, 14–29. San Francisco: KQED Books, 1995.

Worpole, Ken. *Dockers and Detectives.* London: Verso, 1983.

Zaremba, Eve. "A Canadian Speaks." *Mystery Readers Journal* 9.4 (1993–94): 45–47.

Žižek, Slavoj. *Looking Awry: An Introduction to Jacques Lacan through Popular Culture.* Cambridge, Mass.: MIT Press, 1991.

INTERVIEWS

Note: Quotations attributed to authors, agents, and editors that are not followed by page numbers refer to interviews conducted by telephone, e-mail, or letter specifically for this project.

Authors

Barnes, Linda. Telephone, December 12, 1995

Bowers, Elisabeth. Letter, November 23, 1994.

Cornwell, Patricia. Letter, January 14, 1996.

D'Amato, Barbara. Letter, December 12, 1995.

Dawson, Janet. Telephone, November 28, 1995.

Forrest, Katherine V. Telephone, December 12, 1995.

Grant, Linda. Telephone, December 18, 1995.

Hager, Jean. Letter, October 14, 1995.

Hayter, Sparkle. E-mail, October 21, 1995.

Hornsby, Wendy. Letter, November 27, 1995.

Jacobs, Nancy Baker. Telephone, November 25, 1995.

Jance, J. A. Telephone, November 16, 1995.

King, Laurie R. Letter, October 22, 1995.

Knight, Phyllis. Telephone, December 9, 1995.

McGregor, T. J. Telephone, November 25, 1995.

Muller, Marcia. Telephone, November 27, 1995.
O'Callaghan, Maxine. E-mail, November 18, 1995.
Paretsky, Sara. Letter, November 27, 1995.
Piesman, Marissa. Telephone, November 27, 1995.
Pincus, Elizabeth. Letter, November 27, 1995.
Scoppettone, Sandra. Telephone, October 11, 1995.
Singer, Shelley. Telephone, November 22, 1995.
Spring, Michelle. Telephone, April 29, 1996.
Stabenow, Dana. Letter, November 25, 1995.
Taylor, Jean M. Letter, January 11, 1996.
Trocheck, Kathy Hogan. Undated letter, 1995.
Wesley, Valerie Wilson. Telephone, November 15, 1995.
Wingate, Anne. E-mail, November 10, 1995.

Editors

Boersma, Karen. Editor with University of Toronto Press; former publicist for
    Ballantine, Delacorte, Dell. Telephone, July 30, 1996.
Cavin, Ruth. Editor with St. Martin's. Telephone, April 8, 1996.
DeSanti, Carole. Editor with Dutton. Telephone, April 15, 1996.
Freed, Sarah Ann. Editor with Mysterious Press. Telephone, April 8, 1996
Grann, Phyllis. Editor with Putnam. Telephone, May 1, 1996
Kirk, Susanne. Editor with Scribner. Telephone, April 11, 1996.
Rosenstein, Natalee. Editor with Berkley. Telephone, May 2, 1996.
Woods, Marian. Editor with Henry Holt. Telephone, May 8, 1996.

Agents

Able, Dominick. Telephone, April 11, 1996.
Childes, Faith. Telephone, April 12, 1996.
Curtis, Richard. Telephone, April 8, 1996
Friedrich, Molly. Telephone, April 11, 1996.
Jackson, Jennifer. Telephone, April 3, 1996.
Protter, Susan Ann. Telephone, April 10, 1996.

Index

311

Compositor:	G & S Typesetters, Inc.
Text:	10/15 Janson
Display:	American Typewriter Medium
Printer & Binder:	BookCrafters, Inc.